CYBER SQUAD
LEVEL 1

by
A.K. Mocikat

A.K. MOCIKAT

Cyber Squad - Level 1
Copyright © 2021 by A.K. Mocikat

All rights reserved. Printed in the United States of America. No part of this book may be used or reproduced in any manner whatsoever without written permission except in the case of brief quotations embodied in critical articles or reviews.
This book is a work of fiction. Names, characters, businesses, organizations, places, events and incidents either are the product of the author's imagination or are used fictitiously. Any resemblance to actual persons, living or dead, events, or locales is entirely coincidental.

Book Cover design by Ivano Lago

CHAPTER ONE

Everyone stood still. Waiting. On the lookout.

For once, no one spoke. If it weren't for the wind blowing into their faces and the dark clouds moving over the wintery sky, one might have thought that the scenario had frozen – which would have been annoying, but nothing too unusual.

But that wasn't the case this time. Everyone was so focused, so determined that even the most notorious chatters had fallen quiet.

"This is it, people," an assertive voice said, breaking the silence. "All or nothing!"

Some heads turned and looked at the speaker while others kept staring into the lush woods surrounding the castle. Not far away, crows circled high in the clear, crisp air, waiting for the feast to come.

During the last siege, some noob smartass had thought it would be funny to throw fireballs at the crows while waiting for the attack. Although it was indeed hilarious to watch the animal NPCs[1] first burst into flames and then fall to the ground in the form of fried chicken, the fun for the smartass had only lasted for a couple of seconds.

Then he had dematerialized in front of everyone's eyes.

The guild leader had removed him from the group and therefore the campaign. Sieges like these weren't the right time for silly jokes. This was serious business.

All or nothing.

Kai agreed with that. If they won the battle, it would

catapult every one of them into the Top K. The top one thousand players of the game, worldwide. The best of the best. This was not only cool because it would display on their tags, it also came with unique loot, 100k gold and a mansion in the Mountains of Valaria.

They had to win.

Kai froze. For a second, he thought he had spotted movement between the trees, but it was just the wind rustling through old leaves. A snowstorm was coming.

They all had played the campaign so often, they knew the signs that indicated such a storm. And it was very likely that the enemy was waiting for exactly that before they attacked. It was a common tactic after all.

But for now, no enemy movement was to be seen, and the medieval style music playing in everyone's heads had a neutral and relaxed tune.

Kai looked up and studied his brothers and sisters in arms, standing in disciplined rows on the broad outer walls of a massive fortress.

The walls alone were so thick that two mounted guards could easily patrol them next to each other. They surrounded a huge courtyard and, in its midst, an impressive, medieval keep. It should be easy to defend a place like this, yet it wasn't, and everyone standing there knew that only too well as they looked at each other – and the vast gaps between them on the wall.

The anticipation was almost tangible. Many of them had been playing almost non-stop for the last five days to achieve this great victory. And now it was so close.

The timer in the upper right corner of Kai's HUD[2] showed that there was less than an hour to go. All they needed to do to win was hold their ground.

Defend this keep. At any cost.

"Remember," Red's voice filled everyone's head. "Stick together with your assigned team, no matter what. No solo maneuvers. Check if you have enough health potions in your quickslots. Make it easy for your healers to keep you alive."

He was an impressive figure. Sitting on his large, black stallion with fiery hooves and glowing red eyes. It was a premium item from the store, and a very expensive one.

Some items weren't achievable through grinding or farming – they had to be bought for diamonds. Which were only attainable through real money.

It was all about status, in the real world and in the digital one alike.

Red's tall and broad, overly masculine silhouette was dressed in black, ornamented armor. His handsome face hid behind a massive black helmet with two fiery horns at the top.

Above the helmet, his name was displayed in bright blue: Redrum666. And his level: 799 – the highest level achievable in the game. After that, only better gear would make a difference in stats.

On view above his level and visible to everyone was his title: Emperor.

He was the highest-ranked player in this campaign. And he had to keep this title till the campaign ended, then he would win. And with him the whole Blue team, which mostly consisted of one guild.

"Check your inventory, guys," another familiar voice added. It belonged to Cloudgirl69, the second in command in the campaign and the guild – and Red's spouse. At least in the game, since none of them would ever meet in real life. Apparently the two of them liked to play dirty on his coastal estate, if they weren't busy raiding, looting, killing dragons or leading campaigns.

"Everyone needs at least three flaming oils and two fire trebuchets slotted. If you don't have them, go to the vendor in the keep and buy some. But hurry."

Even when she was bossy, her voice always sounded sexy. And rumors were that she was a hot redhead IRL.[3]

But if that wasn't the case, her character in-game was enough to make everyone's blood pump when they looked at her. Her elven body was shapely, and the silver armor revealed more than it covered. Of course, armor like that would be ridiculously useless on a real battlefield, but those were details no one cared about. Besides, her character class was Sorcerer and they used magic shields instead of heavy armor. Everyone knew that.

"Don't forget to protect the aether-fire siege equipment, no matter what," Red said.

Kai felt a soft poke in his side. He turned his head and looked into the beautiful, unearthly face of a female Dark Elf. She rolled her reddish, oversized eyes.

"They're such posers, both of them," Kai heard his friend Stan over a private channel, which simulated a whisper. "Who do they think we are? Bloody noobs? Every idiot knows to protect the aether fire shit!"

Stan's deep voice, with its heavy Australian accent, stood in stark contrast to the graceful elven girl, dressed in brown, tight-fitting leather. A collection of silver knives and daggers was strapped to her light armor, and a huge red-glowing bow was attached to her back.

VRRPG gaming had come a long way since its early days. Every player could select a voice for their avatar which would speak what they wanted to say in an almost natural way. Because of this it had become very difficult to tell if a player was male or female in real life. However, some players chose to use their own voice, or at least what they heard as their won voices in their heads. Stan was one of them. He wanted to be clearly recognizable as a male in real life.

"Everyone knows they're posers," Kai said with a chuckle. "Now shut up and focus! We need to win this!"

"And we bloody will!" answered the elven girl with the deep voice.

Kai's character was a handsome Battlemage who would have looked like a Viking if he didn't wear his helmet. He wore purple-black heavy armor that shimmered and had a flaming great-sword. But he could also cast fireballs and summon lightning. LVL 799 was displayed above his head. He was one of the best players in the guild.

"You see anything?" he asked his friend. The Thief class had 20% better eyesight by default.

"Nope," the Dark Elf next to him answered. "There isn't shit out there."

"Hm. Strange."

It was odd indeed. The HUD showed that the campaign would end in 58 minutes and 15 seconds. What was the enemy waiting for? If their opponents wanted to win this, they needed to hurry. Important battles like this one could last for hours. Especially if one faction sieged a keep that another was defending fiercely.

Maybe they'd decided that the campaign was lost and had left it to do something else in-world instead of attacking?

His thoughts were interrupted by an excited voice yelling into the main channel.

"They're inbound! They're coming! Shit, there are so many of them!"

"Who? Where?" Red asked, trying to keep his voice calm.

"North-east!" Serene559, one of their scouts, answered. "Yellows *and* Purples!"

"What?" Red couldn't hide his irritation. "Damn cheaters! Ok, everyone, north-eastern wall. Deploy the counter-siege engines. Move!"

Suddenly everything was moving hectically. Stan made a gesture with his hand, and his mount, an oversized lizard, spawned right under him. Kai did the same, and within the blink of an eye, he was sitting in the saddle of a huge leopard. The mount let out its characteristic growling hiss when he spurred it, then it followed Stan at breakneck speed. The castle was so huge that it would take way too long to run from one end to the other, which was why everyone was summoning their mount and hastening toward the action.

Seconds later, the walls vibrated under a massive

impact.

The normally relaxed, medieval-inspired music everyone could hear in their heads was replaced by one of the battle themes. Its sound alone made Kai's heart pound and his stomach tingle in anticipation.

The enemy had begun the siege. That was not good at all. If his team wasn't able to set up counter-siege equipment on the walls within the next minute, the damage might be already too high to hold the outer walls of the fortress.

Kai swore inwardly, spurring his leopard on even more. *Why had Red made such a beginner's mistake?*

Yes, it was true that 90% of attacks happened at the front gate. It was wooden and much easier to breach than the stone walls. But it was also easier to defend. An experienced campaign leader at least considered an attack from the flank.

"Oh bloody fuck," Stan moaned. "We're so screwed."

Everything shook under another massive impact.

"Aether-fire!" someone yelled in the main channel. "They got fucking aether!"

"How many units?" Red asked.

"Eight… maybe ten."

"What?!"

Aether-fire, which glowed blue, was the most powerful weapon in the game. Such siege engines were extremely difficult to come by and therefore very valuable. Two or three of them could decide a battle. Red's guild had five, which was a lot. But ten?

"It's because the fuckers have teamed up against us," Stan said dryly. "We're toast."

"Not yet," Kai answered, jumping off his mount, which disappeared into thin air. "We still can do this!"

He had arrived at the wall that was under attack. Looking down, he doubted his own words and began to agree with his friend on the matter. They were going to be toast. Burned toast.

"That's a motherfucking Zerg[4] down there!" one of

their teammates with a clearly puberty-pitched voice cried out.

Kai and Stan exchanged a look.

"Toast," the Dark Elf repeated.

At least fifty enemy players had gathered at the northeastern wall of Castle Black Rock. Players of both enemy factions, recognizable by their purple and yellow game tags. It wasn't against the rules, but it was highly frowned upon if two factions teamed up against one. They weren't even supposed to communicate with each other and couldn't share a voice channel. But experienced players knew how to work around such obstacles. When a massive army attempted a coordinated attack, they were called a Zerg. A term almost as old as gaming history itself.

Kai felt goosebumps as he watched the enemies crawling seventy feet below him, like a hive of raging fire ants. The world around him was fake, a digital construct created by a powerful game engine, but the adrenaline and sweat produced in his body were real. He felt his heart beating faster.

Then he gave himself a mental push. Standing there like a noob and watching the hostiles approach wouldn't help anyone.

Stan had already begun setting up his siege engine, and Kai did the same.

He only had to think *Open Inventory* and the HUD changed. Semi-transparent, so he still could see what was happening around him, the inventory opened and displayed everything he was carrying with him. With his eyes, he focused on the *Siege Equipment* tab and picked one of the weapons stored there.

A massive trebuchet began unfolding right in front of him, directly on the castle wall, which was now shaking under the impact of all kinds of projectiles: rocks, fireballs, ice and the dreaded aether-fire.

"Wall integrity at 43%," Red shouted. "Hurry up, people!"

It took a couple of seconds until Kai's machine was fully set up and ready to use. Then his HUD changed again, and now he was looking through the POV of the trebuchet.

A red circle showed the impact radius. He moved it over two enemy catapults and fired.

Glowing blue fire emerged from his trebuchet and flew in a massive ball toward the targeted enemies. They saw it and tried to evade, but they were too slow. Everything around them erupted in a cloud of deadly, blue flames.

"Ha!" Kai shouted, watching the life stats of the burning enemies he just had hit diminish at a crazy speed.

That was exactly why everyone feared aether-fire. It would sear your flesh from your bones within seconds if you didn't use countermeasures, such as a cleansing spell, in time.

Satisfied, Kai watched as two of the opponent players dropped to the ground, their bodies turning into piles of ash. Their siege engines were ablaze and would be destroyed within ten seconds if someone didn't use a repair kit on them.

Stan fired his stone catapult at the two players who had survived Kai's aether-fire and were trying to repair the valuable machines. The rocks smashed both of them into pulp.

"Woohoo!" the Aussie called out. "Maybe you're right and we have a chance after all!"

"Careful, they're gonna target us now!"

Kai moved his trebuchet a bit to the right and adjusted its aim to hit the next enemies. It took a few seconds and made him extremely vulnerable to attacks. Of course, the other side wasn't dumb and would target their aether-fire as well.

"Don't worry. I got you," a calm, female voice behind them said.

It was LifeSupportForYou2, a LVL 799 player and a top-notch healer.

The sorceress wore a majestic, gold-glowing robe and held a staff with a moving snake head on its end. She performed a gesture with her arms and a huge shimmering dome appeared around Kai, Stan and the other team members close to them.

Just in time.

Two glowing fireballs, one aether and one regular, hit the shield and disappeared.

"Shield integrity at 73%," the healer said calmly. "Finish them off."

"Yes, ma'am!" Stan said, and he and Kai fired their deadly loads on the fire ants below.

With LifeSupport protecting them, they were practically invincible, at least until she ran out of Mana, and that could take a while with her.

The tables began to turn as the two friends and other members of their team unleashed the full power of their defense. The Zerg quickly grew smaller in number, and the hostiles left their organized formation and started running around manically, trying to repair blazing siege equipment or revive fallen players.

Kai laughed. "Look at them! Who's toast now?"

Suddenly, the shimmering shield protecting them disappeared.

Surprised, Kai saw an assassin appearing from a dark cloud that had given him stealth. The black-clad hostile butchered LifeSupport with his dual-wield blades. It was over within two seconds. Not equipped for close combat, the healers were vulnerable to blade attacks. The shield only protected them from projectiles. Cloaked enemy players could easily pass through it and assassinate anyone inside.

"Well, damn," LifeSupport said dryly while her virtual body sank into a puddle of her own blood.

Kai was stunned. Where had this Purple assassin come from? As long as the walls and gates were intact, no one could enter a keep.

"What the—"

He was interrupted by a yell.

"Breach!" Serene559 warned. "They've breached the gate! They're flanking us!"

"Wankers..." Stan swore in disbelief.

The Zerg had been nothing but a massive diversion. While Red's team rushed to the north-eastern wall to defend it against an enemy force that far outnumbered them, a small, tactical unit had breached the gate. Now, yellow and purple tags swarmed into the fortress.

Kai let go of his siege engine, drew his flaming sword and attacked the assassin. They had twenty seconds to revive LifeSupport before she was kicked out of the campaign.

"Retreat inside the inner keep!" Red commanded. "Now!"

Furious, Kai slashed at the assassin with his sword, which was almost the same length as his body and would have been impossible to lift even for a well-trained man in real life. The hostile parried with his daggers but would withstand the much stronger, heavy attacks only for a few seconds.

"You heard him, mate," Stan said, running off along on the wall. "We need to retreat!"

"Damn it, Stan!" Kai growled, irritated. "I need your help here!"

"Sorry mate," his friend said, disappearing into a dark cloud that would cover him from enemy fire until he reached the inner fortress.

Kai swore, then focused.

"Cast *Spell of Clairvoyance!*" he addressed the game system, and a glowing oversized eye appeared over his head. Just in time.

He had anticipated that the assassin would try to disappear again and attack him from the shadows. With his spell, he had cut off the hostile's escape into invisibility. The black-clad figure with the purple tag above his head tried to run but couldn't escape Kai's heavy attack. The flaming sword cut the much shorter and more delicate fighter in two. Blood splatted into Kai's vision but soon faded, allowing him to continue the battle.

He rushed toward the fallen LifeSupport, whose timer

showed that she had only five seconds left to be revived before she got teleported out of the campaign.

Kai produced a Crystal of Rebirth from his inventory and held it over the motionless healer.

"Just a sec, Life!"

"Appreciated."

From the corner of his eye, Kai saw more enemies storming through the gate. They had all stopped attacking the wall and were now rushing inside through the breach. Smart tactic. It would be very difficult to hold the inner keep now.

The crystal glowed bright blue and a timer appeared, showing that it would take seven seconds to revive LifeSupport. In this time, Kai needed to remain motionless and was therefore highly vulnerable to enemy attacks.

He turned and glanced at his trebuchet still standing on the wall behind him. The timer above it showed fifteen seconds. If Kai didn't manage to pick it up in time, the highly valuable machine would disintegrate and be lost.

He looked back at the fallen healer. Five seconds. He could do it.

Further down the wall, he saw some of his team members rushing toward the massive doors of the inner fortress. Maybe he was an idiot for not leaving Life behind and getting himself to safety. But it would have been a shitty move to do that. Besides, if they wanted to win this, they needed her.

Suddenly, multiple arrows hit him from the side. Thanks to his heavy armor, they caused just 10% damage, but as long as he was reviving LifeSupport, he couldn't activate any countermeasures.

Two seconds.

He held on – once she was up, she could heal him easily. More projectiles hit him but didn't cause him to fall. But then he was kicked off his feet. A massive fireball had hit him from behind.

Looking down, he saw that he was burning, the fire causing heavy but not lethal damage. He jumped back to his feet and saw at least ten enemy players storming the wall and charging at him.

"Fuck me…"

"So long, Kai," LifeSupport said from behind him while her body disintegrated, removing her from the campaign.

Now it was too late to turn around and run to safety. Kai knew that he was screwed.

He lifted his sword and lunged at the attackers who surrounded him, throwing everything they had at him. Within seconds he was on fire again and had been slashed by several melee weapons. Irritated, he saw his life stats diminishing at such a speed that he could hardly see the numbers running down his HUD.

Then it was over. Everything turned gray and blurry as he first sank to his knees and then collapsed. The sad theme every player dreaded so much played in his ears, indicating that he was dying. A timer appeared in his field of view, counting down from twenty. Now other players had twenty seconds to come to his aid and revive him.

Of course, no one would come. What was left of his team had gathered inside the fortress where they would take a last, desperate stand. They wouldn't win this. Kai was convinced about that. He saw more and more enemy players run by him as his vision turned darker with every second. One of them took the time to stop and teabag[5] him.

"Seriously?!" Kai shouted, even though he knew that the enemy couldn't hear him. A broad grin crossed the face of the character – a barbarian dressed in furs – as he flipped Kai off before following his buddies.

Kai swore. He heard the noise of collapsing wood and saw his precious aether-fire trebuchet disintegrating next to him.

Great, just great, he thought.

Then everything turned black, and some text appeared in his vision.

You have been removed from the campaign.

CHAPTER TWO

Grayish-purple mists surrounded Kai, thick and impenetrable. He could move his body again, the death stupor inflicted on him after being lethally wounded had passed. But everyone knew that it was pointless to try and go anywhere while in the mists. It was a loading screen, and therefore the mists were infinite, or at least they appeared so.

Did you know? Enemies highlighted in red have a higher LVL than you. Proceed with caution!

The message blinked in Kai's field of view and he grimaced. Those stupid hints that appeared in loading screens were ridiculous. You had to be a total noob playing a video game for the first time not to know any of the glorious advice given there.

The sad music faded and was replaced by a more cheerful, neutral tune. Finally, the mists dissolved as if sucked in by invisible vents and a new environment opened up around Kai.

There were colossal mountains with snow-covered tops, azure-blue waterfalls rushing down picturesque ravines, and reddish beams of light from a low afternoon sun were reflected in a lake so beautiful that it could only exist in a fairy tale – or a video game. A soft, warm wind blew in Kai's face as he materialized. The air was filled with birds singing and gorgeous mountain flower scents.

Kai pulled off his helmet and long, blond hair fell over

his broad shoulders. Although he had suffered lethal wounds only moments ago, his athletic body was now fully healed and he was back to his usual stats. He hadn't felt more than a tickle on his skin when the enemy swords and fireballs had hit him. It wasn't possible to experience severe pain or any injuries suffered in the game on one's real body, which was safely resting in another world – the real one. Nevertheless, the death experience was never a pleasant one.

Kai sighed, turning away from the breathtaking view and toward the estate. He stepped off the teleportation landing platform, which was the only way to access the place, which was located on a steep mountainside. The heavy iron boots made a loud clacking noise as he walked along the cobblestone pathway. It would be absolutely impossible to sneak up on anyone wearing such armor, but that wasn't what his class was designed for anyway. If someone wanted to play a sneaky character, they would pick the Assassin or Thief class, such as Stan had.

Kai frowned. He couldn't help but feel upset with Stan. He had believed they were not only battle buddies but friends. Instead, he had let him down and run off. Although Kai knew that the other player had most likely taken the right decision, since they both would have died if he had stayed, he was still disappointed.

He hoped his team would win, though, even if, after his forceful removal from the campaign, he wouldn't get the XP or advance to the Top K. He would rather see his people win, the guild he hung out with every day, than the damn Yellows and Purples. Teaming up like that? Two against one? That had been anything but fair play. Rather a bully tactic.

Kai pushed open an old iron gate and entered the courtyard of a medieval castle, built from dark gray stones. Somewhere high above in the deep blue sky circled a majestic eagle, its characteristic shriek echoing from the mountains.

The estate was named Eagle's Nest and had cost Kai a shitload of money. Real money, as the more impressive private residences couldn't be acquired for gold, which was the currency earned for accomplishing missions and quests in the game. They only came for diamonds. Kai's house had cost him 300 diamonds, which was 15k Bit-Dollars, almost a third of what he paid as rent for his room every month.

But since he hung out more in his virtual home than his real-life one, it was only fair. Eagle's Nest had a massive main building with two floors, a main hall, four bedrooms, and a dungeon in the basement. An impressive tower loomed next to the house. 70 feet high, it offered a magnificent view over the lands of Arcania, which consisted mostly of mountains, valleys and lakes. The residence was bigger than the apartment building Kai lived in IRL, yet compared to other in-game estates it was rather humble. He knew players who owned fortresses, while others called entire tropical islands their own.

"Soon," he told himself for the hundredth time while dropping his helmet to the ground. It dematerialized before hitting the floor; he knew it would show up again in his armory.

He looked at the timer on his HUD. The campaign would still be going on for over thirty minutes, provided his team didn't get their asses handed to them before that.

It wasn't worth hanging around and waiting. He had been up almost all night to support his guild and needed to try to get at least two hours of sleep now before he had to get up.

"System," he said. "Initiate log-off process."

"Initiating log-off," an automated voice replied. "Please stand still."

The statement was redundant, since he couldn't move, even if he had tried to. Glowing red rings appeared all around his virtual body, holding him in place while a huge timer countdown appeared, almost filling his entire field of view.

5 - 4 - 3 -2 -1...

First the pleasant sounds of the birds and waterfalls faded and the music stopped, then the world around him warped as if he were about to be pulled away at an impossible speed. Lights turned into ribbons rushing by him, then everything turned dark.

"Log-off completed," the disembodied voice said. "Have a wonderful day!"

Kai opened his real eyes.

**

As always, everything was blurry at first and his body felt numb, almost as if he had woken from a deep slumber. In fact, when a player entered VR, their body entered a similar state to sleep. That didn't apply to the brain though. Everything that happened in VR was perceived as real by the brain, which was why long game sessions were exhausting instead of invigorating.

Kai blinked, then stretched himself, yawning. He didn't even realize how tired he was. His tongue felt like a piece of sticky sandpaper. He hadn't drunk anything for hours.

Slowly, he sat up in his bed. It had been day when he had laid down and connected to the game, now it was pitch-black night. He felt the familiar pull in his neck when the cord hit its maximum length.

His movements showed routine when he lifted his hand behind his head and unplugged the cord from the port in his body. Like almost everyone else, he had a neuro-plant installed right under his cortex, connected to his mid-brain and nervous system. It was accessible via a small port on his upper neck, right under the skull. The contact was similar to a USB device but much smaller. However, it was easy to connect the cord. Since the contact was magnetic, it basically slipped into place by itself as soon as it came close. But most users plugged themselves in so frequently that they could have stuck the cable into the contact while they were sleeping.

Kai yawned again. He briefly considered getting up and finding himself some snacks from the kitchen, but then decided otherwise. Instead, he grabbed the soda bottle standing next to his bed and drained it. Then he let himself fall back onto the bed.

He badly needed some sleep. It had been a damn long session that had ended with a very dissatisfying result for him. Tomorrow, he had another seemingly endless work-day. The thought of it made him grimace in dread. But there was also hope. Maybe tomorrow he would finally get the good news he was waiting for.

Why was it taking them so long? It should have been a no-brainer. He had scored by far the best in his test group. It had to work out this time!

Kai tried not to think about that now. He needed to rest. Or he'd accidentally fall asleep on the job tomorrow and cut his finger off, or, worse, get fired.

Fortunately he was so sleepy that it took him only seconds to fall into a deep slumber.

CHAPTER THREE

Less than three hours later, Kai woke from a dreamless sleep. More precisely, he had been woken up. By the sound he probably hated most in the entire world: his alarm clock.

Slowly, he opened his eyes, his lids feeling heavy like lead.

"Ugh," he said, sitting up and holding his head.

It was 9 a.m. and daylight filled his small room. He hadn't bothered to close the drapes yesterday. Outside, the sky was overcast with gray clouds hanging deep between the even grayer tenements surrounding the one he lived it, which, too, was gray, of course.

The system noticed that he was up, and the alarm stopped.

"Good morning, Kai," a female computer voice said in a soft and at the same time bossy tone, which was typical for her. "Do you wish me to snooze?"

"Nope, thanks Alessia. I'm good."

"As you wish," the AI answered while Kai got up from the bed and walked across his small room to the window. "The forecast promises another beautiful day today. Only mildly cloudy with highs of 71 degrees. Chance of rain, 60%. I suggest taking an umbrella."

"Hm," Kai answered, still sleepy, staring through the dirty window. The weather forecast was basically the same every day, all year long. Like in his virtual home, he lived high up, on the 18th floor. But the views in the two worlds couldn't be more different.

There wasn't a green speck to be seen anywhere, no majestic mountains or azure waterfalls. Instead, identical, gray high-rises as far as he could see.

"Alessia, check emails," he said after staring into nowhere for a moment.

"No new emails," the AI answered at once.

Kai clenched his fist and bumped it against the window frame in frustration.

What the hell was taking them so long?

"You have forty minutes before you need to leave, if you want to catch the train to Central Plaza and be in time for work," Alessia reminded him, her voice still both soft and bossy.

"Right," Kai said, giving himself a mental push. There was no point in standing there and gawking mindlessly. If he got to work late he would lose his job, and if then the email didn't bring the news he was hoping for, he'd be in trouble.

"Is the bathroom free?" he asked.

"It is," Alessia answered. "Carol left it less than a minute ago."

"Thank goodness," Kai said, opening his drawer and looking for fresh underwear.

If Carol was in the bathroom, it could easily take an hour until she left it. And she reacted in anything but a friendly way if someone tried to rush her.

He found a pair of boxers but no matching socks. It was time for laundry again. He hated doing laundry!

One day he would get a housekeeping robot that would take care of all this shit for him. He told himself that every day.

"I would advise not to waste time, though," the AI said. "There's movement in Jax's room. He might beat you to it if you don't hurry up."

"Oh crap."

He quickly grabbed two socks that didn't match at all together with his boxers and stormed to the door.

He made it to the bathroom just in time. Jax was already approaching along the hall. The way he moved suggested he had to be even sleepier than Kai, or maybe the drugs he frequently consumed in the evenings hadn't worn off yet.

Jax noticed Kai rushing into the bathroom and shot him an angry glance. "Son of a bitch!"

"Sorry!" Kai mumbled, locking the door behind him. "I'll be quick, I promise."

"You better be," Jax said, now right outside the door, a threatening undertone in his voice.

He was a head taller than Kai and weighed double as much, from the look of him. Although the massive amounts of weed he consumed usually made him lethargic rather than aggressive, he was certainly not the type of guy you wanted to mess with.

Kai removed his clothes and stepped under the shower. First he heard the unnerving noise the showerhead always made upon activation that sounded like a human sigh, then water began sprinkling over his face and body. It was only lukewarm.

Kai swore inwardly while grabbing his shampoo. That meant Carol had used up all the hot water again. Kai had two minutes max until the water turned ice-cold. And he hated cold showers.

Luckily he was used to being quick about his morning business in the bathroom. He managed to wash his hair and body just in time before the water turned unpleasantly cold.

The apartment Kai lived in was in poor condition, with mold in the bathroom and kitchen, windows that wouldn't shut properly and a constantly leaking faucet. The AC had been broken since the day Kai had moved in almost three years ago. Yet the place was so expensive that he had to share it with four other people. Besides Carol and Jax, there were also Caprice and Lizzy, a couple who slept in the living room because the place had only three bedrooms.

All of them were as different as people could be, but they

usually got along somehow.

Kai sighed, stepping out of the shower. It was only temporary. At least, that was what he had been telling himself since day one.

He walked in front of the mirror and looked at himself.

His real-life appearance couldn't be more different than the character he played in *The Scrolls of the Ancients*, or TSOTA, his favorite game that took up most of his time. Kai was a short, skinny guy with thick, black hair and deep-brown eyes that could appear almost black. He lifted his arm and inspected his non-existent muscle mass.

He'd made the decision before to start visiting the gym and get some massive biceps and abs, like his character. Maybe that would get him laid eventually. But staying at home and hanging out in VR was so much more comfortable and exciting that he quickly forgot about his glorious plans.

Besides, his goal was a different one and he did everything to achieve it. And it was nothing too unusual not to ever have sex at his age. Most of his friends never had – at least not in real life. Although sometimes, when he could hear Caprice and Lizzy through the paper-thin walls...

Kai flinched as someone banged at the door so forcefully that it shook.

"Did you flush yourself down the toilet or what's going on?" he heard Jax's annoyed voice. "I don't have all day, man!"

"Give me just a sec!" Kai answered.

He had to hurry. Not only did he risk pissing off Jax if he kept staring at himself in the mirror, but he would also miss his train to work.

Quickly, he grabbed his toothbrush and finished his morning body hygiene routine in less than a minute. Although his dentist recommended he use floss, every time Kai visited his office, he skipped it today. There wasn't enough time, and he hated flossing anyway. His hair was still moist from the shower, but he would let it air-dry on the way, like every day.

When he opened the door and peeked outside, the

big guy was gone. Kai heard him humming in the kitchen and hurried back to his room. The kitchen was too small for two people at once, but Kai didn't store anything in the antiquated, constantly leaking fridge anyway. Whenever he bought something, it would be gone the next day, so he had given up and ate on the run instead.

"You have twenty minutes to catch your train, Kai," Alessia's disembodied voice greeted him once he was back in his room.

That would be a close call, as always, but he would make it.

"Alessia, check emails," he said while grabbing his jeans and a random t-shirt from his closet.

It didn't really matter which one he wore, they were all as nerdy as the next one, all displaying superheroes and video game logos.

"No new emails, Kai," Alessia said.

Sometimes it seemed to him as if there was a hint of snark in her voice, although he knew personal AI shouldn't be capable of expressing such moods.

Kai pressed his lips together. Hopefully he'd hear from them once he was back home.

He grabbed his bag and left the room.

***

A musty odor welcomed Kai as he left the apartment and locked the door behind him. The lights in the long hall were broken and flickered in an unpleasant, frantic way, and the neon red sign at its end said XIT. Someone had battered the E years ago, and no one had bothered to fix it. The smell always reminded him of a mixture of fried eggs and wet socks. It was anything but pleasant, but he had gotten used to it over time. Although sometimes he wondered where it was coming from. Carol claimed that Mrs. Blunt, the cat lady who lived in the last apartment on the left, had dropped dead one day, and now she and her five or so cats were slowly decomposing behind the door. Kai thought that was a pretty macabre and sad story. Besides, why would a decomposing corpse smell like eggs and wet socks?

He passed the two dozen identical doors at a quick pace before he reached an iron gate at the end of the hall. He fished his ID card from his messenger bag and held it against the sensor next to the gate. It clicked and opened, letting him pass. He sighed in relief. Sometimes the sensor was broken, and it could take hours and dozens of angry phone calls to the community management until someone came and fixed it – provided it wasn't a weekend.

The gate shut behind him as he approached the elevators. Two identical gates marked the entrances to the two other halls leading away from the staircase and the elevators in the center. Although often broken, the security measure was a blessing for all residents, as break-ins and violent robberies were common in the area.

"You gotta be kidding me!" Kai said as he reached the elevators.

Out of order was blinking on the control panel between the two doors. He swore and began running down the stairs. He had to hurry now if he wanted to catch the train. Better down than up, but still, it was exhausting and took ages to run down the 18 flights of stairs.

The elevators were broken at least once a month, and Kai and his roommates constantly debated if the maintenance guys were total idiots or if the management had them use spare parts of the lowest quality.

Kai was a strict supporter of the first theory, and halfway down he was confronted with proof for that opinion once again. An overweight middle-aged man dressed in a sweaty polo shirt with the housing community's logo on its back was tinkering with a control panel located a few inches above the floor. The first thing Kai stared into when coming down the stairs was the man's plumber's smile.

Kai wrinkled his nose. Why, why in all worlds did guys like this always do that? It was almost like some unwritten law, as indisputable as the law of gravity or the theory of relativity.

He didn't bother to stop and ask the man if the elevators would be fixed by tonight. Chances were high they wouldn't be. Ascending the stairs to the 18th floor after a long day of labor was going to be a pain in the ass.

After what felt like an eternity, he finally reached the ground floor and hurried to the exit. Thick beads of sweat had built on his forehead and he was out of breath when he pushed the double door open and stepped outside. Although the air felt moist and smelled slightly sour, it was still much fresher than the stale air inside the staircase. Kai took a deep breath and hurried away.

It was a ten-minute walk to the train station – at a fast pace. Which meant that he would just about make it. The clouds hung deeply between the gray concrete tenements, all of them identical and only distinguishable by the huge numbers on their facades, their various shades of corrosion, and the graffiti decorating each of them.

Kai saw other people leaving the apartment blocks and hurrying to the train station. Some of them wore various kinds of uniforms or clothes displaying corporate identities, others were dressed in business attire. But there were also a lot of people to be seen who didn't work at all.

Groups of men and women loitered around benches or in doorways, most of them drunk or high at this early hour. Some held beer cans, others vaped or smoked weed. Shady individuals strolled through the pedestrian areas – the whole community complex containing a couple dozen such buildings as the one Kai lived in was a pedestrian area. Whoever had designed it many years ago must have thought it idyllic, but in reality it felt like a prison.

Most people, however, stayed inside. If they didn't need to go to work, they wouldn't leave their homes for days and weeks, especially since everything was delivered by drones nowadays. The sight of them flying and buzzing in the sky was so common that no one even noticed it anymore. They were as normal as birds had been in earlier times.

Kai saw two guys high as fuck argue about something and hurried away. The last thing he needed now was to get into trouble and miss work as a result. Although no law enforcement could be seen, the whole area, which was known for its crime, was monitored by extensive CCTV. Some cameras hung openly on street lanterns or house facades, others were integrated into drones that pretended to be just another harmless delivery automaton but instead kept a digital eye on everything and everyone.

Nevertheless, the area was anything but safe, which was why Kai never left his house after dark – no one did.

It's only temporary, he told himself again and again, and the hope that this was true drove him every day instead of letting him sink into lethargy like most people he knew.

A thick raindrop fell onto his forehead and he looked to the sky. It would start raining at any moment. Luckily he was almost there. He could already see the massive concrete and chrome building with the oversized Plexiglas windows – the station.

He ran and made it just before the stray raindrops could turn into a waterfall and soak him. He shook his head about himself inwardly. Why did he never manage to bring an umbrella, even though Alessia reminded him about it every time?

He didn't have time to contemplate if he was an absent-minded genius or simply a moron. A digital signal mimicking the traditional gong formerly heard on train stations clang from the speakers, indicating the train was about to enter the station. Kai hurried, taking two steps at once on the escalator, and arrived at the platform just as the train entered the station.

Contrary to the fancy monorails, skytrains and subways in the city, this train was old and almost appeared like a relic from an ancient, bygone era. It still used the traditional two rails and was annoyingly slow. It took forever to get to the city, but for Kai, like for so many others, it was the only way to reach downtown and his job. Like an ancient colossus, it came to a halt and the doors opened with a loud creak. Kai and the hundreds of others waiting on the platform rushed inside, hoping to find a seat.

Actually, Kai didn't have much hope of finding one. Most days, the trains were hopelessly overfilled, and he usually stood squeezed in between the other commuters, smelling alcohol, cheap perfume and sweat. But today, he was lucky.

When he boarded, he spotted an empty seat two rows away from him. Quickly, he made his way there and let himself fall onto the musty, worn-out cushion seconds before another guy could claim it. The man shot him an angry glance, and for a moment, Kai was sure he would start an argument about it, but then he turned away, a tired expression of resignation on his gray face.

Kai leaned back and watched the monotonous buildings of the district he lived in rush by as the train reached its top speed. Everything appeared blurry in the heavy rain drumming against the dirty window. No one spoke. People either stared at their mobile devices or gawked at the little screens and displays mounted directly in front of every seat or hanging from the ceiling or in the door frames. The bigger ones showed the news, informing people about the latest, horrifying incidents they were supposed to be scared of, while the smaller individual ones displayed commercials. Each device showed something different, depending on the person sitting in front of it.

The neuro-plants everyone wore connected to the train network automatically when passengers entered the vehicle. Within seconds, the system retrieved all available information about the implanted individual and showed them exactly the kind of ads and commercials that were of greatest interest to them. If someone had been browsing sneakers the day before, they would see advertisements for the latest models the big brands had to offer. Others would see ads for skin cream, romance novels, or the brand-new Italian-style espresso maker. The system would even know when a person had skipped breakfast and torture them with commercials from the biggest fast-food chains for the whole trip.

No one complained though, and people were so used to constantly being bombarded with ads that, most of the time, they didn't even notice them. When getting a neuro-plant, you had to sign a waiver that would allow the manufacturer to collect data and use it to enhance your experience and make your daily life easier and more pleasant.

Kai was usually too much occupied with his own thoughts and daydreams to even notice what the system was trying to sell him. Today, ads for floss, a water heater and the new Robo-Batman movie ran past him unnoticed while he was daydreaming about how he would celebrate when he finally got the email. Later, the system tried to convince him to sign up for a virtual gym membership. For only 1k bit-bucks extra a month, it would even come with a personal trainer AI that promised to get him into shape in no time.

"Become your dream self," the commercial promised with a silky female voice that only Kai could hear thanks to his neuro-plant. "Become better than your avatar in *The Scrolls of the Ancients*."

The mention of his favorite game made his head jerk up, and Kai realized that he had dozed off. The movement of the train and the gray monotony outside had made him fall asleep. He peeked at his watch and saw that it was only 20 minutes till he reached his destination. If only commuting was always like that. Then it would be more bearable.

Kai assumed that last night's long gaming session and the sprint to the train station had made him tired. He yawned and stretched himself, but then he straightened up as something he had never seen before caught his attention.

"Kai," the screen addressed him directly, a friendly but

assertive, male voice speaking to his neuro-plant. "Do you wish life could offer you more than it does? Are you made for greatness? Don't waste your time or time will waste you. Join the Cyber Squad!"

A skillfully edited sequence of well-known video game characters flashed over the screen while a dramatic score reached its crescendo. The colorful Cyber Squad logo appeared, and the voice continued.

"The adventure of your life is waiting for you, Kai! Send us your resume today. Become a hero!"

Kai stared at the screen in surprise. Of course he knew what Cyber Squad was, but he had never seen one of their recruiting ads address him directly.

Outside the window, the scenery began changing drastically as the train left the suburbs behind and approached the city. Majestic skyscrapers soared into the heavens. The closer the train came to the center, the brighter the world became. Usually, Kai loved staring out of the window and watching the city before the train disappeared into a tunnel for the rest of the journey. But not today.

Today he felt distracted by the personalized ad he had just seen.

Cyber Squad was the name of the biggest and most famous company providing quality assurance in the gaming industry. In earlier times, a job in QA was the least glamourous gaming position imaginable. While the coders did the magic and the level designers created worlds, the guys sitting in QAs were mostly losers, nerds dreaming of becoming a game developer one day. They were the lowest of the low in the food chain, looked down upon by the cool guys who actually created the games.

But those times were long gone.

Now, all games were played in VR. And since almost everyone had a neuro-plant, people logged into the virtual worlds using the implants in their brains – like Kai did every day. Although the game developers and hardware manufacturers claimed otherwise, connecting your brain into VR and especially the Net wasn't without danger.

Glitches and bugs, annoying in earlier decades, could cause brain damage or even death when experienced in neuro-plant-induced VR. Countless horror stories circulated on the web, although it was almost impossible to prove if any of them were true.

Over the last twenty years, VR had become more and more important in people's lives and now dominated all other entertainment forms. It was the easiest way to escape reality, with countless virtual worlds to explore. People rarely went outside anymore for many reasons. Why would they if the virtual worlds were so much better than the real one? They were worlds in which everyone could be whatever they wished to be and experience everything imaginable without limits. From vast MMORPG[6] worlds to simulations of everyday life – just better –, everything was possible. Some ten years ago, VR had been declared essential by the UN and had to become accessible to everyone, no matter their social status. Governments funded basic versions of neuro-plants and consoles to access the virtual world.

Not surprisingly, as a result of this the gaming and VR industries had become the most lucrative in the world, and even the smaller developers were worth billions on the stock market. It had made their lobby incredibly powerful. And the lobby didn't like it when reports of people dying horribly because of glitches and malfunctions made it into the news. Which was why most such stories were rumors and nothing more.

Nevertheless, the Cyber Squad was famous. Those guys jumped in when shit hit the fan. In a time when glitches and bugs could turn into deadly traps, quality assurance had become a high-risk job.

It was a job Kai didn't want to have. Yes, apparently they paid very well, and yes, he was an excellent gamer with an impressive overall Gamerscore.

The Gamerscore was like a virtual fingerprint. The neuro-plant collected data about all activities a gamer performed, what games they played, what achievements they got and much more. All of this was summed up in the player's Gamerscore on X-Perience, which was the standardized VR entrance platform every player had to use if they wanted to play games online.

Kai loved nothing more than VR games. But at the risk of brain damage or his life like the Cyber Squad guys? Nope.

Besides, he had other plans for his life, and he had been working hard over the last 24 months to achieve them.

The train entered the tunnel, and the magnificent city was replaced by darkness.

CHAPTER FOUR

Fifteen minutes later, the train arrived at the underground station of Central Plaza. Kai exited and followed the crowds on the escalators all the way up to the Skytrain station, a hyper-modern building. Made almost completely of glass, it appeared to float high above the streets of southern downtown. Fully automated, the high-tech monorail train arrived right on time, as it always did.

Kai hopped on, ready to enjoy the last five minutes of his daily commute. The Skytrain was a completely different travel experience than the train he used to get into the city.

Much less crowded, it offered a comfortable seat for every passenger. The air was pleasantly conditioned and scented. Most people here wore expensive business attire. This was the heart of the corporate world, and it showed everywhere.

Outside, high-rises of impressive architecture flew by, adorned by oversized billboards. This was a world he only could dream of. Even if his plans worked out, he would never become part of this society that seemed almost like a different world. Or maybe he would? Nothing would be impossible once he made it into the league.

Noiseless, the train reached the next station and Kai's final destination. It took him almost one and a half hours from his home to his workplace. That sucked, but it was only temporary. And the five-minute Skytrain ride cost him more than the rest of the commute, but it was the only way to reach the place. Well, he could walk for another twenty-five minutes instead, but he only did that when he ran out of money and couldn't afford the Skytrain.

Moving quickly, he descended the escalator and entered the huge mall he worked at every day.

***

Kai's job sucked. He hated it.

He hated every day, every hour, every minute. For some reason, it always seemed as if time went by much slower here than in VR. Hell, even the dragging daily commute went by faster than being here. It didn't matter if it was slow or busy, the days always took forever.

"Is there something exciting in this corner, invisible to me?"

He heard Hana right behind him and flinched.

"No, I'm sorry," he mumbled, then hurried away. But not fast enough.

"Then why are you standing around and staring into nothing?" Hana threw after him angrily. "It's not what I'm paying you for, is it?"

Kai looked at her, a remorseful, shy smile on his face. He knew that had worked best to soothe her before. But not today. She glared at him, hands on her hips.

Damn it. He knew that look. She would fire him if he didn't get a grip on himself. Hopefully by tomorrow he would gleefully tell her that he quit, but as long as he couldn't be sure, he needed to keep this lousy job. Kai sighed inwardly, then walked up to the table closest to him. The patrons sitting there gave him a displeased look. They'd obviously been waiting for him to serve them for some time.

He took their order and then rushed past his boss, who was still standing there, watching him Argus-eyed.

Working as a waiter in a restaurant truly wasn't what he had dreamed of for his life, especially given his degree in mathematics, but he kept telling himself that it was only temporary.

He knew very well that he could consider himself lucky that he had even this shitty job though. Most of his friends were unemployed, like almost 50% of the population. After the second industrial revolution, which had happened almost two decades ago, millions had lost their jobs. What had been called a "revolution" had been nothing else but the complete automatization of almost the entire manufacturing and service industries. Nowadays, most jobs were done by robots and AI, and there were only a few industries left that still required a human workforce. As a matter of fact, the hospitality industry wasn't one of them.

Almost all restaurants, bars and hotels were fully automatized, leaving only a few human engineers to maintain the functionality of the machines. However, there were some upscale restaurants that still hired human personnel for their kitchens and for service. They were mostly frequented by elderly patrons who had the required money to spend, since the prices were easily 500% higher than in an automated place. Those people happily paid the prices for the simple luxury of experiencing dining as it used to be in earlier decades. Most of the patrons even tipped generously, although it wasn't required or asked for.

Fuji, the restaurant Kai worked at, was part of a chain by the same name and specialized in upscale Japanese cuisine. The only reason he had even got the job wasn't a qualification or a hard-working attitude but his looks, plain and simple. Fuji only hired Japanese, and if none were available, then people who could pass as such were the next best thing.

Kai looked nothing like a Japanese. His dad had been Thai and his mom from Ohio. They had both passed away when he was five years old. He grew up with his grandma, who had died of cancer shortly after he had graduated from high school. The money she left him had helped him through college – to achieve a degree that had proven to be as useful as a hole in the head. Kai had no siblings, and the only family he had left were distant relatives who lived on Ko Pha Ngan, a tiny island in the Gulf of Siam, and whom he had never met.

Although he was too nerdy and shy to know it, Kai's face was handsome with its Asian-Caucasian features, but he was too short and skinny to be considered attractive. Not that it made any difference, since most social interaction took place in VR anyway, and there he could take any shape he wanted.

Kai wasn't actually his real name but a nickname given to him by his parents at birth. It was a Thai tradition he had never really understood but, he didn't mind it, since his real name was Kelvin Suksan, who sounded like a total dork to his ears. Kai was nice. It could have been a Viking name and it fitted the characters he liked to play in VR. He just needed to keep his mouth shut about what his name meant.

Translated from Thai, it meant "chicken". He would never understand why his parents had chosen that name, but he showed them respect by wearing it. Apparently, it was considered completely fine in Thailand. However, after being mocked mercilessly in high school when his classmates found out the meaning, he usually said it meant "warrior" when someone asked. He liked the nod of appreciation that appeared on people's faces when he told them, and no one ever bothered to look it up.

Of course, Hana, his manager, was neither blind nor stupid when she hired him. She had looked him up and down, a condescending smirk on her face, then said: "You'll do."

She'd been proved right. Most patrons either didn't notice or didn't care that he was different.

But they noticed when he was doing a crappy job, like today. No matter how much he tried, he couldn't focus. He was too nervous because of the email he was expecting. The email that was supposed to change his life.

He forced himself to snap out of his daydreams and brought the patrons their drinks. Walking away from the table, he glanced at the artful clock on the wall, which resembled a setting sun.

Oh God… it was only 1 p.m. This day was going to take forever!

***

Miraculously, he managed not to get fired, although he could tell that Hana was toying with the thought in her head, judging by the icy, displeased looks she had given him all day.

Whenever he had had a short break, he'd peeked at his mobile device, hoping it would show him the email he was waiting for, but instead all he had gotten today was a stupid newsletter from a virtual gym he would never visit that was trying to sell him protein drinks. It was driving him nuts that he still didn't have an answer.

On his way back, Kai could hardly sit still on the train. He felt so anxious that he couldn't focus on anything. He didn't even notice that the system showed him the same ad as in the morning again. The one that had tried to recruit him for the Cyber Squad. Nor did he pay attention to the government announcement that was broadcast to everyone's device every day at 10 p.m., informing them about the curfew.

"Stay inside. Stay safe!" a fatherly voice said in the ad, followed by a montage showing footage, numbers and statistics that warned of all the dangers that could befall an individual if they disrespected the authorities' orders. Crime, sickness, germs and many more dangers were lurking outside, particularly at night. Why more at night than during the day, no one asked, of course. Over time, most people had become accustomed to staying inside and were perfectly happy with this lifestyle. Some claimed it was a tool for control, but Kai didn't waste much thought on such theories. He preferred to stay inside anyway. After all, the dull gray outside world that smelled of routine and obligations couldn't compete with VR.

Finally, after what seemed like an eternity, the train reached his station and he exited, tired and frustrated.

It was 9:45 p.m. and dark when he left the brightly

illuminated building. He quickly made his way through the desolate canyons formed by the massive tenements looming everywhere in the dark, starless sky. When Kai had first moved here after college, he had gotten lost a couple of times. Now his legs walked him home on auto-pilot even if he was distracted, such as today.

An unpleasant wind was blowing in his face, promising more rain, when he arrived at his building. It was only when he entered the main hall that he remembered about the elevator. A vague hope spread inside him that it might have been fixed during the day. After all, he had been gone for twelve hours. *That should have been enough time, right?*

Of course, it wasn't fixed.

Kai sighed.

It's only temporary, he told himself over and over again while ascending the stairs. When he finally arrived upstairs he was soaked in sweat and his heart was racing. The lights in the hall leading to his apartment were even more temperamental than they had been in the morning and flickered like in a horror movie, but at least the security door worked. He would never forget that night a bit over a year ago he had had to spend on the staircase after the door had malfunctioned and wouldn't let him pass.

The familiar odor of eggs and wet socks greeted him when he dragged himself down the hall and finally entered the apartment.

Loud neo-punk music came from the kitchen as well as giggles. Caprice and Lizzy occupied the tiny space, cooking and making out. It seemed miraculous to Kai that the place hadn't burned down yet. Maybe it would one day. His other two roommates were at home, too. He could hear Carol on the phone in her room and the smell of weed coming from Jax's room. Kai was the only one in the household with a job and ambitions. The other four lived off their parents and the universal income the government provided.

Theoretically, no one needed to work if they didn't

expect much from their lives. But Kai did. He knew exactly what he wanted.

"Good evening, Kai," Alessia said when he entered his room and threw his bag on the chair at his desk. "I hope you had a pleasant day."

"Another day in paradise," Kai answered sardonically, wondering if there was some hot water left for him. The back of his t-shirt was moist with sweat, and he could smell that his deodorant had given up on its job during his ascent to the 18th floor.

"I'm happy to hear that," the AI answered, and, as so often, Kai couldn't tell if she was being sarcastic or not. Sometimes he was sure she was mocking him, but according to the developers this was impossible.

"You have mail, Kai," Alessia continued after a second, and he jerked his head as if someone had electrocuted him.

"From whom?"

"I think it's the email you've been waiting for. Would you like me to read it to you?"

But Kai had already pulled his mobile device from the pocket and was staring at it. The email must have arrived during his climb up the stairs. Waves of cold and heat hit his exhausted body, pumping it with adrenaline, as he stared at the sender's name and email address.

This was it. This was what he had been waiting for. A mixture of excitement, anticipation and anxiety filled him as he opened the email with shaky fingers.

Kai had to sit down after reading it.

CHAPTER FIVE

"Come on, man," Stan said, kicking dirt with his feet, which spread in the air with a perfect particle effect. "Stop being such a bore! You can't hide forever!"

Kai looked up and shot his friend an irritated glance. "Thanks for your understanding. You're a true sweetheart."

He turned his attention back to the blacksmith crafting station and continued forging the sword he was working on. It would be a pretty shitty sword, but it didn't matter. Once finished, he would melt it down again and start over anyway.

He and Stan were in the courtyard of his castle, high up in the mountains. Sun shone on their perfect bodies and a pleasant breeze blew the scent of mountain flowers to their noses while the eagle circling high above them in the azure sky let out a characteristic shriek.

Stan was wearing his favorite avatar again, the stunningly exotic-looking Dark Elf girl with the slender body and glowing eyes. He balanced on the battlement, ignoring that it dropped down more than 300 feet only inches from his heels, then jumped from merlon to merlon light-footedly. His Thief character class came with a boost of +25 to light-footedness, which allowed him to pull off all kinds of acrobatic poses.

"I mean, yeah, I know it sucks, mate," he said with his deep voice and Aussie accent that didn't fit the body at all. "But you have to look at the bright side."

"And that would be?" Kai asked, slamming the hammer

down on the forge in frustration, his exaggerated muscles gleaming in the sunlight.

"Well, you have more time to play TSOTA."

Kai's eyes narrowed. "Seriously?"

"Bloody heck, yeah. You even could become Emperor in a campaign. I'm sure the guild would support you, even Red."

"A dream come true."

The Elf rolled her oversized eyes, turned around and began jumping from merlon to merlon in the other direction. "Stop being such a crank!"

"It's a hot day and you're working hard," came a soft, female voice from behind them. "Would you like me to bring you refreshments, my love?"

A young woman of stunning beauty had approached them from the castle. Her thick, flaxen hair was arranged into an artful braid that hung down below her waist. The blue gown she wore perfectly showcased her feminine curves and was of the same color as her bright eyes. An affectionate expression was displayed on her roundish face, which was covered in light freckles.

"No, thank you, Freya," Kai said, not looking at the woman but stubbornly staring into the flames of his forge.

"As you wish, my love," she answered, then slowly walked back to the house. Stan turned his head and followed the smooth movement of her hips with his eyes for a moment, then continued his acrobatic exercise. He wasn't just doing it to pass the time. Every jump and pirouette he made advanced his acrobatic skill level. In a similar way, Kai's mindless hammering and forging of cheap swords advanced his crafting and stamina skills.

"You know, I'll always be jealous that you got that sheila[7]. She's so much hotter than mine," Stan said as the NPC disappeared inside through the heavy wooden door.

Every player could court and marry an NPC if they wanted. The AI generated non-player characters would move into a player's house and take care of their needs. NPCs of both sexes were available in all racial and character classes the game had to offer. Most players had a virtual spouse that would cook for them and tell them how amazing and heroic they were. However, the game wouldn't allow a player to hurt or abuse such NPCs.

Sex was off the table, too. The game didn't permit any acts of a sexual nature, and the NPCs and player characters alike didn't even have genitals. More precisely, it wasn't possible to undress them further than down to their underwear.

"Almost like in a real marriage," Stan used to joke about the sexless life in the game.

Stan was around forty in real life and had apparently been married until his wife had dumped him for another man with more drive and a better income. He had spent most of his time in VR ever since.

Although *The Scrolls of the Ancients* did not allow sexual acts between players or with NPCs, there were, of course, countless games and virtual worlds that did. In fact, it was how most young people had sex nowadays. VR intercourse was safe and allowed people to live out any kind of fantasy or fetish imaginable. The flesh was virtual, yet the arousal players experienced was very real.

Kai ignored his friend's lecherous comments about his virtual wife and kept hammering, as if draining his avatar's muscles of energy could change anything.

"Come on, Kai," the Dark Elf said after a moment had passed. "You can't hide forever. We need you on the trial. You're one of the best, and you know it. Apparently, the Blade of Oblivion drops at the final boss. You always wanted that one, didn't you?"

Kai stopped his work and sighed.

His friend was right. He couldn't hide forever. Killing time wouldn't ease his frustration. Quite the contrary.

The email had not been what he had been expecting and hoping for.

Two weeks ago he had applied for the NightStalk e-sports team for the third time and had now been rejected. Even though he had beaten all other players who had applied. He had been the best by far. It was completely incomprehensible why he had been rejected.

Dear Kai, the email had said. *Thank you so much for applying for the NightStalk e-sports team. We appreciate your interest and enthusiasm. However, even though you scored exceptionally, we regret that, at this time, we can't offer you a slot in the team. Your profile is not quite what we need. We encourage you to apply next year, however... blah blah blah, yadda yadda, sincerely, Mr. Prick.*

The message had crushed Kai. He had been training for months. All his hopes for a better life had been resting on being accepted into a high-class e-sports team. NightStalk was one of the most popular MMO shooters in the world. Its top players had become rich and lived in huge mansions. But even the lower ranks of professional players earned a very decent amount. More in a month than what Kai earned in a year at Fuji, provided Hana didn't fire him. Thankfully, he had been off for the last two days or she would have fired him for sure, as depressed and demotivated as he was.

On the other side, why would he even bother anymore? Maybe he should simply spend his time in VR. There were enough free-to-play games out there that he could play without having an income.

"Come on!" Stan was persistent. "The trial starts in ten minutes. They're holding a spot for you and I won't leave until you come with me."

Kai smiled. "You're a pain in the ass."

The Elf jumped from the battlement and approached him, a wide grin on her face. "That's my middle name. Now grab your armor and let's go!"

***

Five minutes later, they joined the others in the lobby of the event. Ten other players were already there, waiting. All of them were members of the guild, including Cloud69, Serene559, LifeSupportForYou2, and, of course, Red. They all were wearing different avatars than at the battle for Castle Black Rock a few days earlier. The campaign had been PvP[8] and required completely different skills, specifications and equipment than a trial, which was PvE.[9] Red's character was a massive Orc covered in heavy armor. As always for such an event, he would be one of the two tanks.

Cloudgirl had chosen a stunningly beautiful DPS[10] sorceress with flaming-red hair, and Serene was a Rogue-class archer. Life would be one of the two healers required for a trial, of course, since she was the best healer the guild had to offer. Stan had changed from his beloved Dark Elf into a Warrior-class damage dealer. He was one of those players who always chose female characters, but unlike his Elf, this one wasn't pretty to look at. She was bulkier than a bodybuilding champion, and the heavy armor completely covering her frame left her feminine curves to the imagination. A massive two-handed sword was strapped to her back.

Kai had chosen a DPS of the Paladin class. His tall and graceful knight was equipped with sword and shield and was an excellent damage dealer, yet not squishy. He could take more damage than most DPSs and was therefore almost like an extra off-tank. Long blond hair stuck out from under his helmet, and his eyes shimmered cold-fire blue.

Everyone who had been invited to join in today was a seasoned high-level player wearing only the finest equipment that dropped in the most challenging dungeons and arenas.

No wonder, as what the group intended to accomplish was serious business. The Dark Lair was the newest trial, only released the previous week. Trials were basically nothing else but more advanced and challenging dungeons designed for teams of twelve players instead of the classic formation of four that went into group dungeons together: two damage dealers, one healer, one tank.

To be effective, a trial needed two tanks, two healers and eight damage dealers. The Dark Lair was challenging for experienced players on normal difficulty and hardcore on veteran difficulty.

And that was exactly what the group was attempting to beat today. It would be extremely tough, but the best loot in the game dropped at exactly such instances.

Shortly after they arrived, a message flashed up in Kai's field of view.

Redrum666 has sent you a group invite. Do you want to accept?

He accepted, and a second later the right corner of his HUD showed the gamer tags of all twelve players in the party, as well as their character class, level and life stats. The red health bar was at full capacity for all players, but that would no doubt change soon.

Finishing his last preparations before the game started in less than five minutes, Kai felt excited. Maybe Stan was right after all, and a challenging distraction like this was exactly what he had needed.

"Have you ever heard of Cyber Squad?" he asked his friend to pass the time until the gates to the dungeon opened.

Stan spun around and looked at him. "Sure have. Those guys are badass! Why?"

"I saw an ad on the train the other day. Apparently they're recruiting."

"Oh wow. Was it personalized at you?"

"It was. Addressed me directly by name."

Stan whistled, then drew his huge sword and began swinging it, practicing different forms of attacks and blocks.

"Then you caught their attention. Are you gonna apply?"

Kai shrugged. "I never thought about it. But I had very specific plans with my life until two days ago. Not anymore–"

His friend stopped his practice and grabbed Kai's shoulder instead. "Don't even think about it, ok?"

"Why?"

"Have you been living under a rock, mate? It's one of the most dangerous jobs in the world. The easiest way to get killed or turn into a drooling vegetable."

"It also pays well…"

"That's true. But is money really worth the risk? I mean, we all should be grateful for what those guys are doing. But becoming part of it? No chance in hell–"

"Ok, team, let's do this," a familiar voice interrupted. Red and a few others were already standing at the gate, where a holographic timer was counting down the last minute. "Check your equipment one last time and go to the vendor if you need health, stam or mag pods.[11] This is gonna be tough but we can do it!"

Some people mumbled their agreement, but otherwise everyone was deeply focused. For most of the players gathered there, it would be the first time that they entered a new trial on veteran mode. Everyone was excited.

When the countdown went down all the way to zero, the heavy iron gate opened with a rattle and the players stared down a dimly lit tunnel leading directly into a dark cave. Cold wind smelling of death and decay hit their faces as they marched through the gate, and the neutral music of the lobby turned into a dark tune of suspense.

CHAPTER SIX

The path descending into the darkness was narrow and only allowed the players to walk in single file. Silence filled the cavern, the only noise coming from the water dripping from the massive stalactites, some of them 30 feet or more. The wind whistling through the rock formations had something menacing about it and, at times, sounded like whispers in the dark.

Somewhere deep below, the sound of fast running water indicated an underground creek or maybe even a river. From time to time, a quick scurrying noise reached Kai's ears and made his skin crawl. It was his first time in this dungeon, but he had read everything about it when it was released. Even if he had not, the sound was a very well-known one to every RPG player and experienced dungeon explorer. Spiders. Huge ones. And lots of them.

It took the party a couple of minutes to descend to the bottom of the cave. Red used the time for a lecture.

"Ok, let's talk about mechanics," he said in that smug tone typical of him. "Who of you have done this trial before?"

About half of the party answered with a 'yes', the rest kept quiet. Usually, Kai and Stan agreed that the guild leader's sermons about mechanics were annoying as fuck, but in this case Kai was all ears. He had heard that some of the bosses in this dungeon were extremely tough, and every experienced player knew that learning the mechanics of each boss was crucial for beating the more challenging dungeons and trials. Like most others who played this game regularly, he knew the boss mechanics of all important dungeons by heart, which was why he usually hated Red's lectures.

"The first boss is pretty standard, a little warm-up, so to speak. The main tank, aka me, will draw his attention while the off-tank focuses on the adds. Cloud, Serene and Eldritch will eliminate the adds as they keep coming while the rest of you go straight for the big, fat son of a bitch. All clear?"

"Yes, sir!" Stan said with exaggerated enthusiasm.

Kai chuckled. Sooner or later, his friend would be thrown out of the guild if he continued mocking Red like that. Stan had been trying to convince Kai to form their own guild for months, but Kai was hesitant. It would be a lot of work, and he would rather spend his time slaying monsters and enemy players instead of organizing shit.

Just before they reached the bottom, Kai noticed a glitch. The rock formations they passed to their left flickered for a second then changed their shape. That was nothing unusual, though, and players were more than used to such occurrences. Some games were glitchier than others, but *TSOTA* usually ran relatively stable. However, it was especially after new content or updates were released that glitches could sometimes occur. Environmental flickers such as the one Kai had just witnessed were harmless and common, as were occasional clipping bugs. Kai just hoped they wouldn't encounter more severe issues. There was hardly anything more frustrating than not being able to finish an instance because of a showstopper bug.

Following the others, Kai jumped from a ledge into the arena-like bottom of the cave. The ledge was just high enough that it didn't cause more than 10% damage when jumping down, but it was impossible to climb back up. On one side the arena was confined by rocks and on the other by a cliff. A typical point of no return in a game. From here on, there were only two ways to leave the dungeon: as a victor or as a corpse. There was also a third option: abandon the instance and logging off. But that was out of the question for a serious player with honor in their bones. After all, everyone hated quitters.

The music changed from a slow tune of suspense to a faster and more dramatic score. It indicated that they were approaching a dungeon boss. And they didn't have to wait long.

The tapping noise grew louder, followed by a bone-chilling shriek. Then eight oversized legs, each one as tall as a tree, appeared behind a rock formation.

"Get ready!" Red commanded.

Everyone in the team drew their weapons; swords, bows, fireballs. Illumination spread through the cave and made it appear even more impressive, having been hidden mostly in darkness.

The shriek grew louder and a spider of the size of a mammoth appeared from behind the rocks, rising to its full height. Its multiple eyes glowed red and its gigantic maw showed oversized fangs and drooled.

The sight gave Kai the creeps. He hated spiders. Yet, for some reason, game devs loved throwing them at players as often as they could. There was hardly a creature more common in RPGs than the giant spider. And this one was a particularly frightening specimen.

A tag appeared above the spider's head.

The Guardian
Dungeon Boss/Arachnid
2500000/2500000

Even for high-class damage dealers with a DPS rate of more than 20k, it would take a while to bring this beast down.

"Careful, he's gonna pounce! Roll dodge!" Red warned.

The hairy spider legs tensed, then the monstrous arachnid leaped into the air and jumped right onto the group. Kai performed a roll dodge evasive maneuver and dove into safety as one of the legs crashed onto the spot where he had been standing just a second ago. Only now he noticed that all eight legs ended in razor-sharp, black claws. Most likely a one-hit death strike if a damage dealer got hit by it directly.

But the team was well-versed and no one had got hurt. So far, so good.

Kai felt his heart pounding as a wave of pleasant adrenaline rushed through his body. Red drew his sword and performed a class-specific attack to taunt the monster. Immediately, the Guardian turned his attention to the tank and began slashing at him furiously, using its four front legs. The tank took a blocking stance, covering his body with his shield.

He maybe was a pompous asshole, but Kai had to give Red credit for being an excellent tank. Yellow numbers appeared above the shield, indicating the damage the boss did with every hit: 7k, 15k, even 25k. A squishy DPS would be instant toast.

Now that the arachnid was occupied, Kai and the other damage dealers launched their assault.

His sword outstretched, Kai performed a combo of three consecutive attacks, aiming at one of the spider's back legs.

5000, 3700, 8000, Critical! 16500 appeared in red above the monster as he hit it.

Not bad!

More numbers flashed all around the massive boss as the other damage dealers hit it with all they had.

"Watch out for the adds!" Red called out. "Use AoEs[12] on them!"

Not stopping his attack, Kai turned his head and saw at least two dozen spiderlings approach. About the size of a Great Dane, some of the 'little' arachnids came running from the dark corners of the cave, their feet making that uncanny noise on the stone floor that every RPG player hated. Others came down the stalactites or descended on silk threads from the ceiling.

As instructed, the three dedicated damage dealers and the off-tank turned their attention to the spiderlings. The Sorceress cast a powerful ice AoE attack that slowed the swarm down while the other two began slashing through the arachnids that looked almost as disgusting as their big-ass counterpart.

Convinced his teammates would do their job just fine, Kai turned his attention back to the boss.

After taking heavy damage for a minute, the Guardian stopped attacking the tank, stood up on its back legs and let out a bone-shaking shriek.

"Careful, the fucker's gonna spit!" Red warned.

Too late. The Guardian had already opened its horrible mouth and released a massive cloud of green and clearly venomous ichor.

Just before the spider's nasty DoT[13] attack could hit Kai and the fighters closest to him, a luminous shield appeared around them. A ranged attack, the venom bounced off the shield and disappeared.

"Thanks, Life!" Kai called. He didn't even have to look to know it had been her who had cast the protective spell. Life was by far the best healer he had ever encountered.

"You're welcome," she answered, with that calm attitude typical of her, while simultaneously casting a healing spell over the players engaging the adds who were taking a fair amount of damage.

The Guardian tensed its legs again, then pounced into the group attacking it. Kai roll-dodged into safety easily, but Renegade1617 wasn't so lucky. He was still a relatively new player who had been playing *TSOTA* for a couple of months and only got into the guild because he was buddy-buddy with Red. One of the oversized spider legs hit him straight in the chest and the razor-sharp claw impaled him.

Renegade shrieked, then his body turned limp and gray. On his HUD, Kai saw that the guy's health bar had dropped to zero. To make his insta-death appear even more frightening, the Guardian lifted the impaled body up and smashed it against the wall.

"Whoa," Stan said. "That's a bloody badass move!"

"Haha," the now disembodied voice of the fallen warrior said dryly. "Can someone please revive me?"

"On it," the off-healer said, already on the move to his fallen comrade.

"Don't–" Red tried to warn his teammate, but it was too late.

As soon as the healer came close enough to revive the dead Renegade, the Guardian lashed out and impaled him as well.

"The fuck!" the healer shouted angrily. "You wanted to share that mechanic with the rest of us when exactly, Red?"

"Shut up! I didn't expect any of us would fall. This boss is supposed to be a warm-up, not a wipe!"

"We're far from a wipe," Life chimed in calmly. "Focus, everyone!"

She was right. The giant spider was down to almost 50%. The DPS was doing a solid job.

Performing his roll-dodges had drained Kai's stamina to 35%, so he accessed his quickslots and used a stam pod. Back to 100%, he performed another attack combo, landing a critical hit of 21000.

A second wave of spiderlings appeared as the boss fell below 50% health. Kai saw them crawling at frightening speeds from all directions. But suddenly they froze. They were set back a couple of meters, unfroze, then kept running toward the party.

Kai furrowed his virtual brow. That was the second glitch within less than ten minutes. And it was never a good sign if NPCs glitched.

He focused his attention back on the boss spider, which again stood up on its back legs, ready to spit another round of venom. The huge, drooling maw opened and green ichor appeared – then it suddenly froze in mid-air.

As did the Guardian.

The gigantic arachnid had frozen. Erect on his back legs with venom at his mouth, he made a disturbing sight.

Moans and sighs of frustration could be heard from the team.

"Ah, come on," Stan called out. "That's rubbish!"

"What? What happened?" asked the dead healer, who was in the twilight zone and couldn't see what was happening around his dead body.

"The game froze," Kai said, looking around.

After a brief inspection of the cave, it was apparent that it wasn't only the Guardian that had frozen. All the spiderlings were motionless in the middle of their attack mode, and even the sound had stopped. No running water could be heard. Only the dramatic combat music kept going, which made glitches like this even more annoying.

For a moment, everyone remained in combat stance, waiting for the game to unfreeze and the spider to continue with its attack.

When nothing happened, they slowly began standing at ease and sheathing their weapons.

"So, what now?" someone asked.

Red shrugged. "We wait for it to unfreeze."

"Pff, as if that ever happened before," Stan said.

The guild leader shot him an irritated glance but said nothing.

"Can someone please revive me, for heaven's sake?" the dead healer sighed.

"Hang on," LifeSupport said, approaching the two fallen players.

"Sorry, not working," she added after a moment. "The crystals won't work."

"Ugh. Fuck my life," the healer said.

"Why?" Stan complained, stepping beside Kai. "Why does it always have to happen with freshly released content? Why can't they drop a finished product for once?"

Kai grinned. "You've been around for a while, dude. Can you remember it being any different?"

"Nope. But–"

Huge, red glowing 3D letters appeared in the air filling the cave.

"*Attention, players currently located in the Dark Lair,*" a feminine AI voice read the writing aloud. It came from everywhere at once and was impossible to mute. Whatever the game system was attempting to communicate had to be of the highest importance.

Everyone jerked their heads. The ones who had begun chatting with each other fell silent. Glitches were common, but announcements like this one were not.

"*We are currently experiencing an unusual occurrence in this location,*" the voice continued while the words flew through the cave. "*We ask you to keep a distance from NPCs as much as possible. Remain calm and stay where you are. Please, do not log out of the instance or the game. I repeat, **do not** start the log-off process **under any circumstances**. Help is on the way. Please remain calm!*"

The party members stared at each other in disbelief. Stan's broad face formed a surprised O.

"What in the bloody fucking hell?"

"I know," Kai said. "Odd. Very odd."

An uneasy feeling crept up Kai's spine. Standing in this huge, dark cave, surrounded by motionless spider NPCs that appeared as if they were waiting for the right moment to strike and finish everyone off when they least expected it, felt anything but comforting. The feeling became even stronger when he glanced at the frozen giant spider, hovering above them, its front legs outstretched, ready to impale anyone who was stupid enough to get close.

Although *TSOTA* was a virtual world, driven by algorithms and a powerful game engine, it appeared as real as the world outside. If it weren't for the HUDs, tags and the player's ability to access their inventory or the game menu using their minds, it could have been real. The players could feel cold and warm and even a breeze on their virtual skin. They could see and hear everything that happened around as they would in their real body. And they even could smell the scents of wildflowers or exotic fruits and odors coming from monsters and wild animals.

Players couldn't feel pain, yet they felt an unpleasant sensation when taking damage or dying, and as far as their bodies outside of VR were concerned, everything was as real as it could be. Players' bodies produced adrenaline when in battle, sweat when sprinting, endorphins when they got rewarded for a heroic quest, and arousal when they encountered mature content.

But they could also experience stress, fear, panic, and even shock. Which was why Survival Horror games came with explicit warnings. It wasn't uncommon for people to die of heart attacks or exhaustion while experiencing adventures in VR.

The most dangerous thing that could happen was when the log-out process malfunctioned for some reason. The player's brain was directly connected to VR via the neuro-plant. It wasn't possible to simply pull the cord out and exit the simulation. The log-off process was a highly complicated procedure no user really understood. But the fact was, if the shit hit the fan, there wouldn't be a back door with a bright glowing exit sign like in a movie theater. The system would begin an emergency log-out if it noticed the player's brain's signals were running amok, which could indicate a stroke, heart attack, or another emergency in the real world. But in most cases, it would be too late by then.

That was the reason why the system message had made Kai feel so uneasy. His intuition was telling him that something was wrong here. Very wrong.

"Ok, guys, you heard the lady," he addressed the group. "Back away from the NPCs, especially the boss. Group up in the corners!"

Kai, Stan and a few others backed away as far as possible from the giant black menace and its minions, but Red, Cloud, Serene and the rest stayed where they were.

"Relax," the guild leader said, displeased that Kai had taken the initiative to get the party to safety. "Nothing's gonna happen. It's just a glitch."

"The *leave instance* option is jammed," Serene said, concern in her voice. "Have any of you ever seen something like that?"

Kai opened the menu to see for himself. The *leave instance* option was grayed out and not clickable for him too.

"Nope," Kai said. "And I don't like it. Who knows how long we'll be stuck here."

"Shit, I need to cook dinner for my kids. I can't stay here forever," Cloudgirl said.

"Well, fuck that, I'm out of here," the healer declared. "I'm not gonna hang out in the twilight zone in a broken dungeon forever. I'm logging off."

"The system said we shouldn't do that," Kai said.

"Screw the system," the healer said.

A second later, his tone had changed.

"Um… it won't let me."

"It won't let you exit the game and VR?" Stan asked.

"I'd shake my head but I can't because I'm fucking *dead*!" the healer said.

"Guess we're stuck here then, whether we like it or not," Red said. "We could explore the dungeon a bit and see if we find some hidden stuff we would otherwise overlook when in combat. Maybe there's hidden loot or secret passages."

"I'm not sure if that's a good idea," Kai objected. "The physics might be glitched, too. That would make it dangerous to fall off a cliff or something like that."

"Pah," Red said, now visibly annoyed. He stepped up to the frozen Guardian and kicked the giant spider in one of its hairy legs.

Suddenly all hell broke loose around them.

Without any warning, the Guardian came back to life. Letting out a bone-chilling shriek, the arachnid spewed the venomous green ichor over Red and the other players standing close by. It happened so fast that none of them had time to evade the attack, block, or cast a damage shield.

On his HUD, Kai saw how the health bars of all affected players had dropped by 30% and then continued going down due to the DoT nature of the poison.

"What the fuck!" Red screamed while the two others began shrieking frantically. "It burns! Oh my God, it burns like hell!"

All three dropped to the ground, convulsed in pain. Real pain.

There couldn't be any doubt about that.

Everyone else stared at what was happening in disbelief and shock.

"Kai," Stan grabbed his friend by the arm and pointed at the Guardian's health bar. "Look!"

Not only was its health bar back at 100%, it had also turned from red to gold, and so had the whole name tag of the dungeon boss. Gold meant that the enemy was invincible. Usually players had no other choice but to run when they encountered a monster with a golden tag in the world. But this was a closed dungeon. There was no place to run!

"We're so toast," Stan whispered, his usual snarky attitude gone.

Kai froze as he saw that the spiderlings were back in the game, too. And they, too, were golden.

"Shields!" he called out. "Stack together!"

He surprised himself the second the words left his mouth. His heart was racing and existential fear threatened to overwhelm him, yet instead of being paralyzed by it, he took control of the situation.

The party members who were still standing followed his command and quickly gathered in one place, back to back. The first wave of spiderlings approached them, their huge fangs moving in their frightening maws, their multiple eyes glowing menacingly. Kai jerked his shield and bashed it into the three spiders closest to him. Two were thrown to the ground without taking any damage, but the third fell over the cliff into the darkness.

"What should we do?" Eldritch asked in a fearful voice. "They're invincible!"

"Throw anything at them that will stall them," Kai replied. "Ice, caltrops... anything! We need to buy us some time!"

On his HUD, Kai saw that the life stats of the three affected by the poison were now dropping rapidly. He glanced up and saw why.

The giant spider had moved directly over the three figures on the ground and was hitting them with its front legs, doing heavy damage. The two damage dealers would be down to zero in no time, and even Red, who was a tank, wouldn't sustain such an attack for much longer.

What in the hell is happening here?

It seemed like a nightmare, something none of them thought could ever happen in real life. Such stuff was supposed to be confined to urban legends, nothing more. And yet...

Kai got a grip on himself and stopped staring at his friends being butchered.

"Heals! We need heals! *Now!*"

"Sorry, I can't be of much help," the fallen healer replied, oblivious to the dramatic scenes happening around him. "Hey... the log-off... it's working!"

Life slammed her staff on the ground and a cloud of glowing particles appeared around the three fallen team members.

Kai sighed in relief. At least the heal worked. It saved the two DPSs just in time before their health bar reached zero. But it was only a temporary reprieve. If no one stopped the Guardian, the three would die. And so out of control was the system at the moment, that wouldn't mean anything good.

"I need to get closer to cast a stronger heal!" Life said, her usual almost stoical calmness gone.

Meanwhile, the spiderlings were about to overrun the members of the group who were still standing.

A sharp pain ran like a bolt through Kai's body, and he thought he would pass out. Never before had he experienced anything even remotely close to that. He winced and looked down at himself. A spiderling had bitten through the armor on his leg as if it were made of straw and was now ramming its fangs into his flesh. Kai's health bar began dropping as venom sprayed into the wound. For a second, panic threatened to overwhelm him as all kinds of horror stories shot through his mind, about people actually dying in VR or having their consciousness trapped forever. It was true... it was all true.

Then his survival instinct kicked in and his reflexes took over. He had been playing this game for hundreds of hours. He could beat such spiderlings in his sleep, golden or not.

Kai rammed his sword into the spider, which answered the attack with a furious hiss but otherwise didn't take any damage. Then he performed a power attack with his shield. The arachnid let go of his leg and rolled toward the cliff, hissing even more aggressively. But Kai wasn't willing to give it a chance to get up again. He charged at the spiderling and kicked it off the cliff.

"We need to push them off the ledge!" he shouted. "That's our only chance!"

A cloud of glowing particles surrounded him and he saw his life stats rising again. But the pain remained.

What the hell... How was this possible?

The three team members on the ground had stopped screaming and were now moaning and whimpering in agony and fear as the Guardian kept attacking them.

Suddenly a horrifying scream filled everyone's head.

"Oh my God... oh my God... what's happening?! No, no, no..."

It was the healer's voice. His body was just about to disappear, yet not like in a normal log-off process. It flickered and glitched in shades of red, green and purple, like a broken piece of 3D graphics.

The healer screamed again, and this time his scream faded out in an eerie way as his body disappeared from the game.

"Shit!" Stan's voice was filled with terror. "He's gonna pounce! He's gonna fucking pounce!"

Kai broke free from the horror that had temporarily frozen him after they witnessed the tragedy of the healer. His friend was right. The Guardian was preparing his pounce attack. As everyone had witnessed, the game mechanic was devastating when everything was running according to set parameters, but right now nothing seemed normal. This was by far the worst glitch Kai had ever seen or heard of.

Petrified, he watched as the giant spider flexed its legs. The tank might survive the attack but the two damage dealers certainly would not. And who could tell what would happen to a player that got killed under such crazy circumstances? His gut was telling him that this was not good. Not good at all.

Then everything happened in a blur. Without thinking any further about what he was doing, Kai bashed two spiders about to attack him with his shield, staggering them. He consumed a stam pod and a shield buff potion from his quickslot and charged toward his fallen comrades.

"Are you insane? What are you doing, mate?" he heard Stan call out after him, aghast.

Kai ignored him. From another quickslot, he consumed a potion that buffed his strength and speed by 30%. The massive arachnid jumped, three of its oversized claws aiming directly at the players still convulsing on the ground. Thanks to his buffs, Kai fell into an insane sprint, then he activated *Shield Bash*. It was a special attack that came with the Sword & Shield specialization, which he had leveled up to its maximum.

Using his momentum, he bashed his shield into the

spider leg coming down toward Serene, who lay closest to him. It was as if he had run against a massive tree trunk with his shield. The impact robbed him of his breath, and he bounced backward. Yet, while falling to the ground, he saw that his attack had had an effect on the monster. His momentum had been enough to make the arachnid stagger before it could reach the ground. The giant claws missed the three people on the ground by mere inches when the Guardian finished his attack, leaving all three miraculously unharmed.

Kai sighed in relief.

That was close!

But he didn't have much time to enjoy his successful kamikaze rescue mission. With a furious shriek that made Kai's blood run cold, the arachnid turned its attention toward him.

"Oh crap…" Kai said, staring into the spider's multiple, hateful eyes.

"Kai! Run!" Stan yelled in panic. "Run! For fuck's sake!"

It became clear why he was panicking. Aiming at Kai, the giant spider was about to pounce again.

What is this? Kai thought, struck by fear.

Usually, boss AI followed a strict mechanic, a certain pattern of attacks. As they had seen before, the pounce happened as a scripted AoE attack, *not* as a counterattack against a single unit. This was almost conscious. This was revenge.

"KAI!" Stan yelled in despair.

Still on the ground, taking cover under his heavy shield, Kai crawled backward frantically. He wore heavy armor and was a warrior, and therefore lacked the agility to jump up and evade the area of attack. His feet scuffed up dirt as he desperately tried to get away, seeing the massive, hairy body jumping into the air and directly at him. He wouldn't make it. He saw it at once.

Maybe his shield and armor would prevent him from being impaled, but it was doubtful. The boss mechanic made this attack an insta-death for a damage dealer, possibly for any player.

Paralyzed, he stared at the razor-sharp claw coming down at him.

Suddenly something incredible happened, something no one expected.

Right in the center of the cave, only a few feet away from where Kai was staring at his demise like a deer caught in headlights, a portal opened.

Yet it wasn't like a portal any player of *TSOTA* had ever seen in this game. It appeared completely out of place in a medieval and fantasy-inspired setting. A glowing ring, it showed what was behind the graphics of the game, as if someone had opened a curtain, revealing the reality behind an illusion. The grid of the game engine was visible behind the portal. Numbers, vectors, algorithms.

Figures materialized in the portal, creatures consisting of code, like digital specters. Yet they quickly took shape, and when they stepped into the game world, they wore human bodies.

Staring at the portal with an open mouth, Kai realized that the spider had stopped its attack. He should have been impaled by now.

He moved his head, and it felt as if he were stuck in glue.

Lag. Massive lag.

The realization shot through Kai's mind like a bolt. The Guardian hadn't stopped its attack. And the game hadn't frozen. The FPS[14] rate had dropped to a minimum.

Kai saw the giant claw still falling down toward him, aimed directly at his chest, but it was in ultra-slow motion now.

The figures jumping through the portal weren't affected by the lag, however. On the contrary. While everyone and everything moved as if fallen into a honey pot, the newcomers moved lightning fast.

There were six of them. Two female and four male

avatars, who looked nothing like any character design available in the game. Rather, they appeared as if they had used the portal to jump into the action from a completely different game. Their slim, graceful bodies and extravagant clothes would have fitted into a world such as Ultimate Fantasy XXVII.

While Kai's mind tried to process what was going on, the newcomers didn't waste any time. One of them stormed toward him. A girl. The most stunning one he had ever seen.

Kai knew how absurd this thought was the millisecond it entered his mind. He was about to get impaled, yet he had time to realize how breathtaking she was.

Slim and tall with long, delicate limbs, her unnaturally white, straight hair ended in black tips and flew behind her like wings as she sprinted toward him. She leaped forward, reaching behind her back. A sword appeared in her hand, so huge that she couldn't possibly have carried it sheathed on her back.

She slid over the ground, swinging the sword in a way that would have been physically impossible in the real world. Mesmerized, Kai stared at her youthful face, which had the typical delicate features of an Ultimate Fantasy character. Her big eyes were like glowing amethysts and black lipstick covered her perfect lips.

Just before the claw could impale Kai, her sword cut through the massive spider leg as if through butter. The lower part dissolved into fragments, and a second later nothing indicated that it had ever been there. The arachnid staggered in slow motion. Only now did Kai see that the other members of his savior's team had attacked the remaining legs of the giant spider.

The girl grabbed him by the shoulders and pulled him with her, out of harm's way, as the Guardian's massive body began tumbling to the ground.

After dragging him a few feet, she let go of him and straightened up. Her eyes sparkled as she looked down on him.

"Don't worry, you'll be fine," he heard her say in a soft,

female voice.

Kai stared at her. She was a young woman in real life! Her graceful appearance could have been an avatar for a male player... if these guys were even players at all. He knew he would never forget that voice.

Then he realized that he must look like a total dork, staring at her, his body moving in slow motion.

"Thank you," he said.

She smiled briefly, then turned her attention elsewhere and leaped away. Kai stared after her as she ran to her team. She was dressed in black and white, wearing a white top that left her belly open, shiny black pants and heavy boots. Black gloves covered her hands all the way up over the elbows. The oversized sword disappeared as she sheathed it behind her back.

With a shriek, the spider collapsed. The moment it hit the ground, it turned into pixels and then vanished as if it had never been there. The lag stopped as the FPS shot up to over 200.

Kai gasped for air. The low FPS rate had felt as if something heavy had been sitting on his chest.

Still lying on the ground, he looked around. Was it over? He noticed that the spiderlings, too, had disappeared, just before they would have overrun his friends.

His savior and her team were standing in the middle of the cave, remaining silent. Most likely they were communicating with each other over a private channel.

Who were these guys?

Kai had an idea but didn't have time to think about that now.

A bone-shaking roar echoed through the cave as huge, hairy legs appeared behind the rock formation where the spider had shown up originally. A second later, it rose to its full height, hissing viciously. Its name tag and stats were golden, and it was at full health.

Shit, Kai thought. *It's reset!*

And it was still invincible!

The group of strangers didn't seem to be concerned about this, however. Completely calm, they stood at ease, looking at each other, communicating, while the black menace rose above them.

Then one of the guys turned around and addressed Kai's party, whose members stared at them in speechless awe.

"Listen, everyone. Don't move, don't intervene, don't panic. You're safe now. We'll handle this."

"Who are you people?" Stan, who had fallen silent for a change, finally found his voice again.

A smug smile flashed over the man's face. It was of almost ethereal beauty, framed by long, raven-black hair and with pitch-black eyes glowing like dark stars.

"We're Cyber Squad."

Kai's eyes widened. It was them! It was really *them*!

Hissing, the Guardian launched another attack, focusing on the six people right in front of him. With a casual coolness, the Cyber Squad drew their weapons and stood combat ready.

One of them, a little shorter and bulkier than the rest, turned toward Kai's people and lifted his palm. A shimmering barrier appeared, separating the Cyber Squad and the Guardian on one side while leaving the *TSOTA* players on the other – in safety.

He turned to his own team next and a shimmer appeared around them, which could only be some sort of shield of buff. Another of the figures stepped out of the spider's direct impact radius. In the next moment, he summoned something so completely out of place in this fantasy RPG environment that Kai blinked, staring at it.

Three huge holo-screens and a holo-keyboard appeared in front of the man, whose face was hidden under a black helmet. He sat on the ground in front of them and his fingers began flying over the keyboard at an utterly unnatural speed.

What was this guy doing?

The Guardian launched another attack. This time, the monster began its offensive by spitting its venom onto the six people below him. The green ichor cloud didn't reach any of them. With a gesture of his hand, the same guy who had created the barrier summoned an energy shield above the squad. The venom dispersed and disappeared after hitting it.

Before the arachnid could start hitting them with its razor-sharp legs, one of them stepped forward. He was taller than the rest; huge muscles showed through the shiny fabric of his suit, making him appear like a comic superhero. Like the girl had before, he summoned a sword by performing the gesture of pulling it out of a sheath on his back. His was even bigger. In his other hand, a shield appeared.

No doubt this was the tank of the group. After performing a taunting attack, he had the full attention of the Guardian, who immediately began slashing at him. It almost appeared as if the boss had gained even more strength and speed through the reset.

As soon as the arachnid focused on the tank, Kai's savior and two others of her team launched an attack on the spider. They drew their swords and began slashing at the monster with a speed and agility Kai had never seen before. Whatever buffs they were using, he wanted them, too!

But no matter what they tried, the spider didn't take damage, still protected by its golden status of invincibility. The black-haired guy, clearly the leader of the group, turned around to the person with the black helmet, who was still hitting the virtual keyboard frantically.

Now that he felt safe, Kai was increasingly fascinated by what was happening with every second that passed. It almost appeared as if the guy on the keyboard was trying to hack himself into the game – from within the game. This was crazy!

Columns of green numbers ran down his screens: code. Possibly even source code.

The coder briefly lifted a hand toward his leader in an irritated gesture, then kept hammering the keyboard with his insanely fast fingers.

Watching them, Kai realized that this team of six was a slight variation of the classic RPG party: instead of two DPSs, it had three, as well as a tank and a healer. The only class no one would ever find in an RPG was the hacker. It was the only plausible role for this guy that Kai could think of.

The sounds of dozens of arachnid feet echoed through the cave as the Guardian summoned the first wave of spiderlings. Following an unspoken command from the squad leader, two of the damage dealers ran off to greet the critters, leaving only the girl attacking the boss.

Just when Kai began to wonder how the Cyber Squad was actually planning to defeat this menace, the hacker lifted his index finger and a green glow appeared above it. The leader and Kai's heroine exchanged a look, then he nodded at her.

She fell into a sprint and charged toward the tank, dodging the Guardian's furious attacks with the ease and grace of a dancer. The tank extended his shield toward her and she jumped on it. Using his strength and her momentum, he gave her a lift into the air. Like a projectile, she shot up, evaded the spider's gigantic glands with a gracious summersault, and landed on its head.

Kai noticed that he was holding his breath.
What's she doing?

Surprisingly, the Guardian didn't react to her standing on its head at all and instead continued attacking the tank, who parried his slashes with ease. The AI wasn't programmed or prepared for air assaults as no character class in the game was capable of such stunts.

The girl made a summoning gesture and a large dagger appeared in her hand that looked like it was fabricated of black glass. On the ground, the hacker waved his hand as if he was about to throw something at her. But instead of a ball, a projectile, or anything like that, a thin, greenish glowing spool of ribbon appeared in his palm. In the blink of an eye, it extended itself upward and connected with the girl's dagger.

The weapon took on the same shimmering texture as the ribbon. Tiny particles moved inside it.

Kai's jaw dropped as he realized what it was. Code.

She didn't hesitate for a second but rammed the dagger straight into the Guardian's skull.

The monster let out one last bone-shaking shriek as its body trembled. Kai watched, fascinated, as the green code entered its skull and spread through its body like a deadly virus – which it technically was.

A second later, everything was over.

First, the golden name tag disappeared, turning back to the usual red dungeon boss tag. The giant arachnid froze as its massive body flickered and then exploded into millions of tiny pixels, which flew through the cave like particles of glowing green dust, then dissolved. Meanwhile, the spiderlings vanished as if they had never been there.

The girl dropped to the ground where the spider had been only a second ago, her long legs easily absorbing the impact. A smile appeared on her face as she faced the squad leader.

Kai's party woke from their stupor and began applauding and cheering. He looked to his friends and saw an expression of awe and disbelief on Stan's face.

"Wow!" his lips moved, but Kai couldn't hear it.

Instead, blue letters appeared in his field of view.

Removing you from the dungeon in 10, 9, 8, 7...

No, wait!

Kai wanted to say thank you to the people who had just saved their asses. Maybe even talk to the girl. Actually, most of all, talk to the girl.

But there was nothing to be done. Once initiated, the removal process couldn't be stopped.

The usual blur appeared around Kai, and he noticed that the rest of the party was about to be removed from the dungeon, too. Right before he was teleported away, Kai saw a glowing portal appear, and the Cyber Squad left the instance the same way they had entered it.

***

The birds sang and the eagle flew high in the perfectly blue sky, letting out its characteristic scream. A soft breeze circled the mountain top, carrying the scent of flowers and herbs.

Everything appeared unreal to Kai as he materialized back at his estate.

"What in the fucking bloodiest of hells was this?" Stan's voice came from next to him, husky in excitement.

When leaving a dungeon or PvP instance, the game always transported the player back to the last in-world location they had been before entering the event. And since both Kai and his friend had last been hanging out on Kai's estate, it was where they both rematerialized.

Kai faced him. "I have no idea."

Suddenly, he realized how exhausted he was. The adrenaline was wearing off, and he felt as if he had spent days in that dungeon.

"It was the craziest shit I've seen!" Stan said. "Jesus, I thought you were done. I'm glad you're ok."

"Me too," Kai said quietly.

All he was thinking about was that the Cyber Squad had possibly saved everyone's life. And her.

CHAPTER SEVEN

Kai was on autopilot when he walked to the train station the next day. He could hardly process the events that had happened only a few hours before.

After logging out of the game, he had found his real body completely exhausted. Dehydrated and his legs cramping, he felt as if he had just run a marathon – and that being a person who had never seen a gym from the inside in his entire life. When he lifted himself up off the bed, he realized that it was soaked with sweat.

But he only made the most shocking discovery once he managed to get up and walk. His leg hurt. Looking down, he saw that he had a huge bruise above his right knee. Exactly where the spiderling had bitten him!

How could that be possible?

Once he was naked under the shower, he saw that this injury wasn't the only one. His body was covered with bruises, almost as if he had been in a real fight.

When Kai got onto the train that would take him downtown like every day, his head was spinning. Every step he made felt painful. There was only one plausible explanation for his condition.

For some reason, his body had perceived everything that had happened in VR as real. The existential stress he had experienced during the battle with the Guardian and its minions had almost pushed him over the edge. His body had produced adrenaline, sweat, and all sorts of other hormones and substances a human body did when in a life-threatening combat situation.

That alone would have been concerning enough, but how had he received the bruises?

He only hoped that the others were ok. After all, Red, Cloudgirl and Serene had suffered much more damage than him. Kai had been so fascinated watching the Cyber Squad in action that he hadn't even realized that none of the three were moving anymore until they all got logged out of the dungeon. He hoped that it was just a malfunction in the game and that they were fine. After all, none of them had been killed. Kai could remember seeing their health bars in the group section on his HUD.

The unfortunate healer, however, was a completely different story. Kai felt ice-cold when he thought back to the blood-curdling scream the guy had let out when attempting the log-off process. Yes, the dude was a prick who no one in the guild liked – and apparently an idiot for trying to leave the game even though they'd all got the message not to attempt that under any circumstances – but still. No one deserved to suffer serious damage in the real world, or maybe even die as a result of what they did in VR.

Today, Kai hardly noticed anything going on around him on the train. Neither the gray tenements muffled in foggy clouds outside the window, nor the gray faces of the commuters surrounding him. He even didn't notice the commercials trying to sell him whatever the system thought he needed to live a happy life, or at least a less miserable one.

As terrifying and confusing as the whole experience in the dungeon had been, what occupied Kai's thoughts most were the guys who had saved his and everyone else's ass.

The Cyber Squad.

He was fascinated. Yes, those guys had abilities and gadgets no ordinary player ever could dream of, but still, this team of six were easily the best players Kai had ever seen. In fact, he considered himself a pretty good player, otherwise he would never have tried to apply for an e-sports team. But compared to those guys, he was a mere amateur.

And the girl...

His pulse rose just thinking of her.

Yes, he was no idiot and knew very well that it had only been her avatar he had seen. She could be anyone in real life. Although, judging from her voice, she had to be gorgeous.

But the graceful avatar wasn't the main thing he found so attractive and intriguing about her.

Her courage, her coolness, her exceptional way of fighting... not to mention that it had been her who had saved him from being turned into a kebab by a giant spider.

Considering the bruises he had found on his body after the session, he wasn't keen on finding out how it would feel to be impaled when a game experienced such a severe glitch as the one last night.

The thought alone made him feel ice-cold, and he ran his hand over his chest and belly unthinkingly.

Kai closed his eyes for a second, remembering how she had slid toward him, swinging the oversized sword and then cutting off the arachnid's leg before it could hurt him. It had been so impressive... and so smoking hot.

He was that sunken in his own world that he almost missed his station. Frantically, he pushed himself through the other commuters and left the train just before the door closed. Now he needed to hurry so he didn't miss his connecting ride on the Skytrain.

Riding up the escalator, he mostly ignored the colorful 3D ads flashing on the wall next to him. Like the ones on the train, the displays adjusted to the person in front of them, a scanner reading data from each person's neuro-plant. Kai was so used to the constant advertisement overkill that he mostly ignored them completely.

But then he froze as something unexpected caught his attention.

The ad was much shorter than the one he had seen on the train the other day, because the displays on the escalator walls allowed the passerby only a glimpse of an ad, lasting just a few seconds.

It showed the Cyber Squad logo and text in glowing blue letters.

Become a hero! Join Cyber Squad!
Send us your resume NOW.

It almost felt like a bolt hitting Kai's spine. He felt a tingle all over his body as a decision formed in his head.

Once on the Skytrain, he pulled his mobile device from his bag. The system made it easy for him. Being connected to the internet, his device knew exactly which ads had been shown to Kai in the last hours. Whenever he switched it on, it would show him little reminders of the products the system had suggested for him. Web browser, social media, WatchTube – they all accessed data collected by his neuro-plant.

The second push-notice he got was the exact same Cyber Squad ad as the one he had just seen. The only difference was that this time, the *Send us your resume NOW* text was a clickable button.

It took him less than a minute to upload his resume. A few seconds later, he received a text message.

Thank you for your application! We will be in touch shortly! The Helltek Labs Inc. Team

Kai's hand was shaking slightly when he stored his mobile device back in his bag.

Deep inside him, his gut was telling him that what he had just done would change his life forever. He felt a tingling all over his body, like an electric discharge.

Calm down, he told himself while the skyscrapers of downtown flew by him. *All you did was send in your resume. They get thousands of applications every day. Most likely you'll never hear back from them...*

It was true. Finding a decent job nowadays was almost

like finding a needle in a haystack. Which was why most people had stopped trying years ago. And Helltek Labs were the biggest game QA service in the world. Why should they pick him of all people? On the other hand, they had targeted him with their recruitment ads. There had to be a reason for that. Maybe he was a suitable candidate after all?

Kai exited the train and went to work.

On his arrival, he saw Hana lift an eyebrow and watch him with crossed arms as she noticed him limping. He wasn't much slower than normal, and even though his leg hurt, he would do his job as fast as possible, but it was enough to bring a frown to his boss' stern face.

"I fell down the stairs, I'm sorry," he said dryly, which made her knit her perfect eyebrows.

Clocking in, Kai realized that he truly couldn't stand this woman. Who did she think she was?

As always, the day dragged as if in slow motion. Kai caught his thoughts drifting off to the events in *TSOTA*. He wanted to go home, log into the game and find out what had happened and if his friends were ok. Besides, the bruise above his knee made walking and serving grumpy patrons in a restaurant a true pain in the ass.

Kai resisted the urge to pull out his mobile device and check if he had a message from Helltek every minute. It would probably take days, if not weeks, for them to get back to him. If they ever did. And Hana would fire him if she caught him using his phone during work. Kai was convinced that she was waiting for any excuse that would give her a reason to give him the boot.

Finally, after six hours, he got a fifteen-minute break. He grabbed some ramen from the kitchen and sat down in the tiny room that served as a break room for the employees.

Kai couldn't resist any longer. He pulled out his device and took a peek.

There was a new text message. And, to his surprise, it was neither an ad nor a reminder to pay some bills.

It was from Helltek.

Wow, that was quick!

Full of anticipation but also anxious, he opened the message.

Kai dropped his chopsticks as he read it, and the noodles he was about to shove in fell back into the steaming bowl. All interest in the ramen forgotten, he jumped to his feet and headed for the door.

"Where do you think you're going, Kai?" Hana asked icily as she saw him heading for the exit.

Instead of replying, he flipped her off. She sucked in her breath so forcefully that he could clearly hear it while opening the door. It brought a grin to his face.

"You're f–"

He turned around and smiled. "I quit."

***

"Ok, ok, slowly, please," Stan said. "You did *what*?"

"I flipped off my boss and quit."

"Yeah, that's badass. We'd all love to do that at some point. I'm proud of you, mate. But that's not what I mean." He paused for a second, then yelled. "You did *bloody* what?"

As so often when they had nothing better to do but chill, they were hanging out at Kai's estate. Kai used the time in his virtual home to manage his inventory, repair his equipment and practice his skills on dummies or a parkour course he had set up in the courtyard.

"Wow," Kai said, browsing through the new items in his inventory. "I received a full armor set that would have dropped in the Dark Lair. And the sword! In platin!"

Platin was the highest level of gear in the game. It only dropped at the final boss in the most difficult dungeons and arenas on veteran mode. A full set was extremely difficult to come by. Kai's excitement grew when he focused on the set and the full description appeared.

Set of Arachnophobia (Platin)
Armor: 5000 per piece
Class: Heavy
Condition: Perfect
Pieces: 5/5 – Bonus feature unlocked!
When wearing the full set, you gain 20% extra health, 20% extra stamina, and 100% resistance against any poison.
When taking any kind of damage, you have a 15% chance of spawning a Guardian. The Guardian will fight for you for 20 seconds or until killed. Cooldown: 30 seconds.
Enjoy the arachnophobia in your foes' eyes!

That was an epic set!

Right after logging into the game, Kai had received a message from the system.

Yesterday, the Dark Lair experienced an unexpected incident, which we deeply regret. Despite our best efforts, sometimes the code experiences unforeseeable glitches. Rest assured that all issues have been fixed and that *TSOTA* is as safe a virtual environment as it can be. We apologize for any inconvenience and hope you enjoy the little gift we placed in your inventory. The *TSOTA* Team.

"Yeah, I got it, too. It's cool," Stan said. "Now stop deflecting. You did fucking *what?*"

"I applied for the Cyber Squad," Kai said, trying to sound as casual as possible. Even though he was playing it cool toward his friend, he was so excited that he wanted to shout the news all over the Cydonian realm.

"Why the hell would you do that?" Stan asked in disbelief. "Are you insane?"

Kai equipped his new gear and closed the inventory. He looked at his friend, who was wearing the breathtaking Dark Elven avatar again. The expression of confusion and dismay on her face looked as real as on an actual person's.

"You witnessed yourself what those guys are capable of, didn't you? I've never seen anything like it in my entire life."

"That's true, but–"

"Besides, I didn't get the job yet, so relax. All they did was invite me to an interview."

Stan frowned but said nothing.

"Most likely, nothing will come of it," Kai said, shrugging.

In truth, he very much hoped that something would come of it. A new job. The coolest job in the world. Playing games for a living, equipped with buffs and gear any ordinary player could only dream of.

"Hm, guess you're right," his friend said. Then he chuckled. "But it didn't stop you from flipping off your boss and quitting!"

"Man, I hated it there so much. Besides, the interview is tomorrow at noon. Hana would never have given me a day off, and if I stayed away, she would have fired me. So, screw her."

Stan laughed, hitting Kai's shoulder. "Well done, mate."

Kai looked down at himself, inspecting the new armor he had equipped. "Wow."

He summoned a mirror from his inventory, and it appeared right in front of him. The gleaming sunlight in the courtyard reflected in it.

The mirror was an item most players chose to carry in their inventory at all times, even though it took three slot points and was a premium item that had to be bought with real money. After all, when equipping new gear or a new costume to cover the gear, everyone wanted to check if it made them look like a badass or an idiot. Like the majority of VR games, *TSOTA* was a 100% first-person experience with the user becoming the character they played. This made it impossible to look at yourself in third-person, like in earlier times.

Kai liked what he saw in the mirror. Very much. The armor set had been designed with incredible details. It looked as if it had been crafted in shiny, black chitin and was ornamented with artfully sculpted spider reliefs.

Although it was heavy armor, it felt surprisingly light and allowed more agility than other sets usually did. Yet somehow it didn't feel right wearing it. Like a stale, unpleasant taste you couldn't get rid of, no matter how much water you drank.

"It's an amazing set," Stan acknowledged, watching how Kai posed in front of the mirror. "I got the medium version and it looks even better. And the stats… Jesus fucking Christ! It's probably the best set in the game! The Guardian it spawns is a tad smaller than the one we fought but still a frightening sight."

"Don't you think it feels wrong somehow, though?" Kai asked.

"What do you mean? It suits you perfectly!"

"No, I mean… somehow it feels like blood money. They paid us off so we'd keep quiet about what happened."

"Oh, that… yeah."

They both fell silent for a moment. No one in the guild had seen any of the players who had suffered heavy damage yesterday. Which was suspicious, because Red and Cloudgirl in particular spent almost all their days in the game. It wasn't like them not to show up all day and not send a message to anyone. Kai had a very bad feeling about that.

"I'm sure they're gonna be fine," Stan said, as if he sensed Kai's concern. "This is a game, after all. Not real. Everything that happens to you here can't affect your actual body."

He parroted the mantra game devs and publishers repeated over and over, and most players believed it. Luckily he and the rest of the crew hadn't got injured.

Kai frowned, thinking about the bruises on his real body. He didn't tell his friend anything about it because he didn't want to concern him. He also knew that Stan was lying to himself with what he was saying. His friend knew all too well that accidents happened. Otherwise he wouldn't think that the Cyber Squad was such a dangerous job.

"So, what do you think, pal? Shall we put our new gear to the test in PvP? We could smash some noobs in a couple of Death Matches." Stan's voice revealed excitement about the prospect, and the big eyes of his elven avatar gleamed.

"Sure, why not?" Kai smiled.

"Cool! I'll check in the guild to see if we can find two more people to go in with a full team. This is going to be epic! Watch how everyone runs when our big-ass spiders spawn!"

CHAPTER EIGHT

The next morning, Kai woke up before Alessia could activate the morning alarm. And that even though he had set the alarm for two hours earlier than usual. Today was a big day and he wanted to be sure to have enough time to master any obstacle reality could throw in his way. From an occupied bathroom to the train being late.

It turned out that he was the first one up in the apartment, and not only was the bathroom free but there was even enough hot water for him to enjoy his shower for once.

"I would suggest classic, semi-formal attire for a job interview," the AI said as he stood in front of his open closet, staring inside and wondering what to wear. Usually, he didn't give much thought to it and simply chose something clean that matched well enough not to let him look like a total dork.

Why is it so much easier to look good in VR than in real life?

He knew why. A perfectly shaped body looked good in almost anything. His avatar even looked great when naked. Something he couldn't say about his real self...

After a moment of contemplation, he decided to listen to Alessia and put on a pair of blue jeans and a long-sleeved, plain shirt. He didn't own other shoes but sneakers, but he did pick the least worn pair.

"You look formidable, Kai," the AI said, and he wondered once again if that was a hint of sarcasm in her voice. "Good luck at your job interview!"

He left the apartment and was delighted and surprised to find the elevator operating. Maybe that was a good omen. At least he wouldn't show up at the interview with sweat stains on his shirt.

It was so early when he exited the building that the street winding through the tenement canyon was almost empty. The usual drunks and drug addicts loitering on the corners and around benches were apparently still sleeping off their hangovers.

Fifteen minutes later, Kai was sitting on the train downtown. He was so excited that he could hardly sit still during the whole ride. It wasn't the same route as his usual one to his old job. Instead, he had to change trains twice before he was heading to his final destination.

It was in the outskirts of the city, about forty-five minutes from downtown, but in the opposite direction to where Kai lived. And the neighborhood couldn't have been more different either. Instead of run-down tenements, Kai saw impressive buildings of glass and chrome, every one displaying a unique architecture. Some of the biggest tech companies and research facilities in the country were located in this district.

Looking around in awe, Kai made the twenty-minute walk from the train station to Helltek HQ. Once there, he couldn't help but stare with an open mouth at what was lying before him. It was huge. Much bigger than he had anticipated. At first, all he could see was the exquisite glass architecture of the main building, erected in the center of the facility. The premises were surrounded by massive white walls with barbed wire on top. Every couple of feet there was a camera, and security bots were patrolling the site.

A bit intimidated, Kai went up to the main gate, which was operated by two human and two artificial guards, of which one resembled a canine. He introduced himself and presented his ID, as instructed in the email that had come with his invitation to his job interview.

While the human guards checked his ID and ran his face through a scanner, the four-legged robot approached and inspected him almost like a real dog would have. Kai had heard about those models. Apparently they were designed to detect hidden weapons, narcotics and explosives. They were also much faster than they looked.

Kai still remembered that when he was a child, people actually used to have real pets: cats, dogs, and others. No one had them anymore, though, and no one could really say why. Maybe because a pet robot could be simply switched off when its owner didn't want to take care of it? It didn't need food either, or a regular visit to the vet. Kai had had an artificial hamster a couple of years ago but eventually got bored with it, and now he couldn't even remember where he had put it.

After a moment, the guards cleared him and he was good to go inside.

"Just go straight ahead," one of the men said in a bored tone. "Enter the main building and get checked in at the reception desk. You can't miss it."

Kai's heart was pounding as he approached the impressive and slightly intimidating main building. Above the main entrance, *Helltek Labs Inc.* was shimmering in oversized, holographic neon letters, which were changing their color every few seconds. Before entering, Kai looked around and noticed that this was by no means the only structure on the premises. Other, smaller buildings were close by, arranged around a Zen-style artificial lake and a park-like green area. Behind it stood buildings that looked like residential structures yet were not comparable with the gray, basic houses Kai was used to living in. The entire facility had the vibe of an ultra-modern campus.

Automatic glass doors opened, and Kai entered the building. He found himself in a huge entrance hall with white marble floors and glass walls. Pleasantly scented, cool air greeted him. It felt so clean that he almost felt refreshed by simply breathing it in. He approached the front desk. The woman sitting there was young and gorgeous.

"Hi. How can I help you?" she asked in a friendly tone

that faked interest. Her blond hair was pinned up artfully, and her eyes were green like fresh spring leaves. A color that couldn't possibly be natural. She wore a tight white dress and a pin with the company logo on her chest.

"Hi... um, I'm here for a job interview," Kai said, trying to sound less nervous than he was.

"Ah, yes. You must be Kai," she said after glancing at her screen. "Please take a seat over there. Rachel will be right with you."

She pointed at some white lounge chairs near the window. Kai nodded and walked over to them. More than 30 minutes early, he took a seat. He had been so anxious that something might go wrong on his way there that he had calculated in some extra time. Now he would have to wait. Nervous as he was, thirty minutes would feel like an eternity.

Sitting down, he noticed that the chair was surprisingly uncomfortable, one of those designer furniture pieces that had the sole purpose of looking good and nothing more. A 3D hologram shone in the glass wall right next to him, showing a sequence of several promo videos for Helltek and the Cyber Squad. Kai forced himself to watch the sequence over and over again because otherwise his gaze would wander back to the gorgeous receptionist, and he didn't want to appear like a creep.

Luckily, he didn't have to wait long. Only ten minutes later, the unmistakable sound of high-heels on a marble floor echoed through the hall.

Kai looked up and saw an elegant woman approaching. She was in her early thirties and dressed in a black pencil skirt and a red blazer. Brown-reddish locks were pinned up into a loose bun and blue eyes sparkled behind highly fashionable glasses.

Kai's heart skipped a beat when looking at her. Was she even wearing anything under her blazer? It didn't look that way. He felt sweat building up behind his ears and hated himself for it. He was used to seeing the prettiest creatures imaginable in VR, yet he rarely got into contact with beautiful women of flesh and blood. And they had a much stronger effect on him than their virtual counterparts.

"Welcome to Helltek, Kai," she said in a friendly, slightly husky voice. "I'm Rachel from HR."

"Hi!" he said, jumping up. "Nice to meet you."

He put on his most winning smile and tried as hard as he could not to show how nervous he was.

"If you'll follow me, please," Rachel said, turning around.

Kai did as he was asked and couldn't help but notice her heart-shaped ass under the tight skirt and her pretty legs while walking after her. No doubt, this was a woman who spent every night at the gym. But then she opened the door that led from the entrance hall to the main area of the building, and Kai's attention shifted from her to what was lying there.

When approaching it, he had noticed that the building was curved, but it was only now that he saw that it was actually round. Shaped cylindrically, it stretched at least six stories up and probably the same amount down. It was difficult to tell at a quick glance since; instead of a staircase, the building had a ramp that wound through the whole structure like an oversized helix. The center was decorated with artfully installed plants and flowers that were hanging from the rim of the walkway. In the middle, two transparent elevators transported people up and down.

Rachel turned her head and smiled. "It's impressive, isn't it? The architects were inspired by the Getty Museum in New York."

Kai nodded, though he didn't know what the Getty Museum was as he had never been to New York. In fact, like most people, he had never been anywhere. The only place he went was VR. But he didn't want to seem like an idiot, so he pretended as if he knew what the HR lady was talking about.

Instead of approaching the elevators, she took the walkway up. Following the alluring scent of her perfume, Kai peeked down and noticed that the building had at least as many stories underground as it had above. He saw employees using the ramp, the lifts and the glass catwalks connecting the main areas with the elevators in the middle. Most were in their twenties or thirties and well-dressed. Some wore business attire, others more casual clothes, and they all made Kai feel like a loser from the suburbs – which he technically was.

Only half a story up, Rachel stopped in front of a glass door that opened for her automatically. They entered a spacious office with panoramic windows that allowed a beautiful view over the whole campus and the Zen-style park. She sat down behind a modern desk made of milky plexiglass and pointed at a chair facing it.

"Please, make yourself comfortable," she said with a smile, crossing her legs, before looking at her computer screen. Sitting down, Kai tried everything not to stare at her chest, but her outfit made that a difficult task.

"Thanks for sending us your resume, Kai," Rachel said after studying something on her screen for a moment, most likely his profile. "It appears you're a perfect candidate to work in game QA."

"Am I?" he said, surprised, feeling like a total moron the moment his words left his mouth.

Rachel chuckled.

"Yes, indeed. You have a degree in mathematics and an exceptional overall Gamerscore. Your gamer reputation is that of a team player who is considerate of others. You always put the well-being of your team over your own score. *TSOTA* is your favorite game, but you're an allrounder with excellent skills in shooters, strategy games, and more."

"Um, yes," he said, not knowing what else to say.

None of this had been part of his resume. They must have pulled it from his X-Perience profile, which was like his fingerprint in the VR gaming world. It made sense for them to have done so.

"I can also see in our internal report that you've already

come into contact with one of our teams," Rachel continued, pausing for a second while reading something. Then she raised an eyebrow. "It was one of our Level Ten squads, in fact. Those guys are pretty impressive, aren't they?"

Kai stared at her. He hadn't expected the conversation to go in this direction at all. It began to occur to him that Helltek already knew everything about him and that this conversation with the HR lady was a pure formality. Obviously they were able to access all his game protocols if they wanted, and they'd also noticed his player signature during the incident with the glitched giant spider.

"Yes, they are," he answered after a moment had passed.

"Was the encounter with our team the reason why you sent us your resume?"

"Yes and no," he answered truthfully. If they already knew everything about him, he might as well be honest about his intentions. "It was like the final motivation for me to give it a shot, but I'd been playing with the thought for a while."

Rachel leaned back in her chair and studied him.

"Can you elaborate on that?"

"I've seen your recruitment ads on the train and–"

"Ah, yes," she interrupted him with a smile. "We target suitable candidates deliberately by using your neuro-plant data. Glad to hear you received the message."

Kai stared at her for a moment until he realized how stupid he must look. He cleared his throat before speaking.

"You targeted me? Why?"

"We're always in need of fresh talent. Your personality profile exactly fits what we're looking for. Plus, you're an exceptional gamer. You should be playing in a pro league. I'd say it's our luck that e-sports didn't work out for you." For a brief second, her sweet smile had something sharkish. "And finally, you don't have any close relatives. The only family you have left lives in Thailand, is that correct?"

"Yes…"

"Splendid."

"Why does that matter?"

"Before we go into that, let me explain precisely what it means to become part of the Cyber Squad and an employee of Helltek, ok?"

"Sure."

Her smile widened, and she showed perfectly shaped pearl-white teeth. "Helltek offers an exceptionally high wage. Even at Level One, you will earn 50% more than what you got in your old job."

At this point, Kai wasn't even surprised that they knew exactly how much he had earned at Fuji.

"But that's really just for warm-up. Your salary will increase exponentially. That means, at Level Two, you'll earn double as much as you got at Level One. At Level Three, we will double what you got at Level Two, and so on... You're a mathematician, so I don't need to do the math for you and tell you that there's a *lot* of money to be made here."

She chuckled about her own wittiness before she continued. "Furthermore, we offer full health coverage, including dental and mental care. When you reach Level Two, we will welcome you as a resident on our campus, where you will receive an apartment of 1500 square feet and free access to our internal fitness and wellness facilities."

"Wow," he said. "That's incredible!"

"It is, right?" Rachel snickered. "I know that you're a smart boy, Kai. Which is why I know what you're thinking now. Go ahead, ask."

"Where's the catch?"

Her sweet smile turned sharkish for a second again, and it occurred to Kai that maybe she was wearing such an outfit for the precise reason that it would distract him from brief glimpses of her other self. Or was it her true self?

"You're right. Naturally, there's a catch," Rachel replied. "After all, nothing in life comes for free, isn't that so? Not even death is free as it costs you your life. No respawn!"

Again she chuckled at her own joke, and Kai forced

himself to join the fun.

"The catch is that this is a high-risk job, plain and simple. We wouldn't pay such competitive wages if it wasn't," the HR lady said. "In times of neural VR gaming, bugs and glitches aren't just an annoyance. They're potentially deadly threats. We are responsible for eliminating those threats."

She paused for a second to let what she had just said sink in, then she continued. "Cyber Squad keeps millions of players safe every day. This is your chance to become part of something bigger, Kai. This is your chance to become a hero."

Kai had to admit that her words created a tingling sensation in his spine. He had always thought of himself as a loser or at least nothing special. Yet this incredibly hot woman looked at him and saw something else. Hero material. Could she be right about that?

"What do you think? Does that sound good or what?"

"It does," he admitted. "Can you explain to me just what makes the job so high-risk?"

"Thanks for asking! We pursue a policy of full internal disclosure here, although I will have you sign a waiver before you leave that will prohibit you from making anything we discuss here public. Just so you know."

"Ok."

"Awesome! To keep it simple, the urban legends are true. It's not only bugs and glitches coming from malfunctions of internal game code but also malware attacks or hacks that can cause serious threats to a player's – or tester's – health. I'm not a techie and therefore can't go into details now, but trust me, once you start with us, you get an in-depth technical briefing. But in brief, because your brain is directly connected to VR and therefore the game and its code, bugs can cause damage to your brain and body while they're connected. But I don't think I need to tell you that. You've experienced it yourself."

He thought of the bruises he had found all over his body and shivered.

How did she know about that?

Rachel raised a perfectly shaped eyebrow as her face took on a knowing expression. Then she continued.

"Of course, we take all necessary safety precautions. The health of our testers is dear to us and has the highest priority. But sometimes, unfortunate incidents happen. You have to see it like this: our Cyber Squad encounters terra incognita on a daily basis. You guys are like test pilots trying out the craziest and most adventurous machines. No one knows what will happen when a human brain connects itself to a brand-new virtual world. It can be dangerous, yes. But it's also exciting, an adventure. And a lot of fun!"

Although he knew that what Rachel was playing on him here was basically a sales pitch, Kai couldn't help but feel more and more excited with every word that came from her gorgeous mouth.

He always wanted more from his life than any of his friends. He was ambitious. He wanted a challenge, a purpose, excitement, fun. And money.

With every second that passed while he sat there and listened to the Helltek HR lady, he increasingly realized that this was probably the only chance he would get to achieve all he wanted. It was a once-in-a-lifetime offer. There were risks that came with it, yes. But wasn't life itself risky? After all, it was a one-way trip to death anyway.

"If anything should happen, we always have our own medical team on site. We also pay for full rehab should it ever become necessary. But you will have to sign a liability waiver together with your contract. You will agree that you knew what you were signing up for." She winked. "It's also the reason why we prefer candidates who have no living relatives, at least none within US jurisdiction. So what do you think? Any questions?"

She looked at him with a bright smile and expectation in her big eyes.

"I… um…" Kai said, not knowing what to answer. On the one hand, he was completely sold, excited about how his life would change if he signed up. But on the other hand, it also felt a little bit like signing a contract with the devil.

Rachel hadn't said it up front, but it was clear to him that in the worst case scenario, working for VR game QA could be lethal.

"Don't worry," Rachel replied. "You don't need to give me an answer now. After all, I'm not trying to rush you into anything. And we have thousands of candidates to choose from. How about you go home to the suburbs, give everything thorough consideration and then call me tomorrow?"

**

Less than ten minutes later, Kai was standing outside, back in front of the impressive glass tower that was Helltek HQ. His head was spinning. The conversation with Rachel had only lasted thirty minutes but had turned his world completely upside down.

While he had been inside, the sun had broken through the omnipresent clouds and was now heating up his black hair. Kai inhaled deeply. Even the air here felt fresher.

Slowly he began making his way back to the gate. After a few steps, he stopped and turned his head. He studied the vast green area to the right of the main building. The park was beautiful with its blooming trees and exotic flowers. A curved wooden bridge led over the pond, its water shining a bright, almost unreal blue in the sunlight. Behind it, he could see that the residential buildings had huge windows and extensive balconies. Another bright blue shimmer indicated that there was a pool between them.

Besides that, there was also a restaurant, a bar and several cafeterias, as Rachel had explained to him.

This wasn't a job, it was a dream. An opportunity of a lifetime. His only chance to escape the gray hopelessness of the tenement wasteland he was forced to live in now.

It came with a price. A deadly price if things went

wrong. But that didn't necessarily mean they *would*. And, no risk no fun, right?

With a sudden, sharp move, Kai spun on his heel and walked back inside the HQ.

The girl at the reception desk raised her eyebrows in surprise when she saw him enter the hall.

"Can I help you? Did you forget something inside?" she asked.

"Yes," he answered. "I forgot to sign my contract."

CHAPTER NINE

Kai was excited as never before in his life when he arrived at Helltek the next morning. He had hardly slept in anticipation of his big day.

Rachel came to welcome him. Today, she wore tight black office pants, high heels and a white blouse that was similarly revealing to the blazer she had been wearing the day before. She was accompanied by a young man with spiky platin blonde hair.

"Kai, this is Topher, your team lead," Rachel said, introducing the two young men. "He will explain everything to you and show you around. I'll come by later, bring you your badge and the completed paperwork. Have fun, guys!"

She smiled like a cat, then rushed off, her heels clacking on the marble floor.

"Welcome to the squad, rookie," Topher said, a crooked grin on his face. "Follow me!"

He waved his hand and headed toward the main area of the tower. Kai followed him, and this time they walked straight to the elevators in the center of the building.

"I've seen your Gamerscore and reputation," the team lead said while they waited for the lift. "Pretty impressive. When Rach showed me your profile, I immediately said: I want this guy in my team."

"Thank you," Kai said. "I'm really excited to be here."

"Wait until you see our VR pods," Topher said with a smirk. "It will blow your mind."

The elevator came, and they got in.

"What you see here are mostly administrative and management offices," he said, pointing upstairs while the glass cabin rushed down. "The testing facilities, the labs, and basically all the fancy stuff are located underground."

Kai watched the surroundings with curiosity as the elevator arrived on the basement level and the door opened. The design here was different than in the glass tower above, with anthracite walls illuminated by diffuse bluish and yellow lights. It reminded Kai of a spaceship corridor.

They approached a black double door. Topher grabbed his badge from his belt and held it against a sensor on the side of the door, and it opened noiselessly.

"Welcome to Helltek. What you will discover now is what the company really is about. This is the underground and the heart of Helltek, or the Bowels, as we call it here."

They entered a long, dimly lit hall at a fast pace.

"This area is where all Level Ones and Level Twos work. There's a common area, with a cafeteria and some rooms to play and chill between assignments. Your clearance will allow you to move freely within the Level 1-4 areas, but everything else is off-limits for you. For now."

"Which level are you?" Kai asked.

"I'm Level Five," Topher said proudly.

"Oh wow. As a team lead I thought you'd be a Level Ten."

Topher stopped for a moment and looked Kai in the face. Kai gulped, concerned he had offended his boss after knowing him for ten minutes on his first day.

"Those guys are heroes," the team lead said with honest admiration in his voice. "Level Ten is almost godlike in these halls. You'll see for yourself. Only the best of the best reach that level, around 0.1% of us. I doubt I'll ever get there, and neither will you."

"I saw them in action," Kai said, relieved, following Topher as they continued down the hall. "They were really impressive."

"Yeah, I saw in your profile that they saved your ass in

TSOTA the other day."

"How do you guys know about that?"

Topher laughed. "Oh, please. You really don't know? Your neuro-plant records everything you do in-world or off-world. Same as many other big companies, Helltek has legal access to that data. What you witnessed was a major incident that would easily have killed all players involved if it wasn't for our team. Did you suffer bruises? A headache? Nausea?"

"Yes," Kai answered, perplexed. "I don't quite understand how that's even possible–"

"Oh, you will," Topher interrupted him with a grin, his dark brown eyes sparkling with amusement. Or was it mockery? "And you'll learn much more over time. Today you'll learn that you know nothing. At least about the true nature of VR. Ready?"

The team lead halted at a black door. Without waiting for an answer, he opened it and both young men entered.

Kai stopped short and stared into the room with surprise. He wasn't sure what he had been expecting, but certainly not *this*.

Topher had made their entrance so dramatic that Kai had believed they would be entering something like the inner sanctum of Helltek. The place where all his questions would be answered.

Instead, they were standing in a locker room.

The team lead watched Kai's face filling with a 'what the hell?' expression, then he started laughing.

"Sorry, man," he said, clapping Kai's shoulder. "Your face was priceless. Too funny!"

"Um…" Kai didn't know what to say and felt his cheeks turning hot.

Topher laughed more. "Don't worry, we play this stunt on every newbie. You expected whatnot, and instead I brought you into a locker room, huh?"

"Yeah, pretty much," Kai said with a shy smile.

"Well, this isn't just any locker room. Watch!"

He held his badge against a sensor close to the door and then pressed some keys on a pad next to it. A soft click came and all lockers began opening simultaneously. It was only now that Kai noticed that they didn't look like normal lockers at all. Crafted of anthracite metal, each of them was at least three times the size of a normal locker. In fact, they looked like sci-fi versions of them. This became even more apparent when reddish lights in and around the dark storage containers flicked on.

A smug expression on his face, Topher walked to the middle of the room and Kai followed him, more and more startled by the minute. Black suits with red markings on them were stored inside the tall, deep spaces, every one draped in a way as if it were standing upright by itself, or as if there was an actual person filling them.

Kai opened his mouth but wasn't sure what to say, so he closed it again after a second, hoping he didn't look like a complete idiot.

"They're cool, aren't they?" Topher said, extending his arms like a magician who had just performed a breath-taking trick.

"Yes," Kai answered. "What are they?"

"This," Topher answered, walking toward one of the suits, "is your new work uniform, my friend."

Now Kai's jaw dropped, and he didn't care anymore if he behaved like a dork or not.

"Are you serious?"

"Dead serious." The reddish light reflected in Topher's eyes and made them gleam mysteriously. "Come on, take a closer look."

The suit looked like an impressive high-tech piece. As Kai moved closer to inspect it curiously, he noticed that the outer coating was a matte-black, rubber-like material. Various tubes and wires stuck out of it at several points, and there appeared to be ports where cords or wires could be directly connected to the suit.

"Wow," Kai whispered, carefully stretching out his hand to touch this lucid dream of every nerd in the world. Topher didn't stop him and simply stood next to Kai, an amused grin on his face.

The material felt cold and soft under Kai's fingertips. It definitely wasn't rubber, but also not leather or anything like that. When touching it, he could feel that there was a harder material under the coating; plates and bars of some sort, maybe made of aluminum.

"That's incredible!"

"Ha! Right? Wait until you wear it. Which is why we came here, actually."

"What are they for?" Kai asked with excitement. "I mean, do all testers wear them?"

"The lower levels, yes. Levels Four to Nine wear different models. And when you see the gear a Level Ten has, it'll blow your fucking mind!" He made a gesture as if his head had exploded. "As to why. Simple. Protection, but that's not all. The suit might look like Batman cosplay, but it's an engineering marvel. It protects your physical body from damage. It keeps you alive."

He pressed a button and a mechanism slowly moved the suit out of the locker toward him and Kai, then he pointed at the ports. "We hard-wire you into the system when you enter VR and monitor even the slightest change in your body functions. The suit will automatically balance your hormones and soothe your nervous system in case it gets fired up too much. It will also absorb most of the damage your body would take, like the bruises you suffered."

"That's incredible!"

"And that's not all. Ever seen Dune?"

"The video game? I love it!"

"Actually, it was a movie first, and before that a book. You know, one of those paper thingys your grandparents used to read before VR took over everyone's entertainment. Anyway, our gimps here are basically designed the same way. They'll keep you alive, absorb your sweat, keep your body at a normal temperature. The suit will even provide you with fluids and nourishment through the ports so you can easily stay in VR for a couple of days straight, up to a week."

Kai stared at him with wide eyes.

"Yeah, we call them gimps here," Topher laughed. "No idea who came up with it, but the name stuck."

"I can stay in VR for up to a week wearing that? Without to have to log off at any time?"

Kai began to think that this could only be a dream. It couldn't be real. This was too good to be true! It was science-fiction!

"Oh yeah, easily. Wait, did Rachel not tell you that we do that all the time?"

Kai shook his head.

Topher rolled his eyes. "Those damn pencil pushers never do their jobs properly. If we were as sloppy as them, people would drop like flies. Well, yeah, some assignments last for multiple days in a row. But you won't be enlisted for them until you reach Level Two."

"That's amazing! I bet if people outside could have such suits they'd be willing to spend a fortune on them."

Topher grinned. "They'll have them eventually. These are prototypes. CyberWear, the company that developed them for us, have been working on a model suitable for the public for years. It won't take much longer now. But, pssst, you didn't hear it from me!"

He pressed his index finger against his lips and winked.

"So, are you ready to take your gimp for a test ride?" he added.

"Hell yeah!"

"Ok. You need to strip out of everything. No underwear, no socks. There are some instructions right here." He pressed his finger on a glass panel by the door of the locker and it sprang into action, showing a 3D hologram of the suit. "I'll give you some privacy and wait outside."

He clapped Kai's shoulder and left.

***

Even following the instructions, it took Kai more than ten minutes to get the suit on. Topher had been right. It felt awkward at the beginning, especially since the 'gimp' was framed on the inside, which made Kai feel stiff when he walked. For some reason, Kai had hoped he would look sexy – like Batman – when wearing the suit, but instead he felt and looked rather clumsy.

When he opened the door and walked outside into the dimly lit hall, Topher was leaning against a wall, waiting for him, a cup of coffee in his hand. He, too, had changed and was now wearing an identical black suit to Kai's.

The team lead looked Kai up and down and nodded.

"Well done, dude. You did everything right and it only took you ten minutes." There was a slight air of mockery in his voice. "How does it feel?"

"A bit strange, to be honest…"

Topher stepped toward him and pushed a button on Kai's shoulder.

A hissing noise came and Kai stiffened. The suit began tightening around him as the air stored inside was pressed out through a valve on his side. Kai looked down and watched in awe at what was happening. Just when it began to feel claustrophobic and the fear that the suit would suffocate him struck him, the shrinking stopped.

The high-tech clothing had adjusted to his body perfectly. To Kai's surprise, it felt much better now, almost like a second skin.

However, this clearly had a downside. Inspecting himself, Kai felt embarrassed. Being skin-tight now, the suit showed off his body proportions all too clearly – in a not very flattering way.

Topher chuckled, noticing Kai's dismay.

"Yep, that's why the company has a gym on the premises, personal trainers included."

He moved on, indicating for Kai to follow him. Taking a closer look at his new superior, Kai noticed that Topher's body posture and way of moving revealed that he was in pretty good shape. He looked much better than him when wearing one of the suits.

"That's only half the truth, of course," the team lead said, turning the corner and walking down another hall. "Naturally, everyone wants to look acceptable when gimping up, but it's even more imperative to have a good diet and do enough exercise. The healthier your body, the lower your probability of taking heavy damage. Visiting the gym three times a week is mandatory here."

He looked at Kai.

"Let me guess, Rachel didn't mention that either?"

"Nope."

"Well, you know now," he said, a slight irritation in his voice.

They approached a double door with a sign next to it that said *Level 1-4 Medical Center*, and it opened automatically for them. Kai squinted his eyes for a second because it was so bright in there compared with the rest of the underground part of Helltek HQ. In fact, it only came to Kai now that even after a short time down here, he had completely lost his sense of what time it was. It was probably still morning, but he couldn't be sure. No wonder the employees called this part of the facility the Bowels.

Yet the sickbay looked completely different from the rest of the floor. It was brightly illuminated with walls painted in white and blue. A young nurse approached.

"What's up, Topher?"

"I'm bringing you a rookie."

The girl gave Kai a friendly smile. "Ah. You're getting your ports?"

Kai shrugged. "I guess so."

"Don't worry, it sounds worse than it is. You won't feel anything."

She waved her finger, indicating for him to follow her. They entered a small room with an examination chair in its center. The nurse pointed at it, and Kai took a seat.

"Now place your hands in front of you on the markings. Make sure your fingers align with them," the nurse said, and Kai did as asked. "Exactly. Perfect."

She stepped to a control panel next to the chair and pressed some keys. Kai flinched as a mechanism sprang into action and two metallic tubes closed around his hands and wrists.

"No fear, it'll be over in a second," the nurse said in a soothing tone. "I'm Nell, by the way."

"Nice to meet you, I'm Kai."

"What a nice name!"

"Yeah, it's a Viking name," he said with a smile.

"Oh really?"

Kai flinched again. "Ouch!"

He couldn't see what was happening under the tubes, but something had stung him – in both hands. Nell had moved to a screen mounted on the wall, where Kai saw a 3D model of some hands... his hands?

"That was just a little injection," she said. "This way, you won't feel anything from now on. Relax!"

Kai tried to. He leaned back and took a deep breath. He hated needles, and from the feel of it, that had been a pretty big one.

"What exactly are the ports?"

"Ugh," Topher, who was standing in the doorway with crossed arms, chimed in. "Did the office drone not tell you that either? What are they even getting paid for?"

"Right?" the nurse said with a chuckle, then she looked at Kai to explain. "As we speak, the machine is injecting tiny polymer-carbon tubes into your wrist veins, which will be used as permanent, durable entrance ports to your body."

Kai didn't like the idea of tubes in his veins at all. "Like what you get in the hospital?"

"Kinda. Just better. You won't feel them once they're in and the entrance cannula is only three millimeters thick. You'll hardly even see it."

"It's necessary to inject whatever your body might need at any time into your system. Remember what I told you earlier about Dune?" Topher added.

"Do you have those, too?" Kai asked, suddenly scared he would pass out, imagining how this machine that had his hands in a firm grip was inserting stuff into his veins.

"But of course!" Topher held his palms up, and Kai could see tiny plastic rings protruding from his wrists. They were transparent and so small that Kai hadn't noticed them until now.

The machine hummed as it slowly released its grip and the tubes over his hands opened.

"All done!" Nell said with a bright smile. "See? Wasn't bad at all, was it?"

"No, it was no problem," Kai said, inspecting his hands. His skin was reddish around the little rings sticking out of his wrists, but otherwise he couldn't feel anything.

"Ok, let's go," Topher said, clapping impatiently. "It's time for you to meet the squad and then go for a test run."

"Come and see us anytime if you need anything," Nell said, waving as Kai left, following Topher.

Back in the seemingly endless corridors, they encountered two young women walking in the opposite direction, chatting cheerfully. Kai's heart skipped a beat when looking at them. Both were wearing the same suits as him but with purple stripes on the shoulders and sides instead of red ones like his – and they looked breathtaking in them.

They interrupted their conversation and smiled.

"Hi Topher," the taller one of them said. She was blonde and had a round, freckled face.

"What's up, ladies," he answered casually as they passed

them.

"Those two are part of the V-Life crew," the lead explained to Kai. "And they're both Level Four, so don't even start dreaming about it."

"What?" Kai felt caught. "I–"

"Yeah, right," Topher laughed. "You'll get used to that sight. Girls in gimps are omnipresent here. Try not to act like such a nerd, ok? I mean, we're all nerds here, but still."

Kai wasn't sure what to answer, so he just nodded. A moment later, they had arrived. Topher opened a door and they entered a spacious room.

It was long and dimly lit. Judging from its shape and size, it could have been an office space, big enough to accommodate a dozen desks and people working there.

Yet this workspace had no desks since the people working here didn't require any.

Instead, eight chairs were positioned on both sides along the walls, facing each other. The furniture – if the word even applied to those things – was like nothing Kai had ever seen before.

Formed ergonomically, the metallic silver chairs were shaped in a way that allowed the person occupying them to lie down at an angle of 20 degrees instead of horizontally. The part where the head and shoulders were supposed to rest was integrated into an alcove.

Five of the chairs were occupied by people wearing the same kind of suits as Kai and Topher. Their bodies lay still and their eyes were closed. It was clear that those guys were connected to VR, but the way they were connected had hardly anything in common with how Kai and everyone else he knew entered the virtual world.

"Good morning, everyone," Topher said, entering the room and spreading his arms theatrically. "Let me introduce Kai, your new squadmate!"

No one answered. Which was only natural since the people in the chairs couldn't hear him when in VR.

"Ha, aren't you the most hilarious guy in the world?" a sarcastic voice answered from the back of the room.

"You know I am," Topher said with a grin.

"Oh yeah, everyone around these sacred halls knows."

It was only now that Kai noticed that the VR stations weren't the only equipment in the room. The sarcastic speaker emerged from behind a desk that was surrounded by screens and holograms and other high-tech stuff Kai had never seen before.

She was a woman in her early thirties, from the look of her, with wild, curly red hair standing in all directions as if she had been electrocuted. A strange pair of goggles was strapped to her forehead. Unlike the motionless figures in the chairs, she was dressed in normal clothes, although her style was rather... unique, to put it mildly. She wore camouflage cargo pants stuffed into lime-green Doc Martens boots. *Fuck you, you fucking fuck* was printed on her t-shirt, with a skeleton hand flipping off whoever dared to look at her. She had the vibe of an eccentric rock star, or a crazy scientist, although her white lab coat indicated the latter.

"So, you're the noob?" she asked, squinting an eye while looking Kai up and down.

"Kai, that's Lex, our squad operator," Topher introduced them.

"Aka the person who keeps your skinny little ass alive," she said, smirking.

"Hi," Kai said, startled. Every time he thought his experience here couldn't get more unreal, he was proven wrong.

"She's a bit crazy but overall a doll," Topher said with a wink.

"And you're a jerk," she answered, winking back, then turned to Kai. "Alright, kiddo, let's plug you in, shall we?"

She grabbed something from her desk, which looked so messy it might have been the inspiration for chaos theory, and approached him. It looked like a portable scanner of some sort, but Kai wasn't sure about that. Everything seemed to be different down here.

Lex turned his head to the side and held the device against his neuro-plant.

"Just to be certain that we have your exact signature," she explained. "It can be scrambled at times when coming over the wire."

Kai had no clue what she was talking about but tried to put a knowing expression on his face.

The device beeped softly. Lex pulled it away and nodded approvingly.

"Ok. I assume he's getting Misha's seat?" she asked Topher while pointing at an empty VR station to her left.

"Yep," Topher answered.

"Make yourself comfortable, kiddo," Lex said, walking to the chair. "You're gonna spend more time here than anywhere else… well, at least your body will."

She typed a code into a control panel located in the alcove part of the VR chair, and a bunch of displays and lights sprang into action. Kai felt his heart pounding as he approached the chair. For some reason, he was suddenly filled with the paralyzing fear that he would die in this seat. Or suffer whatever fate had happened to his predecessor, Misha.

Remember, you know what you're signing up for, he thought, recalling Rachel's words, coming out of her pretty, catlike face.

Do I really?

He saw Lex raising an eyebrow and gave himself a mental push.

Here goes nothing, he thought, sitting down clumsily.

The chair had special perforations for his arms and legs, and as soon as he placed his limbs there, the suit clicked into place, as if it had become one with the device. The magnetism, or whatever tech stood behind this, kept him in place, and it felt surprisingly comfortable. Almost like floating.

"This is so your muscles can relax and don't cramp in

longer sessions or under stress," Lex said, then pointed at the lights, displays and diagrams above Kai's head. "The system will constantly monitor your vital functions, and I keep an eye on all data back in my little she-cave. If anything goes wrong, we'll know about it within seconds. You're actually much safer here than in your home environment. Hold your hands still."

Kai heard a click and felt a soft burn in his wrists as two metallic wires were plugged into the contact ports the friendly nurse had implanted less than an hour ago.

The headpiece wasn't a pillow, rather it was designed to hold his head in place when he rested it there, and it had an opening for the back of his head and neck, where his neuro-plant access was.

"All right, you're almost good to go, sweetie," Lex said, petting Kai's cheek nonchalantly. "The wire that will enter your neuro-plant in a moment and deliver you to the land of dreams is a tad bigger than what you're used to, but don't worry, it only hurts a little the first time."

Topher, who had meanwhile walked over to the empty chair next to Kai, laughed, shaking his head. "I need to remember that one."

"You're welcome," Lex grinned, then she turned her attention back to Kai.

"Ok, Kai, ready?"

"Ready."

"What kind of name is Kai, anyway?" she asked, pressing some keys in the station above his head. "Is it Thai?"

"No," he said quickly. "It's—"

But he didn't have time to finish his sentence as his life changed forever.

CHAPTER TEN

A sharp pain ran through Kai's skull like a lightning bolt as the connector entered the neuro-plant port in his head.

For a millisecond, the world around him froze, then he felt like he was flying backward through a tunnel – at light speed. Just when he thought his consciousness would be ripped into shreds, he stopped.

To his surprise, he found himself back in the room he just had left. Kai furrowed his brow, looking around, but he quickly realized that this wasn't the same room. It was a virtual version that had been designed to look similar. Its layout and coloring were the same, but instead of Lex's she-cave, the rear part was equipped with comfy-looking lounge furniture. Colorful posters decorated the walls, most of them showing famous video games or superheroes.

"I know, the first couple of times, the entry might feel pretty rough to you," Topher said, materializing in an armchair. "It's because the test equipment runs on way more powerful machines than anything you can find outside. The processor power is insane, but necessary. In ordinary environments an FPS rate drop is annoying, for us it can pose a serious threat. But you'll learn that soon enough. Come on, take a seat."

Kai sat down and Topher continued.

"I summoned the crew – they should be here any moment to meet you. Then we'll proceed with your training. You're an experienced VR user and gamer, so many things will come naturally to you. Other stuff will be new for you, and pretty exciting."

Looking at the team lead, Kai noticed that his virtual appearance looked different to the guy he had met outside VR. Although a relatively handsome young man in real life, Topher had chosen an avatar that looked like an idealized version of himself. He was taller and leaner, with broad shoulders. His face was more symmetrical and smoother than his real one, and his eyes shone like black marbles. No doubt there were perfect abs hidden under the fashionable, form-fitting shirt he was wearing. Kai looked down at himself and found his own body to be rather boring.

Topher noticed Kai inspecting himself and chuckled.

"No worries, this is just a default avatar. You can customize yourself later. When testing a game environment, you will usually be assigned an appearance that is a default for the game, same as when you play an ego-shooter at home, for example. As you know, single-player and co-op games usually have default characters which are only marginally customizable. However, everyone at Helltek is encouraged to create a virtual persona and stick to it when outside a game or inside an environment that allows customization."

Kai remembered the Cyber Squad that had entered *TSOTA*. How out of place they had appeared in the midst of the high fantasy-themed RPG. Had those been the virtual personas of those people?

"This here is a safe environment located on our internal servers with no access from the outside," Topher said. "We usually test single-player games offline unless necessary. As soon as we enter the Net, things can get pretty rough at times."

"Why?"

Topher's overly handsome face turned very serious.

"Because there's more shit out there than you can even imagine. In fact, no one would play virtual games online if they were aware of *what* is actually out there."

Kai felt his neck hair standing up as an ice-cold shiver

ran down his spine at Topher's words. It felt absolutely *real*. Way more real than anything he had ever experienced in VR until now.

"What is out there?"

Topher grinned.

"Patience, young Padawan. You'll learn that soon enough. We don't want to scare the crap out of you on your first day," he added with a wink after remaining silent for a moment.

Before Kai could ask any more questions, the door opened and five young people entered.

The team lead waved his hand. "Here they come. Meet your Cyber Squad, Kai. Guys, this is our new Level One."

Four young men and one young woman approached him. They all were dressed in identical black combat suits. Those were not the VR suits every one of them was wearing on their real bodies but originated from the game they just had exited. All of them looked extremely badass.

"Hey Kai, what's up?" the young man walking in front of the others greeted him. "I'm Marco, DPS."

He extended his hand in a fist bump and Kai responded. Marco was an athletic guy with brown skin and fire-red hair that hung over his left eye.

"And those are: Josh, tank," he pointed at a guy who looked way too lanky to be a tank. "Then there's Francois, healer – don't mind him, he's Canadian."

"And you're an asshole," the other answered with fake offense and a slight French accent.

Marco ignored him and instead introduced the only girl in the team. "The lady is Claudia, also DPS."

Claudia smiled, sitting down on a couch facing Kai.

"Nice to meet you!"

She had curly, brown hair bound into a ponytail and lively hazel-colored eyes.

"And last but not least, Viktor, our tech," Marco finished the introduction.

Viktor, a pale guy with black hair and piercing eyes, lifted his palm into a minimalistic greeting while his mouth twitched into an even more minimalistic smile.

"Oh, and you've already met Topher," Marco added after they all had sat down. "Our master and commander."

"Damn right," Topher answered with a grin, then turned serious. "Ok, now that we're all here, let's get to business. You guys know we're on a tight schedule. How's it going out there?"

"The game runs surprisingly smoothly so far," Marco replied. "We only ran into some minor issues and made tickets for them."

"Don't jinx it," Claudia said, rolling her eyes.

"Our squads are the external QA, the testers that investigate the shippable game for security risks," Topher turned his attention back to Kai. "Game devs have their own QAs that check the games for bugs while in development. We're the first ones who actually play them."

"Yep, we're the cool guys," Marco nodded.

"But that's only half of the services Helltek provides," Topher said, ignoring Marco's interruption. "The way more glamorous – and dangerous – half is in-game intervention. The name Cyber Squad is no coincidence. We're like virtual special unit squads. If the shit hits the fan somewhere in one of the countless online worlds frequented by hundreds of millions of players each day, they call us. In times where any bug or glitch can easily turn into a deadly menace, special elite forces are needed to clean up."

An expression of pride and excitement spread over everyone's face as he spoke. Kai could feel the enthusiasm spreading over to him. The skin on his neck prickled, as it always did when he got excited. Only later would he fully realize that when plugged into the Helltek system, he experienced everything exactly as he did in his real body, down to the tiniest detail.

"However, they won't deploy you on such missions

until you reach Level Five," Topher said after a short moment of silence had passed, and the others nodded knowingly.

"Our teams usually consist of six players. Three damage dealers, who we call DPSs, one tank, one healer and one techie. Just in case you're wondering what that is, it's nothing other than a coder. A programmer who can influence the game code on the run if necessary."

Kai nodded. "I've seen one in action. It was impressive."

"Gang, our newbie here has had the pleasure of encountering a Level Ten Cyber Squad in-game," the team lead said.

All heads turned to Kai in surprise.

"Ah man, I would love to see those guys in action some day!" Josh said dreamingly.

"Which team did you encounter?" Claudia asked.

Kai shrugged. "I have no idea –"

"I think it was Alpha," Topher interrupted.

"What?!" Josh cried out. "How cool is that!"

"You *have* to tell us how it was," Claudia begged.

"Later," Topher said. "I want to brief him with the basics and then have a quick test-run in-game."

"I assume I'll be DPS?" Kai asked.

"According to your gamer profile, that's your preferred class and what you're best at," Topher answered. "Besides, it's the role that has become vacant in our team."

Suddenly, an uncomfortable silence spread in the room like an unpleasant smell, and everyone looked downcast.

"We mostly use the classic roles when testing RPGs," Topher said quickly, noticing his team's reaction. "Right now, we're testing a co-op shooter, so everyone basically functions as DPS. But I believe it'll be easier to show you everything than trying to explain it. I just wanted you to meet the family before we continue."

Topher rose from his chair. "You guys can go on with the map you started. If everything runs smoothly, Kai will be able to join you after lunch."

"Aye, Captain," Marco said.

Kai watched as they all got up from their seats. Then, one after another, they performed a gesture with their hands, as if activating something on an invisible screen in front of them. With one blink after another, the squad had vanished.

"You're lucky – this is a great team," Topher said with a smile and pride in his voice once they were gone.

"I bet!" Kai answered genuinely. Manners were often rude among gamers, and he hadn't expected such a warm welcome as he had just received.

Topher, too, now began moving his fingers in the air as if using an invisible touch screen.

A blue HUD appeared in Kai's field of view.

"This is your personal tester UI[15]," the team lead explained. "It doesn't look much different to any game HUD but has some special features."

Curious, Kai took a closer look.

Name: Kai
Level: 1
100/100
Team: 76B
Team Lead: Topher B.
Game: n.a.
Progression: 0/1000
Available Features: Dev mode, Console, God mode

"What does progression mean?" Kai asked.

"That's your progression to Level Two," Topher explained.

"How do I progress?"

"Mostly through grinding, really. You get points for every day you're here, for every level played, every bug you report, et cetera. But, of course, there's more. You get extra points for certain stuff, and those are what will make you rise like a rocket through the ranks."

"What kind of stuff?"

"If you open your menu in the left bottom corner, you'll find the Q&A button there. It contains files with hundreds of pages of intel about your job, Helltek, Cyber Squad, game testing in general, and the ranks and how you climb them. Basically, whenever you do something extraordinary, the system will notice and record it."

"Such as?"

Topher shrugged.

"Stick your neck out for a teammate. Discover unique issues and document them. That kind of stuff. And, of course, there are also the tournaments that can boost your score."

"What kind of tournaments?"

The lead chuckled. "You'll see soon enough."

"Ok," Kai was pumped and ready to jump into any adventure waiting for him. Then he remembered one more question that had interested him since the beginning. "How long does it usually take to reach Level Two?"

"You can't wait to get all the benefits, eh? I can't blame you," Topher said. "Usually about a year. But some overachievers make it in a few months. Some never."

Kai's face fell, and Topher smiled.

"But I have full faith in you, to be honest. Ok, let's jump into the game. I'll explain the really important features of your HUD on the run. You can open and close it by thinking, by the way. There are only very few functions that have to be activated 'manually' by using a gesture. Try thinking *HUD OFF*."

HUD OFF, Kai thought, and the HUD vanished from his view.

"Splendid! Now switch it back on again. I'm logging us into the game."

HUD ON, Kai thought, and the HUD was back in his FOV.

A message appeared in his vision, blinking:

Logging you into game_secure_dev-mode. 3... 2... 1...

CHAPTER ELEVEN

The room around Kai dissolved into pixels and bits, and for a second he was in complete, white emptiness. Then countless fragments rushed toward him, like a jagged wave of confetti, and began forming an environment, the millions of pieces clicking together to create a piece of art of seemingly impossible complexity. Kai blinked as he stood in a completely different, virtual world than the one he had been in only a moment ago.

He looked around in awe. The graphics were 100% photo-realistic. Everything around him seemed as real as it could be. Even if Topher hadn't mentioned it before, Kai would have known that this game could only be a shooter.

It was a tradition going back decades, all the way back to the early years of gaming, which demanded that shooters were always required to use groundbreaking technology, at least the AAA ones.

Kai didn't know what game this was, but it looked absolutely stunning.

He stood in the middle of a street in a beautiful, futuristic city. The skyscrapers were of unusual architecture and were much higher than the highest in the real world, almost defying gravity. Less than a mile away, a spectacular building loomed amidst the skyscrapers: a gigantic black pyramid, seemingly of glass.

Yet one thing was unusual and like nothing he had ever seen before or expected when entering a virtual world.

Everything around him was frozen. Futuristic cars

stood completely still. High above, a shimmering monorail seemed frozen in time. It took him a second to realize that there was also no air movement whatsoever. It felt more like a sterile lab than a city – a gigantic open-air lab.

But the most curious sight was the people.

The pedestrians on the sidewalks stood still. Not just frozen in time or like machines cut off from electricity. They stood unnaturally upright, with their arms spread, forming a T.

Kai had heard of that but had never seen it before. It was the so-called T-pose, the state game NPCs remained in when in dev mode. The realization struck him all of a sudden and filled him with excitement: he was in the game engine editor!

The times when game engine editors had been open-sourced to users to create mods were long gone. Nowadays, every game studio kept its editor locked up like Fort Knox.

Nevertheless, rumors existed that there were virtual worlds on the Dark Web that had been created with illegally obtained sandboxes. Those were dark and extremely violent places, where no rules applied, if any of the stories circling around in the gaming community could be trusted.

"Cool, huh?" Topher said, suddenly right next to him, ripping him out of his chain of thought.

"Yes!" Kai said. "It looks amazing. Are we in dev mode?"

Topher nodded.

"That's exactly where we are. I assume you've never entered a game this way before?" Kai shook his head. "The reason we do that is because it's the safest way to enter a game that hasn't been thoroughly tested yet. If something is really off, it will often show in dev mode. Take a look!"

He pointed behind them, and Kai saw an NPC that was very different to the others. The male figure, dressed in a futuristic business suit, was flickering. Upon closer inspection, Kai noticed that the figure wasn't just flickering. His arms were moving up and down from his T-pose into a casual one, as fast as a hummingbird's wings.

"Congrats!" Topher said. "Not even a minute in the game and you can report your first bug. Using your UI, open the menu and select 'report'. It will give you an option to take a screenshot. Try to capture it as closely as possible. It will display your exact position automatically when the report is sent to the game studio. This looks like a minor issue to me, and the answer we get will probably be: *Close. Known, shippable.*"

"Known, shippable?" Kai asked, focusing his HUD on the hummingbird man to take a picture.

Topher laughed.

"The dreaded 'known, shippable' is the reason why games are almost always buggy as fuck when they're released. Such little issues as this one will most likely never be fixed, no matter if they release a patch or not. But we report them anyway. It's our job – and good for your progression score."

"Got the pic," Kai said.

"Awesome, now open 'description' and describe in a few precise words exactly what you encountered. Once you've opened the description field, you can simply think what you want to write in there. Pro tip: try to keep your dirty thoughts out of your mind when doing so."

He winked, then laughed on seeing Kai's startled face.

"Happens to the best of us at times. Anyway, in this case, an appropriate description would be something like: *NPC breaks T-pose*. Once you've filled it out, you can assign a priority to the issue. In this case, it should be the lowest, priority 1. It's the green field."

Kai did everything as instructed and was amazed at how smoothly it went. It seemed like an easy enough job so far.

"Ok, now, don't select 'send' yet. It's absolutely imperative that we test every issue that we encounter in the sandbox in-game as well before we send the ticket off. Sometimes things look like a trifle in the editor and are a major issue in the game. That's one of the reasons why massive bugs can stay unnoticed by the dev teams. Simply select 'save draft' for now."

"Got it."

"Good. Ready to jump into the game?"

Kai smiled. "So ready."

Topher walked onto the sidewalk, then grinned. "Little advice. You might want to get off the road first."

Kai did as he was told and quickly moved to the side. Just in time.

Suddenly, everything around him came to life. Not slowly but from one blink to another.

Warm sun rays fell on his face, and the airstream from the cars rushing by hit his skin. Topher had been right. If Kai had stayed on the street, he would have been run over by a couple of vehicles, which sped down the virtual street much faster than they were allowed in real life. He most likely would have died or at least taken heavy damage, depending on how the mechanics of this game worked.

Kai lifted his head, amazed by the incredible details of this world. Someone bumped into him and cussed him out. The pedestrians were in as much of a hurry as the cars.

He noticed that he now had another HUD that overlay his tester UI, the actual game HUD. It was a typical shooter HUD, showing his health and ammo stats as well as the weapon he had equipped, a pistol. But there were also some abilities displayed which seemed to be game-specific, such as 'scanner', 'rush', 'drone', and a few others.

Turning his head, he saw Topher watching him attentively. The team lead was now wearing the same black combat suit as the others from his squad had when he had met them. Somehow its design seemed familiar to Kai, but he couldn't recall where he had seen it before.

Topher pointed his finger behind them and Kai saw the flawed NPC. It showed similarly erratic behavior in-game. It was moving more like a broken robot than a human being, whereas the other NPCs appeared 100% human.

"Take another screenshot, attach it to the report with

the comment that the NPC is broken in-game, too, then send it off."

"Done," Kai said a few seconds later.

At the same moment, he saw numbers on his tester HUD move as his progression ticked up.

Name: Kai
Level: 1
100/100
Team: 76B
Team Lead: Topher B.
Game: Behind Blue Eyes 3
Progression: 1/1000
Available Features: Dev mode, Console, God mode

Ugh, he thought. It would take a long time to advance to the next level indeed.

"Don't worry," Topher said, almost as if reading Kai's thoughts. "It'll go quicker than you think."

"This world looks fantastic," Kai said. "What game is it?"

"It should show up on your UI, doesn't it?"

Kai checked his UI, which was partially covered by the game HUD.

"You can adjust its size in the menu to fit your field of vision better."

Kai did and now saw the information better. The tester UI showed he was teamed up with Topher and also the title of the game.

"*Behind Blue Eyes 3*?"

"Yeah, it's brand-new. Due for release in the fall," Topher said.

Kai could hardly hide his excitement. "I played the first two and loved them!"

Topher grinned. "We know. Why do you think they assigned you to my team?"

"That's awesome!"

"Well, you'll notice that testing a game isn't actually the same as playing it for fun. I know testers who got so fed up with shooters that they can only work on RPGs now. And vice versa. Others have been assigned to V-Life."

"I knew I'd seen the suits before," Kai said.

"They're awesome, aren't they? Everyone looks like a badass wearing them," Topher agreed.

For a moment, both of them had turned into nerdy gamer fanboys.

"Alright, now I'll show you the most important thing you're gonna learn today. Actually, it's the most important thing for any tester in any game."

Kai looked at him in anticipation.

"My friend, you're going to learn how to open and use the console," Topher said in a tone as if he was about to reveal the biggest secret of the universe. "And the best thing is, it's universal! Once you learn how to access it, you can use it in *any* game."

"Ok..." Kai said slowly. "What exactly is the console?"

Topher let a beat pass before he spoke to show the importance of his next sentence.

"It's basically your super-power. And will save your ass more than once. You'll see. It might even save your life."

Kai watched and listened attentively. Although he wasn't much older than him, Topher almost appeared like a sage to him at that moment.

"They told you this is a high-risk job, didn't they?" he asked.

"Yes, I signed a waiver."

"The gimp you're wearing in real life now will protect your body from most injuries, but the thing is, there's no protective suit for your brain. Severe glitches in a game can cause brain damage, seizures, strokes, or even death."

Kai felt his hair standing up. All juvenile casualness was now gone from Topher's voice.

"I'm not telling you that to scare you," he said. "I want you to understand that this isn't a game. Well, of course, *this* is a game. But our job isn't."

"I understand." Kai tried to make his voice sound firm.

"And if it weren't for the console, testers would drop like flies. Which is the reason why the commands are universal and can be applied to any game, no matter the developer. By entering our system earlier, the console clearance has been added to your neuro-plant automatically. It's a tiny but highly encrypted piece of code. Every game will automatically recognize this sequence and give you console access. Think *OPEN CONSOLE*."

Kai did and saw the result instantly.

The game HUD vanished and was replaced by a command-line interface with a blinking black cube at its end.

"Whoa," Kai said. "Is that..."

"Yep, it's your personal open sesame into the game engine."

Kai felt a bit overwhelmed. Game engines were like the holy grail of every game developer, strictly secured by many security measures. For a gamer fanatic like him, entering the command-line of a game engine was like Christmas. Or sex. Or both at once.

"What do I do with it?"

"Do you see the virtual keyboard in front of you? You actually need to type in the command. You can't just thought-command the console."

"Ok, what do I type?"

"For now, you'll only be able to use two commands, but those are essential. One is *>enter_dev_mode*. It will instantly stop the game and bring you back to the secure dev mode we just came from. However, keep in mind that there's no dev mode in multiplayer. At least, not like this."

"Makes sense," Kai thought out loud.

"The other one is your life insurance, Kai. *>enter_god_mode*."

"Woohoo, I can enter god mode?" Kai was in utter fanboy mode now.

It happened from time to time that hackers implemented the god mode cheat – which made the player immune to any damage- into popular games, but this was usually highly illegal and could result in a permanent ban from X-Perience, which was basically a ban from online gaming. To legally enter god mode at any time – that was a dream!

Topher smiled. "Yes, you can. Type it in."

Kai did. The console closed instantly after he hit enter on the virtual keyboard.

But nothing changed. He still felt and looked exactly the same.

"Yeah, I know, everyone thinks they'll instantly turn into Superman but that's not how it works," Topher laughed. "Step into the road. Go on!"

Kai hesitated for a second. Even though he knew that this was only a virtual world, Topher's warning about how dangerous unfinished games could be had stuck in his brain. But then he saw the team lead watching him, gave himself a mental push and stepped into the busy street.

Two futuristic sports cars raced toward him, and Kai needed all his strength of will not to leap out of harm's way. He couldn't prevent himself from clenching his teeth and grimacing though.

The cars didn't slow down a bit or try to avoid him. Obviously the AI was programmed to strictly follow its path here, no matter what. Suddenly just as they were almost within touching distance of Kai, they both crashed into an invisible obstacle at high speed. Due to their momentum, the impact was so massive that the vehicles were completely destroyed.

"Sweet, isn't it?" Topher said.

Kai laughed. "It is!"

"God mode creates a boundary around you which is impenetrable. There's another mode that would show you the exact vectors, but you don't need access to that. At least for now. And there's this... watch!"

He stepped into the street in the midst of the speeding cars. But instead of hitting him or an invisible obstacle, they simply passed through him, as if he were a ghost.

"Clipping mode," Topher said, spreading his arms. "There's much more, but only higher-level techs have access to that. The best of the best can fix the code on the run."

Kai remembered the hacker with the Level Ten team he had witnessed in action and nodded.

"Ok, let's go and try to kill some stuff," Topher said.

"Do we always use god mode?" Kai asked.

"Nope. It's only for speed runs and emergencies. Otherwise, we're supposed to test all aspects of the game, taking damage, dying and respawning included. Besides, god mode can be tricky in MMOs. Sometimes it interferes with the game mechanics and won't function as it should. Come on!"

The game HUD was back in Kai's field of view, and some text flashed through his vision.

New Objective: Enter the target area and eliminate all hostiles.
Optional: Stay unnoticed.

Kai followed Topher, who was sprinting ahead. They both ran through the seemingly endless maze of glass and chrome with inhuman speed, and Kai noticed how incredibly realistic the rays of light appeared when reflected from the glass towers and hitting his eyes. Turning his head, Kai could see his own reflection in the windows they sped past. Even his default avatar looked great in the black combat suit, which was iconic for the game series. Slowly, the environment changed from a city of light, beauty and perfection to a shadier area with older and lower buildings.

Contrary to most RPGs, stamina dropping when sprinting wasn't an issue in shooters, and they quickly arrived at the destination marked in red on the 3D mini-map displayed in the right lower corner of the HUD.

Entering restricted area!

"We're not shitting around with stealth gameplay, we're going full Rambo," Topher said. "I want to see you in action."
"Copy that!"
"You take the left, I'll take the right flank. This is one of the first missions in the game, so it should be a piece of cake… but before we rush in, please disable god mode. The command for that is >*exit_god_mode*."
Kai did as he was asked.
"Done."
They took off in opposite directions. The target area had a very typical design for this kind of game. The objective marker pointed at a run-down warehouse, surrounded by containers, trucks and other obstacles which could be used as cover.
"You know the game mechanic from the previous installments," Topher said directly in his ear. "Scan the area first, then attack. So far, the scanning has proven to be the buggiest feature in the game. Let's see how it goes for you."
Kai ran into cover behind a low, half-collapsed wall, then activated the scanner. His vision changed into something that vaguely resembled infra-red but was more than that, just as he remembered from the last game. Two dozen figures appeared around the compound and inside the warehouse, highlighted in red. Additionally, their bodies showed their blood vessels, and they appeared like creatures consisting of blood and neural systems. When Kai focused his vision directly on the closest one, he saw data running over his field of view.

Thug
Faction: Implant Harvester

Health: 360/360
Condition: Good
Danger: Moderate

Scanning over the other hostiles, he saw similar stats. The blood vessels were interrupted by augmented body parts. Some of the hostiles had one or more prosthetics and other body modifications.

"Attack when you're ready and I'll join in," Topher said.

Quickly, Kai opened the weapon and character menu to see what he had there.

Name: Kai
Faction: Guardian Angels
Rank: Rookie
Health: 1000/1000
Armor: 600/600
Weapon Equipped: Pistol
Ammo: 300/300
Abilities:
Angelblades: Turn your arms into swords
Rush: Allows you to move ten times faster than a human (duration: 10 sec/cooldown: 10 sec)
Scanner: Detects hostiles
Drone: (locked)

Kai smiled. Oh yeah, he remembered the Angelblades. They were one of the most fun features the game had to offer.

In the lower right corner, he saw the stats of his cyborg body, equipped with titanium legs and arms, silicate muscles and other gadgets that came in handy in combat. The status of his synthetic spider-silk body armor was at 100%. He was as ready as he could be.

Usually, he wouldn't have given that much thought to details and simply stormed the compound, but this time, after all, he was playing with his boss, so he wanted to make a good impression.

Topher had said he wanted to go in full Rambo. Kai wasn't sure what that reference meant, but he understood the context. It was his favorite way to play a shooter: jump in and kill everyone.

Kai drew his pistol and leaned out of cover. The HUD now showed a crosshair that moved slightly when he aimed it at an enemy. He focused his cybernetic eyes on the thug and automatically zoomed closer. Now that he had exited the scanner mode, he could see the man's face close up. His brown hair was moving in the summer breeze and sweat had formed on his forehead. An unkempt beard spread over his lower face yet left a shiny metal jaw uncovered. One of his eyes had been replaced with a red-glowing eye prosthetic.

What an ugly son of a bitch, Kai thought.

Yet, at the same time, he was amazed how perfectly human the NPC looked. Nothing in his appearance or movements looked artificial in any way, and Kai had to remind himself that this was nothing but an AI-powered construct.

Kai pulled the trigger. Three consecutive shots hit the man straight in the face. Blood sprayed in all directions as the man's health bar dropped to zero and he collapsed.

Headshot!
Critical hit!

"Well done!" Topher acknowledged. "Now let's party."

He was right. The party started immediately.

Alarmed by the shots and dead body, several thugs turned in Kai's direction and opened fire.

Again, he leaned out of cover and shot. His bullets struck down a bulky man with metal legs who was approaching him swiftly. It was too difficult to aim for the head when the target was moving, so Kai focused on the torso. After the fourth hit, the man collapsed.

An experienced player, Kai knew that staying in his

cover would be a bad idea. Game AI had come a long way and wasn't as stupid and easily outsmarted as it had been in earlier times, especially in AAA shooters.

Two hostiles tried to outflank him. He leaped out of cover and activated *Rush*, which made him run ten times faster than any human NPC, although only for a limited time of ten seconds.

That was more than enough to sprint into cover behind a corroded container. Bullets riddled the cracked concrete behind him, but he was way too fast to be hit. A second later, he was in cover and eliminated two more hostiles from there.

Euphoria filled him.

This is nothing but a dream job!

He felt an impact and a current ran through his whole body as if he'd been electrocuted.

Shit!

One second of losing focus had been enough to get hit. This game had a high level of difficulty! He ducked, avoiding getting hit again just in time as bullets riddled the container above his face.

Red numbers flashed through his vision, then:

Suit integrity at 75%!

Kai activated the scanner and saw two snipers on the roof aiming at him.

Not good. Snipers could cause heavy damage.

His augmented ears indicated footsteps from behind. Turning his head, he saw two more hostiles approaching from there. If he stayed where he was and tried to kill the snipers on the roof, they would get to him and cause heavy damage before he could take them out. He had to move.

Kai leaped out of cover and activated Rush once again, charging the two thugs trying to ambush him. This was the perfect occasion to test melee combat.

With a thought, he activated Angelblades.

Two long, razor-sharp titanium blades emerged directly from his wrists. Shimmering in the sunlight, they had turned his hands into deadly weapons.

Kai thrust them simultaneously into both approaching attackers, impaling them from the abdomen up to their necks. Blood sprayed into his face, clouding his vision, but it then quickly turned translucent before it vanished. Still on the move, Kai ripped his blades out from the two dead bodies and roll-dodged into the next cover.

Good old roll-dodge came in handy in almost every game.

Still in Rush mode, he leaned out of cover and took aim at the two men on the roof, ten times faster than them.

First he eliminated the one with the sniper rifle with three headshots, then shot his companion in the chest. The man's health sank to 150/360. He wasn't dead yet, but he'd lost his balance and fell from the roof. The impact with the ground smashed him, finishing him off.

"Sweet!" Topher commented.

Kai saw him approaching from the flank, eliminating two hostiles in his way with his rifle.

"The front yard is clear, let's finish off the rest inside. Did you encounter anything out of the ordinary?"

"Not sure," Kai said. "It might be that the scanner didn't show me the two shooters on the roof, but I'm not sure. Maybe I just didn't notice them."

Topher nodded. "Ok, we check that once we cleared out everything. Keep your eyes open."

He ran ahead toward the side entrance of the warehouse and kicked in the door with such force that it fell off its hinges. Activating the scanner again, Kai followed him into the building.

Inside, it was dark. The few windows had been covered with black paint to hide whatever shady business the gang was conducting in this facility. But as Kai remembered from the previous games, darkness was no problem for his augmented cyborg eyes. They adjusted to night vision automatically.

A slight bluish glow appeared around him and Topher as they took cover behind iron pillars. Glancing at his teammate, Kai saw that his eyes were glowing in neon blue. The iconic eyes were what had given the game series its name.

Objective updated: Rescue hostages!

Kai activated the scanner once again and inspected his surroundings. Five hostiles were marked in red. In the rear part of the building, another seven figures were marked in green. The hostages they had to rescue.

"I get the hostages, you kill everyone," Topher instructed. "If we don't split, the dude guarding the hostages will start killing them and the objective fails. I've played this many times," he added with a chuckle.

"Ok," Kai said, "Run. I'll cover you."

Without wasting time, he left his cover and sprinted toward four of the thugs who were located in his close proximity. The fifth one was on the other side of the hall and was probably the one guarding the civilians.

Kai opened fire and struck down the hostile closest to him while on the run. Only three to go, two of whom were hiding behind an old, corroded machine. The third one, however, could pose a bigger challenge than the rest. When Kai ran his scanner over the bulky man, he saw:

Gunnar Thorne
Faction: Implant Harvester
Health: 600/600
Condition: Excellent
Danger: High

He wasn't quite a boss, but he had a name, which always indicated that the hostile NPC was at least a heavy grunt.

Kai rolled out of cover, was on his feet lightning-fast

and lunged at the two thugs.

Silicate muscle structure integrity at 60%

The text flashed over his HUD as he directed extra energy into his legs and jumped – impossibly high.

With ease, he leaped over the cover the two hostiles were hiding behind and executed them from above. Another bullet hit him, this time in his side.

High-caliber impact! Suit integrity 20%. Biological tissue damaged.

It felt like a bolt had hit him. Surprisingly real – and unpleasant. His health bar dropped by 30%.

Damn, this Heavy was equipped with some exquisite high-caliber weapon.

Despite the damage he had just taken, he landed on his feet and reached cover just in time before he could take another hit. Kai reloaded his gun and waited for the hostile to advance. In most cases, the AI of mini-bosses was scripted to do that.

He was right. After shooting two salvos at him, the Heavy left his position and advanced. High-caliber projectiles crashed into the corroded machinery Kai was using as cover. It was clear that it wouldn't withstand such a barrage for long.

Kai decided to go full frontal – or do a Rambo, as Topher had called it. He jumped forward and opened fire on the hostile.

Not able to aim as precisely on the move as he would have from his cover, he focused his attack on the Heavy's torso instead of the head. He managed to land three direct hits, and his opponent's health dropped by 35%.

Shit, that wasn't enough. Not nearly enough.

The NPC returned fire, and again, Kai experienced an unpleasant sensation as bullets hit his chest, hip and left leg.

The damage report flashed through his view, but he ignored it. It was all or nothing now. Another one of his bullets hit the man in the chest and made him stagger.

Critical hit!

This was his chance. Kai dashed forward and activated his Angelblades once again. The AI anticipated his move and the man lifted his augmented metal arms to parry the attack.

Instead of trying to stab him, Kai came to a sudden halt right in front of him and used the full momentum of his speed to kick the thug in the abdomen. The man staggered again, leaving his defensive posture for a second.

It was enough for Kai to finish him off.

Using his arm blades like oversized garden scissors, he activated the full force of his augmented muscles and chopped off the hostile's head. It flew through the air before hitting the wall behind while the body collapsed, bleeding and throwing sparks.

Kai took a deep breath. That was way too close for his taste. The damage report showed that his health had dropped below 50%, and his injured body parts felt stiff. Most modern shooters and other action games were designed way more realistically than in earlier decades. There was no automatic health regeneration, and the player experienced damaged body parts as a handicap until he got them fixed.

"Well done!" Topher said, walking toward him.

Objective Completed! All hostiles eliminated. Hostages saved.

An in-game visual message popped up in Kai's field of vision, replacing his HUD. He could see a female face, semi-transparent, with a stern expression. Her almond-shaped artificial eyes glowed neon blue, and she appeared beautiful and intimidating.

"Excellent work, rookie," she said with a cold yet sexy voice. "The High Archangel will be very pleased. Return to HQ for further instructions!"

A chilling smile showed on her face and she disappeared.

Kai remembered the actress from the previous installments. Although most NPCs were engine-generated and designed by artists, the main characters in AAA games were usually portrayed by famous actors.

"In real life, your approach might not have been the smartest," Topher said with a grin. "But who cares, right?"

"In real life, I'm not a killer cyborg either," Kai answered. "Sadly."

Topher snickered, then studied the dead enemies and nodded. "You're a good player, no doubt. I'm sure the squad will be excited to have you in a tournament."

"What are the tournaments?"

"Once every three months, one of the multiplayer games currently being tested is picked, and all squads participate in a tournament. The higher your team and you personally score in such competitions, the more level progress you earn. It's a great way to boost your level-up a bit. Helltek tests the multiplayer components of each game this way." Topher paused, then asked, "Did you notice anything out of the ordinary?"

Kai shook his head. "I don't think so. Everything functioned as it should have."

"Good," Topher said, walking to the main exit of the warehouse. "Let's get out of here before it resets."

"Why will it reset?"

"Let me put it differently: let's get out of here before I reset the scenario. We're going to test it again and see if the scanner works properly or if it doesn't show the snipers on the roof. It's always important to reproduce such issues. Unless it's something as minor as the T-pose bug earlier, we always reproduce. If you can reproduce the same issue exactly the same way four times in a row, we call it 100% reproducible, if it's two times, it's 50%, and one time is 25%. If you encounter something out of the ordinary but cannot reproduce it, you report it anyway but add the note *cannot reproduce*."

"Ok," Kai said. "That makes sense."

"Yes, it does when it comes to professional testing. But trust me, you're gonna hate it in no time," Topher said. "Ok, let's do exactly the same thing again. Reproduce your steps as precisely as possible, clear?"

"Clear."

They had reached the edge of the event area and once again stood in the glaring sun in the midst of the breathtaking mega-city.

New Objective: Eliminate all hostiles.

CHAPTER TWELVE

"Welcome back."

Slowly, Kai opened his real eyes. His eyelids felt heavy, as if he had woken up from a deep slumber, and he noticed a slight throbbing in his temples. It took him a moment until he could see clearly.

Lex looked down on him, one eye squinted.

"Hi."

She turned her head and nodded toward someone Kai couldn't see. "Babyface's alright."

"Good," he heard Topher's voice. "He did really well in there."

"Oh, I know. I have an eye on everything you guys do, remember?"

She rolled her eyes, then turned her attention back to Kai. "Ok, let me unplug you. If you experience any dizziness or headache, don't worry about it. That's normal in the beginning. Our machines here are way more powerful than what you're used to from ordinary VR gaming. Your brain needs to get used to it."

Lex stepped closer, grabbed the cord attached to Kai's skull and pulled it out with a sharp, smooth movement that revealed routine.

He sat up and noticed that the dizziness already began to vanish.

"How was your first time?" Lex asked with a smirk, crossing her arms.

"Great! It was fun," Kai answered, stretching his limbs.

"Don't worry, you didn't suffer any damage," Lex said. "There shouldn't be any bruises or anything like that. But I guess you noticed that taking damage can feel pretty uncomfortable. That's because we test all games on high intensity. Usually, players won't experience even half of it. But we need to know if it gets too much."

"Kai found three bugs on his first test run," Topher said. "Not bad for starters."

"That's cool, dude," Marco chimed in.

Kai hadn't noticed him until now because he was leaning against the wall close to the door. Looking around, Kai saw that all the pods around him were empty. The rest of the squad had not only left VR but the room.

Surprisingly, Marco didn't look that much different in real life to his VR avatar. He wasn't as tall and athletic and his brown skin wasn't as smooth, the proportions of his face not as perfect, but he wore the same red-dyed haircut and a cocky grin on his face.

"Kai, I asked Marco to accompany you to the cafeteria and show you where you can get some lunch. You should find the others there."

Only now did Kai notice that his stomach was rumbling. He felt as if he hadn't eaten in ages.

"Come on," Marco said. "I'm starving."

Kai followed his new teammate, and they left the room.

"So, how do you like it here so far?" Marco asked as they walked down one of the endless halls that looked all the same to Kai.

"It's great!" he answered.

"A dream job?"

"Yeah."

Marco chuckled. "We all thought that at the beginning."

Kai looked at him in surprise. "Is it not?"

"Oh, it sure is! I mean, it's really cool what we're doing here and the pay is fantastic, once you hit a higher level. It's just not necessarily a dream *dream*, you know?"

"Um... what do you mean?"

"You'll see soon enough."

Although he was curious as hell, Kai decided not to pry for now. Apparently there were things around here people chose not to talk about. On their way, they passed several other testers wearing the same gimp suits as them, although with different colors on their shoulders. Some of them greeted Marco as they passed by, others ignored them. Kai noticed that some wore everyday clothes over their suits, mostly long shirts or vests, many women in particular. He could understand why. The suit was so tight that it almost felt like walking around naked.

"There's a small cafeteria on every underground level and a big one up on the campus. The food is basically the same everywhere, but we go to the big one as often as we can to get some daylight. It can get pretty grim down here at times, you know?" Marco explained after a moment of silence. "But no matter where you go, stay away from the hot dogs. They're–"

He made a gesture as if he wanted to stick his index finger down his throat and stuck out his tongue.

Kai laughed. "I'll try to remember that."

"I don't know what they're putting in there. I mean, a hot dog should be the easiest thing in the world to make, you'd think. But, nope."

They arrived at a huge double door, which slid open when they came closer, and they entered a spacious area. Kai paused for a moment, surprised by what he saw. The cafeteria wasn't at all what he had expected. It was decorated to resemble a 1960s diner, but everything was in bright neon colors. LED light chains illuminated the walls in pink and blue, and every few feet, a colorful moving hologram portrayed a character from a famous video game. One corner was dominated by an oversized screen showing one of the countless Avengers movies. Glimpsing at it, Kai wasn't sure if it was part 14 or maybe 16.

The place was filled with people, all young, all wearing

gimp suits. Some covered their bodies with shirts and other everyday clothes. At a quick glance, it appeared that maybe 70% were male.

Although most were occupying the tables and booths spread around the room in groups, some preferred to be by themselves, indicating this by wearing headphones. Mobile devices weren't allowed inside the testing facility, and Kai had left his with his bag and clothes in the locker room. He noticed that most tables were designed for six people. Most likely so the squads could spend their lunch breaks together. J-pop music played from invisible speakers, and the air was filled with chatter and occasional laughs. The whole atmosphere reminded Kai of the cafeteria at the college he used to attend, just way cooler – and weirder.

"Yeah, I know, it's a bit odd," Marco said, noticing Kai's puzzlement. "First time I came here, I thought my eyes would get cancer and fall out, plop!"

He made a gesture with his hands as if his eyes had exploded.

"I mean, everything is dim and grim in the halls and corridors, and then you walk in here and feel like you've fallen straight into an anime. Don't ask me why. But apparently they hired some expensive af designers to decorate the cafeterias and other common areas, and that's what they came up with. It's kind of a shock, especially when you grew up in the prospects like me and are used to real life being gray on gray. But don't worry, you get accustomed to it quickly. Come on!"

He clapped his shoulder and pointed at a queue that had gathered at the food distribution point in the center of the room.

"How do I pay? I have nothing with me," Kai asked after reaching for his wallet in his pocket and realizing that he had neither.

"Oh, didn't they tell you that at HR? All food and drinks are on the house."

"Guess not. But that's awesome!"

Free food? This was getting better and better.

"Ugh... let me guess, Rachel?"

"Yeah."

Marco rolled his eyes. "That chick. Great boobs, no brain."

Kai stared at him with an open mouth. No one dared to openly speak like that nowadays. Especially not in a work environment.

Marco laughed, grabbing a tray.

"You're looking at me as if I've just committed all seven deadly sins at once and am on my way straight to hell."

"Well, technically you have," Kai said.

"Not here, man. This is the video game industry. And we're the Cyber Squad and not some snowflakes. Besides, I got that straight from Claudia. Ask her what she thinks about Rachel. Her theory is that Rachel dresses in such a slutty way to distract from the small print in the contract she gave you. And it works – we're all here! Not in hell but at Helltek."

Kai grabbed a tray and stood behind Marco in the food line. He didn't want to admit that Rachel's trick had certainly worked on him.

"Why is the company called Helltek anyway?" he asked instead.

"Because of the Twins of Hell who own it," Marco said with a mischievous grin.

"Huh?"

"Gregor and Marie-Louise Hell, never heard of them?"

"No..." Kai blushed.

"They founded and own Helltek. They're German or Swiss, or something like that. Apparently, in German, Hell means bright. Funny, huh? They also happen to be twins. Their Daddy founded Orbis Software, which is where their money came from originally."

"I had no idea!" Kai said. Orbis Software was the third-biggest games developer and distributor worldwide.

"Yeah, naturally we test everything Orbis develops,

publishes and distributes. Coincidentally," Marco winked.

They had reached the food distribution point. It was organized like most contemporary restaurants. A couple of dishes were presented on a bright and colorful display, and Kai could choose one by simply pointing at it. He noticed that everything besides the hot dog with French fries consisted mostly of vegetables, quinoa, tofu, lettuce, and other super-healthy stuff. Apparently it was important to Helltek's management to provide their employees with healthy nutrition. Considering what Marco had said about the hot dog earlier, Kai suspected that it was only on the menu to create the impression that the employees could choose fast food if they wanted.

After a moment of consideration, he chose a sweet-and-sour vegetable stir fry and watched the robot behind the counter prepare it swiftly.

"Hey, look here!" Marco whispered, poking him with his elbow.

Kai turned his attention away from his food being prepared and to his new friend.

"Over there!" Marco said, moving his eyes several times to the left and wiggling his eyebrows, indicating that was where Kai should look.

Kai followed Marco's line of sight and saw a group of seven girls entering the cafeteria.

"Try not to stare, idiot!" Marco laughed. "Maeve will notice and wipe the floor with you. Literally."

Kai tried to follow the advice but found it difficult not to stare. Those girls were not only different from any he had ever seen in real life, they also stuck out from the other testers gathered in the cafeteria. All seven wore clothes over their gimp suits, but not loose T-shirts or sweaters like the rest of the crew. The girls were dressed in skirts, boots, stockings, blouses and tank tops, all black and white.

Contrary to most other female testers Kai had seen so far, who wore no or only a little makeup, these girls wore enough to paint the entire walls of the cafeteria with it. Black eyeliner, black or deep red lipstick and white powder covered their doll-like faces. All of them had similar layered haircuts in raven-black, blue or pink. The group seemed like they had come straight from an anime cosplay convention.

"Pretty sexy, huh?" Marco said.

"Who are they?"

"We call them the Hot Squad, but only behind their backs, of course. All of them are Level Seven. They test Japanese survival horror, such as the *Inside Evil* series and the latest *Muted Hills*. The girl in the front, Maeve, is their team lead."

Kai studied the girl with fascination. She was maybe a couple of years older than him, but he couldn't be sure with the amount of makeup she wore on her face. Her long hair was raven-black, and her pale skin and big eyes gave her the look of a Gothic Lolita.

Walking by, she noticed Kai's stare, looked up and winked.

"She's mostly into girls, but apparently she gives young, cute guys a chance from time to time. You might fall exactly into her category of prey," Marco grinned and clapped Kai's shoulder.

Kai felt heat rushing to his cheeks. "What... me...? I'm not cute."

Marco laughed heartily.

"Your food is ready, sir," the cooking robot said, bringing Kai back to reality. He grabbed his plate and followed Marco, who had chosen a quinoa burger and was already on the move through the cafeteria. They stopped at a booth occupied by three people who could only be his fellow teammates Josh, Francois and Claudia.

It had become clear to Kai that it was customary here to create one's avatar as an idealized version of yourself, yet still resembling your real-life appearance. He would take that into account and refrain from the Viking persona he liked to use otherwise.

All three people looking up at him from their meals were very similar to their virtual counterparts, yet not quite as perfect.

Josh was even more lanky and skinny than his avatar, with huge nerd glasses and hair that needed a cut. Francois had curly brown hair and a distinctive nose. Claudia had clearly made her virtual version taller and slimmer than her true self. She was a short, curvy girl with a freckled face and lively eyes. She wore a gray blouse over her suit.

"Hey guys," Marco said, letting himself fall on the bench next to Claudia. "Look who I found!"

"Sit with us, Kai," Claudia said with a friendly smile and pointed at the empty seat next to Josh. "How was your test run?"

"Pretty good! I'm excited to join you after lunch."

"Topher thinks he did pretty well, so I guess he did," Marco said with a shrug, then he began wolfing down his meal. Kai tried his stir-fry and was surprised at how good it actually was.

"We're excited to have you on our team, Kai," Claudia said. "Isn't that so, boys?"

The others mumbled something in agreement, then Francois asked: "I assume our Master and Commander stayed behind?"

Marco chuckled. "What else did you expect?"

They all exchanged a knowing look, and Kai suddenly felt left out. These people had maybe known each other for years. It would take time until he was truly one of them.

Claudia must have noticed something in his face and explained.

"Topher, to whom we refer lovingly as Master and Commander, is in love with Lex."

Kai raised his eyebrows in surprise. Lex wasn't unattractive, but she was clearly very weird.

"That's not all," Marco jumped in. "Whenever possible,

they–"

He formed a ring with the thumb and forefinger of his left hand and moved the index finger of his right hand back and forth through the ring. The others snickered.

"Especially at parties, when they're drunk," Marco finished.

"Aha," Kai said, not quite sure what to do with this information.

"We think he wants more, but Lex says he's too young and immature," Claudia said in a conspirative tone. "She's 38 and has a PhD in neuroscience."

"What level is she?" Kai asked, impressed. Thinking back to the woman with the wild, red hair and vulgar T-shirt, he would never have guessed that.

"None," Claudia replied. "The operators don't enter VR and therefore don't level up."

"And what about you guys?"

"I'm Level Two," Claudia said with pride.

"Same," Francois chimed in.

"I'm *almost* Level Two," Josh said, a bit embarrassed.

"I'm just that far away from Three," Marco made the 'little bit' gesture with his thumb and index finger. "I hope to reach it at the next tournament."

Kai nodded and continued eating. This world was still very strange to him, and he realized that it would take a while to settle in. But so far, he loved everything about his new job.

"Tell us about the squad that saved your ass in-game," Josh begged. "I can't believe you witnessed Level Ten Alpha in action!"

"They were pretty impressive," Kai said, remembering the scary yet exciting event.

"Are you kidding? Those guys are the definition of badass," Josh said. "They're damn heroes!"

Everyone nodded in agreement in a sincere way that surprised Kai. The Alpha squad he had met really must be something special.

Then Claudia grinned at Josh. "Especially Rogue, huh, Josh?"

Josh blushed but said nothing.

"Our Josh here has been crushing heavily on Rogue for a while now... same as every other nerd around."

She rolled her eyes, then added. "In my opinion, she isn't that special, but apparently I'm lacking something between my legs to fully appreciate her."

"Who's Rogue?" Kai asked. Though he had a pretty clear idea who Claudia was referring to. A memory flashed into his mind. The girl with the white hair and black tips, sliding toward him and hacking off the gigantic spider claw just in time before it could impale him. The more he learned about the dangers in VR, the more he was convinced that she had saved his life.

"Rogue's one of the two girl members of Alpha," Claudia said. "If Alpha are considered super stars around here, then she's the supernova among those stars. Probably only exceeded by Raven, who's their squad leader."

"Does her avatar have long, white hair?" Kai asked.

"Ha!" Claudia called out. "There goes another admirer!"

For a brief moment, Kai saw a spiteful expression flash over Claudia's face, then her look turned back to the calm friendliness he had seen so far.

"So, what exactly happened in that game you met Alpha?" Josh wanted to know.

Kai briefly described the events with the giant spider that had gone out of control and how the Cyber Squad had saved the day.

Everyone listened in silence, clinging to Kai's words.

"I eat my hat, if that was a simple glitch," Francois finally said in his slight French accent once Kai had finished.

Everyone nodded. Suddenly the whole group had turned dead serious.

"Yeah," Marco agreed. All his cockiness and happy-go-lucky attitude had vanished from his face and voice. "It's getting worse out there, if you ask me."

"What do you mean?" Kai asked. "What's out there? Topher mentioned something to me earlier but didn't elaborate."

"There's some really scary shit out there on the Net," Marco answered.

"Like what?"

Marco moved his head closer to Kai. "We don't know anything official, of course. After all, we're all low levels and only test games on our internal servers."

"Technically, we're all still rookies, not just you," Josh said.

"Hey, speak for yourself, dude," Claudia scorned him jokingly.

But the topic had brought an undoubted nervousness into everyone's attitude, although they tried not to show it. Anxiety, almost.

"What *is* out there?" Kai kept digging, feeling how the hair on his arms stood up.

"Illegal mods on the Dark Web," Marco said, lowering his voice. "Malware that can infect your neuro-plant with all kinds of nastiness and totally screw you up. Hackers who specialize in attacking game code, causing mayhem."

"What kind of hackers?"

"Various kinds. Some act out of maliciousness and the joy of destruction, but they aren't the worst. Way more dangerous are the organized conglomerates. Some are hired for industrial espionage, others have anarchistic motives. They believe that VR enslaves people and needs to be destroyed, or some bullshit like that."

"But that's still nothing compared to rogue AI," Claudia said.

Kai stared at her. "You gotta be kidding me!"

Yet everyone glanced back at him in deadly seriousness.

"There's no such thing as rogue AI on the Net... that's an urban legend," Kai said, getting more insecure with every word that left his mouth. "Or not?"

"You should ask Viktor about it," Marco said. "He'll tell you stories that'll give you nightmares and make you wonder if you ever want to connect yourself to VR on the Net again."

"Once he's ready to talk to you," Claudia added. "He's a bit… different. Which is why he rarely spends his lunch break with us."

"And finally, there are the ghosts," Francois said.

"The what?" Kai was still hoping his new colleagues were pulling a newbie prank on him, but their serious faces made him doubt that more and more with every second.

"Have you never wondered what happens to people who die while they're connected to VR?" Marco asked, his voice hardly more than a whisper now. "And especially those who fall into a coma in real life while connected? What happens to their consciousness?"

Kai wasn't sure what to answer and remained silent. This was getting crazier by the minute!

"There are stories that such people are trapped in VR, or at least digital imprints of them," Marco said. "And now comes the killer: we don't know for sure, but we believe that the Level Ten squads aren't simply game testers like we are. They're the ones who deal with all the shit out there others believe doesn't even exist. And Alpha is the most hardcore of them all."

Everyone remained silent for a moment, and Kai's hope that all of this was only a prank faded entirely.

"You're serious, aren't you?" he finally said.

"Hey," Marco lifted his hands. "You asked, we answered."

The others nodded, and Kai swallowed hard.

"Well, that's scary," he finally said.

Marco laughed, and suddenly the mood at the table switched back to normal again, as if the sun was back after hiding behind a thick, black cloud for a moment.

"You said it, man. But don't worry, you won't even be sent out into MMOs before you reach Level Four, so you're good.

For now."

"Yeah, it's the reason I don't play online in my spare time anymore," Josh said.

"What spare time are you talking about?" Francois threw in dryly.

"Ok, I believe it's time for us to go back," Claudia said, nodding at the big digital wall clock above the food distribution area. "We don't want Master and Commander to be upset with us."

"Right. He should be done with eating 'lunch', too, by now," Marco said, wiggling his eyebrows, and Claudia rolled her eyes.

They returned their trays and empty dishes to the distributor and made their way to the exit. Kai's head was spinning. During the thirty minutes his lunch break had lasted, he had been bombarded with more information than he had wished to gain. Game glitches and bugs were bad enough, but malicious malware, hackers, rogue AI... ghosts?

Something was telling him that this was only the tip of the iceberg. His new friends hadn't told him all they knew, not at all. And he was more than curious now to hear what the mysterious Viktor had to say.

He got disoriented again once they were outside of the screaming colors of the cafeteria and in the Bowels. Kai was glad he could follow the others as he would never have found his way back to the testing room on his own.

They found Topher standing next to Lex's she-cave while she was sitting behind her desk, resting her legs on its edge. There was undoubtedly something intimate in the body language of those two, and now that he was aware of it, Kai wondered how he hadn't noticed it before.

"There you are," Lex greeted them. "Ready for your baptism of fire, Kai?"

"Ready," he answered.

"Splendid! I'll throw you guys into one of the advanced levels on hard mode. Should be fun to watch," Lex said with a hint of sadism in her voice.

"Hooray," Francois said in the dry tone typical for him, and they all went to their pods.

Kai noticed that Viktor was already there, waiting in his pod with his arms crossed. His pale blue eyes studied Kai with curiosity, and Kai was stunned when he realized that Viktor was the first person he had ever met who actually looked much better in real life than in VR.

No doubt, this was a very strange guy.

Kai felt a little nervous when he took his place in the pod he had been assigned before. The level he had played with Topher earlier had been more of a beginners mission. He was determined to give a good performance in the campaign Lex was about to throw them into now. It was clear to him that he wanted to reach Level Two as quickly as possible, as that was apparently when the fun really started in this job.

"Place your hands in the depressions, Kai, palms down," Lex said, approaching him. "Exactly like that, good boy."

Kai felt a sharp pain for a second as two metal tubes connected to the ports in his wrists. The nurse had done such a good job that he had already forgotten the ports were even in his body.

"Just in case your adrenaline runs amok," Lex said, petting his cheek. "It can get pretty rough out there."

"I'll be fi–"

Before Kai could finish his sentence, the operator had plugged him in and his consciousness was sucked into VR for a ride he wouldn't forget any time soon.

CHAPTER THIRTEEN

Entering game... Please wait... Loading...
Behind Blue Eyes 3. **Secure_dev_mode, build 322B.**

The infinite space of white vanished and Kai found himself in a room with large windows offering a spectacular view over the same majestic city he had seen before. Seemingly endless rows of glass towers lined up till the horizon, reflecting a blood-red afternoon sun that was about to set in the west. A long way down, several lines of transportation buzzed with traffic. Futuristic aircraft cruised between the high-rises which mile-high facades functioning as oversized billboards.

In close proximity, the gigantic black pyramid stood out with its unique architecture. From the previous installments, Kai remembered that this was the center of power in this world. He wondered how many decades it would take until real-life cities would look like that, if ever.

The room itself was decorated like a lounge, with tasteful, black furniture. It was the game lobby.

Waiting for players to join... Please stand by.

He had been the first one to be uploaded and needed to wait for his team. After a moment, Claudia materialized, then Marco, and then the rest.

"The view is pretty, huh?" Claudia said.

"Yes, it is. I love this game!"

She chuckled. "Give it a couple of weeks and you'll love to hate it."

"How long have you been testing it?"

"A bit over three months now," Claudia said. "We got three more months to go, then it needs to be ready to ship, no matter what."

"Alright, squad," they heard Topher's disembodied voice. "As our veterans here know, the co-op version of the game only allows a team of four. Marco, Claudia, Josh and Kai will team up and play the campaign. Viktor will keep an eye on the code and Francois an eye on Viktor – the usual."

Kai's game HUD sprang into action, showing him grouped up with the other three, while his tester HUD below showed the complete squad of six.

"I didn't even know the game had a co-op modus," Kai said. "That's awesome."

"It's a new feature that came with this installment," Marco explained.

Viktor sat in one of the black leather armchairs, his legs crossed and his hands folded. Like all others in the room, his avatar was dressed in the iconic black combat suit, and his eyes had been replaced by the neon-blue cyborg eyes the game series took its name from. He studied Kai attentively without saying anything, and the unnatural eyes gave his stare something eerie.

Kai looked into the large mirror which was attached to the adjacent wall. He too was dressed the same way, and the same unnatural eyes stared from his unfamiliar, generic face. It was about time to exchange this boring avatar for something custom-made to match the others.

Initializing campaign...

Everything froze briefly, then the lobby dissolved and was replaced by a different surrounding.

Kai found himself sitting in a row with the others, strapped to his seat by a safety belt. It was dark, and the slight shaking of the black-walled cabin revealed that this had to be the interior of a plane. His teammates were seated next to him, but there were also at least a dozen NPCs with them, all dressed in the same attire, their eyes glowing an unsettling blue.

A woman stood in the middle of the cabin. Although seemingly dressed the same as everyone else, for some reason she looked way sexier than the rest. Kai recognized the actress who had been playing Nephilim, an important character in the game in the previous installments. Apparently there was an illegal mod on the web that would make her appear naked at all times, but Kai would never dare to try such a thing – besides, it would somehow feel wrong.

"Attention, Angels," Nephilim began her briefing with her unique voice that was both stern and sensual. "We're about to enter one of the most challenging and dangerous missions since the founding of our unit. I'll be honest with you, it's going to be tough... and many of you will die–"

"Oh, for Christ's sake, can we cut the crap, please?" Claudia sighed. "I know you guys like staring at her bosom but we've seen this cutscene how many times now? A thousand?"

"We need to be sure we didn't miss a bug here," Marco grinned.

"Actually, it has been only 37 times, but you're right," Viktor said, joining the conversation. The console with its holo keyboard and screen sprang into action and his hands flew over it, while his face didn't change its bored expression.

The cutscene froze and Nephilim disappeared. Suddenly the safety belts were unfastened and the back hatch of the aircraft was open.

"Thanks, Viktor," Claudia said, getting up. "Who writes such shitty dialogue anyway?"

"Game writers," Josh answered. "They earn a lot of money."

"Not as much as us once we hit a high level," Marco said as he jumped up and hurried toward the open hatch.

Without slowing down, he leaped outside into the darkness – and let out a horrible scream, as if he were falling to his death.

Claudia rolled her eyes. "He's such a clown."

"Yes," Viktor agreed dryly.

"Come on," the girl addressed Kai. "It's part of the game mechanic to jump out there and won't cause any damage."

They all went to the hatch and let themselves drop into the night. Kai followed and stepped into nothing without hesitation. He felt cold air hitting his face, creating an utterly realistic sensation on his skin, and saw a bright silver full moon on the horizon. Then he hit the ground, 60 feet below.

Impact absorbed. Limbs at 90% nominal capacity.

Quickly, he followed the others' example and crouched behind a half-collapsed wall.

"So, what's the mission about?"

"Go in, kill everyone. It's a shooter," Francois said with a shrug and a slight smugness in his voice.

"Smartass," Claudia replied, then explained to Kai. "You should be able to see the area on your mini-map if you activate scan mode. In front of us is a deserted shopping mall with enemy cyborg units called Wasps hiding inside. They're tough motherfuckers even on normal mode but Lex sent us straight into hard mode hell, so it's gonna be brutal. To make it even more nasty, the whole area is one massive ticking bomb. We have less than ten minutes to kill all hostiles and deactivate it or we lose the campaign."

"Ok," Kai said. "I'm ready."

"Luckily we've already searched the area for bugs multiple times, so there shouldn't be any clipping issues or other glitches," Marco said. "This test is all about AI behavior in combat. Am I right, master?"

"Right," Topher's disembodied voice answered. "Kai will team up with Claudia. Josh protects Marco's ass. Now, move!"

"Yes, master."

Topher laughed. "One day I'll simply leave you in VR

over the weekend, Marco. You'll see."

"This way," Claudia nudged Kai's arm, then ran ahead.

New Objective: Eliminate all hostiles.
Time to Detonation: 9:59

His vision changed from night-black to a ghostly blue, which simulated the enhanced vision of his cybernetic eyes. It was a pretty cool effect, similar to night vision and yet unique.

As always when playing this game, he wondered what it would be like to be a mighty cyborg – or any kind of hero. Like the guys from Level Ten Alpha, who apparently almost had a godlike status among the other testers. How did one become someone like that?

Sunken in thoughts, he bumped right into Claudia, who had stopped at the corner of a ruined building that looked a bit like the remains of a former fast-food restaurant. In his blue vision mode, he could now clearly see how desolate the area was. Something horrible must have happened to have left this world so shattered.

"Careful, rookie," Claudia said, then chuckled. "You know you need to buy me a drink first, don't you?"

Kai gasped for air and was glad that his avatar didn't have the ability to blush. At least not in a shooter. There were games and simulations specialized in human interactions which could simulate much more than that.

"Um... I'm sorry. I didn't mean to–"

"Shut up, I'm just messing with you." She was clearly amused.

Kai had to admit that she looked pretty hot in her cyborg state, but so did everyone.

"Look," she pointed toward a massive building in front of them.

It had the architecture of a shopping mall, being rectangular and five or six stories high. As was typical for such buildings, it had no windows on the outside. Huge cracks in the facade were visible in many places and the plastering was crumbling everywhere. The setting looked like something straight out of a post-apocalyptic scenario and stood in stark contrast to the shiny city of lights in which most of the former games took place. 'Peachtree Mall' was still painted above the barricaded main entrance of the massive building. The letters were faded and only readable due to Kai's enhanced vision.

"If you turn on scan mode, you should see the snipers on the roof," Claudia continued. Kai did as he was told and could clearly see two red-highlighted figures on the roof. Those two were completely different to the thugs he had encountered earlier. They were highly augmented human killing machines.

Hostile Cyborg
Faction: Wasps
Role: Sharpshooter
Status: Excellent
Danger: Very high

Kai wondered why he couldn't see any more hostiles on his scan.

"Are there supposed to be only two of them?" he asked. "Or is my scanner acting up again?"

"Your scanner's fine. There are more than two dozen of them here, but most are in stealth mode. We only notice them when they attack."

"Oh crap."

"Yeah, but luckily we have plenty of NPCs with us as cannon fodder. We would hear the whole story chatter all the time, but Viktor has turned it off. The main characters are kinda talkative in this game. Anyway, I have a sniper rifle and will take them out as soon as we're in range. You cover me."

"Copy that."

Claudia moved forward and he followed her, trying to be as stealthy as possible. Apparently they weren't going in full

Rambo this time. At least, not yet. Black shadows moved in close proximity to them, matching their speed and stealth. The friendly NPCs.

The front side of the target structure was almost entirely dominated by a huge parking lot, which was empty but for some demolished and burned-out car wrecks. Approaching from there would be suicidal, which was why they sneaked up from the flank, using some structures that appeared to have been smaller stores and restaurants in their heyday as cover. On the mini-map, Kai could see the position of their other two squad members, Marco and Josh. Their life stats showed 100% in the group section of Kai's HUD. So far so good.

Viktor and Francois had stayed behind and were following the co-op team at a distance. Since they weren't part of that team, Kai wondered if they could even be spotted and attacked by the hostile NPCs.

"How's it going over there?" Marco asked over the team com channel.

"We're in position," Claudia replied. "I'm ready to snipe out the sharpshooters on the roof and Kai is covering me."

"Splendid!" Marco said, mimicking Topher's way of speaking. "We're ready for all hell to break loose on us, too."

He wasn't exaggerating. Only seconds later, all hell did indeed break loose around them.

Claudia grabbed the massive rifle which she was wearing strapped to her back and took aim, focusing. After a second, Kai heard two consecutive, muffled shots.

The two highlighted figures on the roof collapsed.

"Great shots!" he complimented Claudia.

"Thanks. I've played this before, you know," she said in an amused voice, then turned serious. "Get ready!"

The NPC closest to them let out a scream of agony as a shimmering blade appeared out of nowhere and impaled him from behind. The cyborg next to him literally lost his head as another phantom appeared right next to him and decapitated him. Blood sprayed from the stump that used to be his neck like a fountain as the body collapsed.

Kai activated his Angelblades and charged the invisible attackers, hacking where he suspected the assassin that had decapitated the NPC to be. He was lucky. In an extremely realistic way, he felt how his swords hit flesh as he chopped through the hostile cyborg's body.

The figure appeared right in front of him, losing his stealth, and he could now see the Wasp's stats.

Critical hit!
710/1000

Holy shit, that's a tough son of a bitch!
The hostile turned around and counterattacked. His face was hidden under a black helmet with a yellow visor which gave his appearance something menacing.

Just in time, Kai parried an attack aimed at his face and kicked the masked figure away to gain some room. The hostile was attacked by another NPC and turned his attention toward him. This gave Kai the opportunity to attack the Wasp from behind. Instead of trying to melee him, Kai drew his pistol and fired multiple shots into the enemy unit's head. Sparks flew through the night as red numbers flashed above the Wasp, indicating his health was dropping rapidly. Finally his head exploded, hit by one last bullet from Kai's pistol.

"Not bad!" he heard Claudia from next to him, where she was melee attacking another enemy who had lost his invisibility. "Be careful. There's two more of them coming from behind. Parry!"

Kai reacted faster than he could even think. He spun on his heels and lifted his arms with the integrated blades defensively in front of his face and chest.

Sparks flew once more as an invisible sword hit him, yet without causing damage.

"Focus your scanner on sound!" Claudia called out. "It's

the only way to spot them when they're cloaked!"

"And you're telling me this only now?" Kai asked, fending off another potentially deadly strike.

"Sorry..." Claudia chuckled, skillfully evading the attack of two uncloaked hostile cyborgs.

"You ok over there?" they heard Marco ask over the com channel.

"Of course!" Claudia replied. "We're gonna have our side cleaned up long before you!"

"Pah!"

Kai focused his scanner on sound as Claudia had instructed and saw soundwaves sparkling in the bluish air when the hostile NPCs moved.

Quickly, he opened his weapon inventory and grabbed the assault rifle instead of the pistol. He aimed vaguely at the soundwaves in front of him. A muffled scream pierced the night as his salvo of high-caliber bullets riddled the torso of an opponent. From this short distance, the weapon outright devastated the hostile's body. Blood sprayed in his face but quickly vanished from his vision, as so often in games of this kind.

"Yes!"

But his triumph lasted only for a second.

A sharp pain pierced through his side as an assassin's blade ripped his flesh open.

Kai tumbled to the side and cried out in pain.

What the hell was this? It felt way too intense!

Warning! Severe damage in biological tissue detected!

You can say that again, he thought, clenching his teeth while his life energy dropped below 50%.

Kai was so distracted by the sudden heavy damage he had taken that he didn't even notice the soundwaves approaching him at high speed. But instead of landing the final blow, the assassin's head exploded right in front of him, covering him in goo.

Still overwhelmed by what had just happened, Kai saw Claudia lowering her rifle.

"Thanks," he said, straightening up. His HUD indicated that his health was still diminishing. The attack had caused bleeding damage.

"That should be all of them for now," she said. "The rest are hiding inside the building. Are you ok?"

"Not sure," Kai said. "That hurt as hell! Is that normal?"

Claudia summoned a med kit out of her inventory and approached him.

"Here, let me fix you up before you bleed to death, rookie," she said, spraying a white mist over his wound.

The effect was immediate. Kai's life stats quickly rose again until the bar stopped at 75%.

"On hard mode, you won't get your full health back and will lose up to 25% with every critical hit," Claudia said, then spoke into the group channel. "Control, Kai took a heavy hit here. The intensity might need to be recalibrated."

"Nah, we're all good," they heard Lex's voice. "We're running hard mode on highest intensity. It might hurt a little more than usual, but Kai's fine. Your body is still in one piece, kiddo."

She laughed.

"Good to know," Kai said, still a bit shaken.

"Other than that, everything ran smoothly on our side," Claudia reported.

"All good on our side, too," Marco confirmed.

"Code looks clean, I can't see anything out of the ordinary," Viktor added in his bored voice.

"Splendid!" Topher said. "You better proceed then. You've got only seven minutes and ten seconds left until the big bang."

"Ok, we group up inside, same place as always," Marco said.

Claudia tapped Kai's shoulder. "Come on, we need to

hurry."

She ran off, followed by the remaining friendly NPCs. After the ambush, they only had three left. Kai followed them quickly and reloaded his weapons on the run, as every experienced shooter player did. They took cover behind the ruined base buildings flanking the mall, which loomed dark and menacing in front of them.

"I've never felt such intense pain in a game," he told his partner, catching up with her.

"I know, it sucks at times, but you get used to it."

"Are you serious?'

"Yeah. Remember, it's not real. It's a trick played on your brain."

If that's so, why are we wearing the gimp suits which are supposed to protect our bodies? he thought, but he bit his tongue instead of saying it out loud.

"Someone has to test the maximum intensity to make sure people playing the game later don't get hurt, if they think they need to play it with the intensity turned all the way up. And that someone is us," Claudia said, not slowing down.

"Makes sense."

The bright moonlight cast long shadows on everything around them. An old dumpster, a corroded car wreck, a burned tree.

If the others hadn't told him that the rest of the hostiles were inside, Kai would have expected another attack any second. Every moving shadow could be a cloaked hostile, ready to strike. The level designers had done an excellent job here. Kai could feel how his body was producing adrenaline, whether he liked it or not. More than ever now that he knew how painful a direct hit could be.

"Yeah, this job is for people with masochistic tendencies," Claudia said with a chuckle. "But, of course, HR don't tell you that."

"No, they definitely don't."

They had arrived at the side of the mall and at an

entrance that said 'Employees only'.

"But don't worry," Claudia continued. "We rarely test on highest intensity. Most of the time it's not necessary. Sometimes we even use god mode. Ok, we'll send the NPCs in first. They'll be ambushed and slaughtered by two hostiles hiding by the door. We rush in and take them out, then regroup with the others in the atrium."

She used the inhuman strength of her cyborg body to kick in the door, then she and Kai took cover at the sides while the three NPCs rushed in first.

All of them were shredded within seconds. It made it easy to determine the hostiles' position. When they stormed in, Claudia took on the assassin on the right, while Kai turned left. The two hostile killer cyborgs were dead within seconds.

A long, dark corridor led them straight into the main area of the shopping center. A view of morbid beauty opened before Kai. Some parts of the vast hall were demolished, and one arm of the building had collapsed and was blocked by rubble. Other parts, however, appeared as if the people who had been working and shopping in the many little stores had just left for a lunch break – never to return again. The remains of clothes still hung displayed behind the windows. Other stores advertised outdated electronics, covered by thick layers of dust. Shattered glass covered the floor and reflected the moonlight shining in through the destroyed dome. One escalator was still standing upright, seemingly waiting for shoppers to take them to the upper area of the building. The other one next to it had collapsed, and its remains decorated the ground like a giant's broken spine. Dust particles hovered in the air, shining in the moonlight. It was clear to Kai the instant he entered the hall that this was a place where some huge shit would soon go down.

The other four were already waiting at a fountain that hadn't seen any water for decades and was instead filled with dried dirt.

"There you are," Marco said, grinning. "Just in case you

didn't know, there's a ticking nuclear bomb here somewhere."

Claudia narrowed her cyborg eyes and flipped him off.

"Let's just finish it quickly, ok?" Francois said. "I hate it when that thing blows off. It gives me the creeps."

"Any issues with the AI so far?" Viktor asked, not looking up from the code rushing over his virtual screen.

"Nope," Claudia said. "Friendly and hostile NPCs worked according to parameters on our side."

"On ours, too," Marco nodded.

"Seems like the pathfinding and trigger behavior works flawlessly. Who would have thought they'd fix that for the new build?" Josh said.

"Ok, let's do this," Marco said. "The hostiles are guarding their precious little bomb way back behind the food court on the second floor. We take the escalator and go in full frontal. We can test the sneak approach on the next run."

They rushed up the escalator. It creaked dangerously and big clouds of dust hovered off it, slowly sinking to the ground. Kai followed right behind Marco and Claudia and was happy when they reached the top without the thing crashing down under their heavy semi-machine bodies. Although he trusted that the others knew what they were doing – after all, they kept repeating laconically that they'd played this game before – he had still expected the escalator to collapse at any second. No doubt that was the level designers' intention.

Upstairs, many of the shop windows were shattered, and glass crunched under their heavy combat boots as they made their way toward the food court. With its scattered tables and chairs and only very dim lighting, the area had something eerie and deeply unsettling about it.

"Four minutes," Viktor said in a tone that suggested he was talking about nothing more concerning than a microwave timer.

Something caught Kai's attention. Out of the corner of his eye he saw a strange shimmer, as if light was shining through the dust-covered marble floor a few feet away from him.

Following the instinctive curiosity of a gamer, he decided to take a closer look without slowing down and losing the others. Experienced gamers knew that such things never appeared coincidentally in a game. If level designers illuminated an area in a slightly different way than the rest, then it usually meant that something was hidden there.

He hadn't gone more than five steps away from the party when something he never would have expected happened.

Suddenly, he fell through the floor. Less than six feet away from the shining light, his boots hit thin air. An invisible trap door. The floor looked perfectly normal, yet there was nothing physical there to step on.

Kai let out a surprised scream as he fell into a world completely different from the game above. Gray and blue beams surrounded him as he plunged by geometrical figures, vectors and numbers. He fell at least 50 feet, but he couldn't tell for sure as his head began to spin and he lost orientation. After a couple of seconds – or minutes, he couldn't really tell – he crashed into a construct of triangles that could never have existed in the physical world. He got stuck in a hellishly uncomfortable position with one leg splayed out at an impossible angle and his arms stuck in the geometrical shapes.

To his surprise, his avatar hadn't taken any damage and his limbs didn't hurt, even though his leg surely would have been at least fractured in real life or a realistic game.

"What the fuck…" he whispered.

"Kai, are you ok?" Claudia asked over the group channel.

"Yeah," he answered, looking around. "I somehow fell through the floor. I don't know where I am."

"Dude, you fell out of the game," Marco said. "Control, we have a massive clipping glitch here."

"I see it," Lex replied. "Kai, my boy, it's only your first day here and you're already trying to escape the Matrix?"

"I… um…" Kai looked around.

Whatever this was, it seemed to be endless. The geometrical figures spread out in all directions. Lights flickered erratically and below his stuck body opened an abyss that appeared to have no ground. The atmosphere had something utterly surreal about it.

Of course, he knew what clipping bugs were. They appeared quite frequently in a variety of games. Mostly, however, clipping issues concerned NPCs who could get stuck in the walls or fall through the floor when killed. In MMOs, players sometimes got stuck in objects and had to reload to free themselves. But Kai had never experienced anything like *this* before.

"Can you move?" Claudia asked.

"I don't think so. I'm pretty much stuck, but even if I could, I'd just fall into the abyss."

He wondered if it would be dangerous to actually fall into the abyss. What would happen to him if he did?

"Guys, you plowed through this whole map multiple times. How come you missed a clipping bug of such proportions?" Topher asked.

"Maybe because it wasn't there the last time?" Marco replied.

"It's possible it came up with the latest build," Lex agreed. "You know how game devs are. They fix one thing and break another."

"Viktor, activate secure dev mode and try to get him out of there," Topher said. "If it doesn't work then we reset the whole campaign."

"On it."

All of a sudden, it felt as if all weight was gone from Kai's body. But he wasn't floating either. He noticed that he was frozen and couldn't move. In the midst of the vastness surrounding him, this effect gave him an unpleasantly claustrophobic sensation. It sounded absurd in his head, the moment he thought it, but it was the only way he could describe what he was experiencing.

Then he was moved while his body remained static, almost as if dragged and dropped by an invisible, oversized cursor. He clipped through the geometrical formation that had been holding him in place in a similar way to how the cars had gone through Topher earlier today, then he was moved upward at high speed, like in an invisible elevator. Looking up, he couldn't see any hole or trapdoor through which he could have entered this strange place. There only was the same vastness as in all other directions.

Just when he was starting to wonder how they were planning to get him out of there, he clipped through the floor and was back in the dim lighting of the demolished shopping mall.

His team stood a few feet away, waiting. Guns in their hands and unnatural eyes glowing in the dark, they made an impressive and intimidating sight, yet to someone who had just been dragged through the bowels of infinity, they appeared comforting.

In secure dev mode, the dust particles that had formerly been dancing in the beams of moonlight were now still. Behind the food court, several figures stood in T-pose. They were hostile NPCs, waiting to be set back into action and ambush anyone who dared approach them.

"Hey buddy," Marco said, a strange seriousness in his voice. "We thought we'd lost you. Forever."

Kai gulped. He had no idea clipping bugs could be so dangerous!

Claudia rolled her eyes and gave Marco a push. "He's bullshitting you. That's not a black hole out there, or anything like that."

Kai could feel his body again as his feet hit the ground. The invisible cursor had let go of him.

"Yes, but it's still a serious issue," Viktor said. He was sitting on the ground and had multiple holo-screens glowing in a greenish light in front of him. "If you go too deep, it can rip your avatar into shreds and send your mind into a state of shock. And who wants that?"

For the first time, a smile appeared on his face, and it was a chilling rather than a friendly sight.

"Right," Topher chimed in. "Which is why we take such massive clipping issues very seriously. Congrats, Kai, you just found your first Severity Five bug. Open your tester UI and write a ticket."

Kai began documenting the issue he had just discovered the way Topher had taught him earlier.

"Don't we need to reproduce it?" he asked.

Marco and Claudia shook their heads while Topher's disembodied voice answered him.

"No. This is such a severe issue that even if it occurs only one in a hundred times, it needs to be fixed. Usually it's a level designer who screwed up, but sometimes the problem lies in the code."

"Not our concern," Marco shrugged, then clapped Kai's shoulder. "Well done, Kai!"

"Thanks!" Kai said, sending off the ticket.

His Progression stat in the tester UI changed to 8/1000. He had earned five points simply by falling through the floor. Kai grinned.

"Ok, let's jump back into game mode and finish this crappy level – so we can test it all over again," Marco said.

Instead of answering, Viktor pressed some keys on his console and the game sprang back into life again. The dust particles danced in the moonlight as if nothing had happened. The T-posing NPCs behind the food court had vanished, turning back into stealthy assassins, lurking in the dark.

"Sometimes, it feels a bit like Sisyphus' labor, no?" Francois said as they approached the darkness behind the demolished restaurant, weapons at the ready.

"As long as no one tries to eat my kidneys I'm ok with that," Marco shrugged.

"Eww, what the hell are you talking about? That's gross," Josh said.

"Not the kidneys, the liver," Viktor said. "And it was Prometheus who had it eaten. Sisyphus was the one with the rock."

"Huh?"

"Google it," Viktor ended the discussion.

Kai smiled as he listened to his new teammates bantering. They really seemed to be a nice crew.

It should have been impossible to sneak up on anyone chatting like that, but all games were programmed this way. Whatever players discussed in a party, the NPCs couldn't hear.

"We got five of them waiting for us here and another six inside the movie theater behind the food court. It's where they set up their bomb," Marco explained to Kai. "And that shit blows up in less than three minutes."

"We're not gonna make it in time," Francois said fatalistically.

"No big deal," Topher intervened. "We need to test the bomb explosion on hard mode anyway."

"Yay."

Without having to look, Marco lifted his arm and extended his blade, which shimmered silver in the little moonlight that had made it all the way back there. Out of nowhere, a sword appeared that would have cut his head off if he hadn't parried in time. Josh fired his gun into the air where the blade had come from, and red-flashing numbers indicated that he had hit his target. Marco lunged forward and slashed seemingly blindly into the air, yet his blades slashed the hostile cyborg who was sneaking up in stealth mode.

Kai watched, impressed, but then reminded himself that those guys knew the game so well that they could play it in their sleep – literally.

"Watch out, Kai," Claudia warned. "Three o'clock!"

Spinning around, Kai activated his scanner. At first, he couldn't see or hear anything. But then he saw the slight movement of soundwaves, indicating a phantom approaching. He charged forward, drawing his blades, lightning-fast – and managed to impale the enemy through his abdomen. The unpleasant sound of metal cutting through flesh could be heard.

Critical hit!

Red numbers counted down so fast that a human eye could hardly see it, then they stopped at 100/3500.

Finish off enemy?
Y/N

Hell yeah! Kai thought, quickly selecting Y.

Next to him, Claudia had engaged another hostile, while Marco and Josh had made short work of the last Wasp in the darkness.

Suddenly Kai lost control over his body as the game took over for him and maneuvered him into a scripted finishing sequence – and a spectacular one. He jumped up, high in the air, with inhuman speed, then descended on the struggling enemy like a bird of prey. His legs performed a perfect split while both his blades rammed into the hostile's skull from above, slicing down his neck and through his whole body, cutting him in two.

"Whoa," Kai said when the scripted sequence had ended and he gained control back over his body, his bloody handiwork finished.

That had been ultra-realistic and brutal.

He turned around and saw that the others had finished the job, too, and were already on the move. No one had noticed his spectacular stunt. Or maybe they've seen it so often that they simply didn't care.

Pleased with himself, Kai wanted to follow, but Viktor called after him.

"You missed something here, Kai. Maybe you should write a ticket."

Kai looked down at the bloody mess that had been a soldier only seconds ago and furrowed his brow.

The bloody mess was twitching and moving erratically.

The body was split in two, surrounded by blood, organ tissue and metal pieces, yet both parts moved as if the killed NPC was trying to walk. It was a highly disturbing sight that made Kai's stomach churn.

He forced himself to stop staring and to keep cool.

"What do I write in the ticket?" he asked Viktor, opening the menu in the tester UI.

"We call this a ragdoll," Viktor explained. "It sometimes happens with dead NPCs, although this one is a particularly interesting case. I assume it was triggered because of your finishing move. Make sure to reproduce it the exact same way later."

"Ok."

"Hey, what's going on back there?" Marco called back. "We got less than 90 seconds left."

He and the rest had already advanced to the heavy doors of the movie theater.

"Kai found a ragdoll," Viktor said as he, Francois and Kai quickly closed in on the others.

"Damn it! You're a bug magnet!" Marco laughed.

"Seems the special melee finishing animation triggered the behavior."

"Oh shit, something's telling me Master and Commander will have us test every damn NPC on this level," Marco groaned.

"Let's use Rush and assault the remaining NPCs as quickly as possible. We still can do it easily," Claudia said.

They all activated the inhuman speed ability and sprinted into the movie theater. Kai, who was still a bit behind after writing the bug ticket, hurried after them as fast as he could. He entered the huge, black-walled hall and saw that Marco, Josh and Claudia hadn't bothered to use the stairs but had leaped down to the lowest part instead, their cyborg limbs easily absorbing the impact. There they engaged the remaining six hostiles, killing them quickly. It didn't matter if they had played this level many times before or not, those people were exceptional players, there could be no doubt about it.

When Kai arrived downstairs, there wasn't much left for him to do. Marco ripped open the curtains that covered the screen. And there it was: the bomb.

It wasn't very big but nonetheless looked impressive and nasty, with its neon-green glow and blinking lights. The lower part had the classic yellow symbol for radioactivity printed on it to make it clear to even the dumbest player that this was a nuclear device.

Josh was already leaning over it.

"We did it," Marco smiled. "It's a mini-game to disarm it and not a big deal once you figure out how. When Josh is done the boss will appear, a mech that will crash through this wall."

He pointed to their right.

"We haven't tried him on hard mode yet and he's a badass son of a bitch, but we'll manage... unless you fall through the floor again."

"I'll try to watch my step from now on, I promise."

"All done," Josh said, straightening up, with pride in his voice.

The green glow vanished from the bomb and it made a sound that indicated it was powering down. The timer stopped at 00:19 seconds.

Everyone readied themselves for the boss that was expected to crash through the wall. But nothing happened.

"What the fuck?" Marco scratched his head after they waited for a couple of seconds.

The team members exchanged surprised looks.

"Seems we have a showstopper here," Claudia said.

"Um... guys," Josh pointed at the bomb.

They had been so focused on the boss who didn't show up that none of them had noticed that the bomb had reactivated itself. The menacing green glow was back, and so was the timer.

"I thought you disabled it, Josh!" Marco said, irritated.

"I did!"

They all looked at the timer.

4...
3...
2...
"*Merde*," Francois said dryly.
1...

For a very brief moment, everything froze, then moved in slow motion. Kai saw how the bomb turned into a raging fireball, which quickly expanded. Josh was closest to the detonation and was consumed by the fire first. Eyes wide with horror, Kai witnessed how the flesh burned off his body, leaving only bones and metal augmentations. Then the rest of him disintegrated into ashes.

The fire expanded rapidly, and even though the scripted sequence played out in slow motion, it happened extremely fast. Kai didn't even have the chance to react in any way before the fire hit Marco and then him.

An unbearable pain shot through his body as he felt the fire consuming it, burning through his flesh, vaporizing his blood, melting his metal parts. It felt 100% real and sent his mind into a panic.

Just when he thought he would go insane, it stopped.

Black infinity surrounded him and he heard the game's iconic title music, played in a slow, incredibly depressing way.

You died.
Critical mission failure.
The nuclear blast was so powerful that it reached and devastated Olympias City.

**There's nothing left of you to be reconstructed.
(No save point reload possible on hard mode.)**

Slowly the darkness around Kai faded and he found himself back in the game lobby. Yet his mind was still in a frenzy. Back in his avatar's body, he collapsed to the ground, shaking. Blood rushed through his head and buzzed in his ears with such intensity that he thought his skull would burst.

Far away, he heard voices and recognized his teammates sitting on the floor, too. His vision was so blurry that he only recognized their shapes.

He was suffocating. There wasn't enough air...

His heart was racing, pounding so hard as if it was about to burst through his chest at any second.

"Kai," he heard a sharp, commanding voice. He thought it was Lex, but he wasn't sure. "Kai, listen to me. You're fine. Do you understand? It was an illusion... God damnit, he's going into shock. Initializing cocktail!"

Kai felt a burning pain in his wrists. For a moment, he thought he was dying.

Have you never wondered what happens to people who die while they're connected to VR?

He heard a voice echoing in his mind. It could have been Marco's, but he wasn't sure.

"I'm dying..." he whispered.

"No, you're not."

He could breathe again. Clean, cool air filled his lungs. He opened his eyes – and found himself back in the real world.

Lights were blinking all around him in his pod and he could see Lex's frowning face.

"What happened to me?" Kai asked, confused.

At the same time, he was astounded how quickly his body and mind had gone back to normal. It almost seemed like waking up from a bad dream, with the nightmare that had been horrifying only a second ago now fading away.

Lex's stern expression turned friendly and she smiled,

petting his cheek.

"He's here, he's fine," she said, pulling the plug out from his skull while the tubes released his wrists. "No worries, kiddo. It's all good. Your mind was tricked into believing the explosion was real and went into a state of shock. I'm sorry you had to experience this on your first day. It's the reason you wear this suit and have those–"

She lifted her hands and pointed at her wrists, yet her skin was smooth and pale. Where Kai and other testers had had their ports implanted, she had nothing.

"I feel like shit," Kai said, sitting up and inspecting his own wrists, which had been released from the chair. The skin around the ports was red and felt burned.

Topher approached him and clapped his shoulder. "Don't worry, that's normal after a cocktail injection. You did great in there! Amazing performance."

"Thanks... I guess."

He still felt confused and as if someone had mangled him. And he now understood why this job was considered high-risk. What would have happened if Lex hadn't watched out for him and given him the injection in time? Would he have died? Or gone insane?

"It's not usually like that around here," Topher said. "And it certainly wasn't what Lex meant when she said you were getting your baptism of fire. You not only demonstrated remarkable skills as a game tester in there, you learned the hard way why we dress up like gimps. Certainly not for fashion reasons."

"Ha! Who knows," Lex threw in with a grin.

"You mean, I would have been burned if not for the suit?" Kai asked, stretching his limbs. Everything felt normal.

"Well, not to a crisp like your avatar," Lex said. "But you might have suffered burns on your real body. When the human mind is tricked into believing what's happening is real, the body might react as if it had suffered real injuries. It's a fascinating phenomenon science hasn't fully explained yet."

Great...

"What the fuck, Topher?" he heard Marco's voice behind him.

Kai turned and saw the other testers waking up. Marco's dark eyes gleamed angrily.

"That was way too intense!"

"Yes, we know that now," the team lead replied calmly. "We'll write a report to the dev studio advising them to curb the intensity on hard mode."

"That was too much," Claudia complained.

"Agreed," Francois said. "I hate this stupid bomb on normal and casual mode, but this? *Merde...*"

Josh nodded in agreement. Only Viktor remained calm and silent.

Topher lifted his hands. "Ok, ok, noted. But you guys know full well that it's our job to test exactly this. It's an unpleasant experience for you, but you have a safety net. The players out there don't. If the game had been shipped like that, people could have been hurt."

"Kai got hurt," Claudia said.

"No, I'm fine," Kai said quickly, wondering why the experience had sent him into shock and simply made the others angry. "I'll get used to it, I guess."

"You will," Topher said. "Next time won't be half as bad."

"There's also a major showstopper issue in there," Marco said, calming down a bit. "The boss didn't show up. Instead the bomb reset itself. Total bullshit."

"Yes," Topher replied. "Since it only appears on hard mode, we won't test that again until the studio sends us a new build with a lower intensity."

"I'll see to that at once," Lex agreed.

The lead smiled at his team. "How about everyone gets ten points and the rest of the day off?"

The testers exchanged a look and Marco grinned.

"Now we're talking."

CHAPTER FOURTEEN

When Kai left the sickbay, he found Josh waiting for him in the corridor.

"Thanks for waiting for me," he said. "I'd get lost around here by myself."

"No problem," Josh answered. "I know exactly how you feel. There are still parts of the facility I get lost in too. You wouldn't believe how huge it is when coming here for the first time, right?"

"How long have you been working here?" Kai asked as they walked down the endless hall together.

"Almost sixteen months now," Josh said, then sighed. "I know what you're thinking. You're thinking I'm a loser because I'm still a Level One after all that time."

"No, not at all! Why would I?"

Josh squirmed visibly as he led Kai to a row of elevators he hadn't noticed before. "Because most testers reach Level Two after twelve months, some much faster. And I'm still here."

Kai wasn't sure how to answer, so he remained silent while they waited for the elevator to come.

"I have one month left to reach the next level before they fire me," Josh continued, clearly embarrassed. "But I'm really close now and will hopefully gain enough points with the next tournament."

"I'm sure you will!" Kai tried to put as much confidence as possible into his voice to cheer up his new friend.

The elevator door opened silently and they entered the silvery cabin.

"I'm sure *you* don't need to worry about your progression," Josh said while they rode upward. "You did amazing today! I can tell you're an overachiever."

Kai laughed. "No, I'm not. I've never achieved anything in my entire life. Besides, I got fried in there pretty badly, remember?"

Goosebumps rose all over his body, thinking of what had happened only an hour ago. The horror he had experienced while his mind believed he was dying.

"That could have happened to anyone," Josh said. "The game devs are insane to set the intensity that high! What did they say in the med lab?"

Kai shrugged. "Apparently, I'm good. No damage taken."

Right after dismissing them for the day, Topher had sent Kai to see the medical staff and let them check him out. Everyone else had left for home, but since he was the only one who didn't live on the campus and had to commute back to the city, Josh had agreed to wait for Kai so they could go together.

Nell, the friendly nurse, had frowned after Kai told her what had happened, then took him to an examination room, where she ran some tests on him. Well, she had stuck him into a machine that ran the tests and simply checked the results. Everything seemed ok and she told him to go home and get some rest.

"No more VR for you today, ok?" she had told him with a stern voice. "And if you experience anything odd, call us immediately. Sometimes the cocktail can show side effects up to twelve hours after injection."

The elevator stopped, and when the doors opened, bright daylight hit Kai's eyes. He squinted, not prepared for this, then followed Josh outside. To his surprise, they weren't at the HQ building anymore. Instead, they had left the underground facility via a base building, which was easily a quarter mile away from the round glass tower, looming in the center of the premises.

Kai followed Josh through the beautiful park and lush

gardens and studied the adjacent buildings with interest.

"Is that where the employees live?" he asked.

Josh nodded.

"The buildings around the park and the pools are reserved for the higher levels, with the Level Nine and Ten penthouses at the top. Level Two to Four testers live in the more modest buildings at the back, which have no such spectacular views. But I bet any of the apartments there are still much better than anything you and I have ever lived in."

Kai snickered, thinking of his smelly, moldy apartment he had to share with people who were even bigger losers than him.

"Oh, I have no doubt about that."

"I *so* hope I'll reach Level Two soon," Josh said dreamily.

"You will," Kai said with a comforting smile.

He wondered how long it would take him to be admitted here in this environment that appeared like a paradise compared to the tenement desert he had to live in now. They passed a modern two-story building which was the main cafeteria of the compound. It had a stylish outside area shaded by huge, white canvases shaped like sails. Several people were sitting there, enjoying a break in the mild afternoon. Some wore black suits while others were dressed in plain clothes.

At first, it had felt outright strange to Kai when he had disrobed from the high-tech suit and got dressed back into his normal clothes. Almost as if something was missing. He was amazed at how quickly he had felt comfortable with wearing the extravagant tester uniform, especially since he had felt so awkward in the beginning.

Suddenly, Josh grabbed his arm and stopped abruptly. Kai turned his head and looked at his friend in surprise. He saw an excited expression on Josh's face, his cheeks blushing.

"What?"

"There," Josh said, pointing to their left with his chin. "There she is!"

Curiously, Kai looked into the direction Josh was pointing, and his heart skipped a beat.

About 300 feet away, on the wooden bridge crossing the pond, stood a figure. It was a woman, leaning against the railing and looking down at the lilies and lotuses on the sapphire blue water.

She had her back turned toward them but Kai recognized her anyway. He knew it was *her* the instant he laid his eyes on her.

Her body was tall and slender. Straight white hair reached down almost to her hips, the black tips moving in the afternoon breeze. She was dressed in extravagant designer clothes, all black and white. Black top, short white leather skirt and knee-high boots. A tattoo covered her left arm all the way down from her delicate shoulder to her wrist, but Kai couldn't see what it was at that distance.

He held his breath, mesmerized.

"Is that..."

"Yeah," Josh answered, his voice filled with awe. "That's her. That's Rogue."

Kai could hardly believe what he was seeing. The moment he had seen her in VR, he had been convinced that she was gorgeous in real life. But this sight blew his mind. She looked exactly like her virtual counterpart. Kai couldn't see her face, but he was convinced that it was even prettier than the VR version.

"She's incredible, isn't she?" Josh said dreamily.

"Yeah." Kai didn't know what else to say but to agree.

"Her real name is Alice, you know?"

A man stepped out of the shadow of a nearby tree and approached her. He was tall and had long, raven-black hair that seemed so perfect it almost looked unreal. He wore a long, black designer coat and below it a silken, white shirt that was unbuttoned half the way down.

Kai recognized the man as well. He, too, had been part of the Level Ten squad that had stormed *TSOTA* the other day.

"And that's Raven," Josh said with a sigh, watching how the man placed his arm around the girl's slender waist.

"Are they...?"

"Yes. Well, kinda. No one really knows. But the fact is, the guy is a total prick."

Kai didn't doubt that for a second. One look at him and he knew that he couldn't stand Raven. There was so much hubris in his posture. A cold ruthlessness showed in his body language.

"We should go," Josh said after a moment. "We'll miss our train."

Kai realized how stupid the two of them must look. Two nerds, total losers staring at the girl who was undoubtfully the Cyber Squad's supernova – and her boyfriend.

Kai shot one more glimpse at her, then he and Josh hurried away and approached a side entrance of the compound Kai hadn't noticed until now.

"This is the fastest way to the station," Josh explained.

"Why are they so pretty?" Kai asked after a moment of silence.

"Huh? What do you mean?"

"Rogue and Raven. They look almost unreal."

"Not sure. I guess that comes when you're a multi-millionaire. They can afford the fanciest stuff," Josh said with a shrug.

"They are?"

Josh looked at him as if he were an idiot.

"Of course they are! You can do the math yourself and figure out how much they make per month. And those two have been doing the job for years. All Level Tens have penthouses here, but they also own huge mansions outside the city. Autonomous cars and all kinds of other shit... They can afford to look any way they want."

***

Kai felt unreal when he reached home two hours later. Everything in the tenement district and the apartment he lived in was still completely the same as when he had left. Time seemed to stand still here. Nothing ever changed.

Yet he had changed.

Deep inside, he knew that he wasn't the same person as he had been twelve hours ago when he had left his home to begin his adventure as a tester for Cyber Squad.

"Good evening, Kai," the AI greeted him when he entered his room. "How was your first day at Helltek Labs Inc.?"

"Splendid," he answered, absent-minded.

"I am glad to hear that," Alessia said. "I would love to hear more about your new job sometime."

"Sure," Kai said, not even noticing what a strange statement that was for a personal AI.

He dropped his stuff and went straight to the bathroom to take a shower. There, he carefully inspected his body. For a moment, he feared he'd find burns there or other horrible wounds as a memory of the dreadful explosion flashed through his mind. But there was nothing.

Apart from some of the bruises that were still visible after the incident in *TSOTA*, his body showed no signs of any injury. Kai sighed in relief, enjoying the warm water running down his skin. He lifted his hands and inspected the ports on his wrists. The skin around the tiny tubes was still irritated, but other than that, he couldn't even feel they were there. Kai had no idea what the 'cocktail' that had been shot into his body through these tiny openings had actually been, but he was convinced that it had saved him from greater damage.

On his very first day at Helltek, he had learned firsthand why this was considered a high-risk job. What he had experienced in VR had been absolutely horrifying, and a part of him was telling him to forget about the whole thing and never go back there again.

He sure as hell wouldn't listen to that part.

Of course he'd go back there tomorrow. Maybe it was stupid. Maybe it would eventually cost him his life or turn him into a drooling vegetable. But the opportunities offered to him at Helltek were better than anything he'd ever dreamed of. Besides, he couldn't remember when he had had so much fun in his entire life. Disregarding the disturbing incident at the end, this had been the best day ever. He'd had a blast!

A smile on his lips, he left the bathroom and went back to his room. Behind their doors, he could hear his roommates do what they did every day – which was nothing in particular with their lives. In fact, they were vegetables already, even though it would surely never occur to them. And if it did, then they wouldn't give a shit.

It's only temporary.

He had been telling himself this for years, and now he knew it would soon become true. All he needed to do was perform well and reach Level Two as quickly as possible. Kai hoped it wouldn't take him as long as Josh, but even if it did, then he would accept it. It didn't matter how long it took him, all that mattered was that he eventually made it. And he would.

Back in his room, for a moment he considered jumping into VR and into *TSOTA*. He was dying to tell Stan all about his adventures. At least, as much as he was allowed to. The waiver he had signed clearly stated that he wasn't allowed to talk about anything specific concerning his job and Helltek.

Not the technology, not the testing procedures, nothing about the unreleased games he was testing – and most of all, nothing about the potential risks he was facing.

Acting against this instruction would lead to an instant termination of his contract, and he sure as hell wouldn't risk that at any cost. Especially since he had learned that his neuroplant recorded much more about him and his daily life than he would have ever expected. And Helltek could access this data at any given time.

After battling with himself for a moment, he decided to follow the nurse's advice and skip the VR for today. Instead, he lay down on his bed and relaxed, thinking.

Kai's head spun when he recalled everything he had learned in the previous hours. As if the job, the suits, the tech, and daily business as part of the Cyber Squad wasn't exciting enough, there was so much more.

What the others had told him at their lunch break had outright blown his mind. Hackers, rogue AI... ghosts? It seemed that every rumor and urban legend about VR and using it while connected to the Net was indeed true.

Kai was excited to learn more about all those mysteries. But he also felt anxious. Was it really possible to get stuck in VR and become a digital ghost?

He was only now starting to realize how tired he was. Although it was still early in the evening, he was feeling his eyelids become heavier by the minute.

Everything he had seen and experienced today had been mind-blowingly exciting. But if he was honest with himself, the most exciting thing was seeing *her*.

Kai's heart started beating faster when he remembered Rogue – Alice – standing on the wooden bridge. She was perfect.

A dreamy smile crossed Kai's lips.

But then he reminded himself who he was and who *she* was. Rogue was the supernova, a member of *the* Level Ten squad. She was clearly the most beautiful girl he had ever seen – and filthy rich.

Whereas he... he was just some nerd. A Level One.

He had to stop himself crushing on her before it was too late. After all, he needed to focus on his new job and not dream of a girl he could never have. Not only would a girl like her never feel attracted to a guy like him, she had a boyfriend – of course.

Girls like her always did.

And if that wasn't enough, her boyfriend was the best

of the best of all Level Ten squads. A fucking hero.

Kai sighed.

Yes, he needed to focus on the more achievable things for now. Reach Level Two. And stay alive while doing so. It was a long way to go considering the current status of his tester UI.

Name: Kai
Level: 1
100/100
Team: 76B
Team Lead: Topher B.
Game: Behind Blue Eyes 3
Progression: 18/1000
Available Features: Dev mode, Console, God mode

Yet the last thing he thought about before drifting off to sleep was her black and white hair blowing in the wind.

CHAPTER FIFTEEN

"Oh, hey Kai. Welcome back!"

Lex was the only one already there when Kai entered the testing room the next day. It was shortly after 8 a.m. He had decided to show up extra early and take care of his VR appearance first thing in the morning.

It had required him to get up at 4:30 a.m., but he didn't feel tired at all. On the contrary, he felt full of energy and motivated like never before in his life.

"Good morning, Lex."

She got up from her desk and approached him. Kai looked at the taller woman as she approached him. Today she wore pink tartan pants and a black vintage-style t-shirt. 'Electrohead' was printed on it as well as a graphic showing a head that was half skull and half machine. Her red hair stood out in all directions and made Kai wonder if she ever brushed it.

Lex stopped a few feet away from Kai and studied him for a moment, her arms crossed.

"Topher and I took bets yesterday if you'd show up again or not," she eventually said.

"Why?"

"Because after what you experienced yesterday, chances were high we would never see you again."

"Seriously?"

She shrugged.

"Of course. Do you think it was a coincidence that we sent you into one of the most challenging levels the game has to offer? On hard mode? And highest intensity?"

She winked, her blue eyes sparkling in amusement, then continued.

"I meant it literally when I said this was going to be your baptism of fire, kid. It was a test. We wanted to see what you're truly made of and if you're the right guy for the job. Turns out you are."

"So, the malfunction in the game… the explosion, that was intentional?"

Lex chuckled.

"Nah, I would never mess with the game code in such a way. That *was* a coincidence. But if you ask me, a lucky one."

Kai could hardly believe what he was hearing. He wasn't sure what to say and decided to remain silent before he said something that offended her. His intuition was telling him that Lex was the wrong person to mess with.

"Don't look at me like that," she said, laughing, then she slowly walked back to her desk. "I'm not your enemy, Kai. I'm here to keep your ass as safe as possible while you risk it in there every day."

She pointed at the alcoves.

"It was a lucky coincidence because yesterday you got a taste of it, of what this job here really is. About 60% of testers never show up again once they experience something like that for the first time, for one reason or another. I have to admit, I'm surprised you're here, and delighted. You showed great potential yesterday. I see you climbing up the ranks in no time."

She jumped up with surprising agility and sat on her desk, facing him and letting her boots dangle in the air.

"Thanks, I guess," Kai said slowly. "But what do you mean by one reason or another?"

"Ha! I knew you were a smart cookie, and you pay attention," she smirked, then turned serious. "Most have their pants full after such an experience and decide to quit. Others… well, let's say they can't make that decision on their own anymore."

Her words made Kai feel ice cold. It almost seemed as if someone had turned the AC down several degrees.

"Like my predecessor... Misha?"

"Exactly like him."

Kai was almost scared to ask.

"What happened to him?"

"What happens to many sooner or later," Lex shrugged. "Brain damage. Helltek carries the costs for a nursing facility in such cases."

The temperature in the room seemed to fall even more as Kai listened to the words coming out of her mouth in a nonchalant way. They stood between them like a frosty barrier for a moment, then Lex smiled.

"So, what brings you here this early? We usually don't start before nine. Well, obviously, I do, because I don't have a life."

"I thought I'd come early and create my avatar."

"I like your initiative! And look at you... you even managed to put on the gimp correctly by yourself. Some people need days until they get the hang of it."

Lex jumped off her desk and grinned.

"You're such an adorable little gimp." Kai's cheeks turned fire red, and she burst out laughing. "Come on, I'll plug you in and upload you into the character editor."

He walked to the alcove assigned to him and took a seat while Lex activated the complicated machine. It came to life with a soft humming sound, and lights of various colors and shapes sprang on all around him. The whole machinery reminded Kai more of a jet cockpit than a VR docking station.

"Alright, sweetie-pie, you're good to go," she said after a moment. "Do me a favor and keep away from bombs and trapdoors this time."

"Which side were you on?"

"Huh?"

"In the bet with Topher?"

Lex grinned then shot him into VR before he could say anything more.

***

Welcome to the Helltek character editor, Kai!

He found himself in a brightly lit room with stylish furniture and an oversized mirror covering an entire wall. The location seemed like a dressing room in an expensive designer boutique. One of those places in downtown that he had passed by so often, knowing he would never set foot inside. Although, if he was honest with himself, he would have had no idea what to buy in such a store anyway. He was perfectly happy in jeans and nerd shirts.

Please select your personal styling assistant. Do you wish to be served by a male or female associate?

The question caught him off-guard.

"Um… female?"

He could have slapped himself the moment the words left his mouth. What was he thinking? Surely Lex was watching and would make fun of him if he behaved like a dork in here.

Too late.

A beautiful, blond woman in an expensive-looking dress materialized in front of him. She looked so perfect that she reminded more of a Barbie doll than an actual person.

"Good morning, Kai," she said in a silky voice. "I'm Elle, your personal styling assistant. I'm here to help you choose the avatar that will be your VR persona from now on."

"Hi," he answered, not knowing what else to say or do.

"Feel free to ask me anything at any time," the NPC said. "I'm here to help."

"Ok."

"First, let's decide on your sex. Would you prefer a male or female appearance in VR?"

"Male," he answered, surprised by the question. Yes, of course, it was customary in games that some people chose an avatar of the opposite sex. His friend Stan was a prime example of that. Kai had a couple of female avatars himself. But in a professional environment, that would seem odd to him.

It was only now that he noticed that he couldn't see a reflection of himself in the huge mirror.

I've been a vampire all this time and didn't even notice, he thought with a smirk as the default avatar that he had seen yesterday appeared in the mirror.

The person looking back at him was naked but for his underwear. Although it was a generic default character, it still had a much better shape than his real body.

"Please select your height," the assistant said when a scale appeared next to him in the mirror, ranging from 5' 5" to 6' 5".

Only 5' 7" in real life, Kai selected 6' 0", which always had been his dream height.

"Now choose your preferred frame."

Six different body types appeared in the mirror, from skinny to athletic to overly muscular to fat.

For a second, he was tempted to select the overly muscular one, but then he decided to go for the athletic build. His avatar in the mirror adjusted, and he already liked what he saw.

"Would you like to have a penis or a vagina?" the NPC asked next.

Kai almost jumped back when he saw two versions of the body he had just chosen. They were both naked now, and one showed male and the other female genitals. He was grateful that the Helltek avatar system didn't feature blushing as he pointed at the penis.

"Please select the size and shape of your genitals," the NPC said, unmoved.

Kai saw himself confronted with five different shapes of penises and quickly pointed at the one in the middle that seemed average to him... well, maybe slightly above average.

He could only imagine Lex and Topher laughing their asses off as they watched him feeling awkward while using this editor software.

As soon as he had picked his size, he noticed – relieved – that his body was dressed in underwear again.

"You will be able to adjust your facial features, your skin, hair and eye color," the assistant said. "Before we continue, I would like to inform you that it is customary at Helltek to choose a virtual appearance that resembles your real-life one. You are not required to do so by any means. However, please note that over 99% of Helltek employees use an avatar based on their true self."

Kai already had noticed that and, of course, would follow everyone else's example.

There goes my beloved Viking persona, he thought with a sigh.

"With your permission, I will access the employee databank and upload your picture into the Helltek avatar editor," the AI continued.

"Sure, go ahead."

His reflection in the mirror began changing until it showed Kai's face on the body he had just created. Looking at himself, he was stunned. Since when did he look so good? Or was it the more athletic body that made the difference?

His unasked question was promptly answered.

"I took the liberty of optimizing your appearance according to contemporary beauty standards," the NPC said.

Dang, not quite him after all.

Studying his virtual reflection, he noticed that his skin was smoother, his face more symmetrical, his nose smaller. His hair shone in a perfect black, and he had a different, highly fashionable haircut. Kai smiled at himself, showing sparkling white teeth that would have made any model in a toothpaste commercial jealous.

"Would you like to make any adjustments to your appearance?"

"No," he replied. "This is perfect. You did a great job on me!"

She smiled, yet it was without any warmth or soul. "I am excited to hear that! Let's pick some clothes for you then. You are free to choose from more than three hundred different styles and over ten thousand pieces of clothing."

Instead of the mirror, a collage of various different styles appeared in front of Kai, ranging from fashionable suits and formal attire over casual streetwear styles to outfits resembling famous video game, anime or comic characters.

Kai instantly felt overwhelmed.

He had no real sense of style and was unsure what to pick. His first impulse was to pick something casual, similar to what he liked to wear in real life. But then he realized that was a stupid idea. Here, he could be whatever he wished to be. He could dress himself in attire he would never be able to afford in reality. He thought about how incredibly cool and badass the guys from Level Ten Alpha had looked and what an impression they had made on him when they appeared.

Kai began trying different styles. Whenever he picked something, it appeared on his body. He tried a tuxedo, a designer suit with a hat, a neo-punk outfit, and dozens of different styles from video games and anime. He even tried to dress up as Batman but felt embarrassed the second he saw himself and quickly switched to another style. The more time he spent with the clothing editor, the more insecure he felt.

Who would have thought that endless possibilities could cause such a headache?

It turned out that it was much easier to pick something if you were limited by money and imperfect body proportions. If you could choose from anything, how were you ever supposed to make a decision?

He realized that he had no idea how much time he had

already spent in there. 20 minutes? An hour? Two?

No matter how long, he should probably hurry up. After all, he was being paid for bug hunting and not playing fashion model. But what to choose?

"If I may offer assistance," the NPC said. "It might help if you try to think of who and what you would like to represent with your virtual self. Would you like to appear fashionable? Sexy? Cool? Extravagant? Badass?"

"Badass," Kai answered without hesitation.

The display changed to a variety of superhero and game character costumes.

Looking at them, all of a sudden, Kai knew exactly what he wanted.

"Do you have the combat suits from *Behind Blue Eyes*?"

The assistant flashed her artificial smile.

"But of course."

That same instant, Kai was dressed in the iconic black suit.

He grinned, studying himself in the mirror. Could anything be more badass than that?

***

"There you are," Lex said when he opened his eyes back in reality. "I thought you would stay in there forever. You're worse than most girls."

"I'm sorry," he said while she unplugged him. "I had no idea how long I was in there. There was no timer or anything."

"Almost three hours," she said dryly.

"Ugh… shit."

He sat up and saw that all other VR pods were occupied. The rest of his squad was doing what they were paid for: testing.

"Should I join the others?" he asked.

Lex shook her head, her wild hair flying. "There's no point now. They're in the middle of a campaign. Topher took your place."

"Oh." Kai felt embarrassed.

Lex waved her hand, walking back to her she-cave. "Don't worry about it. It's good for him if he joins the testers from time to time so he doesn't forget how the actual job works. Why don't you go upstairs, grab some coffee and get some UV light? You can join the others after lunch."

He smiled. "Thank you."

"Down the hall, then turn left, and then left again," Lex said while Kai walked to the exit. "You'll find the elevators there."

Kai nodded and opened the door. Just before he could leave, she called after him.

"Oh, and Kai… nice choice in there."

He beamed.

"Thank you! It was a tough choice with so many options to pick from. But I simply love the outfits from the game."

"I'm not talking about the outfit. You basically picked another gimp suit, just a little bit cooler," she said with a mischievous grin. "I'm talking about your genitals."

Kai felt hot blood rushing into his cheeks and fled the room, her laughter following him.

***

His cheeks burning, Kai hurried away down the seemingly endless hall. Had Lex really watched him in the character editor, or was she just messing with him? Although it had been explained to him that the operators watched and monitored everything a squad did in VR, it still felt like an intrusion into his privacy.

On the other hand, he should have expected something like that. After all, he had noticed more than once by now that people inside Helltek showed a very different attitude to anything he'd ever seen before. Was it the constant danger of the job that made people become like that? So hard-boiled and blunt?

He was so deep in thought that he, of course, took the wrong turn and ended up at the infirmary instead at the elevators.

"Crap…" he scratched his head.

Why did everything look the same here? And why did no one bother to put up signs? This was almost like a dungeon in a game.

For a moment, he considered going in and saying hi to Nell, the friendly nurse. But he was interrupted by excited voices coming down the hall toward him. Turning around, he saw three people and a stretcher. Two young men and one woman, dressed in scrubs, were rushing to the infirmary. A motionless figure in the black tester suit lay on the stretcher.

"We're losing him! We're losing him!" one of the medics yelled. "Brain activity failing!"

"God damnit!" the other man cried out. "Not again!"

"Out of the way, idiot!" the woman snapped at Kai, who was standing there in the middle of the hall, staring – like an idiot indeed.

Kai jumped out of the way and let the medics pass and enter the infirmary. He caught a glimpse of the man lying on the stretcher. He was hardly more than a boy, by the look of him, three to four years younger than Kai. His eyes were wide open, yet they stared into nowhere, frozen in terror. Crimson ribbons of blood ran down from his nose and dripped onto the floor.

Then the group was inside the medical facility and the door shut.

"We need Dr. Simmons here *now*, where the fuck is he?" he heard an agitated voice from inside. "Patient is flatlining! Prepare the defibrillator!"

Kai remained motionless for a moment and stared at the closed door. His body was ice cold while his mind tried to process what he just had witnessed. Was that poor boy in there dying? What had happened to him?

The realization struck him like a frosty whip. What he just had seen was the other side of Helltek. The dark side. The ugly side. The deadly side.

He had no idea how long he stood there, eyes wide in shock, until he finally got a grip of himself and moved on. Just before he turned the corner, he heard steps behind him. Looking back, he saw a middle-aged man in a white physician's coat and a nurse hurrying toward the infirmary.

Kai could only hope they came in time and that the boy would make it.

Trying to shake off the image of the pale face with blood running down its nose, he eventually found the elevators and entered one of the cabins. With trembling fingers, he pressed the up button and leaned against the wall as the elevator noiselessly set itself into motion.

That could have been him on the stretcher. Yesterday, or anytime in the future if he was unlucky.

Yes, the job was fantastic and the benefits stellar, but was all of that worth it in exchange for risking his life?

The elevator arrived on the ground floor. Kai stepped outside and took a deep breath of fresh air. The sun was shining and warmed his skin as he approached the glass structure housing the main cafeteria. The pleasant warmth and beautifully designed compound made him feel a bit more at ease.

When he arrived at the cafeteria, what he had experienced down in the Bowels almost seemed like a nightmare and something that could never actually happen here, in such a pleasant environment. Yet, deep inside him, a chill remained. A nudging doubt. Fear.

Is this really worth it?

He asked himself the question again while entering the cafeteria.

It was still too early for lunch and not many people were around. Only a couple of testers and other personnel sat spread around the huge dining area at tables or in lounges. Some alone, others in small groups. Most were dressed in the black tester suits.

After what he had just witnessed, Kai wasn't hungry at all. His stomach felt rather like a cramped, ice-cold knot. And the thought of coffee made it cramp even more.

For a moment, he stood in the entrance area of the beautifully designed, ultra-modern building, not sure what to do. Then he realized that he must look like a total moron and set himself into motion.

Kai approached the hot beverage station, which was labeled as such with a huge 3D hologram of a steaming cup circling above it. He wasn't in the mood for coffee, but maybe they had some green tea.

Studying the display, he decided to go for hot cocoa instead. It was a rather childish and totally not cool beverage, but no one was around to see what the machine filled in his cup, and he felt that this was exactly what he needed after the incident at the sickbay.

Smelling the hot chocolate pouring into the cup, he instantly began feeling better.

Kai grabbed his beverage and took a sip right in front of the machine. The hot liquid spread a pleasant warmth in his stomach.

Sunken in thoughts, he turned around abruptly – and bumped into someone who was stood behind him.

The unexpected collision made him drop his cup and spill the warm liquid all over himself. A delicate hand rushed forward and caught his cup in mid-air before it could hit the ground and create an even bigger mess – with an agility and speed like he had never seen before.

Kai looked up and only now saw who he had bumped into. He froze and his heart seemed to stop for a moment.

It was Rogue.

She wasn't dressed in the extravagant clothes he had seen her in the day before but was wearing a tester suit instead. Well, at least, Kai assumed it was the model the Level Tens wore, as it looked completely different from the gimp suit he and everyone else was wearing. With its mixture of silver and black and shiny fabric material that reminded him of chitin, it was more like something astronauts in sci-fi movies wore.

However, it was as tight and form-fitted as a second skin and displayed her slender body in a breathtaking way. She was taller than him, at least 5' 9", and he had to look up to see her face.

When he did, it was as if the sun had appeared behind thick clouds after a month of non-stop rain. It hit him like a lightning bolt and filled him with previously unknown warmth.

Alice's face was slightly different to her virtual one but even more beautiful. Its delicate features and pale skin had something elfin about it, framed by her long white hair with the black tips. Dark blue eyes shone down on him. Eyes that were so deep, he instantly felt like drowning in them, and he didn't mind at all.

"Oh my gosh, I'm so sorry!" she said, and recognizing her voice sent shivers down his spine. "I hope I didn't burn you! Are you ok?"

He tried to say something but no words left his mouth, so he simply nodded like a total dork. It was only much later, when recalling the encounter to the very last detail, that he would realize that she had caught the cup with an outright impossible speed.

She handed him the cup and smiled. Her smile was the most beautiful thing he had ever seen.

"Hot chocolate," she said. "That's my favorite, too."

"Really?" He forced the word out and would later hate himself for such a dumb reaction.

She chuckled. "Yes, really. But don't tell anyone, ok?"

Kai gulped as she squinted her left eye into a conspiratorial wink.

She stepped past him and activated the beverage machine, which prepared two cups of cocoa.

"You must be new here. I've never seen you before," she said, handing him one of the fresh cups. "I'm Alice."

He took the cup and finally managed to behave like a civilized human being again instead of like a drooling monkey.

"Kai."

"Pleased to meet you, Kai," she said, giving him another smile that turned his knees to jelly. "I'll see you around."

Her cup in her hand, she walked off toward the exit. Kai stared after her with an open mouth. Every one of her steps was graceful perfection.

"Don't even start dreaming about it, dude."

A mocking voice behind him made him jump and spill his cocoa again.

Completely baffled, he turned around and saw Marco behind him, a huge grin on his face. He and the others from his team had entered the building through the side door. The rest were now standing at the food distribution point, yet he was certain that every one of them had witnessed his encounter with Alice. Kai's cheeks turned fire red and he hated himself even more.

"She's gonna rip your heart out and eat it for breakfast," Marco said, shaking his head. "You wouldn't be the first one."

"I… um… it was nothing. I accidentally bumped into her and spilled my coc… coffee."

"Right," Marco said while pulling down his left lower eyelid with his finger. "Nice try. But it won't work. That chick is miles out of your league. Miles as in from here to Timbuktu. Got it?"

"Yeah. But I didn't try–"

Marco laughed and walked back to the others. Kai sighed.

He grabbed some napkins and cleaned the cocoa from his suit. It turned out that the outer fabric was fluid repellant and that his little accident wouldn't leave any stains. He had been told that the gimps were automatically cleaned and disinfected in their lockers every night, but having brown stains on it for the rest of the day would still have been embarrassing.

Kai joined the others who had gathered at a table by the window. Judging from their faces, they had all witnessed him talking to Rogue and were ready to mock him.

"There he is, our Casanova," Marco said mischievously. "Here the second day and already trying to hook up with the hottest girl around."

Claudia rolled her eyes and an irritated expression flashed over her face.

"She isn't *that* hot. You guys are all the same."

"Right," Francois agreed. "Way too skinny if you ask me."

"What are you talking about?" Josh said. "She's a goddess!"

"Oh Josh," Claudia chuckled.

"I didn't try anything, really," Kai said. "It was a coincidence."

He tried desperately not to show how excited he was about the encounter. It already felt like a surreal dream.

The only one not participating in the banter was Viktor. He didn't get any food or drink either, and instead just sat there with crossed arms and a slightly bored, aloof expression on his face. Kai wondered why he was even there. After all, the others had told him that Viktor rarely socialized with any of them.

"Here comes the master," Marco said, pointing at the door with his chin.

"Nice of him to join us," Kai said, surprised.

"He usually wouldn't," Marco explained. "But he said he has something important to tell us and that we may as well do it during lunch, especially since Kai spent some quality time with the character editor this morning."

"Stop being a dick," Claudia said, then turned to Kai, her usual kind expression back on her roundish face. "It happens to everyone. Lex had to outright drag me out of there or I would have wasted the whole day."

"Why is the editor so detailed?" Kai asked.

"You mean, why can you pick a cock?" Marco said. "Several reasons. For one–"

"Hey gang," Topher said, approaching them.

He grabbed a chair and pulled it up to the table, which was, like most, made for six.

"Hi Topher," Kai said. "Sorry it took me so long in the editor. I lost track of time in there…"

The team lead waved his hand.

"No big deal, Kai. But what I'm about to tell you is."

"Is it about the tournament?" Josh asked, his voice filled with anticipation.

Topher nodded.

"The email about the tournament went out this morning, and–"

He paused for a second to create suspense. Even Viktor turned his head and gave him his full attention.

"–and this time they picked *Behind Blue Eyes 3* for the next tournament."

"Yes!" Marco called out.

Claudia clapped her hands, and Josh and Francois exchanged a high-five.

"I knew it!" Claudia said. "I told you we'd be lucky this time. I was feeling it in my gut!"

"Famous female intuition, huh?" Marco mocked her, which made her flip him off in a playful way.

Everyone was excited.

"This means a great chance for our team and for every one of you individually, guys," Topher said. "We'll put in an extra hour of practice every day until the tournament next week."

Then he turned his attention to Kai and explained.

"Every three months, they pick a different game to test the multiplayer in a tournament. Of course, the teams who are currently testing the chosen game have a big advantage over the other participants because they know the mechanics in their sleep."

"And that's us," Kai said, feeling the others' excitement spread over to him.

"Among others. We're not the only squad testing this game, of course."

"But the others suck!" Marco laughed.

Topher grinned. "I wouldn't say it so drastically... but, yes. I want you guys to win the low-level challenge. You have a realistic shot there."

"Hell yeah," Marco agreed.

"You really are a lucky bastard, Kai," Francois said. "Some people have worked here for years and never get to play the game they test in a tournament. And you'll have your first one after a week."

"Tournaments are so important because they can boost your progression tremendously," Topher said.

"I'll reach Level Two!" Josh said dreamily.

"Alright," Topher said. "I suggest you finish your lunch quickly and jump back into your pods. We not only have a game to test, we have a tournament to win."

Kai was grateful that he was off the hook from being mocked, at least for now. The others began chatting about the upcoming tournament and seemed as excited as little children.

He didn't understand all of what they were saying, but he was sure he would learn the specifics in time. And he knew for a fact that he was an excellent player when it came to multiplayer shooters. Judging from the way Topher had glanced at him, the team lead was well aware of that, too.

The excitement about the tournament and his encounter with Alice made the horrible scene he had witnessed earlier appear like a bad dream that was already fading. Yes, the job was dangerous, but it was worth it.

It wasn't only the benefits, the money, the fun, and the possibility to participate in tournaments that were like e-sports on a smaller scale.

No, Kai also knew that he would stick around for *her*, no matter what. How else would he ever be able to see her again? Maybe talk to her?

Yes, he was well aware that she was lightyears out of his league. Unearthly beautiful, she was a hero among Helltek employees and a multi-millionaire. Not to mention that she already had a boyfriend who was as pretty, cool, badass and rich as her.

And yet… it couldn't hurt to dream. Could it?

CHAPTER SIXTEEN

By the end of the week, Kai was convinced that time could pass at different speeds. It wasn't only a feeling, it had to be a fact.

While the days – and weeks, and months – had dragged like they were stuck in glue when he was working at Fuji, his first week at Helltek had rushed by at light speed. He could hardly believe it was already Friday night when he exited the train and hurried home to make it back in time before curfew.

Over the last couple of days, he had played through the whole game three times, repeating every level over and over again. The others said that *BBE3* was a well-developed game. Compared to others they had tested, it had very few bugs. That was laudable of the studio and made their job safer than in many other games. The downside was that they progressed more slowly if they didn't find bugs.

Kai had scored 48 points in his first week anyway, which everyone agreed was pretty good. Topher said that Kai was doing a great job. Apparently he was attentive and not only had an eye for details but a deep sense for level design too, which made him discover issues more easily than most.

They only discovered small issues. Minor glitches, such as AI clipping through obstacles or pathfinding errors, broken shaders, T-poses, or a slight FPS drop when too many particle effects were involved – which was a very common issue every gamer had encountered one way or another. The scanner kept acting up in several scenarios, and Viktor claimed that it was something embedded deeply in the code and that, most likely, the studio wouldn't be able to fix that in time and would ship it as it was.

As long as it was no major issue that could pose a threat to the players or turn into a showstopper, studios often decided to ship the game and fix the smaller issues with a patch – or sometimes they wouldn't.

On Thursday they had delivered a new build which had curbed the high intensity to an acceptable level, and the showstopper Kai and his team had encountered had been fixed. It still was very unpleasant to receive damage or die when playing the game on hard mode and at the highest intensity level. But in an email accompanying the latest build, the devs claimed that this was by design.

Gamers who chose to play new-gen shooters on hard mode expected a thrill. Damage at death had to come with a price. However, the intensity was bearable now, and neither Kai nor his crew had encountered any horrifying incidents such as the bomb on his first day.

Whenever they found an issue, the testers tried to reproduce it at least four times to deliver a result that was as accurate as possible. This was the part of the job most game testers disliked, but Kai didn't mind it. It had an analytical aspect that he, as a mathematician, could relate to. And it was even fun for him to try to reproduce everything as thoroughly as possible.

"Give it a couple of weeks," Marco had commented, laughing.

His colleague probably was right about that. So far, everything was new for Kai, and it was all exciting and fun. He had decided to not think about the risks that the job could bring anymore but instead focus on the good and fun aspects. And his goals.

Kai wanted to reach Level Two as quickly as possible. It was his way out of the tenement slums he was forced to live in now. His only way. And he was determined not to mess that up.

Even though his pay was almost double what he had

earned at Fuji, it still wasn't nearly enough to move out of the moldy place he shared with his stoner roommates and move into a better apartment, maybe one by himself. The opportunity Helltek offered in giving their employees apartments on the campus was incredibly generous. Even with Level Two income, Kai could hardly have afforded to live in a better place. Maybe he could have moved into a tiny studio apartment, but certainly not in a better district or closer to his workplace. One of the reasons Helltek offered apartments to their employees was that they could be at work in five minutes and therefore spend more time testing instead of commuting for hours every day, such as Kai and Josh were forced to do. Right now, Kai spent more than four hours on public transport every day. Time that was completely wasted and energy draining.

Usually, when he came home in the evening, all he could do was take a quick shower and then go to bed. He hadn't been in VR all week. Kai wondered how his online friends were doing and hoped everyone was alright. He still didn't know what had happened to Red and the other players that had been affected by the horrifying incident with the giant spider in *TSOTA*.

Kai shuddered, imagining what could have happened if the Cyber Squad Level Ten team hadn't stepped in just in time. And remembering what those guys were capable of sent chills down his spine.

Especially when he thought of *her*.

He hadn't seen Rogue since the accidental bump in the cafeteria. Every moment he didn't spend in VR but in the real world on Helltek's premises, he kept watching his surroundings attentively in the hope of eventually spotting her somewhere.

It was a foolish hope, and he knew it. Even if he managed to see her somewhere on the compound, he still wouldn't have an opportunity to talk to her again. What purpose would he have? He was only a Level One tester, a freshly hired noob, whereas she…

What reason could she ever have to talk to him or interact with him in any way? It was a very lucky coincidence that he had bumped into her the other day. Something that most likely would never happen again. No wonder his team was mocking him about it.

Yet he couldn't help himself. He had been thinking about the encounter over and over again. Recalling every single detail. Like watching a video, replaying it a hundred times.

It was only in retrospect that he had noticed what remarkable speed and agility she had shown when catching his cup. It had been so remarkable that he wasn't sure if it had happened that way or if it was his brain playing tricks on him, remembering details that had never happened that way.

In his mind, Kai saw her hand lash out, fast as a snake. The more he thought about it, the more he was convinced that it couldn't possibly have happened the way he remembered.

Alice was amazing enough as she was, he didn't have to equip her with inhuman speed in his imagination. And yet…

You really have to stop thinking about her, idiot, he told himself for the millionth time. *It's pathetic.*

Kai sighed, walking down the hall toward his apartment, the unpleasant odor of eggs and wet socks hitting his nose, like every day.

It's only temporary.

Yes, it was only a matter of time. He only had to achieve another 952 points and then he would leave here once and for all and never look back.

Hopefully, the tournament next Wednesday would give him a huge boost. Everyone in the team seemed convinced that they would score well, and Topher was pushing them to their limits in after-hours training sessions. Although he meant well, it was exhausting.

Today, Kai was so tired that he didn't think he'd even make it under the shower. He would collapse into bed and fall fast asleep as soon as he entered his room.

Fortunately, his roommates were busy with their usual, meaningless business when he entered the apartment, and no one bothered him when he walked down the hall to his room. They didn't even know that he was working at Helltek now. And even if they did, they probably couldn't care less.

"Good evening, Kai," Alessia greeted him when he entered his room. "Did you have a pleasant day at Helltek?"

"Mhm," he answered.

Could it be that the personal AI had become more talkative lately? Or was he imagining it? He wasn't sure, and he didn't really care.

"You can always share your thoughts and experiences with me, Kai," Alessia said with her typical neutral voice that seemed to hide sarcasm. "You know that."

"Yeah, yeah," he mumbled, falling on his bed.

He didn't even bother to undress. Within seconds he was asleep.

**

"You wanker."

Kai laughed. "Yeah, I missed you, too."

Only seconds after he had logged into VR and *TSOTA* the next day, Stan had sent him an angry message.

Now the stunning Dark Elf girl was standing in the courtyard of his estate, glaring at him, her arms crossed. Her facial expression looked surprisingly real, and very feminine. It was a look every guy in a relationship knew well.

"Where the bloody hell have you been, Kai?"

"I was busy. I'm sorry."

"As you should be! I was worried."

Kai winked. "How sweet of you."

"Asshole."

"Ok, I get it. I could have sent a message. But I was away all week and when I came home, I was too tired to go into VR."

"So, you got the job with Cyber Squad?"

"I did! And–"

"And that's exactly why I was worried about you! I thought you'd been killed there. Or worse."

And you weren't so wrong about that, Kai thought. Instead, he smiled cheerfully.

"It's really not as dangerous as everyone thinks it is. Actually, it's pretty awesome."

"You need to tell me all about it!" Stan said, excited like a little boy.

Kai did. He told his friend as much as he was allowed to. About Helltek, about the amazing people he'd met, the incredible technology the testers used, the crazy cafeteria serving free food, the beautiful compound, the high-tech suits the testers wore – and what they had nicknamed them.

That had made Stan laugh out loud.

"Seriously? They call them gimps? That's hilarious!"

They had left Kai's estate and were now riding through a gloomy swamp. Stan had a quest here and had asked his friend to join him and help him beat the world boss. He had tried it a couple of times on his own over the last week and failed every time. Kai felt guilty about having left his friend in the dark about his whereabouts and was more than happy to comply.

"And the girl testers? Do they wear those gimps, too?" Stan asked.

"They sure do."

"Whoa," Stan's avatar took on a dreaming expression. "Maybe it's not such a bad job after all."

Kai rolled his eyes. "Really? Of all the amazing stuff I've told you about, that's what excited you most?"

"Hell yeah," he answered with a shrug. "Girls in gimps. Sounds like pure porn to me."

Kai laughed. "Now that you say it… but I assure you, the girls working there are badass."

"Oh I bet. The sheilas that were part of the Cyber Squad

that saved our asses looked smoking hot."

You have no idea, Kai thought.

He hadn't told Stan about Alice, and he wasn't planning to. It was bad enough that his teammates were mocking him about his obvious crush. He didn't want Stan to chime in on that. Besides, somehow, she felt of too high value to include her in a conversation like this. It felt disrespectful.

The further they advanced into the swamp, the darker and gloomier it became. Toxic green fog circled above the muddy waters that covered the lower parts of the leafless, mangrove-style trees. Carcasses and bones stuck out of the shallow water in many places. Now and then, they passed dead warriors, who had been mutilated and must have died a horrible death. The closer they got to the location that was marked with a red skull on the mini-map, indicating a powerful world boss, the more it became clear that the monster lurking here had to be particularly nasty – and dangerous.

Dark clouds veiled the low afternoon sun, turning its reddish rays into an unearthly, purple light. Suspenseful music made the scenery even more eerie, holding a promise of great dangers ahead.

From time to time, they encountered some smaller creatures, such as anacondas, poisonous fire-lizards or giant ticks, but unless they attacked them, Kai and Stan ignored them. They weren't here to waste their time on low-level trifles. They were here for the big guy.

Kai was enjoying simply playing a game for a change instead of testing and scanning it for issues. It felt relaxing. Although, admittedly, he had to restrain himself from looking out for bugs. At one point, he saw some particle movement that seemed off to him. Not long after, a crocodile made swimming movements on land. Seeing it, he felt the urge to open his tester HUD and write a ticket.

This made him wonder if he could theoretically open the console in this game, if he wanted. After all, Topher had told him that the console was universal and that the code sequence to activate it had been attached to his neuro-plant signature. So, theoretically, it should be possible, right?

Could he jump into the sandbox of this game? Or, even better, activate god mode? He made a mental note to ask Topher or Lex next week.

"Earth to Kai," Stan said, amused. "You there?"

"Huh?" he twitched.

"I said, I was wondering how long you'll bother to hang out with your unimportant friends in *TSOTA* anymore, now that you've moved up into the ranks of the cool guys," Stan said snottily.

"Ha, I'm far away from being one of the cool guys there," Kai assured him. "I'm a total noob. The good stuff comes with reaching Level Two, and I'm light years away from that."

"Don't downplay yourself, mate. You're one of the best players I've ever seen. Everyone in the guild has been talking about what you did in the spider lair. You're a bloody hero."

"I didn't do anything special. I would have been toast if not for the Cyber Squad."

Stan stopped his mount and turned his head to Kai, a serious expression on his virtual face. "That's a pile of rubbish and you know that. You saved those three on the ground."

"Any word from them?" Kai asked.

For some reason, he had avoided asking that until now. After what he had learned during the last couple of days, he feared the worst.

Of course, he hadn't told Stan about his disturbing experience with the death sequence on high intensity. That was a part of his job that had to remain confidential.

"Oh, right! You don't know!" Stan said, clapping his forehead. "Apparently Red, Cloudgirl and Serene are fine."

"Thank God. What did they say happened to them exactly?"

"I have no clue."

Stan shrugged, spurring his mount. He continued on

the narrow path, wriggling through the deadly swamp, and Kai followed him.

"What do you mean?"

"I mean that no one's spoken to any of them since the incident. Apparently all three have been banned from X-Perience. The guild has received a written message from Red saying that he's stepping down as guild leader. And that's that."

Kai didn't react. At least on the surface. Luckily, it was much easier to hide one's feelings when inside an avatar than in real life.

In truth, he found Stan's words deeply concerning. After all he had learned over the last five days, this sounded more than fishy.

"Why have they been banned?" he asked.

"No idea, mate. Apparently some glitch. Hopefully they'll be back soon."

Kai stared at his friend, wondering if he really believed that, or if he simply chose to believe it.

Chances were high that this was a cover-up and that something serious had happened to the three players damaged during the glitch. Thinking of the bruises he had suffered, Kai could only hope that they were alright.

Have you never wondered what happens to people who die while they're connected to VR?

Kai heard Marco's voice echo in his head and suddenly felt ice-cold.

"And what about the healer?" he asked after a moment.

"Ah, that guy. No one knows."

"He's just gone?"

"Yeah. Maybe his account was locked, too. Or he had enough of it after the experience. Frankly, no one liked the guy anyway, so no one really misses him. Dude was a cunt."

There's some scary shit out there.

Kai shook off the uncanny feeling getting a grip on him.

It was fascinating how easily people believed what they were told.

Then he realized why everyone was so proud to be a part of Cyber Squad. It was their job to prevent stuff like this from happening to anyone. They were the ones standing on the line between oblivious players and all the dangers lurking on the Net in VR.

"Ok, we're almost there," Stan said, pointing ahead.

They approached a steep cliff, overgrown with lush plants and an unsurmountable obstacle. It formed a half-circle around the target location. The path they had followed ended there.

Stan halted his mount and descended. Kai scanned the area, following his friend's example. He had never been here before. The whole swamp was a remote area, far away from any main quest. They were the only players here. Often people would gather around world boss spawn points, waiting for others to join in before they engaged the challenge. World bosses were tough enemies and designed to be challenged by groups of players. However, it wasn't impossible for two or three experienced, well-equipped LVL 799s to beat such monsters.

"So, what's the mechanic?" Kai asked.

The green swamp fogs were so thick here that he could hardly see anything, especially since the light was now fading rapidly. No doubt they were poisonous. Thanks to the Set of Arachnophobia they both were wearing this wouldn't bother any of them though, as the set gave 100% resistance against any poison.

"Um, we go in and kill the ugly wanker?"

"That's a fantastic plan."

"Thank you."

"Do you have any details to share, maybe? The next spawn point is a ten-minute ride away, and if we both die, chances are high no one will come and revive us. What do you want with this boss anyway?"

"The achievement for beating all world bosses in Tamuria."

Kai whistled. "Ambitious. How many do you have so far?"

"Three."

"Of how many? Twenty?" Kai asked with a laugh.

"Eighteen. It doesn't matter since you're gonna help me with the rest. You owe me."

"For what?"

"For fucking disappearing for a week."

Kai sighed. "Fine. Let's do this then."

He drew his sword and approached the area surrounded by the cliffs. The music changed from suspense to the combat theme assigned to the swamps of Tamuria.

Only now did he notice a huge cave entrance. Countless skulls and bones were piled up in front of it. Humanoid ones. Some still had rotting flesh attached.

An unpleasant odor hung in the air. For some reason, it reminded Kai of the stench in the hall of his apartment building. He wrinkled his nose.

The level design suggested that the monster would emerge from the cave, and it didn't take long for that to happen.

After taking a few steps, they heard a furious roar echoing from inside the cave. Kai had heard such roars before in this game and had an idea of what was lurking inside.

A second later, he received confirmation.

Following another roar, a massive figure emerged from the mists circling the cave. Its head was bald, and it had pointy ears and gray-green, wrinkly skin. The body was humanoid in shape, yet at least twelve feet tall. It was dressed in a stained leather loincloth, leaving the rest of its overly muscular body on display.

The creature opened its broad mouth, showing long, razor-sharp, yet crooked teeth as it let out another bone-shaking roar. Its hands were so huge that they could easily crack Kai's or Stan's skull, if they got ahold of either of them. But right now, the monster was holding a massive club spiked with rusty metal fragments, swinging it menacingly. Its more than impressive arm muscles flexed. It was ready to attack.

A red tag appeared above the creature's head, identifying it as

Biwak
Swamp Troll
(500000/500000)

"Damn," Kai said. "That's an ugly son of a bitch."

"Yep. You said it," Stan confirmed. "And pretty strong."

"Half a mill health… this could take a while."

Quickly, Kai opened his inventory and buffed himself with health and stamina boost potions.

"Ok. Let's do this."

"The swamp mists are poisonous, but thanks to our awesome armor we don't need to give a shit about that," Stan said with a grin.

"But if the smelly bastard lands a direct hit on your head with his club, it's an insta-kill, so be careful," he added.

Before Kai could answer, the swamp troll attacked, letting out another horrifying roar, its maw drooling. Apparently it was expecting to add more bloody bones to its collection.

It would be disappointed.

Kai stood still and watched the massive body of his opponent charge toward him. The troll wasn't intending to take prisoners and instead was swinging his club aggressively.

At the very last moment, Kai dodged.

Pirouetting on one leg, he avoided the attack. The monster rushed past him, and now it was on him not to waste any time. He swung his sword and stabbed the swamp troll in the back.

Critical hit! 25000!

"Woohoo, well done, mate!" Stan called out, skillfully dodging the attack himself.

"Yeah, only 475000 hit points do go," Kai said dryly. "Does he have adds?"

"Sure does," Stan said while simultaneously attacking the troll's side with his dual wield daggers.

Red numbers rushed down at high speed, indicating minor damage. "There's gonna be some poisonous fire lizards. Piece of cake."

"Ok, you throw AoEs on the lizards and I'll take care of the big guy," Kai said, dodging another swing of the massive club.

He countered with his sword, then blocked a strike from a giant hand with his shield.

The troll staggered for a second, which gave Kai the time to swing his sword into a heavy attack. He landed another critical hit. The monster was down to 88% health. If it followed a typical boss mechanic, the adds would spawn when the troll lost 25% of its health.

Biwak swung the club into a heavy attack. Kai roll-dodged out of the area of impact. But when the club hit the ground, the impact was so massive that the soil shook, creating an AoE. Kai and Stan both got stunned, and a timer in his field of vision indicated three seconds.

While this was hardly more than the blink of an eye, it was enough time for the troll to lash out and kick Kai with its leg, which was the size of a huge tree trunk.

The momentum ripped Kai off his feet and made him fly against the cliff. Damage numbers rolled through his view. The assault had cost him more than 20% health and the impact had stunned him again. Not wasting any time, the troll charged toward him.

Shit, Kai thought.

No wonder Stan had been unable to beat this opponent by himself. The bastard stunned and then landed devastating blows with its club.

But Kai was lucky.

The damage he had taken triggered the special feature his armor set provided. With a blood-curdling shriek, a giant spider spawned right next to Kai. It wasn't as huge as the Guardian, but it was at least the size of a cow.

Now his limited-time familiar, the spider instantly attacked the troll. Kai watched with satisfaction. This feature came in real handy. It had been even more fun in PvP when he and Stan had tested it the other day. He couldn't help but snicker while watching how the enemy players had run away, chased by his own giant spider.

Against a world boss, it was pretty clear that the spider wouldn't do much damage, but it would keep the troll occupied – at least for a bit. Kai doubted that the mini-guardian could sustain more than two hits from the massive club, and since the boss had a poison mechanic, it was highly probable that he was immune to poison himself.

Kai jumped up and activated *Lunge*, an ability that came with the Sword & Shield specialization. He lunged forward, performing three long steps and jumping up. Using the built-up momentum, he stabbed his sword in the troll's side with full force, draining 50% of his stamina.

Critical hit! 29000!

It brought the troll down to 71% and triggered the adds.

Eight nasty-looking swamp lizards attacked them from all sides.

"Your turn, Stan!" Kai called out. "Take care of your pets!"

"On it!"

A metallic sound could be heard as the Dark Elf threw caltrops in the air. They exploded before hitting the ground, covering the approaching lizards with sharp metal shards that caused damage and slowed them down.

Stan exploited this and jumped at the lizard closest to him using the dual-wield *Whirlwind* attack. Flesh, blood and bone shreds flew in all directions as he turned the lizard into twitching pulp.

Meanwhile, Kai kept hitting the boss with all he had, rotating the special attacks of his character and weapon classes. The giant spider kept the troll occupied, although its health bar was down to under 25%. One more hit and the spider would be done.

But at that moment, another shriek could be heard and a second spider spawned right next to Stan. He was under attack from three lizards at once and was taking damage, which had triggered the spawn mechanism of his spider.

"You ok?" Kai called while stabbing his sword in the troll's guts and twisting it sharply, landing another critical hit.

"I'm good, I'm good," Stan replied, desperately trying to fend off the attacking lizards.

The troll let out a bone-shaking roar that sounded like a surprisingly convincing mix of pain and anger. Down to almost 50%, the boss AI suddenly switched into a state of frenzy.

It first smashed Kai's spider to the ground, killing it off, then it turned its full attention to Kai.

Kai swore inwardly, cursing his friend for not telling him about this important mechanic. In a desperate attempt to fend off the troll's frantic attacks, he lifted both his sword and shield upward, crossing them. The troll hit with such force that it surely would have been a killing blow if it had hit Kai's head instead of the sword and shield. Yet it still made Kai stagger back.

Luckily, Stan's spider attacked the boss from behind. Before the troll could hit Kai again, it turned its attention to the mini-guardian. Kai regained his balance and was about to hit the boss with full force when he heard his friend call out.

"Kai! Help!"

Turning his head, he saw that Stan was stuck in

climbing plants, which were growing in the misty swamp water. They wiggled around his feet, clearly alive. Probably also poisonous, but at least that was something neither of them needed to be concerned about. Without the poison resistance, this boss would surely be impossible to beat for two players. It was tough as it was, without a tank and a healer.

The plants had instantly got a firm grip on the Dark Elf, immobilizing her and dragging her into the water while the lizards continued the attack. Kai left the troll occupied with the spider and stormed toward his friend. But the troll wouldn't let him go that easily. It swung its massive leg and kicked Kai in the side. Again, Kai flew against the cliff.

At that moment, he was glad that he wasn't testing the game and that there wasn't any kind of glitch going on. Instead of experiencing any pain, all he felt was a tingling in his body as he hit the rocks. But his health dropped below 50%.

"Damn it!"

"Kai! I'm being eaten alive here!" Stan complained. "Do something!"

"It was your glorious idea to come here in the first place!"

Kai got up and used a health potion, then hurried to his friend. This time he was smarter about it and tried to run in a circle around the troll so he didn't get hit again – only to get stuck in the plants on the other side.

"Argh!" he called out in frustration, yet he didn't waste any time. With his sword, he quickly cut through the plants climbing up his legs. It took him valuable seconds, and when he finally was on the run toward his friend again, it was too late. He saw Stan's health bar drop to zero as the lizards overwhelmed him.

"Why, thank you," Stan said, anything but amused.

Kai turned around and saw that the troll was still busy with the spider, but it was only a matter of seconds until the monster destroyed the arachnid.

There were still three lizards left; Stan had managed to

kill the rest of them. Kai engaged the reptiles, hitting them with all he had. If he managed to revive Stan while the troll was still busy with the mini-guardian, they had a realistic chance of beating the boss. His own spider was on cooldown, and so was the ability to take another healing potion.

It was funny. Fifteen seconds sounded like nothing. But if it was the cooldown between two healing potions, it could last an eternity.

Kai cut through the neck of the last remaining lizard, watching its health bar drop to zero, then leaped to his fallen friend.

"I got you!" he said, summoning one of the crystals out of his inventory that were used to revive a fallen comrade.

As the crystal fired up and immobilized Kai during the process, he saw, from the corner of his eye, that the troll was about to land the final blow on the spider. With one last shriek, the arachnid fell to the ground and dissolved.

"Oh, fuck."

Stuck in the reviving process, Kai saw the troll swing its club and ram it down on his head.

Everything turned gray as his health bar disappeared. Kai fell right next to his friend.

"That went well," he said.

They were both shrouded in twilight and could hear the dreaded music that always accompanied death in this game. Why did all games have such a theme? It almost seemed as if the game developers were sneering, implementing a feature everyone hated.

"I don't think it was that bad," Stan said.

"We're both dead and there's no one to revive us, so I'd say it was bad," Kai replied. "So, what now?"

"We revive at the spawn point and try again."

Kai would have rolled his eyes, but he had none in his current state of death.

"And ride the entire way back here? That'll take ten minutes. No way! Let's do something else."

"You owe me!"

"Ok, fine," he sighed. "But only one time, ok?"

"Pinkie promise!"

***

Hours later, they were back at Kai's estate and were both busy checking their inventory. Kai jokingly called this doing housework chores. Every RPG player knew that it could take up to an hour to go through one's inventory, checking all new loot for usefulness. Both of them had gathered a massive amount of loot today after killing three world bosses.

Of course, Stan's pinkie promise had been worth nothing, as always. They had died two more times before they'd finally been able to beat Biwak, the swamp troll. Every time, they had had to ride the ten-minute distance from the spawn point to the cave.

Just when Kai was about to get upset with his friend, they had finally beaten the monster. Now that he was going through the loot the boss had dropped in detail, Kai had to admit that it had been worth the effort. He'd got several high-value armor pieces, 5k gold and a weapon.

Biwak's Club (Unique)
Two-handed/Blunt
LVL Requirement: 799
DPS: 25000
Bonus: A direct hit has a 35% chance of stunning the target.

That was pretty decent. Kai could use it for his Barbarian class character.

Besides, both had got the monster trophy, of course.

Those unique collectibles dropped when beating a world boss or a dungeon boss. Like every high-level player, Kai had dozens of similar trophies on display in his house. He already had an idea for where to put Biwak's head. There still was some space on the walls in the dining hall.

They both worked through their inventory in silence for a while. With routine, Kai categorized the loot into three different folders. One was for stuff he would keep for himself and maybe use someday. The second was for valuable stuff that was worth being brought to a vendor to make some coin, and the last one was for junk that he would break down for resources and crafting experience.

"So, what now?" Stan finally asked. "Want to go on a quest together, or would you prefer some PvP?"

"I think I'll call it a day," Kai said, still browsing through his inventory.

"You what?" Stan stared at Kai with his big elven eyes.

"I haven't eaten anything today because I jumped into *TSOTA* first thing in the morning, and I bet my RL body is starving. Besides, I'm really tired. The job at Cyber Squad is exciting but also pretty challenging, and the four-hour commute every day is killing me."

"Oh, ok," Stan said, disappointed. "But you'll be here next Saturday, won't you?"

"Sure thing," Kai replied. "Is there something particular going on next Saturday?"

"Hell yeah. The guild is going on a dragon hunt! There's a new dragon dropping with the DLC next week and we want our guild to be one of the first to get the trophy. Apparently it will also drop platinum loot. You in?"

"Of course! When did I ever say no to a dragon hunt?"

"Awesome! We need you more than ever now that Red and Cloudgirl are gone."

"Who's leading the guild now?"

"LifeSupport took over."

Kai raised his eyebrows in surprise. So far, he had found

Life to be rather quiet. She had never given him the impression that she wanted to be in charge of anything. It had seemed as if she was content with healing and supporting others.

"Yeah, I know. I didn't expect that either," Stan shrugged. "But when she came forward, no one objected. And her first idea was to beat the new dragon, so, of course, everyone is excited."

"I'll be there," Kai promised with a smile.

"I heard you say you're hungry, my love," a soft voice behind him said. "I cooked you a meal."

He turned around and saw Freya, his NPC wife, standing behind him, a cheery smile on her face. Her flaxen hair moved in the slight summer breeze and her eyes sparkled with unquestionable devotion. She held a steaming bowl in her hands that contained venison stew, judging by its delicious smell.

Kai felt his stomach rumble and knew that it was his real stomach reacting to the alluring scent. In RL, he had never tasted venison and probably never would.

"Thank you," he said, reaching out for the food. The instant he touched the bowl it vanished and was added to his inventory. Spouses' home-cooked meals could be used as stamina buffs before going into combat.

The NPC gave him a saccharine smile. "I'll be in the house if you need me."

She turned around and slowly walked back to the house, her round hips moving in an alluring way.

"Damn, what I would give for a woman like that in real life," Stan said dreamily.

Kai laughed. "Really? Don't you think the NPCs are a bit dull?"

Admittedly, until not long ago, he too had thought NPCs like Freya were hot. Now that he had come into contact with breathtaking women in real life, he noticed that NPCs were flavorless, soulless. Mere imitations, consisting of pixels and sophisticated code.

And there was one woman in particular he had met who was more magnificent than any NPC could ever be, no matter how realistic they appeared.

"Dull? Why? Freya is hot as fuck. What else do I need? Well," he added, interrupting his own thoughts. "Of course, the prettiest girls *are* dull if you can't fuck them, you're right about that."

Stan was referring to the sexless life in *TSOTA*, a fact he complained about on a regular basis.

"Not quite what I meant," Kai said.

Bantering and having fun, the friends didn't pay the NPC any more attention.

As soon as Freya was out of sight, her face changed. The dull bliss and devoted smile vanished and were replaced by a completely different expression.

Freya's big eyes narrowed, and a cunning smirk appeared on her lips. All of a sudden, she didn't appear like a soulless construct of pixels and code anymore. She appeared alive. And anything but friendly.

CHAPTER SEVENTEEN

"Alright, gang, this is it," Topher said. "Today is our day."

The squad had gathered in their testing room, and everyone was visibly excited. It was Wednesday morning, shortly after 9 a.m. – the day of the tournament.

"I'm sorry if I pushed you hard over the last week, but you'll thank me when you win today. And I know you can do it."

"That would be sensational," Lex threw in, sitting on her desk and chewing bubble gum. Today she wore ripped black jeans and a black t-shirt with the logo of the game *Steampunk 2020*. The jeans were stuck into her obligatory Doc Martens boots, this pair in pink. "I can't remember a Level One team ever winning the tournament."

"Hey, we're not all Level One," Marco objected, straightening up like a rooster.

"Oh, I forgot. Some of you are even Level Two. Wow." Lex said dryly, then let a bubble plop on her mouth.

"I'm *almost* Level Three," Marco said, visibly miffed.

"Let's focus on the task," Topher said. "Lex is right. It won't be easy for you. After all, you'll be competing with Level Fours, some of whom are close to reaching Five. But your advantage is that you know the mechanics in your sleep and yesterday's training was excellent. You can do this."

A rush of excitement rose in Kai as Topher spoke. Even though he felt exhausted, he was also pumped. The last two days had been hardcore. All of them had had to show up at 7 a.m., which was an inconvenience for the team members living on the campus but a total nightmare for Kai, who had had to get up at 4 a.m. and catch the first train at 5. They trained PvP for two hours before their regular testing schedule began, and later they skipped their lunch break so they could finish early and train again.

For Topher, benevolence wasn't the only reason why he wanted his team to succeed. Tournaments were also important for team leads. The better their team scored, the more progression points the leads gained.

Marco had told Kai that Topher had been stuck at Level Five forever and that he was close to reaching Six. A successful run in the tournament could catapult him there. Behind his back, Marco also explained that they needed to score well for Josh, who was close to being fired. He had overheard a conversation between Topher and Lex the other day, and both had seemed to be convinced that Josh was a hopeless case.

"I mean, sure, he's not the brightest bulb around, but he's part of the family," Marco had explained. "We need to win this for *him*."

Kai agreed. He liked Josh, although admittedly he was by far the weakest player in their team. And the worst tester. Most of the time, he was so withdrawn that he overlooked bugs even if they showed up right in front of his nose. Marco was convinced it was because of Josh's drug abuse. Although it was absolutely forbidden for the testers to consume any kind of drugs, even legal ones such as weed, some, like Josh, had a drug history in the past.

Helltek's no drug policy was so severe for a simple reason: anything that could influence the functionality of the brain could easily become very dangerous when plugged into VR, especially when connected to brand new software full of glitches. The employees were tested once a week, and anyone who broke the policy was fired on the spot.

Learning this, Kai wondered how many gamers out there risked brain damage every day because of drug use. Even though every game came with a warning to only connect to it when sober, nobody gave a damn about that. On the contrary, there were plenty of illegal substances people took to enhance their VR experience, especially when it came to sex.

There's some scary shit out there.

Would people still connect their brains to VR if they were fully aware of how dangerous it really was?

The VR industry was the biggest in the world, not only for gaming but also for all other forms of its use. Communication, information… most students visited virtual classrooms nowadays. It was much cheaper and safer, and no one had to leave the house to attend school. Millions of former office jobs took place in VR.

The more Kai learned about the technology and its economic aspects, the more he was convinced that the vast majority of incidents were covered up. By the industry or maybe even governments.

He thought about his missing guildmates and what had happened to them. Most likely, none of them would ever be seen again.

"Alright, let's move," Topher said, waking Kai from his brooding. "It's almost time for the general assembly."

***

There was much more movement in the halls and corridors than usual. Black-clad figures seemed to come from everywhere, some wearing clothes over their suits, others not. Kai and his team had to wait at the elevators because so many people were going to the surface at the same time. There had to be a staircase somewhere, too, but Kai hadn't discovered it yet, and obviously nobody bothered to use it anyway.

When they finally reached the surface, the sky was cloudy and the humidity high. Kai could feel sweat building up on his skin, yet it was immediately absorbed by his high-tech suit.

They approached a low, round building that Kai hadn't seen until now because it was located directly behind the main tower of Helltek HQ. Yet he would have found it easily. All he needed to do was follow the crowd of testers who were coming from everywhere and entering the building.

Inside, only diffuse light came from well-hidden lamps. Kai's eyes needed a moment to adjust to the semi-darkness. They entered a huge hall decorated with oversized abstract art paintings. This place was not only used for the employees' monthly general assembly but also for press events and other official occasions.

A small stage was located at the rear end. Brightly illuminated, it featured an oversized Helltek logo and, next to it, a holographic blue globe rotating around its axis. It was the CI of Orbis, Helltek's mother company.

The air was filled with murmuring, excitement and a pleasant scent of rose and sandalwood coming from invisible air dispensers. Like all other architecture at Helltek, the assembly hall had Feng Shui written all over it.

While the place was slowly but surely filling up, Kai let his gaze wander over the crowd, studying the people who had come together. There were at least five hundred people there, maybe more. The hall was probably big enough to accommodate over a thousand. Everyone was young, in their twenties and thirties from the look of them. Most were in good or excellent shape and wore fashionable haircuts and clothes over their gimp suits.

It was interesting to study all those people, but if Kai was honest with himself, there was one particular girl he was hoping to see. Her tall figure and white hair should have been easy to spot even in a crowd of such a size, but she was nowhere to be seen. Kai couldn't help but feel disappointed. The thought of her alone made his heart flutter.

Suddenly he could feel eyes resting on him.

Turning his head, he stared into Maeve's gorgeous face. She and the other girls of her squad were standing not far away. Like the other day, they all were dressed up like anime Gothic Lolitas, and their make-up easily stood out in the crowd. A lascivious smile appeared on Maeve's face and she winked at Kai, then she turned away and focused on the stage in the front.

Heat rushed to Kai's cheeks, and he was grateful for the semi-darkness which covered it up. Besides, his co-testers were deep in conversation about the last tournament, which apparently had not gone well for them.

Then he felt an elbow hit his side, and Marco whispered: "There. The Twins from Hell in persona."

Kai turned his attention to the stage. He had been so focused on his search for Alice among the crowd that he hadn't even noticed that two figures had entered the stage. A man and a woman.

They both were blond and dressed in expensive-looking, almost identical business suits. The woman's one had a slightly different, more feminine cut. But both were crafted of the same, black velvet-like material and both wore a shirt of white silk beneath it. It was apparent at first sight that those two people were siblings, most likely twins. Their faces had the same shape with a distinctive nose, bright blue, narrow eyes and thin lips. They seemed to be in their late thirties, but Kai couldn't say for sure. Maybe they were older and had an excellent plastic surgeon.

But the fact was that Gregor and Marie-Louise Hell were impressive figures, if not intimidating.

"They must have an important announcement, otherwise they wouldn't show up in person," Marco said in Kai's ear. "Usually they send one of their management lackeys to hold the monthly assembly."

"Good morning, Helltek family," Gregor Hell began in a smooth voice with a slight German accent. "We are aware that you are all excited about this month's tournament and the progression it will hopefully bring every one of you, which is why we will keep this short and sweet."

He paused for a moment, letting his gaze wander over the hundreds of young people listening to him. A friendly smile played on his lips, which only revealed his smugness when studied closely.

"You are the backbone of this company. Helltek's success is *your* success. My sister and I couldn't be more proud of your achievements that have made this company number one. However, you all know our credo, don't you?"

He lifted his palm to his ear and leaned forward.

"Disrespect the impossible!" some voices shouted.

"What was that?" Gregor asked. "I'm not sure I can hear you!"

Kai noticed Marie-Louise stepping from one foot to the other impatiently. Even though her face didn't show any particular expression, her body language indicated that she would rather be anyplace else but here and wished her brother would get to the point instead of playing games.

"Disrespect the impossible!" more voices shouted, with greater enthusiasm.

A broad smile appeared on Gregor's handsome face. Unlike his sister, he clearly enjoyed being the center of attention.

"Exactly! Disrespect the impossible! Because this is our credo, we are where we wanted to be. On top! We are number one in the VR testing industry. But that's not all! My sister and I came here today to share some big news with you, before you hear it from the media. I am delighted to announce that Orbis, our mother company, has merged with Electronic Entertainment and has become the biggest entertainment conglomerate worldwide. But that's not all. You all know that VR is the future. It's not only entertainment like video games or movies, as it used to be. It's so much more than that! It's a lifestyle. There are massive changes coming up in the next few months and years. Innovations that will change human life – and death – forever. And it's going to be our job – your job! – to make VR a safe environment for everyone at any time. You guys are heroes! I salute you! I applaud you!"

He started clapping, and everyone joined in enthusiastically. Some more than others.

The Twins from Hell exchanged a look, their faces unreadable.

Finally, Gregor continued after the applause had ceased. "We will have more big news for you soon. For now, know that you're a part of something greater. Something much greater than yourselves."

His smile was broad and shiny, yet had something uncanny about it. Almost chilling. However, Kai noticed that most people clung to his words and didn't seem to notice it.

"But I don't want to keep you away from an important event," the CEO said. "Enjoy the tournament, folks! And to celebrate Helltek's success, we've doubled the progression points today, giving all teams a chance of greater progression. Go get 'em!"

He waved into the crowd, then he and his sister left the stage. Marie-Louise's expression was bored. Now that she thought no one was paying attention anymore, she had dropped her friendly mask.

Next to Kai, Claudia and Marco exchanged an excited look, and Topher smiled.

"This is our chance, guys!" he said while the group exited the assembly hall, following the hundreds of people in tight black suits.

"Hell yeah!" Marco called out. "I can't wait to get started!"

"We will *so* whip everyone's ass!" Claudia agreed.

Kai fell a bit behind the others, who already seemed to be celebrating their success before the tournament even had started. He found himself next to Viktor, who didn't seem excited at all.

"What do you think, Viktor?" Kai asked, trying to start a conversation.

"I think this guy is so full of shit it smells all over

campus," Viktor answered, so casually it was as if he were talking about the weather and not running his mouth about the CEO of his company.

"Um..." Kai said, not knowing how to react. Viktor's bluntness had caught him off guard.

But then something else caught his attention. For a second, he thought he spotted snow-white hair in the crowd. He strained his neck, hoping to catch a glimpse of her, his heart pounding. But he couldn't see her anymore.

Get a grip on yourself, idiot, he told himself. *What are you, twelve? Focus!*

And that he would. He knew he wanted to score as high as possible in the tournament. Every progression point brought him closer to a better life. A life away from stinky tenements and on a shiny campus. A life closer to *her*.

***

Entering game... Please wait... Loading...
***Behind Blue Eyes 3*. Secure_dev_mode, build 341A.**

A second later, Kai found himself in the lobby of the game. He had been here so often recently that he didn't even notice the spectacular view outside the windows anymore. Claudia, Marco, Francois and Josh were already waiting. They seemed excited but in good spirits.

It wasn't customary for the techs to participate in tournaments unless the game required six players. The team size for *BBE* was four to eight players. And the memo sent out by the manager organizing the event stated that all teams were required to have five people.

The techs and team leads were supposed to monitor the game closely. The primary goal of the whole event wasn't to offer the testers a good time and progression but to test all aspects of the multiplayer mode. Especially when many matches were played at the same time.

The first four rounds were played simultaneously by all teams, with the Level One and Two teams competing against each other and the Threes and Fours separately. After that, the best teams in each group would compete against each other in a final match. The same happened for the higher levels. Level Tens didn't participate in tournaments as no one would have a chance against them anyway.

Matchmaking in progress – please stand by!

This was it. Kai felt his heart pounding in excitement. He had never participated in something so competitive – and important.

Loading map...
3...
2...
1...

The lobby disappeared and was replaced by a loading screen showing the map they were entering as a 3D model as well as the game mode.

Kai and his friends had played all the maps many times, and he instantly recognized which one it was.

"Jackpot!" he heard Marco say over the comm.

Kai smiled inwardly. This map was their favorite, their home turf, so to speak.

Map: Village
Modus: Capture the Flag
Faction: Guardian Angels

"Excellent!" Claudia called out.

The multiplayer version of the game offered three different modi: Capture the Flag, Domination, and Death

Match.

Kai's team agreed that they preferred CtF or Domination to Death Match. They were easier to practice and to control, whereas Death Match was pure slaughter. The only goal was to kill as many enemy players as possible within a given time frame.

The loading screen vanished, and Kai and his team found themselves in a bleak, desolate area.

As normal for Capture the Flag, they spawned at their flag, which bore the Guardian Angels logo, two neon-blue wings on a black background. The flag was located on the roof of a base building that looked like the ruins of a former supermarket. It was accessible via stairs at the front and two ramps on the sides.

"Ok," Marco said. "We stick to the tactic we've practiced. "Claudia and Francois guard the flag. Kai, Josh and I go hunting. Let's move!"

"Left or right?" Josh asked as they jumped from the roof.

Each map was set up for three teams. At the beginning of the match, it wasn't clear which team had their base where, since that was generated randomly. Although the map featured a variety of buildings, the three flag bases looked exactly the same. This was important for the balancing of a PvP game. The balancing was something the tournament was supposed to test, among other features. It was axiomatic that all three teams should have the exact same chances of winning the match, which would entirely depend on their skills. Players hated only a few things more than poor balancing in PvP.

"Left," Marco decided. "Remember. We're avoiding the marketplace."

"Copy that," Kai answered.

The sky was overcast, and the low afternoon light veiled many of the buildings they passed in darkness. The map was designed to look like a deserted, post-apocalyptic small town or village. Trying to avoid making any noise, they used a back alley behind crumbling base buildings that could have been small shops and businesses in a long bygone area. Behind them were a couple of residences with creaking porches and devastated yards.

The map was huge, and even though they sprinted, it took them more than a minute to pass the center and approach the enemy base.

As soon as the base came into sight, the three slowed down and crouched, making themselves more difficult to spot. The scanning function, which was an important part of the main game, was disabled in PvP and so was any kind of flying drone, which was used to lift a player up onto high buildings in Single Player and Co-op modes. This made sense as the scanner would have made it impossible to sneak up on an enemy, and using a flying drone to flee once the flag was captured would have been lame and bad balancing.

"How's it going at the base?" Marco asked.

"No enemy contact so far," Claudia replied.

She and Francois were lying low, close to the flag. The plan was to ambush whoever tried to steal their flag. Crouching in the shadows made their Blue team tags disappear and meant they were almost invisible to the enemy.

"Copy that."

"Maybe we've been lucky and Reds and Yellows went against each other," Kai said.

That would be the best scenario possible, he thought. And indeed, as they approached the enemy base, it seemed deserted. The red flag with the iron fist logo moved lazily in the afternoon breeze.

"Ok, I'm going to get it," Marco said. "Cover me!"

Kai stayed behind the corner of a destroyed diner, his rifle at the ready, while Josh crouched behind a burned-out car wreck. They watched as Marco carefully approached the enemy base, completely unhindered. He stretched out his hand to grab the flag.

Suddenly his head exploded in a red mist.

"What the fuck!" they heard Marco's disembodied voice

as his remains collapsed.

"Sniper!" Kai called out. "Watch out Josh!"

He looked around, trying to localize where the shot had come from. A rifle muzzle stuck out from a shattered window on the second floor of a building right next to the diner.

"Damn campers!" Marco's voice sounded furious.

"I'll take care of him," Kai said, already on the move. "Wait for my signal, Josh, then run and grab the flag!"

"We've got company here," Francois reported.

"How many?"

"Four Reds."

"God damn it!" Marco swore. "I have fifteen seconds left until I respawn. Hold on there!"

"Engaging them now," Claudia's voice sounded cold and calculated.

Kai kicked in the door and stormed upstairs, where the sniper was hiding. Yet when he entered the room the shot had come from, it was empty.

He reacted lightning-fast, spinning and activating his blades. Just in time before a massive sword could decapitate him. Sparks flew in the semi-darkness of the room.

Being an experienced PvP player, Kai had anticipated where the attack would come from.

Campers usually always followed the same tactic. They hid, 'camping', ambushed an opponent, then quickly hid behind the door or any other suitable cover and waited for the enemy to go after them and storm the room. This one had chosen the most obvious solution and hidden behind the door.

Kai tumbled backward due to the immense force of the attack. The Reds were called Proms in the game and had different standard equipment than the Angels, the faction Kai and his team had been randomly assigned to. They were bigger, bulkier and much stronger, with clearly artificial limbs made of metal.

"Get the flag Josh!" Kai called out over the channel only his teammates could hear.

The cyborg soldiers Kai's team was playing lacked the Reds' immense strength, but they made up for it in agility. Moving much quicker than his opponent could react, Kai performed a roundhouse kick and hit the hostile in the abdomen. The Red lost his balance for a second, which was enough for Kai to finish him off. Activating the Rush ability, he lunged at the enemy and decapitated him with one clean strike, using all his momentum.

"Camper's down."

"We're having a bit of trouble here," Claudia reported. "We've got one of them but Francois is almost done, too."

"Hold on! I'm almost back," Marco said. "Six seconds!"

"*Merde*!" Francois called out.

"…And he's done," Claudia said.

Meanwhile, Kai ran to the window which the sniper had used as a vantage point. Down on the street, he saw Josh grabbing the flag.

"Got it!" Josh called out triumphantly.

Then Kai saw something else.

"Watch out, Josh! Yellows approaching from behind! RUN!"

He had wondered what the third faction was doing. Two hostiles from the Yellow faction appeared from behind a building, where they had obviously been waiting for the right moment, and now went in pursuit of Josh. Those hostiles were smaller and lighter but way more agile than Kai's team. They were of the same kind as the killer cyborgs they had encountered in the dreaded level with the mall and the bomb.

Luckily there were only two of them, which meant the remaining three were guarding their home base. But there was no doubt that they would catch up with Josh at any second. The game mechanics prevented the player carrying the flag from sprinting.

They almost had him.

Kai grabbed the sniper rifle that the enemy he had just killed had dropped and took aim.

Hitting a moving target with a sniper rifle was always a difficult task, but he had to try.

Kai held his breath and pulled the trigger.

And hit the enemy player!

The Yellow froze for a second, then stumbled and fell. Kai hadn't managed to kill him, but at least he had wounded him enough that the hostile couldn't pursue Josh anymore.

Crawling on the ground, Kai saw him reaching for his pistol.

"Don't even think about it, asshole," Kai said.

Quickly, he took aim again and pulled the trigger. This time he hit the enemy cyborg's head, which exploded in a foam of blood and metal shards.

In a tournament, the most progression points came from a victorious match, but every kill gave extra points, and Kai had already eliminated two hostiles.

But he didn't have time to celebrate. The second Yellow had stopped and was now aiming his rifle at Josh, about to shoot the flag carrier in the back.

"Josh! Watch out!"

Too late.

The enemy player riddled Josh with bullets from his assault rifle.

"Ah!" Josh called out as his virtual body twitched in death spasms and then collapsed.

The Yellow used Rush to advance quickly and grab the flag. Meanwhile, Kai saw the first of the fallen Reds respawn at their base. It would be difficult to get the red flag now.

Once again, Kai took aim with his sniper rifle, ready to blow the remaining Yellow into temporary nirvana.

A noise startled him.

He spun and saw another Yellow standing in the door of the room, aiming his pistol at him. The hostile had done exactly the same as Kai earlier: he'd gone to eliminate the sniper before trying to capture the flag.

Kai leaped to the side. He dodged the first bullet, but

the second hit him in the back, causing 25% damage. An unpleasant sensation hit his body, similar to an electric bolt, but nothing compared to what he had had to endure on hard mode.

He didn't waste a second. Rolling, he drew his own pistol and fired three consecutive shots at the enemy player. Looking up, he saw that two of his bullets had hit the target. The hostile had fallen to a crouching position, a gaping wound in his chest indicating heavy damage. Before he could do anything else, Kai was on him and finished him off with a short distance headshot.

He heard an unpleasant popping sound as the bullet smashed the Yellow's head and bloody goo splatted into his vision.

"Are you guys done at our base?" he asked.

"I'm back," Marco replied. "Claudia and I are about to finish off the last of the Red fuckers."

"Ok, cool," Kai said, running down the stairs. "You might want to check the Yellow base, it's pretty much unguarded. With a bit of luck, we can get two flags at once."

"Copy that!"

Back on the street, Kai saw that the respawned Red was about to pick up the flag. Kai drew his assault rifle and riddled the enemy player with bullets, sending him to nirvana for the second time in as many minutes. He grinned, imagining how the other player was swearing and cussing him out.

Activating Rush, Kai leaped for the flag and grabbed it.

"Got the red flag!"

All he needed to do now was survive and bring the flag back to his home base. Which was easier said than done as the Red team could see the position of their flag on their mini-map and would try to retrieve it no matter what. There was no point in sneaking now. Kai took the shortest route home, even though it led him through open terrain.

"I'm back at the base," he heard Josh say. "The others went for the yellow flag."

"Ok." Kai ran as fast as he could. "Cover me! You should see me in a moment."

He turned his head and saw a Red player chasing after him.

"Oh shit, I got one on my tail!"

He could neither sprint nor fire a weapon when carrying the flag. The only way to avoid being shot was to run in erratic zig-zags. Bullets hit the remains of a collapsed building right next to his head, and exploding plaster clouded his vision for a brief moment. Luckily he knew the map by heart.

"We got the yellow flag!" he heard Marco's triumphant voice. "We lost Claudia, but Francois and I are on our way. Hold on there, we can do this!"

"Yeah, they sacrificed me for the greater good," Claudia said with fake pathos in her voice.

Meanwhile, Kai evaded another storm or bullets, but it was close. Next time he wouldn't be so lucky, that was clear. He could hear his pursuer's footsteps on the old, cracked concrete. The heavy cyborg body was impossible not to notice.

Suddenly, Kai had an idea.

He dropped the flag and spun on his heel, lightning-fast. Simultaneously, he drew his pistols and fired in the direction where he anticipated his opponent.

Kai was lucky. One of his bullets hit the puzzled enemy, who hadn't expected the flag carrier to go on the offensive.

Instantly, Kai exploited his pursuer's bafflement and shot him in the face.

He smiled, picking the flag back up. That was his fourth kill. He could imagine his progression numbers moving up as he gained extra points.

Approaching his team's base, he saw Marco and Francois swiftly closing in with the yellow flag from the other direction.

Kai arrived first, and a victorious theme could be heard as he placed the flag on the designated pedestal. The area on his HUD designated to display the team's points shifted from zero to one for the Blue team. Seconds later, it went up to two as Marco and Francois arrived with the yellow flag.

"Woohoo!" Marco cried out. "We rock! Only one more and we win."

It was true. There were two ways to win a CtF match, either by leading when time ran out after ten minutes or when one team scored three points. Kai's team had started out extraordinarily well, outsmarting and outplaying both enemy teams.

"Ok, let's finish this!" Francois said.

"Wait for me," they heard Claudia say. "I'm almost back, seven seconds."

"Ok, what's the plan?" Josh asked.

"They'll either go for all or nothing and attack us full force or squat at their base, trying to defend it at any cost," Kai said.

The yellow and red flags began glowing, then started blinking before they both disappeared, returning to their bases.

"I say, Reds are gonna come at us full frontal," Claudia said, materializing back at the spawn point.

"And Yellows might decide to lay low…or come after us, too," Marco agreed.

"Ok, we shouldn't take any unnecessary risks," Kai said, taking the initiative in a completely natural way. "You guys stay here and keep them at bay. Claudia, you take the sniper rifle and give them a warm greeting. I'll sneak up to the red base and get the flag."

No one objected.

"Sounds like a legit plan," Marco said. "Go get it, Kai! Claudia and I go into hiding and Francois and Josh stay at the flag. That way, when they approach, they'll think there's only two of us who are guarding the flag and not basically our full squad."

"Roger that!" Claudia said, and she and Marco ran off.

Kai took a deep breath. He had presented the plan

without even thinking. It was only now that he clearly realized that it was down to him to win this match for his team.

And he would.

Swiftly, he ran off, back toward the Red base. This time, however, he took the longer path, which provided excellent cover and would make it possible for him to sneak up on the enemies guarding the base. Which hopefully wouldn't be the whole Red team. Then he'd quickly be toast. The full plan was based on the hope that the Reds would take the all-or-nothing approach. There was less than five minutes left now. If time ran out with things as they currently were, Kai's team would automatically win with two flags.

Using a half-collapsed building as cover, he carefully closed in on the enemy base.

Then Kai froze.

He could see all five Red players gathered at the base. They were stood close to each other, exchanging looks, clearly communicating and debating what strategy to use. Two of them were observing the surroundings attentively. Kai ducked into the shadows of the desolate building, avoiding being spotted.

Damn, he thought. *There goes my glorious plan.*

If the Red team decided to squat and guard their flag instead of going on the offensive, there wasn't much he could do. His team would win anyway, but the higher they scored, the better for the team's progression.

"What's going on, Kai?" Marco asked.

"It's a bit crowded here, I'm afraid. The Reds seem to want to hang out and picnic at their base until time runs out."

"That doesn't make any sense! They'll lose, damn cowards."

"Yeah," Kai said. "Oh, wait! They're moving out!"

"Sweet! How many?"

"Four. They're running toward you."

Kai watched the Red team leave their base and disappear in the direction he had come from. No one noticed him. He'd wait another five seconds, then attack the remaining guy guarding the flag.

"Ok, we're ready to offer them a sweet welcome full of surprises," Claudia said.

Just when Kai was about to leave his position and attack the red base, he saw something that made him stop in his tracks.

The Yellow team was inbound. They, too, had waited for the Reds to leave and were now ready to strike. Instead of going for Kai's team, which had dominated the match, they had decided to attack the much weaker Red team. And they, too, were going for all or nothing. Kai counted four Yellow players who would jump the oblivious Red guarding the flag any second. That would make it pretty much impossible for Kai to get the red flag now. But he wouldn't let that little detail stop him from winning the match for his team.

Carefully he backed off, using the building as cover once more, then leaped forward and sprinted.

He couldn't snatch the red flag, but with a bit of luck he could grab the yellow one before their team came back.

"Change of plan," he informed his team. "Yellows are coming for the red flag so I'm going to snatch theirs."

"Copy that. We got company here," Marco replied.

Kai ran as fast as he could. It would be a very close call. By now, the Yellow team had probably killed the guy guarding the red flag and were running back. He had to kill the guard they had left behind and be off and away with the flag before they came into sight.

Luckily, he knew a shortcut.

He took the direct route through the marketplace, which was in the center of the map. The reason they never took the direct route was that the marketplace was trapped with proximity mines. Navigating around them was time-consuming and dangerous, since stepping on them was an insta-kill for any player from any of the three factions. But Kai and his team had played the map so often that they had found a work-around. They weren't sure if it was an exploit or by design, but one thing was certain: it would come in very handy for Kai in this situation.

Instead of running straight into the marketplace and onto the deathtraps lurking there, he took the stairs up to the roof of a two-story brick building. There, he remained still for a second, focusing.

Kai activated Rush and sprinted to the edge of the roof with full speed, knowing that this stunt was all about timing. He needed to jump at the exact right moment. A fraction of a second too early and he would fall onto the landmines. A fraction of a second too late and he would fall off the roof and would have to try again. And that would cost him too much time.

He counted his steps as his cyborg avatar ran with impossible speed, then jumped, directing all his body's energy into his artificial legs – leaping over a distance of almost eighty feet.

He flew over the demolished marketplace and crashed against the building on the opposite side. His fingers automatically grabbed the ledge and he pulled himself up, using his momentum. Without slowing down, he crossed the roof of the building, then jumped down into the street on the other side.

Kai was almost there. He ran through a narrow alley separating two former office buildings and abruptly stopped at the corner. Carefully, he peeked around. He could see the Yellow base from here, as well as the hostile team member guarding the flag.

Kai grinned. He was lucky. The Yellow wouldn't expect him to approach from here and was staring in the direction of the Blue base. Drawing his assault rifle, Kai lunged forward. He shot the enemy on the run before the poor guy had even fully noticed what was going on. Again, Kai activated his high-speed ability and, in a blink of an eye, was at the flag.

"I got it!" he reported excitedly. "I have the yellow flag!"

He spun and ran toward his home base.

"Well done, man!" Marco replied. "We're about to finish off the last commie here."

That meant the game was basically over for the Red team. They wouldn't respawn in time to reach one of the enemy bases, steal their flag and bring it back. The Yellow team could still pose a threat, however. Kai had to reach his base, flag in hand, to seal the deal for their victory.

Looking over his shoulder, he saw that the Yellows had arrived back at their base, one of them carrying the red flag. But as long as their own flag was gone, they couldn't score the enemy flag. Without wasting any time, the Yellow team turned around and pursued him.

"Shit," Kai said. "I got company. Yellows are after me."

"Think you can make it?"

"Not sure. Probably not…"

"Ok, we're on our way!"

Kai expected the enemy to open fire at any second and again began running evasive zig-zag maneuvers. He left the middle of the street and moved closer to the demolished stores flanking the road, trying to use as many structures as possible as cover without slowing down. Again, knowing the map so well came as a big advantage since he knew exactly where to find burned-out car wrecks, corroded dumpsters and other obstacles the level designers had dumped around the map to give the players cover possibilities.

It didn't take long for the Yellows to start firing, and soon bullets were flying all around him.

Not good. He wouldn't make it like this.

A second later, he got hit. Once in his lower back and once in his left shoulder blade. The unpleasant sensation he had come to know so well rushed through his body, and an even less pleasant report flashed over his HUD.

Warning! Severe damage to biological tissue detected!

His health was down to 48%.

Two more direct shots like that and he was done.

Bleeding heavily, his body slowed down even more. On his mini-map, he saw four of his teammates approaching swiftly, but it was improbable that they would make it in time.

Kai needed to change his tactic. Mobilizing all his strength, he pushed forward and dived behind the next street corner. There he dropped the flag and drew his rifle. He had fifteen seconds until the flag disappeared and respawned. If he could hold them off for that long, the others had a chance to arrive and cover him.

He leaned from cover and opened fire. Without having time to take aim, he didn't hit any of his opponents, but at least he managed to slow them down.

Luckily there were only three hostiles chasing him. The flag bearer had stayed behind, and the guy Kai had killed hadn't respawned yet.

Agile as they were, the Yellows, or so called Wasps, broke up their formation and performed evasive maneuvers only the Yellow troops were capable of. But avoiding getting hit slowed down their murderous sprint and bought Kai some badly needed seconds. He kept his barrage up, hitting one of them in the leg and forcing all three into cover. Then he was out of ammo and had to reload.

Quickly, he retreated back into cover and grabbed some fresh ammo from his inventory. Bullets hit the wall, creating deep craters. Kai glanced at the flag – five seconds left until it went back to the enemy base. Without looking, he pointed his rifle out from behind the corner and fired a salvo blindly, then grabbed the flag before it could disappear.

Again, bullets hit the wall he was hiding behind. He was a sitting duck!

Carefully, he peeked around the corner with one eye and saw that his pursuers were close now.

Suddenly one of the Yellows was hit by a large caliber

bullet. Blood sprayed from his neck like a fountain as he collapsed.

"Got you, son of a bitch!" Claudia said.

More shots were fired, and Kai saw Marco, Claudia and Josh approaching.

"Run, Kai!" Marco said. "We got this!"

Kai didn't need to be told twice.

Holding the flag firmly, he left his nearly destroyed cover and continued on his way to the Blue base. Behind him, he heard shots being fired as his friends engaged in a final stand-off with the enemy players. His injuries slowed Kai down by 20%, which made this last part of the dash feel like forever, but it didn't matter. Even if the Yellows managed to wipe out his team, which he doubted, they wouldn't catch up with him in time now. Turning the corner, Kai could see his base. Francois was standing there, waiting for him. The timer in the right corner of his HUD showed that the game would end in 40 seconds.

A moment later, Kai reached the base and dropped the flag on the small pedestal designed for it.

"YES!" he raised his fist in victory.

"*Fantastique!*" Francois extended his hand for a high-five.

Just before their hands could meet, the scenario froze.

VICTORY! CONGRATULATIONS!

The iconic game theme began, yet it sounded different, more triumphant.

Blue Team

3

Red Team

0

Yellow Team

0

The map dissolved around Kai, and so did his injured body.

Removing you from the map. Returning to lobby. Please stand by!

As if I could go anywhere, Kai thought with a grin. For the thousandth time, he wondered why loading screens always stated the obvious.

He could still feel the adrenaline pumping and knew that it was his real body experiencing it. And endorphins. What an amazing success!

A couple of seconds later, he appeared back in the game lobby, and so did his comrades.

"That was fucking amazing, man!" Marco said, approaching Kai and hitting his shoulder. "You basically single-handedly won the game for us!"

"That's not true," Kai protested modestly, trying not to show too much how happy the acknowledgment and success made him.

"It sure is!" Claudia's virtual eyes gleamed in excitement. "Who would have thought, rookie, huh?"

"That was excellent!" Topher's disembodied voice chimed in. "Well done, all of you! But don't get carried away now and focus, ok? There are three more matches to go before you reach the low-level finals. And I know you can do it."

Everyone nodded.

"We can do it," Kai agreed. "And we will!"
Their hands met in an enthusiastic group high-five.

CHAPTER EIGHTEEN

And they did.

They won all their following games. The next one had been a struggle, with one of the enemy teams being aggressive and well-coordinated. They almost lost that one but, with luck on their side, they managed to win it after all with a score of 3 – 2 – 0.

The other two matches were much easier, however, with Kai's team clearly dominating both. It turned out that the tough training Topher had put them through paid off, and knowing the game mechanics so well was an essential element in the formula for their success.

When they went for a quick lunch in the cafeteria, they were the proud winners of the low-level round, which had been for Level One and Level Two teams. This alone was a great accomplishment, especially considering the fact that they had two Level Ones in their team, with Kai being super fresh at Helltek and in the Cyber Squad in general. But they wanted more. They wanted to win the low-level finale. Extra progression points waited for the winning team – and, of course, fame.

But to achieve this, they had to beat the winners of the second group, which only consisted of Level Three and Level Four teams. It wouldn't be impossible to beat the team that won that round, but it would be difficult.

During their lunch, Kai saw that all the screens in the cafeteria were displaying live matches, and the place was full of people watching and applauding. People were mostly watching the high-level matches, but many of them would definitely watch the low-level finale. Most testers had nothing better to do but watch the other matches once their team had been eliminated from the tournament. No one did regular work on tournament days.

Kai wondered what the Level Tens did on tournament days since they weren't participating. Did they watch the others play, or did they have better things to do? If they watched, then maybe *she* would watch him play in the finale. The thought alone made Kai's heart skip a beat.

But no matter if she did or not, Kai wanted nothing more than to win this tournament. Although he was usually a relaxed type of guy, he could become very ambitious in a competitive environment.

He had noticed that his teammates looked at him differently now compared to only a few hours ago. He had proven his value to them, and they didn't see him as the rookie anymore. Even Lex had acknowledged his achievements, although in her own very special way.

"Look at you! You're not completely useless after all," she had commented when unplugging him. Yet the smile on her face showed that she was actually impressed and pleased with him.

"Ok, gang," Topher greeted them when they came back from lunch. "We've got fifteen minutes before it gets really serious. This is your moment to shine."

"Do we know which teams we'll face in the finale?" Francois asked.

Topher nodded. "We do. As usual, when there are three teams needed for a match, the Level One or Two team that scored best, which is you, will compete against the two teams that scored best among the Level Threes and Fours."

"Isn't that a bit unfair?" Kai wondered aloud.

"You could say so," Topher shrugged. "But those are the rules."

"So, who are the teams?" Marco asked.

"Darrel's team and Jason's team."

"Jason as in the Level Four almost Level Five team?"

"Exactly that one."

"Oh crap."

All of a sudden, the mood changed, and everyone looked downcast and discouraged. Kai had no idea who Jason and his team were, but his teammates' reaction told him everything he needed to know.

Topher put his hands on his hips and smiled.

"What did you guys expect? That it would be easy? Of course it wouldn't. Any team that won the Level Three and Four round and got to the finale would have been a challenge. It will be tough, but you can do it."

Josh squirmed. "But Jason's team is *really* good! Didn't they win three of the last five tournaments or something like that?"

"Four of five," Claudia corrected him.

"And I can't remember any tournament when a low-level team has won the finale," Francois said.

"Because it never happens," a sarcastic voice said.

Kai turned around and looked at Viktor, who was reclining in his tester chair, a condescending smile on his handsome face. He was pretty sure that this was the first time he had seen the guy smile.

"And Jason's team has been testing Call of Heroism for almost two years now," Marco said, even his cockiness gone. "They're shooter pros."

"So what?" Lex threw in, sitting behind her desk with her feet resting on it. "So are you. You've been testing this game for months now. You know it like the back of your hand. This is *your* game. Fuck them and their stupid Call of Heroism."

"Lex is right," Claudia said. "What do we have to lose? Absolutely nothing. But we have plenty to win."

Lex pointed her index finger at Claudia and squinted an eye. "That's my girl!"

She jumped up from her chair and walked toward the

pods. "And now go in there and kick some ass!"

***

Once they were uploaded into the lobby, Kai could sense how nervous everyone was. The tension hanging in the virtual air was outright tangible.

Suddenly he had an idea.

"So, this Jason and his team, they only test shooters?"

"Yep," Marco answered. "They're hardcore shooter fans. While most teams are happy for changes in between genres from assignment to assignment, those guys explicitly apply to test shooters. And all of them are almost Level Five. In fact, they *will* be Five after this tournament."

"They are really, really good," Francois agreed. "Let's face it. We stand no chance."

"Not necessarily," Kai said, and everyone jerked their heads and looked at him. "Maybe we need a different approach to beat them than the tactics we've used in the matches so far."

"What do you have in mind?" Marco asked.

"They're shooter pros, which means they can do any common shooter tactic in their sleep. They're probably better than us at every possible tactic and scenario. Yes, we know the maps better, but let's be honest. All shooter maps basically follow the same principles. There's nothing we could do they wouldn't anticipate, if they're really as good as you guys say."

"Tell us something new," Josh said with resignation in his voice.

Kai smiled. "How about we play in a way they don't expect at all. How about we play it with the tactic we'd usually use in an MMORPG match."

Everyone stared at him in surprise. Then Marco grinned.

"You sneaky bastard. I know where this is going and I like it. Keep talking!"

Kai did.

***

Loading map…
3…
2…
1…

Map: Sky Bridge
Modus: Capture the Flag
Faction: Proms

"Fuck me," Marco said while the loading screen displayed the map in 3D. "We are *so* lucky. If it had been a Death Match we'd have been screwed. CtF is our best shot."

"So is the map," Claudia said. "Remember when we played Sky Bridge for the first time? It's pretty challenging."

"It is," Francois said. "And you can fall off so easily. How many times did you fall, Josh?"

"Shut up," Josh replied, sounding embarrassed.

"Let's assume we're even luckier and Jason's sublime team has never seen this map before," Kai said. "With ten different maps the game can choose from randomly and four matches played, the chances of that are high, right? We can use the map as a weapon and lure them into places where they will fall off."

"Assuming they haven't practiced like we did," Claudia said.

"I don't think they have," Marco said. "Jason's guys are so cocksure of themselves, they think they can play every map in every shooter and win. I bet they didn't even bother to practice."

They materialized at the base around their flag, which was waving in the wind. This time they were the Red team, playing the slower, heavier cyborgs. That was another bit of good fortune as the Red cyborgs were sturdier than the other two teams, and for the plan to work out, they would need to sustain as much damage as possible.

The map itself couldn't be more different from the first one they had played that morning. While that scenario had been set in a post-apocalyptic, destroyed village, this map was located in the heart of Olympias City, the futuristic megalopolis that served as the backdrop for the *Behind Blue Eyes* series.

The midday sun was shining brightly, reflected by the gigantic forest of glass towers surrounding them. Its glaring rays were reflected in many places, creating spectacular lighting effects. No doubt the game engine was flexing its muscles here, and the level designers and lighting artists must have been very proud of themselves. Gamers often took no notice of such artful installations, however, and Kai and his team were no different.

The scenario was set high in the sky on top of three high-rises arranged in a triangle that were connected with each other by a massive glass bridge, which gave the map its name. This map had been designed as a nightmare scenario for people with vertigo as the skyscrapers were more than a mile high, and the ultra-realism of the game made it seem 100% authentic to the players. Misty clouds circled between the tops of the highest buildings surrounding the map and a warm wind blew in the players' faces.

What made the map even trickier to play was the fact that it had two levels. Between the faction base and the glass bridge, every building had a hatch leading inside. From there, two tunnels led straight to the other buildings – and enemy player bases. Those tunnels were not made of glass, and so it was impossible to see if someone was approaching from there.

When playing Death Match, all three factions' players basically met at the center platform connecting the three bridge parts leading to the main buildings and engaged in a fierce battle there. Kai's team would have had no chance in such a fight, but in the CtF mode, the chances were even.

"Ok," Marco said as the countdown ended and the match started. "Remember, we stick to the plan. We don't engage, we wait for them to either go at each other's throats or come for us. Then we stand our ground for as long as possible and let Kai do his magic."

"Yes, sir," Claudia said with an obvious grin in her voice. "You almost sound like Topher."

"One day I'll whip your ass, girl."

"Empty promises."

While still bantering, everyone took a position at the point best suited for their designated role.

Claudia crouched at the flag pedestal, her sniper rifle at the ready. Marco and Josh took cover behind AC vents close to the bridge, and Francois crouched behind a vent behind them. Kai focused on the hatch. If someone approached from there, he would hear and see them. If not, then he was ready to jump down and sneak up on the enemy base as soon as they were under attack.

The tactic they were about to try was indeed highly unusual for shooters, which normally only required a straightforward approach to succeed. It was based on the 'hold the line' tactic known from RPGs. Marco and Josh would both play the part of the tank, meaning they would try to get as much of the enemy's attention as possible. Francois' job would be to keep the two alive, at least temporarily. The game allowed every player two utility slots, which were by default filled with two healing sprays and two grenades. Francois had swapped his grenades with Marco and now had four healing sprays. Once he used those up, he could swap with Josh and Claudia, who would try to snipe out the hostiles as they approached over the bridge. She had deliberately chosen ammo that didn't cause lethal damage but had a high-velocity impact that would make the target stagger backward. The goal was to have the map kill the enemy players for them.

While his team would do everything they could to hold

the fort, it was Kai's job to retrieve the enemy flags, plain and simple.

He felt a bit nervous when the game began. Even though it was a team effort, in the end, victory would depend on his skills. He took a deep breath and focused.

We can do it.

"Claudia, can you see anything?" Marco asked.

The map was so cleverly designed that antennas covered the direct views of the enemy bases. Unless they went onto the bridge, the hostiles stayed out of sight.

"Negative," she replied, looking through her scope so that she could see further.

Nothing moved.

"Maybe they went against each other?" Josh asked hopefully.

"It's too early to know that," Marco said.

Kai licked his lips. A gesture that came from his real body as his virtual one couldn't get dry lips when nervous, at least not in a shooter game. The anticipation was tangible.

Finally, Kai spotted movement.

Holy shit, he thought.

This wasn't at all what they had expected.

"They're coming!" he called out.

"Where?" Marco asked. "I can't see anything!"

"Through the tunnel!"

"What? How many? Blue or Yellow?"

This only could mean that their enemies knew the map. At least one of the teams, possibly both.

"Not sure!"

Carefully, he leaned forward and peeked deeper into the hatch and the darkness below. A slight blue shimmer shone in the dark.

"Blue. I'm not sure how many though. Oh, wait–"

Kai froze. He could see shadows moving now. A lot of them. And there was also a yellow glow.

A second later, shots were fired as a fierce battle began

right below their base.

"Blue and Yellow," Kai corrected himself.

"Shit. Both have decided to come for us," Josh said.

"And now they're fighting in the junction," Kai added.

An elfish grin flashed over his face as he had an idea.

He produced a grenade from his quickslot and armed it. Then he leaned down the hatch and threw the grenade deep into the tunnel. A second later, everything was shaken by a massive explosion and Kai got a status notice informing him he had killed three people. A feeling of satisfaction every shooter fan knew too well filled him.

It was no secret among players that there was hardly anything so satisfying in the gaming world as defeating an enemy player. Fighting NPCs was one thing. Fighting real people behind their virtual bodies was something completely different. It was a phenomenon psychologists had been debating for decades, yet, of course, neither Kai nor any of his friends had ever wasted a thought on any of that. All they knew was that it was a deeply satisfying feeling, almost comparable with a good meal – or sex.

"Marco!" he called out. "Take over for me here. Shoot at anything that moves. But be careful, they might try to throw grenades, too."

"And you?"

Kai grinned. "I'm going to get us a flag."

Without waiting for a response, he sprinted off toward the glass bridge. He couldn't tell for sure, but he guessed that each enemy team had sent at least three people into the tunnel, maybe even four. Both had had the same idea to ambush the Red team with full force, which meant their bases were being guarded by only one or two people.

The Red faction didn't possess the Rush ability like the Blues. Instead, they could activate a damage shield. In this situation, Rush would have come in very handy, but Kai had to manage with what he had. Crossing the bridge, he avoided looking downward. The floor was made entirely of glass, or more likely plexiglass. Running over it felt like running over thin air. It was extremely unpleasant and required him to convince his brain over and over again that he wouldn't fall a mile down with the next step he took. Even though you didn't fall all the way down but dematerialized after a couple hundred feet, the experience was still a disturbing one.

When they had trained in this map, Kai had learned that the easiest way was to focus on the high-rises on the horizon instead of looking down. However, neither the bridge nor the platform in the middle had rails. One wrong step meant the end. Until he respawned, of course.

After a few seconds, Kai reached the central platform. It was round and had a radius of about 70 feet. Technically it was part of the bridge as it hung in the air. Seemingly defying gravity, it connected the three buildings with each other via bridges that were hardly more than catwalks.

Bright sunlight reflected from the glass surface and blinded Kai. An effect set by default, designed to make crossing and particularly fighting on the bridge even more challenging.

He didn't hesitate for a second but took the connecting bridge to his left. He couldn't possibly know how many players stood on guard at each base, so it would be better to attack the Yellows, who were more agile but physically weaker than the Blues.

"How's it going over there?" he asked his team.

"Splendid!" Marco answered sarcastically. "If you'll excuse us, we're a little busy here…"

A moment later, Kai had a clear view of the Yellow base and couldn't believe his luck. It was empty! Only the yellow flag moved frantically in the wind.

However, his excitement only lasted for a second.

As he hurried to the Yellow base, a massive impact hit his shoulder. Kai staggered and almost fell off the bridge.

Critical hit!

Health 65%!

Looking up, Kai saw movement by the AC vent closest to the flag. The enemy team had left a sharpshooter on guard.
Damn it!
It would have been too good to be true if the base had been unguarded. He didn't have time for a stand-off with the guy. His comrades would respawn any second, and then he'd be toast.
Kai had only one chance to succeed here, and the Red character would help him do the trick: go in full Rambo. He had learned that the reference came from a series of old movies Topher was particularly fond of. It meant a full-frontal assault, no matter the risk and casualties.
Kai clenched his teeth and charged forward, activating his damage shield. Sunlight reflected off the glass and hit his eyes as the sniper moved his scope around the corner. He fired and hit Kai again, this time in his torso.

Critical hit!
Shield capacity 18%!
Health 60%!

The sniper retreated behind the AC vent, reloading. Kai continued his charge at full speed. When he arrived at the cover, the sniper was waiting for him, his long, sharp, samurai-style blade ready to strike.
But Kai didn't give him a chance. Instead of trying to parry with his own melee weapon or seek cover, he rammed the hostile with full force, using his momentum. The much shorter and lighter fighter was thrown back through the air – and fell from the ledge into the metropolitan abyss.
"Yes!"
Kai could hardly believe his insane plan had worked.
Quickly, he grabbed the flag and disappeared into the hatch leading to the tunnel.

In a way, the original plan had been reversed as he had had to improvise. He had wanted to use the tunnel to sneak up on the enemy and take the direct way back over the bridge. Now the tunnel was his escape route.

"Got it!" he informed his team. "I'm coming through the tunnel, so make sure they're all dead by the time I'm there."

"Copy that!" Claudia replied. "We got them all, we think. Hurry up! They'll respawn any second and then screw you from behind."

Kai laughed. "I think I'll pass on that."

"Then move your ass!"

"What do you think I'm doing?!"

He advanced through the darkness and carefully peeked over his shoulder. No yellow gleam behind him – yet.

But it was only a matter of time.

A few steps further into the darkness, Kai took another peek – and saw yellow-glowing eyes approaching. At least two pairs, maybe three.

"Fuck!" he swore as bullets hit the wall only inches from his head. "They're on my tail!"

"We're coming to back you up!" Marco replied.

"No! Stay where you are!" Kai's voice sounded unusually fierce. "Stick to the plan, no matter what. Somehow they know we're the weakest team and are deliberately going for us."

Another bullet almost hit Kai.

"Son of a bitch!"

Anger rose inside him. This claustrophobic, dark tunnel hanging a mile over the ground was bad enough by itself without someone trying to blow his head off.

Then a crazy idea popped into his head.

Kai stopped in his tracks and crouched, turning around to face his pursuers. He could see them clearly now as they approached swiftly. He would have had no chance of reaching the Red base before they got to him, that much was clear.

Without wasting any more precious seconds, Kai brought up his inventory and selected his second grenade. In real life, what he was going to attempt to do would have been certain suicide, but he had played this map often enough to know that the tunnel was designed to be indestructible.

Kai threw the grenade at his pursuers and couched deeper, shielding his head and neck with his titanium arms.

The detonation shook the tunnel but didn't destroy it. But the three Yellow cyborgs chasing Kai were downed in a massive ball of fire.

Kai felt the heat wave approaching him, but his heavy body was strong enough to sustain it without being blown away.

Warning! Fire damage!
Heavy damage to biological tissue!
Shield: 0%!
Health: 19%!

Damn, one more hit and he was done for. And it didn't even have to be a critical one.

Nonetheless, Kai grinned as he jumped up and continued his escape through the tunnel.

His HUD was telling him that two of his pursuers had died in the explosion and the third one was barely standing anymore.

That meant four kills for him in this match so far and hopefully a successful flag run in less than a minute.

"You bastard!" he heard Francois say. "That was incredible!"

"Thanks! I'm almost there!"

He could see light at the end of the tunnel. But then, crossing the junction with the tunnel leading to the third base, he saw something else: glowing neon-blue eyes.

"Watch out, Kai!" Marco, who was standing at the hatch, saw them, too. "Blues are at your ass now!"

"Geez, why do all of them go for us?" Josh asked.

"Doesn't matter," Claudia said icily. "Let's kill them all."

"If they don't kill me first!" Kai was certain that his real body was dripping in sweat by now as the situation turned increasingly stressful.

He wondered if he should keep running or try to engage the enemy.

But he was almost there... only a couple more feet left.

A bullet hit him in the hip and made him stagger.

Health: 2%!

He felt the familiar unpleasant sensation, yet kept running. Miraculously, he was still alive. But now, he couldn't possibly make it up the hatch.

"Marco! Take it!"

He stretched out his hand that was holding the flag, blood dripping down his body and forming a puddle at his feet. Marco leaned down and extended his hand.

Suddenly he heard a loud bang, and everything turned black.

Critical hit!
You died!
Respawn in 15 seconds.

A countdown appeared and the loading screen showed the map.

"Marco!" he called out from the afterlife. "Did you get it?"

For a moment there was silence.

Then he heard Marco's triumphant voice. "We scored!"

Kai sighed in relief.

That was close!

"Fucking amazing, Kai!" Claudia said.

"And now they're trying to kill us... oh *merde*, we lost Josh." Francois was less enthusiastic.

The timer in Kai's vision showed ten seconds. It was

incredible how slowly seconds passed in such a situation. Ten seconds could be an eternity in a PvP match.

"Hold on! I'm almost back!" he said.

Kai felt the urge to bite his fingernails, a habit he had gotten rid of years ago. But in his current bodyless state, he had no fingernails to bite, which, in a way, he was grateful for.

Finally, his penalty was coming to its end and he was nearly good to go.

3...
2...
1...

Kai respawned in the midst of chaos.

***

Josh was down, and so was Claudia. Marco and Francois were still standing, though barely. Both had health at less than 50% and were taking heavy damage from two Blue attackers, who had somehow managed to climb up from the tunnel and were now determined to destroy their opponents.

Kai drew his gun and was about to help his friends when he noticed the third Blue attacker – who was stealing their flag. He had already picked it up and was leaving the platform.

Kai didn't hesitate. Instead of trying to shoot the enemy, he did the same as he had done earlier with the Yellow player: he used his bigger mass and strength and charged into the guy.

The player stumbled and lost balance but somehow managed not to fall. But not for long.

Summoning all the strength in his mechanical limbs, Kai kicked the hostile in the abdomen with full force – sending him flying over the edge and again using the uniqueness of the map to his advantage.

The flag still in his hand, the Blue fell from the platform to his certain death.

Kai grinned inwardly. It didn't matter that the flag

had fallen with the hostile. It would respawn in a couple of seconds, and as long as it was gone, no one could snatch it away from under their noses.

Kai turned around and opened fire at the two remaining attackers. Diving into cover, he hit one of them in the chest, causing critical damage.

Just then, Marco and Francois eliminated the third guy and turned their attention toward the remaining hostile. Even the best player couldn't withstand an attack from two sides for too long, and the opponent was down a few seconds later.

The Blue base flashed on Kai's mini-map, indicating that the Yellows had grabbed the blue flag. At least they weren't all going after Kai's team anymore, but this wasn't good. If they wanted to win, they had to stop the Yellow team from acquiring the blue flag, or…

Kai sprinted forward and jumped down the hatch into the tunnel. Francois and Marco jerked their heads in surprise.

"What are you doing?" he heard Marco's voice as he ran down the dark tunnel with all the speed this faction's cyborgs allowed.

"I'm getting the yellow flag for us," he called back. "Try to patch each other up and hold the base!"

"I'm back," Josh announced, as if it were an accomplishment.

"I'll be there in six seconds. Go Kai!" Claudia added.

The timer on Kai's HUD showed that they still had over four minutes to play, which meant that sitting it out wasn't an option. They had to score at least one more point to win this match. And Kai was determined to make this possible for his team. After all, they had proven that the much stronger Level Fours weren't as superior to them as everyone had thought at the beginning.

Kai speculated that the Yellows were trying to exploit the Blue team's temporary weakness and had gone all-in to steal their flag while half of the Blue team was still in the process of respawning.

A moment later, Kai arrived at the hatch under the Yellow base. This wasn't the time for scouting and sneaking up. Without slowing down, he jumped up and grabbed the ledge, then pulled himself up, while simultaneously activating his damage shield.

His whole body shook as he was hit by a bullet in his shoulder. But the shield absorbed most of the impact, leaving him with a minor wound and only 15% damage.

Lifting his head, he saw that, again, the Yellows had left only one man to defend the base. Most likely, more were about to respawn while the rest would show up on the bridge with the blue flag at any second.

Kai caught another bullet from the defender as he rushed toward him and then jumped him. This time, the Yellow was standing too far away from the ledge to be pushed off into the abyss. But the Red faction had a unique ability, and Kai was about to try it on an enemy player for the first time. Slow but strong, the Red characters had an Execute mode for times when the player managed to get into close combat with the enemy and grab them.

Kai managed it. Ignoring a fresh wound that brought him down to below 60% health, he grabbed his opponent and activated the unique Execute ability. His character wrapped his massive metal arms around the much smaller and lighter Yellow fighter, twisted his neck – and ripped his head clean off.

Completely ignoring the brutality of the attack, Kai dropped the dead enemy player and grabbed the flag.

Just when he was about to disappear down the tunnel, he saw the rest of the Yellow team approaching with the blue flag. Like aggravated wasps, they sped toward him. No doubt at least two of them would pursue him. Not only would they want to prevent him from scoring another point by any means possible, but as long as their own flag was gone, they couldn't score the flag they had stolen either. Which also made them vulnerable to a Blue counterattack, as they no doubt would try to retrieve their flag.

"I'm inbound," Kai said, highly focused, speeding down the tunnel. "They'll be on my ass at any second. Need backup."

"I'm back and on my way," Claudia said. "Josh, come with me."

"But wasn't the plan to defend our base first and foremost?" Francois objected. "You're leaving only Marco and me here. And we're not at full health."

"I'm pretty sure the Blues will try to get their flag back and leave us alone for now," Kai said, peeking over his shoulder. He could see a slight yellow glow at the end of the tunnel.

Damn, those guys are fast!

Following his intuition, Kai ducked and ran in zig-zags as much as the narrow space allowed. Bullets hit the wall to his right. Thankfully the cooldown for his shield was over, and he reactivated it.

He was just in time – a salvo hit his back, bringing his shield down to 45% and his health to 30%.

Not good!

"They're grilling me here!" he called out.

"We got you!" Claudia replied. "Almost there!"

He could see them on the mini-map, approaching swiftly, and a moment later, he could see a red glow advancing in the dark.

"Keep as far to your right as possible," she added. "I don't want to accidentally blow your head off!"

To make it more realistic – and more difficult – the game came with friendly fire by default. Unless the campaign was set to casual mode, which, of course, wasn't possible in PvP.

Kai did as he was told and pressed himself as closely as possible to the wall on his right. He didn't need to look back to know that the two hostiles were very close now. Apparently they had decided to get into melee range and finish him off with their swords.

Projectiles swooshed by him as his teammates opened fire on the hostiles. Still on the run, the Yellows returned the fire and Kai found himself in a storm of bullets. Another direct hit in the back brought his shield down and diminished his health to 18%. One more and he was toast.

"Keep running!" Claudia said. "We'll stall them!"

"Thanks!"

Both Claudia and Josh had stopped and were now crouching, their rifles pointing down the tunnel. Using the rest of his energy reserves, Kai leaped over them and continued running. He could see the light falling through the hatch now. He was almost there.

On the mini-map, Kai saw the Blue base glowing. The Blues had retrieved their flag.

Rushing forward, he watched as Claudia's and Josh's health bars diminished quickly.

Those Yellow guys must be really good players, much better in a stand-off.

He grabbed the ledge and pulled himself up and back into his base, where his remaining two teammates were waiting. A second later, he crossed the platform and planted the flag.

"Woohoo!" Marco cried out enthusiastically. "Eat this, Jason!"

"Good to see our selfless sacrifice wasn't for nothing," Claudia said with a falsely dramatic voice. "Careful, we managed to take out one, but two more are on their way toward the base."

The yellow flag blinked on the pedestal Kai had put it on, then disappeared. The HUD now showed two points for Kai's team and zero for the other two, with 90 seconds left to play.

We can do this!

He crouched next to the hatch, ready to shoot the two approaching Wasps to shreds, but they never showed up. Kai furrowed his brow in surprise. They must have turned around.

A moment later, he discovered why. The Yellow base glowed on the mini-map.

The Blues had first retrieved their flag and then waited until the yellow flag had respawned at its home base to instantly snatch it.

Clever move.

"How long till you guys respawn?" he asked Claudia and Josh.

"Ten secs," she replied.

Kai nodded, turning around and facing the edge of the platform. Out of the corner of his eye, he saw surprised looks from Marco and Francois as he sprinted toward the abyss.

"What the fuck, dude?" Marco asked with a disbelieving laugh as he saw Kai jumping.

Kai closed his eyes. He hated the fall.

It felt absolutely realistic and gave him the creeps. He could feel the wind hitting his face as gravity pulled his body down. He knew if he opened his eyes he would see the ground coming closer at an absolutely terrifying rate.

Finally, the drop stopped as everything resolved around him, and he found himself looking at the loading screen.

Respawn in 15 seconds.

"I figured I should reset instead of using up a healing spray," he explained to his team. "Yellows are busy chasing Blues who are busy getting the flag back to their base, so we should have a breather for at least 30 seconds before they come after us again."

"Good thinking," Claudia said. "Josh and I are back."

"I don't want to jinx it, but I think we're gonna win this!" Marco exclaimed, hardly able to hide how excited he was.

Kai watched his respawn timer creep down as if it was in slow motion. 10 seconds left. 70 seconds left in the match.

"Oh no!" Francois called out. "They're coming!"

"Who?"

7 seconds left.

"Blues!"

Kai swore inwardly, watching the timer that seemed to slow down from second to second. The Blue team knew that their only chance of winning was to get Kai's team's flag. But could they do it in less than 60 seconds?

"They're using Rush to advance quickly!" Marco said. "Take cover!"

"I'm almost back, five seconds!"

"Yellows are inbound, too!" Claudia reported.

"What? Where?"

"Through the tunnel."

"Are the cocksuckers working together?" Francois asked.

"That's what I thought earlier," Marco replied. "Impact!"

The last three seconds seemed like an eternity to Kai, then he was finally back.

Not one moment too early. He found his team under heavy attack from two sides. 60 seconds to play.

Francois was the first to fall. He was about to use a healing spray on Marco, crouching close to him, when a precise headshot struck him down. Marco was next. A hail of bullets first destroyed his damage shield then quickly depleted his health, which hadn't fully regenerated.

45 seconds.

Claudia and Josh were desperately trying to fend off the Yellow team, which was aggressively advancing through the tunnel.

"Throw a grenade at them!" Kai called out, taking cover behind the AC vent closest to the flag.

"We're out of grenades, smartass!" Claudia replied.

Kai remembered that he still had one in his quickslot. He couldn't hit the Yellows without endangering his teammates but he could hit the Blues, who were now advancing toward his position and the flag.

40 seconds.

He threw the grenade. It most likely wouldn't kill them, but it would hopefully stall their advance a bit. That was all they needed now. They just needed to hold the line for a little bit longer.

Kai watched the grenade fly at the hostiles. But before it could explode, one of the Blue players rushed forward and kicked it off the platform. The explosive detonated in mid-air, causing no damage to anyone.

35 seconds.

"Respawn in ten seconds," Marco reported.

"Seven for me," Francois said.

That wasn't quick enough.

Kai watched as one of the Yellows jumped Claudia and impaled her with his sword, and then his comrade finished her off. Josh would be next within seconds.

But Kai wasn't willing to give up. And he sure as hell wasn't willing to let them have the flag.

30 seconds.

Activating his damage shield, he jumped up. But instead of engaging the enemy, Kai grabbed their own flag – just before the leading Blue player could get his hands on it.

For a brief moment, the Blue player froze, puzzled by Kai's action. Then he and his friends opened fire. The flag in his hand, Kai leaped to the side, yet was hit anyway. Several bullets struck him, bringing his shield down to under 50% and his health to 60%.

Ignoring the damage, Kai charged forward to the edge of the platform. There he stopped, teetering over the abyss.

25 seconds.

He turned on his heel, facing his attackers. A helmet covered his face, making it impossible for his enemies to see his grin.

However, they could clearly see the only remaining member of the Red team lift his hand and flip them off.

More bullets hit Kai. With his health right down at 5%, he let himself fall from the ledge and into the seemingly bottomless abyss between the skyscrapers.

Falling, he saw how the frontrunner of the Blue team

reached the platform's edge and looked down at him. Kai only could imagine the rage and frustration the guy must feel.

They had lost and Kai's team had won. The Level One and Two noobs had beaten the far stronger and more experienced Level Four teams.

It would take about five seconds until Kai died from the fall and returned to the loading screen. That meant there would be less than 20 seconds of game time left. After that, the flag would need another five seconds to respawn back on the pedestal.

Which left the enemy players with less than 15 seconds to grab the flag and return to their base. Even using the Rush ability all the way, they needed at least 20 seconds from base to base. Kai knew that – they'd tested it in training.

He grinned broadly as his body dissolved and the game returned him to the loading screen.

The taste of victory was sweet.

***

The first thing Kai felt after opening his eyes back in reality was how exhausted his body felt. Almost as if he had just performed a sprint over a long distance. At the same time, he felt a rush of endorphins, of euphoria.

He wasn't the only one. The whole room was in turmoil as everyone was cheering and laughing happily.

Lex stepped toward him and smiled.

"That was quite impressive, kiddo," she said. "Who would have thought you'd be such a cunning, sneaky son of a bitch?"

Kai laughed. "Thanks, I guess."

She petted his cheek, and even though she played it cool, Kai could clearly see how excited and proud she was.

"Seems I was wrong about you," she said, pulling the cord from his head. "I thought you were a chicken."

Free from the restraint, Kai turned his head toward her

in surprise.

Lex chuckled. "What? Did you believe I didn't know how to use Google?"

She watched him as his face fell apart, then she laughed heartily, grabbing his cheek between her thumb and index finger and squeezed it playfully. "No worries, sweetie. Your secret is safe with me."

Kai nodded, perplexed. He couldn't possibly tell if she was serious or making fun of him.

But he didn't have time to think about that now. Now it was time to celebrate.

CHAPTER NINETEEN

"To the dream team! To us!" Marco said, lifting his glass.

"To us!"

They all lifted their glasses and clinked. Then they downed the booze.

Kai wasn't used to drinking strong alcohol. The first rounds of tequila had burned in his throat, but afterward the nerves there apparently had died off and he hardly felt more than a tickle when swallowing the clear liquid.

The whole group was in high spirits. This was easily the biggest accomplishment any of them had ever achieved in their lives.

"And all thanks to our hero of the day," Marco added, hitting Kai's shoulder cordially.

Kai wasn't used to being the center of attention either. At first, he had tried to play his role in the success down, but neither Marco nor the others would hear any of it.

"I still can't believe you did that," Claudia giggled, slightly tipsy. "Taking our own flag and jumping into the abyss holding it so the others couldn't get it... that was badass. And fucking brilliant!"

Her cheeks were flushed by the alcohol, and her brown eyes gleamed as she looked at him admiringly. For the first time, Kai noticed that she was actually cute.

Of course, she wasn't *her*. But no one was.

"It was," Josh agreed. "Man, I thought we were done, and then that... bam!"

He clapped his fist into his palm.

Kai smiled. Their victorious run in the tournament had catapulted Josh into Level Two and saved his career at Helltek, at least for now. Marco was only 150 progression points from Level Three now, and Claudia and Francois were both solid Level Twos.

Kai's progression had got a massive boost as well. Not only had he achieved victory for his team, but he had scored the most enemy kills in the whole low-level tournament.

Before logging out of VR, he had checked his progression status – as they all had – and was surprised and excited at how he found it.

Name: Kai
Level: 1
100/100
Team: 76B
Team Lead: Topher B.
Game: Behind Blue Eyes 3
Progression: 5341000
Available Features: Dev mode, Console, God mode

That was more than halfway to the next level – his ticket out of his miserable life circumstances and into a dream world.

Actually, he was living the dream already. Sometimes he wanted to pinch himself to be sure all of this was real.

They were sitting at a table in the main cafeteria, drinking and celebrating their success. Even Viktor had joined them, which had surprised everyone since he usually didn't like to socialize. He was sitting on the corner of the sofa next to Francois, drinking only water. He hadn't said anything all evening, instead studying Kai attentively with his pale blue eyes. He didn't even lower his gaze when Kai looked in his direction but kept staring at him. Usually, behavior like that would have made Kai feel uncomfortable, but today he didn't care. He was too happy about their success – or maybe too drunk already.

Outside it had turned dark and the glass building had been artfully illuminated, glowing like an oversized jewel in the night. The building was crawling with people who had all come together to celebrate the outcome of the tournaments. It was customary to have a big party after every such event, and everyone was eagerly anticipating the latest one.

Of course, food and drinks were free, and the rear part of the building had been transformed into a bar serving all kinds of cocktails, spirits, beers and wines. A live DJ was performing on the balcony that led to the second floor. It was accessible via a set of broad plexiglass stairs, but it was off-limits for low-level testers. There was no bouncer or anything like that, just an unwritten rule that upstairs was the place where the Level Tens and the management stayed among themselves on such occasions.

Whenever he felt unwatched, Kai let his eyes wander up the gallery in the hope of spotting *her*. It was foolish and he knew it, yet he couldn't help himself. Just catching a glimpse of her would make this day perfect.

No, actually, it wouldn't. If he was honest with himself, he wanted so much more than just that. Yet it would always remain a dream. Tipsy as he was, he better stop fantasizing about it right now, before his body betrayed him.

Besides, it was stupid, and he knew that very well, too. After all, the place was packed with attractive girls. Kai couldn't remember ever seeing so many in one place. It seemed that everyone at Helltek made a great effort to always look at their best. When Kai looked around the crowd gathered in the cafeteria, he was truly amazed. The place hadn't got enough seats for everyone and many were standing, gathered in groups, laughing, partying. Even the patio outside was packed, colorful string lights and torches creating a pleasant illumination for the party-goers.

Some of the testers were still wearing their gimp suits, but most had changed into their ordinary clothes. From simple jeans and nerdy t-shirts to dresses and high heels, every imaginable style was present.

Most looks were directed toward a group of girls sitting in a lounge only a few meters away from Kai and his friends: Maeve and her team. They had exchanged their gimp suits for mesh and fishnets and looked even more breathtaking than usual. When Kai looked in their direction, he locked eyes with Maeve for a second before quickly turning his attention elsewhere. This woman was making him nervous, and he couldn't tell if it was in a good or a bad way.

It was after 9 p.m., and usually Kai would be sitting on the train at this time, commuting to the depressing place he was forced to live if he wanted to make it home before curfew. But Marco had insisted he crash at his place, while Josh slept on Francois' sofa on such occasions.

Not for much longer though, as he had pointed out a hundred times that evening. Within the next couple of days, HR would assign him a place on the campus, now that he had reached Level Two.

"Let's have another round!" Marco suggested. "Josh, it's your turn to go and bring it."

Josh made a gesture with his hand, mimicking a military salute. Yet, tipsy as he was, it almost looked comical. Then he walked off.

"How about you guys take it a bit slower for now?" Topher asked, approaching the table, a beer in his hand and Lex in tow.

With her wild hair and unconventional clothes, she seemed to be the only woman in the room who didn't give a fuck about her looks. That didn't stop Topher from glancing at her longingly whenever he got a chance, which happened more frequently the more alcohol he consumed.

"You know you're not done for tonight yet, right? None of us is."

"Oh yeah, that..." Marco said, his face looking as if he had forgotten to study for an important test.

"Do we have to?" Claudia asked.

"Of course you do!" Topher replied with a smirk. "Don't tell me you're not excited!"

"Huh?" Kai asked. "What are you talking about?"

"Oh, they didn't tell you?"

"It was supposed to be a surprise," Marco said with a grin while Claudia gave Kai an innocent smile and a shrug.

"What?" he asked.

"As always after a tournament, there will be a small ceremony to present the winners to the crowd," Topher explained. "Nothing fancy. You'll just shake the CEO's hand."

"WHAT?"

Kai didn't like the idea of standing in front of all those people at all. Back in college, he'd been happy if he didn't suffer an anxiety attack when he had had to present a paper.

"Don't worry, you'll be fine. It'll only take a minute," Topher said, trying very hard not to show that he was excited himself. Today's success was also his success. He had reached Level Six and could expect a nice bonus.

On their way to the party, he had taken Kai to one side for a moment to have a word with him.

"I've never seen someone play like you today," he had said. "I take back what I said when you first started here."

"What do you mean?" Kai had asked.

"That you'll never make it to Level Ten. Nothing is impossible."

Now he stood there, tipsy himself and an expression of almost fatherly pride on his face, even though he was only a couple years older than Kai and the others.

A moment later, Josh returned with a small tray filled with tequila shots.

"How about you leave that here and bring a glass of water for everyone instead?" Topher told him.

"But—"

"Do it, dude," Marco said. "We drink the shots once everything is over."

Josh mumbled something and went back to the bar.

Kai agreed that it was better to stop drinking for now, although after what he just had heard, he badly needed another shot. His knees felt like jelly.

When Josh came back with the water, they all downed it under Topher's watch, then waited.

But they didn't have to wait for long as the spectacle began only a few minutes later.

***

The music stopped and Gregor Hell appeared on the stairs. He was accompanied by Rachel and some guys who smelled of management from miles away. They lurked behind Gregor respectfully, however, and let their boss have the show and everyone's full attention. Marie-Louise Hell was nowhere to be seen. Apparently she had better things to do than grace an event such as this with her presence.

Gregor grabbed a microphone, a winning yet slightly condescending smile on his aristocratic face.

"Good evening, Helltek family," he began. "You played a formidable tournament today, which was not only plenty of fun for everyone but helped us finish the multiplayer testing of *Behind Blue Eyes 3*. I'm very proud of you! Although I didn't have the time to watch all the matches, I have been told that many of you put on a remarkable performance. You demonstrated that you disrespect the impossible!"

He paused for a moment, letting the cheering and clapping that had followed his words calm down.

"As always, I will keep it short. After all, you want to enjoy the party and not listen to boring speeches. But, as it is the tradition at Helltek, I want to present the two winning teams to you because I believe they put on a remarkable performance today!"

First, he called the high-level winners to join him on the improvised stage. Topher, Kai and the others had already taken up a position close to the stairs, ready for when the CEO called for them.

Kai watched the high-level team approach Gregor. Four men and two women in their late twenties, all dressed in expensive-looking, extravagant designer clothes. They all were Level Nine and had a good chance of becoming Level Tens in the future. Kai had been told that this team almost always won, which is why they were taking the celebration with a slightly bored dignity.

While they stood there next to the CEO, who praised their accomplishments, Kai realized that there was something odd about the whole group. At first he couldn't put his finger on what it was – then he realized that it was their eyes.

Although all of them were good-looking and well-groomed, their eyes had something chilling about them. They appeared dull, emotionless, lifeless. Like the eyes of war veterans who had seen so much that, eventually, something inside them had broken and turned to stone.

None of them said anything. Gregor shook everyone's hand and dismissed them after speaking to them for a moment. But Kai didn't have time to wonder about the strange looks and behavior of the high-level testers, as it was now his team's turn to be presented.

"I'm very excited to come to today's sensation now," Gregor said. "As many of you have surely heard, for the first time in the history of our tournaments, a team consisting of Level Twos and Level Ones has won the low-level category. These guys have truly disrespected the impossible. Please, show them our appreciation!"

He waved his perfectly manicured hand, indicating that Kai's team should step forward. Kai's legs felt like they were frozen to the ground, but Topher gave him a gentle push and he followed the others onto the stairs, where the CEO shook everyone's hand while the whole room erupted in enthusiastic applause.

Gregor was saying something, but Kai didn't hear any of it.

When he walked up the stairs, his eyes drifted to the balcony. There was a strange tingling in the back of his head that made him lift his gaze and look up. He gasped for air as his eyes met *hers*.

Alice stood at the gallery, leaning against the rail. Her white hair appeared purplish against the festive illumination and the expression in her big blue eyes made his heart race. A slight smile appeared on her beautifully shaped lips and, for Kai, the world around him melted into insignificance.

A pain in his side brought him back to reality and he turned his head. Claudia had poked him between the ribs with her elbow and gave him an irritated glance. Kai realized that it was his turn to shake the CEO's hand, and he stepped forward.

"Exceptional accomplishment!" Gregor said with a perfect smile.

"Thank you, sir," Kai mumbled.

Making room for Claudia, whose turn was next, he glanced up at the balcony again.

She was still there, but she had turned her head to the side. Her attention was now with Raven, who was stood next to her, stroking a wisp of hair from her face with one hand and wrapping the other around her slender waist in a possessive gesture.

Kai felt a stitch in his heart, even though he knew only too well that it was idiotic to feel that way.

Then, as quickly as it had begun, the ceremony was over. The CEO finished talking, waved to the crowd, and disappeared up the stairs, followed by his lackeys. The DJ continued his gig, and everyone else went back into drinking and party mode.

Kai noticed that many people were looking at him and his crew as they walked back to their table. Topher stayed behind, talking with some people Kai didn't recognize.

"Phew," Marco said, letting himself fall into the cushions at the lounge table. "Now that that's over, back to drinking!"

He lifted his abandoned shot and held it toward the group. "To us! Because we're awesome!"

They emptied their glasses, and Francois went to the bar to get the next round.

The alcohol felt good in Kai's stomach, creating a warm sensation and drowning the butterflies that were still fluttering in there.

"Look who Topher's talking to," Claudia said with a grin.

"Ha!" Marco laughed.

"Who's that?" Kai asked, watching the team lead speaking with an athletic guy.

"That's Jason. The guy who's probably fuming because his precious team lost against us."

"Which one was Jason's team?"

"Blue for sure," Marco said. "Those guys were beasts, didn't you notice?"

"I still think they worked together against us," Claudia said. "Which is totally against the rules."

"But we can't prove it," Francois said, returning with the next round of shots. "So fuck it. And them assholes."

"And guess what? We won anyway," Marco said, grabbing another glass.

They drank, and suddenly Kai felt his head spinning. He leaned back on the cushions while Marco, Claudia and the others continued chatting, all in a great mood. Apparently, they were better acquainted with tequila than him. Only now Kai did notice that Viktor had left, leaving his spot empty, his full glass of water still standing there. But right then he didn't really care as the spinning got worse, threatening to turn his head upside down.

He decided that he better go and get some fresh air before he threw up on the table. If that happened, he would probably drop dead of shame.

"I'll be right back," he mumbled, but no one gave it much attention.

When he walked toward the door, he felt like he was on a ship. He could have sworn the floor was moving under his feet. Passing by them, he saw Topher and Lex standing at the bar. Their body language was that of two people who were about to rip each other's clothes off. Kai ignored them.

He couldn't ignore Maeve, however, who stepped into his path, a seductive look on her face. Slightly squinting her eyes and licking her upper lip with the tip of her tongue, she appeared like a cat that had chosen a mouse she wanted to devour for dinner.

"Hi," she said, her voice like liquid silk.

"Hi," he replied, trying to focus his eyes on her and stop seeing two Maeves… though that was alluring.

"You're Kai, right?" she said, her big, black eyes gazing into his. "I'm Maeve. But I'm sure you knew that already. Everyone does."

Massive black eyelashes fluttered as she winked at him while her gorgeous black lips curled up into a smile.

"I couldn't help but notice how you look at me, Kai."

Heat rushed into his cheeks as he stared at her. "No, I… um…"

Kai had no idea what to do. He felt intimidated by this woman who had got very close to him now, but he also couldn't help but stare at her. Admittedly, she was extremely sexy.

Being so drunk that he could hardly look straight didn't help much in the situation. Nevertheless, he also felt a hot feeling in his stomach, slowly spreading through his lower body, which he could only identify as arousal.

She chuckled, moving even closer, and an alluring scent hit his nose. A mix of lilac and patchouli that turned him on and made his tortured stomach revolt.

"You know," she whispered in his ear, "I should have you right here and now. I should eat you up. I like shy little virgins like you."

He stiffened as a wave of arousal and panic hit him at the same time. What should he do?

"I'm not... um, I mean..."

She snickered, her lips so close to his ear that he could feel her breath against his earlobe.

"But of course..."

Maeve moved her face toward his, and for a moment he thought she would kiss him.

"I think I'll wait until you sober up a little bit, though," she said. "No one should say Maeve's taking advantage of drunk, sweet boys. And you want to perform, don't you?"

Kai sucked in his breath as his eyes turned wide. Without him noticing, she had placed her hand between his legs and was squeezing him in a gentle yet demanding way.

Her seductive smile turned into a grin, and she seemed even more like a cat toying with her prey.

Then she backed off and let her fingers, with their long, black fingernails, caress his cheek. "I'll see you around, Kai."

Before he even noticed what was happening, she was gone and he was standing there, left behind in a state of frenzy, confused and aroused.

And drunk.

Now that Maeve was gone, he felt the world around him start spinning again, even quicker than before. The huge room had turned into a carousel.

Out. He needed to get out of there. Get some air.

Quickly, Kai moved toward the door. Fresh, cool night air hit his lungs as he stumbled outside.

Thank God, I've made it...

He kept moving, leaving the cafeteria and the party behind, and ventured into the dark, not knowing where he was going.

But instead of feeling better out in the fresh air, he soon felt even worse. Until, finally, the spinning overwhelmed him. Kai fell to his knees on the grass and threw up into a flower bed.

When he was done, he sat on the cold ground for a moment, trying to catch his breath, then looked up. He was alone. No one had seen him barfing into the artful flower installation. Thank goodness.

Kai hadn't even noticed that he had strayed so far away from the party. Now that he could see and think more clearly again, he noticed that he was in the middle of the campus, at least 300 feet away from the cafeteria. He could hear music and muffled voices coming from there and saw people moving around as the party was still in full swing. Not far away, he saw the pond with its wooden bridge, the water illuminated by hidden lamps. In the distance, the glass tower of Helltek HQ shone in the night.

Kai decided to simply sit there for a couple of minutes and catch his breath. He felt overwhelmed – and not just because of the alcohol.

The tournament, the victory, shaking the CEO's hand, and finally Maeve's incredibly blunt and straightforward way of going after him... It was all a lot to digest.

Was it so obvious that he was a virgin? Or was it simply not usual for men his age nowadays?

The encounter had stressed him out and turned him on. What was wrong with him? According to Marco, every male and half of the females in this company would gladly be in his position. Why did he turn into an idiot with the IQ of a cucumber when it came to women? It was pathetic.

He sighed and shook his head.

Slowly, the world stopped spinning and he could see clearly again. Although the sky was overcast and the moon was hiding behind thick clouds, the artificial illumination was enough to see the park in its full nocturnal beauty.

His ears had also stopped buzzing. He could hear nightly noises now, which he wasn't accustomed to at all, because there was no speck of green around the tenement canyons he called home. Soft wind blowing through the trees, crickets chirping, frogs croaking, someone crying...

Wait, what?

He lifted his head in surprise and listened.

Indeed, someone *was* crying softly, and close by.

Kai looked around, listening attentively. For a moment, the sobbing had stopped, and he almost thought he had imagined it. Then he heard it again. It was coming from the bridge over the pond, but he couldn't see the person because trees hindered his view.

Slowly, Kai got up. He still felt shaky when he made his first steps, but it quickly got better. He decided to take a look. Maybe someone needed help?

The soft sobbing continued as he moved closer, and he was certain now that it had to be a female who was crying. He walked past the trees and stepped onto the bridge.

Kai froze. He couldn't believe his eyes. Had he fallen asleep? It couldn't be her. Impossible.

Yet he was awake, and he would have recognized the waist-long white hair and slender figure anywhere.

It was Alice who was standing there on the bridge, crying.

Seeing her like this felt like a spike in his heart. What reason could she have to stand there, alone, crying? She of all people?

The surprise was replaced by a deep feeling of tenderness. He wished for nothing more but to walk up to her and hold her, to make her tears stop.

Instead, he stood there for who knew how long, silently watching her. Like a creep.

After a moment, she must have heard or sensed something as she stopped sobbing and lifted her head.

Alice turned and looked at him. The illumination reflected by the lake hit her face and made it appear unearthly beautiful. He stared at her.

"I'm sorry," he stuttered like a complete idiot. "I didn't want to scare you... I... I just heard you and..."

She smiled, wiping away tears with the back of her hand. "You didn't scare me. It takes more than that."

"Um, ok... Are you alright?"

She nodded and put on a fake smile, trying to cover up how she felt. It was a good act. If Kai hadn't seen her crying only a minute ago, he totally would have bought it.

Seeing her vulnerable like this made his feelings for her outright explode. So far, he had mostly admired her, her beauty, her courage, her skills. She had almost seemed like a superhero to him. Now, he realized that she was a human being like everyone else. The urge to step closer and comfort her became almost overwhelming.

"I'm fine," she said. "That was nothing."

Kai understood. He nodded, slowly coming closer.

"I won't tell anyone what I saw. Actually, I didn't see or hear anything at all."

She smiled, and this time it was a genuine one.

"Thank you, Kai."

His heart almost jumped out of his chest. She remembered who he was! She remembered his name!

It took him all his self-control not to show how excited this little thing made him. She was the supernova, and he was a nobody. The lowest member in the food chain. He would never have believed she'd even remember their encounter in the cafeteria, let alone that she'd remember his name.

Yet she must still have seen something in his face as her smile turned warm.

"I saw you in the tournament today. It was pretty impressive."

His jaw dropped, but he couldn't help it. Staring at her, he wondered if he had heard right or if she was maybe making fun of him.

But then he looked into her face and saw genuine kindness there. Could it be that she liked him? Well, surely not like that... or maybe a little bit?

Then he realized that he must look like a complete dork, staring at her with an open mouth and visibly drunk. Quickly, he got a grip on himself. At least, as much as he could.

"You... did? Really?"

She chuckled, and the sound of it shot happiness through his body like a bolt of electricity. "Of course. Why wouldn't I have?"

He didn't have an answer to that.

"I like watching the finals when time allows it," she continued. "It feels like an eternity since I was allowed to participate for the last time. You were the best player on the field."

Kai was grateful for the darkness that covered up his blushes as he knew that his cheeks had turned fire-red. Her acknowledging him was almost too much for him to handle. The whole situation felt like a dream. If it was, he hoped he'd never wake up from it.

"Thank you," he finally said, breaking the silence. "I wish I could see you in action sometime. You're so badass."

"But you already have, don't you remember?"

Again, he stared at her. How could she know it had been him, back in the spider liar in *TSOTA*? His avatar looked nothing like him.

"I do," he said. "You saved my life. I think."

She nodded, turning serious. "Most likely, I did."

"Thank you," he repeated, at a loss for words.

He hadn't even noticed that he had come closer to her. She towered a few inches over him, and it wasn't because she was wearing high heels. Her expensive-looking black-and-white boots were flats.

Alice shrugged. "It's my job. No need to thank me."

"You're amazing," he blurted out, and he could have slapped himself a second later. Was he insane? Or was it the alcohol speaking?

A sweet smile appeared on her face that made her look

like a young girl. Kai wasn't sure how old she was, but he assumed she was a couple of years older than him, maybe in her late twenties. It didn't matter to him anyway.

"Thank you," she said. "But things aren't always as they seem, you know?"

"If you need someone to talk to…" Kai said, and again he wondered about himself.

She turned her head away from him and stared out at the water, frowning. "Sometimes, I just think I can't take it anymore."

"What?" He leaned against the rail next to her, and all of a sudden there was an almost tangible intimacy between them. As if they had known each other forever.

Alice sighed. "I can't talk about it, Kai. There's so much no one is allowed to know… Sometimes, all I want is to scream into the void. And there's loss. So much loss…"

"You could quit," he suggested. "You probably have more money than you could spend in a lifetime."

She turned her head and looked at him again. At that moment, the moon appeared from behind a cloud where it had been hiding all night long. It filled everything with a silver light that made the whole situation appear even more surreal than before.

"It's not that easy," she said with sadness in her voice. Her eyes shone at him in the silver light, and so did her hair.

Suddenly, Kai had the crazy idea to lean forward and kiss her. It seemed like the most natural thing to do.

They looked into each other's eyes for a moment.

Then their bubble got pierced violently.

"Alice?" a male voice said from behind them. "There you are."

She flinched as she heard it, then turned away from Kai and toward the speaker. Her body language changed completely as she moved. She straightened up and put on a bright smile.

"Raven," she said.

He approached in a slow, confident way. The tight black-silver clothes showed an athletic yet slim body. His silky shirt was sleeveless and revealed that his arms were tattooed from wrists to shoulders.

"I was wondering where you went," Raven said, studying Kai from head to toe in a condescending way.

He was a head taller than Kai. His long, black hair framed a slim, perfectly symmetrical face. Up close, he seemed even more like an anime character. Kai immediately felt intimidated by his presence.

"I needed some fresh air," Alice said, walking up to Raven. She kissed him, and he placed his hand on her hip.

"Have you met Kai?" she asked.

"I don't think I have," Raven answered. His narrow eyes studied Kai in the same way someone studies a bothersome insect, wondering if he should simply crush it under his heel or rip out its legs one by one first.

"Hi," Kai said, feeling increasingly uncomfortable.

Finally, Raven turned his attention away from Kai and toward Alice. He brushed a wisp of hair from her face before he kissed her forehead.

Something about this guy gave Kai the creeps. He couldn't say what it was, but even if the situation weren't so awkward, he would have felt uncomfortable in his presence. Not to mention the fact that seeing him kissing Alice felt like a fiery dagger in Kai's heart.

"Let's go inside," Raven said, taking Alice's hand.

"Bye, Kai," she said. "Again, congrats on your success in the tournament."

"Bye." His voice was hardly more than a whisper as the incredibly beautiful couple walked off.

Seeing them together, Kai wondered how he could ever have been so stupid and dreamed of landing a girl like her. He sighed.

After moving a few feet away, Raven turned his head one more time and looked back at Kai. His face didn't show any particular expression. It was cool and motionless. Yet Kai understood the non-verbal communication.

Keep away from my girl, or else.

Kai swallowed. He didn't want to find out what 'or else' could mean with a guy like that.

***

When Kai returned to the cafeteria, the party was still going, though many people had already left. Luckily, his friends were still there, sitting at the same table, with a lot more empty shot glasses piled up on the table between them. Kai's stomach cramped when he saw the empty tequila glasses. How was it possible that they could take so much more than him?

"Hey, look who's here!" Marco greeted him, spreading his arms. "We were starting to worry Maeve had sacrificed you to Cthulhu or something."

"Huh?" Kai blinked, confused.

Everyone at the table stared at him, grinning. It took Kai a moment to realize one of them must have seen him talking to Maeve.

"Um, no…" he stammered. "I wasn't…"

"Riiight," Marco said, stretching the word to demonstrate that he thought Kai was bullshitting them. To make it even clearer, he pulled down the lid of his left eye with his index finger.

Kai sighed and let himself drop next to Claudia. She wrinkled her nose.

"Did you barf?"

"No, Cthulhu did," he replied resignedly.

Claudia burst out laughing, and the others joined in.

"Ok, folks," she said after a moment. "This was lovely, but I need to hit the sack."

"So do I," Francois said, yawning.

"We all should," Marco agreed and rose from his seat.

"After all, we have to work tomorrow."

***

Kai was stunned for a moment after they entered Marco's apartment on the campus. The lights sprang on automatically as soon as Marco opened the door, and a female computer voice, similar to Kai's Alessia, greeted them.

"Good evening, Marco. I hope you had a pleasant night. Congratulations on your success."

"Thanks, babe," Marco said nonchalantly with a wave of his hand. Then he noticed Kai looking at him and laughed. "What? She's the closest I've ever come to a girlfriend. Not everyone is a Casanova like you."

Before Kai could protest, Marco playfully poked him with his elbow and walked on.

"Welcome, Kai," 'Babe' said, and after a short moment of surprise, Kai decided not to wonder how she knew who he was. Most likely all systems at Helltek were connected somehow.

He followed Marco through the hall and into the main area of the apartment. It consisted of a spacious living area and a small kitchen. On one side, another hall led to more rooms and bathrooms.

"Whoa," Kai said, looking around.

"Pretty cool, huh?" Marco agreed. He walked to the fridge and grabbed two bottles of water, then handed one to Kai.

"Here," he said. "Figured you need this. I also have aspirin and other shit."

"This place is easily bigger than where I live now. And I have to share it with four other people," Kai said.

"I know," Marco said, throwing himself into an armchair. "It was the same for me when I moved here. I could hardly believe it. It comes fully furnished. I didn't have to buy anything. And this is one of the small ones with a view of the opposite building. You should see one of the higher-level ones.

It'll blow your freaking mind!"

"Why?" Kai asked, sitting down on the sofa. "Why is Helltek so generous?"

"Because they want to motivate us to be the best we can. They only recruit exceptional people, following the quality not quantity mantra. Wanna know why?"

Kai nodded, drinking his water. It felt good in his tortured stomach.

"Because we explore the unknown. You already noticed that VR isn't what people are told it is. If Helltek didn't recruit only exceptional people, their testers would drop like flies. They mean it when they say it's a high-risk job. And it's the reason they pay us so well. So the best people stay."

Kai thought about what Alice had said earlier. That quitting wasn't that easy. He wondered if there was more to it.

"How many people have you seen die or get seriously injured?"

"Personally, not so many, but I've only been here a year and a half. We don't get official numbers either, but rumors are that a severe incident happens every week. At least once."

"Shit…"

Kai remembered the horrifying scene he had witnessed at the sickbay and shuddered.

"Yeah." Marco nodded grimly, then he decided to change the subject. "So, what about you and Maeve?"

Kai sighed. "Nothing, really."

"Come on! We all saw you talking to her. She looked as if she wanted to fuck you on the spot. Lucky bastard! Then you were gone for quite a while. So did you…"

He made a gesture with his hands, clapping his fist against his palm, then chuckled. "Or rather, she you?"

"No!"

"Seriously?"

"Seriously. She was very… blunt. But then decided that I was too drunk and let me go."

"Damn," Marco said. "It means she'll get back to you

eventually. Someone's gonna get laid!"

Kai said nothing. He didn't want to admit that Maeve scared him. Besides, after his encounter with Alice, he wasn't interested in touching any other woman. Even though he knew that was stupid.

"So, where did you disappear to then?"

"I threw up in a flowerbed," Kai said with a shrug.

Marco looked at him for a second, then started shaking with laughter.

For a moment, Kai wondered if he should tell him about his encounter with Alice, but then he decided otherwise. Somehow, he felt that what they had shared was a very private thing. As much as he liked Marco, he wasn't sure that he'd understand.

"Ok," Marco said after he'd finished both laughing and his water. "I need to get some sleep. And you should, too."

He left the room for a moment, then returned with a pillow and a blanket. "Make yourself comfortable. The bathroom is the first door on the left."

When the light was out and Kai lay on the sofa, all he could think about was the conversation with Alice. He smiled, remembering every detail. In his fantasy, her prick of a boyfriend didn't show up and destroy the moment, however. Instead, he imagined how he kissed her.

It would never happen, and he knew it. Raven had clearly shown him that she was his girl and that he didn't tolerate a rival. The guy appeared to be ruthless, and Kai certainly wouldn't want to mess with someone like that. He wondered why good people so often ended up with awful partners. But even if it weren't so in Alice's case, it was very doubtful that she could ever like him.

He sighed and imagined kissing her again before he fell asleep.

CHAPTER TWENTY

The next morning, Kai woke up with an erection. He quickly disappeared into the bathroom for a cold shower before Marco could notice anything and make fun of him.

The shower was nothing like the old, broken thing in the smelly bathroom in his apartment but tasteful and ultra-modern. He could set the exact temperature on a display. When he was done, he knew that this was a life he wanted badly. If only he could gain the next 500 progression points quickly. Too bad the next tournament was three months away, but he swore to himself that he'd use it for a level up.

He and Marco grabbed a quick veggie bagel in the cafeteria, downed it with some coffee, and then went to work.

Topher and Lex were already there and acted as if they hadn't stuck their tongues down each other's throats the night before – and who knew what else. The others arrived shortly after. Everyone was tired and hungover, but Kai was told that it was ok. No one expected them to work at full capacity the day after a tournament. They would only test some routine stuff with a minimum level of risk.

The rest of the week went by quickly and without any incident. When Kai sat on the train home on Friday night, he almost wished he could work over the weekend. His job, although risky, was so much better than anything he could do in his free time in his shitty apartment. Besides, it was only when he was around the campus that he got a chance to catch a glimpse of *her*.

Back home, he remembered that he had promised to join Stan in *TSOSA* that weekend and go on a dragon hunt with the guild. Well, it would at least keep him occupied.

He had no idea that he would get much more than he had bargained for.

***

Stan looked over the moon at seeing Kai online the next day. The Dark Elf girl teleported into his estate, charged up to him and embraced him into a hug.

"So good to see you, mate! I was worried something might have happened to you… or maybe that we're not good enough for you anymore."

"What?" Kai was genuinely surprised. "Why would you think so? You should know me better than that."

"Yeah, I know… sorry," Stan said.

It was only then that he noticed the change in Kai.

Stan straightened up and looked at his friend in surprise. "You got yourself a new avatar."

Kai nodded. "Like it?"

He had woken up early today, at the same time as he usually would to go to work. Not sure what to do with himself, he had logged into the game and decided to create a new appearance for himself. Following what everyone at Helltek did and the example of his avatar there, he designed an appearance based on his true self.

No longer an overly tall and muscular Viking, Kai's new avatar looked very much like him – just an idealized version, of course.

"You look a bit like Keanu Reeves when he was young. Not bad," his friend said slowly, studying him. "Why did you do it?"

"Not sure," Kai replied. "I guess I wanted to look similar to my avatar at Helltek. I spend so much time in his skin now.

It somehow felt right."

"Is this how you look IRL?"

Kai laughed. "I wish. It's an idealized version of me."

Stan shrugged. "That's what VR is for, isn't it? If we wanted to look like our ugly asses, we might as well stay in reality."

Kai nodded, yet his thoughts drifted to Alice, who, in his opinion, looked even better in real life than her avatar did.

"So, are you ready for the big hunt, mate?" Stan asked, yanking Kai out of his daydream.

"Sure am!"

"Good! As it starts in thirty minutes and everyone in the guild expects you to be there. They think you're a hero, you know?"

Kai laughed. "Why would they think so... wait, did you tell them I'm with the Cyber Squad now?"

The Dark Elf gracefully jumped onto the battlement and gave Kai an innocent shrug.

"Maybe..." He paused. "Nothing wrong with that, eh? Why shouldn't they know, I figured. It's not like it's a secret or anything."

"I guess so," Kai said.

"LifeSupport in particular was very interested when she found out."

"Really? Why?"

"No clue. Maybe she wants to apply too? You know what an excellent player she is. And she's such a better guild leader than Red, I'm telling you. Literally everyone in the guild will be there today! It's gonna be the biggest event we've ever had. We'll burn through this dragon wanker like nothing. Ah, I can't wait for the loot!"

As the two friends were sharing their excitement about the upcoming guild event, they paid Kai's NPC wife no attention at all.

Freya stood in the courtyard, her blonde hair flowing in the wind, her unnaturally pretty eyes narrowed. She watched the two in silence.

Watching and listening. As she always did.

***

"How's the new DLC?" Kai asked as they teleported into the area.

"It only dropped Thursday night, so I haven't played it much yet. But so far it looks awesome. A couple of new monsters, two new dungeons, and, of course, the dragons."

"Have you seen one?"

"Yeah, they're flying around the map and come down on you and eat you at any time. Not a pleasant experience."

Kai laughed. "Did you manage to be eaten already? Within less than 24 hours?"

"Shut up…"

Kai laughed more as they materialized into the teleport point of the new area. As the landscape unfolded in front of him, he fell silent, however. This was absolutely breathtaking!

The level designers had outdone themselves in creating a fantastic world full of mountains, ravines, canyons – and active volcanos. The scene was dimmed in reddish light, emanating from the glowing lava slowly flowing down the slopes and reflected by the foggy sky. The music took on a dramatic and foreboding tone, indicating that this was dangerous territory.

In fact, the new area was for high-level players only. It wasn't that no one below level 300 was allowed to enter it. The game was an open world with no set boundaries. But low-level players wouldn't survive an encounter with any creature roaming these plains, even if it was only a lava rat.

Looking around, Kai felt excited. "This is gorgeous!"

"Wait until you see the dragons! I've never seen a dragon so well animated!"

"Did you acknowledge that before or after it ate you alive?"

"Wanker."

Stan made a fake pouting face and Kai laughed. As they approached a huge group of people, he noticed the slight smell of burned wood and glowing coal in the air. Such little details made an atmosphere even more believable. Looking around, he wondered if the DLC had come with many glitches. *Known shippable*, as he now knew, was the developer's code phrase for screwing players up right after release. Although he also knew that it could only be minor stuff, otherwise a game wouldn't pass the quality control checks. He made a mental note to ask Topher if *TSOTA* was tested by Helltek. If so, maybe he could apply for testing it once he reached a higher level. On the other hand, he really liked his teammates and knew that he could consider himself lucky that they welcomed him so warmly in their midst. He hoped he would stay part of this team for as long as possible.

Easily two dozen players had come together on a plateau overlooking a canyon filled with lava. Kai recognized the gamer tags of most of them. It was his old guild, which had apparently gained some new members during his absence to compensate for the ones who had 'left'.

Before teleporting here, Kai had asked Stan about Red, Cloudgirl and the others who had been injured by the Guardian almost three weeks ago. Apparently no one had heard anything about any of them ever since – and no one seemed to care.

Kai found that shocking. But he also knew more than the ordinary players out there. They didn't know how bad it could get in VR. In his short time at Helltek, he had learned enough to have nightmares or to never want to enter VR again. And yet, here he was.

However, he was certain that the accident with the Guardian was an isolated incident. The chances that something like that would happen again in the same game were minimal. And surely the devs had done everything to improve the safety in the game. After all, dead people were bad for business.

Thinking everything through in detail, he was convinced that the people affected by the glitch the other day were either dead or gravely injured. Again, he wondered if he could open the console in this game if he wanted.

Theoretically, it should be possible, right?

"Hey, Kai," LifeSupport said, greeting him in the calm assertive way that was typical for her. "Glad you could join us."

"I wouldn't have wanted to miss it," he replied.

Her sorceress avatar was dressed in the usual white-glowing robes, and the snake head that decorated her staff moved as if it were alive.

She smiled. "And I would have hated to do this without you, Kai. All of us owe you so much. You deserve to be part of this event. It will be... unforgettable."

LifeSupport4You has sent you a group invite. Accept? Y/N

Kai accepted and found himself in a group of twelve, which included LifeSupport and Stan. The rest of the guild had grouped up in two more parties.

Instead of the usual group chat channel, Kai was automatically connected to the guild channel. That way, they could all communicate and coordinate the attack.

"Ok, folks," LifeSupport said. "Mount up and let's go!"

Kai summoned his mount. Today he had picked a flame elemental to fit the landscape. It was a premium item he had bought a while back and never used. But today's endeavor was the perfect occasion to show it off. Most mounts were premium items players had to buy for real money. Such items were similar to when people showed off designer labels on their clothes in real life.

Kai realized that his first paycheck from Helltek was coming up and wondered what he should do with the money. His income wasn't enough to move into a better apartment, so he would probably spend it on some more fashionable real-life clothes and some premium items for the game. It wasn't worth saving up for a new place anyway since his plan was to reach Level Two as soon as possible and leave his current shithole for a better and more exciting life on the Helltek campus.

The whole army rode through breathtaking canyons, over steep slopes and down narrow mountain paths along rivers of glowing lava. Kai could feel the heat coming from those red-glowing fire-rivers. Unless you played as a Dark Elf, who had 100% fire resistance by default as a race, falling into those lava streams would result in a massive amount of damage and certain death if the player wasn't able to escape the flaming trap within a few seconds.

"Are we going to discuss mechanics?" someone in the guild chat asked.

"There's not much to discuss," LifeSupport said calmly. "We go in and kill it."

"Bloody heck, yeah!" Stan said.

"We have two tanks in each party, which makes six in total. Two will take on the dragon, and the rest will focus on the adds. The six healers, including myself, will spread out and keep everyone alive, and the DPSs do what DPSs do best," Life said as they closed in on a mountain top surrounded by lava. "The area is brand new, and not many people have had much experience with those dragons yet. The one we're taking on is the world boss in this region, the strongest dragon in the entire game – and, so far, unbeaten."

Some people murmured with excitement. This was a dream for every guild. To be the first ones to accomplish something like this.

"I would assume he has a similar mechanic to all dragons in the game. He flies up, he lands, smashing everyone who is in proximity, he uses his wings to create wind that will kick you off your feet, and, of course, he spews fire."

"Piece of cake," Stan said, and someone in the group laughed nervously.

It was known that dragons were the toughest enemies the game had to offer. Even the smaller, low-level ones were extremely difficult to kill, and the one they were about to challenge was the king of dragons. What made it even more difficult was the fact that the next spawn point was a several-minute ride away. If someone fell, their comrades needed to help them up before the revive window timer ran out.

Entering challenge area. Maximum player capacity: 36

That was the right amount for three full parties and was the exact number Kai's guild had brought along. Looking at the stats of the people in his group, Kai saw that LifeSupport had summoned only the best players the guild had to offer, if not the best the game had to offer. The lowest level was 588, and Kai knew the guy. He was an excellent tank who had put a lot of time and money into his gear.

They were as prepared for the challenge as anyone ever could be.

Kai felt excitement and anticipation building in his stomach. For the first time in days, he forgot about Alice.

The guild entered the plateau, which was set up like an arena, with cliffs on one side and a glowing lava stream on the other. And, in the middle, waited the 'challenge'.

"Fuck me sideways..." Stan whispered next to Kai. "What is this? Godzilla?"

The comparison was legit. As they closed in, the dragon, who was sleeping, first jerked his head up, opening two huge, red-glowing, malicious eyes. Then he slowly rose to his full height, revealing that he had the size of a four-story building.

A tag appeared above his head, introducing the monster.

Baldurian
Dragon King
10000000/10000000

Its body was pitch black and covered in shiny scales that protected Baldurian from his head to the tip of his long, muscular tail, which ended in a claw and was covered with spikes, each the size of a grown man. Stretching himself, the Dragon King revealed massive wings.

Kai grinned. "Godzilla can't fly. This asshole can."

"Health of ten mill? They can't be bloody serious," Stan groaned.

It would take a long time to take the monster down, even for a team of 36 high-level players.

Kai couldn't wait for the battle to start. It was going to be epic.

But then he stiffened in his saddle.

Out of the corner of his eye, he had seen movement. If that was what he thought it was...

No, no... It couldn't be. What are the chances? Unless...

Kai turned his head to his left sharply and his eyes widened.

"Shit..." he murmured.

The cliffs confining the arena on the left side were glitched. Not just a little bit but massively.

The surface flickered, showing pixels and grid beams for fractions of a second. Like a wave spreading, the phenomenon moved along the whole cliff from one end to the other. The clouds in the sky froze like in a still image as the flickering wave reached the dragon. Everything happened so fast that the others hadn't even noticed something was off. And if they had, they didn't think anything of it.

But Kai had seen it.

This was a glitch of massive proportions. It was impossible for something like that to have passed QA. Someone was tampering with the code.

"Retreat!" Kai shouted, trying to make his voice sound steady and not show the panic he felt. "Turn around and leave the area!"

Several people turned toward him in surprise.

"Huh? What are you talking about? Why?" someone asked.

Kai didn't have time to explain. "RUN! Now!!"

But it was too late.

The Dragon King rose up on his back legs and began flapping his gigantic wings, which were the size of yacht sails.

The effect was immediate. Wind of the strength and speed of a hurricane hit the players and threw them all off their mounts. Before anyone realized what was going on, the dragon opened his gigantic maw and let out a bone-shaking roar. It was so loud that even the rocks in the cliffs trembled. A second later, avalanches cascaded down everywhere – and the biggest one blocked the ravine that was the only exit from the arena.

Kai remembered what his teammates at Cyber Squad had said when he had told them the story of how the incident with the giant spider went down: that it had been no coincidence, no simple glitch caused by a game engine or code malfunction. It had been a deliberate attack.

There's some scary shit out there, he heard Marco's voice repeat in his head.

Kai jumped up and looked around. There had to be something he could do!

The spider had been bad, but this winged monster would grill everyone within seconds before he devoured them. And if their bodies perceived it as real... Kai felt his knees go weak, imagining how it would feel when those razor-sharp teeth the size of pikes crunched his bones.

Or anyone's.

All 36 people would die.

He remembered Topher's exact words on his first day at Helltek:

By entering our system earlier, the console clearance has been added to your neuro-plant automatically. It's a tiny but highly encrypted piece of code. Every game will automatically recognize this sequence and give you console access.

It had been coded into his neuro-plant. And his neuro-plant was always the same, no matter if he entered VR from a pod at Helltek or when jacking in from home. Right?

There was only one way, and he had to try it. It was now or never.

OPEN CONSOLE

He thought the command in the exact same way as Topher had taught him.

And…

It worked!

Kai could hardly believe what was happening when he saw how his game HUD disappeared to be replaced by the tester HUD and the console.

He could have cheered in happiness, but he knew he had to focus now. Opening the console meant nothing in itself.

He started typing into the console, using the virtual keyboard that had automatically appeared at his fingers.

>*tester_emegency_team76B.*

That was an emergency code that every tester at Helltek could use if the shit really hit the fan. He wasn't on the Helltek servers, so he had no idea if it would actually work or not, but it was worth a try. Now the next step.

>*enter_dev_mode*

Kai blinked in surprise.

He had been hoping that that would work, but when it actually did, he was stunned for a second. This was still the same world, the same game. Yet at the same time, it wasn't.

Slowly, he turned around, taking everything in with awe. The world around him had frozen. Other players, the dragon, the sky, the lava streams. It almost felt as if he was standing in the midst of a 3D painting.

Next to him, he saw Stan, frozen in time, as well as the rest of the crew, who had been scattered around the whole arena after the storm the dragon had unleashed with his wings. Baldurian himself stood in the center of the place on all fours. His long neck and tail were stretched out straight, and so were his wings at his sides. Clearly this was a T-pose for non-humanoid NPCs.

He was surrounded by dozens of smaller NPCs, some of which looked like wyverns, some like lizards, and others like humanoid lizardmen. They all were lined up in T-poses like toy soldiers. None of them had been visible when Kai entered the console, so he assumed that they would be spawned eventually. But they were already present in the sandbox, of course, including their pathfinding and the trigger points.

It was only now that Kai noticed that Stan and the others weren't actually frozen. They still moved, yet in super-slow-motion. He could see Stan's eyes blink. His beautiful elven face frowning.

This was absolutely incredible!

But then he remembered why he was here in the first place. Everyone was in danger, including him. Whatever was happening, he had to stop it. But how the hell could he do that?

He remembered the 'magic' the Alpha team was capable of only too well. But he was only a Level One tester. He could open the console and send a bug ticket.

Actually, why not?

He opened the bug ticket editor and typed in a message using his thoughts.

Game engine compromised. Potential hack. Request immediate support.

A second later, he had sent it on its way with the highest priority. Hopefully it would reach the game studio. Or Helltek… or anyone who could fix this mess!

Kai wondered what his friends were seeing now. Was the game continuing for them? Or were they, too, seeing the dragon in T-pose? Somehow he felt like a traveler in another dimension – or a ghost.

Out of the corner of his eye, he spotted something that ripped him out of his thoughts violently.

Something was moving.

He spun around and realized that he wasn't alone in the sandbox. Somebody else was here. Somebody he hadn't expected at all.

She stood at the other side of the arena, looking at him. Her arms crossed. Then she slowly moved toward him.

"Smart boy to enter the console," she said in her typically calm but now also condescending voice. "But I expected nothing less from you, Kai."

He stared at her in disbelief.

"Life... *You* did this?"

LifeSupport spread her arms, coming closer.

"I did. Do you like it?"

He could now see her face clearly as she walked past the lizard toy soldier army. Although it was the same avatar as she always used, he hardly recognized her. Her beautiful features were contorted into a gleeful, malicious grin.

"No!" he shouted angrily. "I don't! Why the hell would you do this?"

"That's none of your concern, little one. You'll be dead in a moment. And so will everyone else trapped here."

"You want to kill all these people? What have they done to you?"

Kai was horrified, yet somewhere deep inside, a cool, calculated voice was telling him to stall her until help arrived.

Slowly, he approached her until they met in front of the T-posed dragon.

She shrugged. "Nothing. Wrong place at the wrong time, I guess. They'll be a wonderful demonstration subject though."

"You were responsible for the spider incident too…"

"Smart boy. You're almost too valuable to be sacrificed here… but it is what it is."

"Why?" Kai asked again, and it wasn't just a stalling tactic. He couldn't wrap his head around what was happening here.

"The people I represent have their reasons," she replied as a virtual keyboard appeared at her fingertips, and they began typing with inhuman speed.

"You're a hacker," Kai said.

"Clueless dimwits might call me so," she said. "But I'm so much more than that."

A greenish, glowing beam expanded from her keyboard and formed a rectangular shape. Then the whole construct sank to the ground. The surface textures disappeared where it made contact with the terrain, creating something like an oversized trap door – leading into nowhere. It reminded Kai of the clipping glitch he had fallen into the other day. But the darkness inside this one appeared way more horrifying.

Satisfied with her work, LifeSupport turned her attention back to Kai.

"It was lovely chatting with you, Kai," she said with a smirk. "I wish we could spend more quality time together, but life isn't always what we wish for, right? I hope you enjoy the barbecue as you're going to be the main course."

Kai wanted to reply with something, but he didn't get the chance.

Again, her fingers flew over the keyboard with incredible speed.

>exit_dev_mode
>terminate_dev_mode_access

Dev_Mode UNAVAILABLE

Kai was back in the game.

She had not only kicked him out of the console, but she had also terminated his sandbox access! How in the world was that possible?!

Everything around him was in turmoil.

He heard screams and the crackling sound of fire. An unpleasant smell of charred flesh was in the air.

The realization struck him like lightning. He hadn't stopped the world when entering the console. That, of course, wasn't possible. By entering the sandbox, he had basically entered a different layer of the game, whereas the main game kept rolling unhindered. Of course, anything else would have been impossible in an MMORPG.

But Kai didn't have time to contemplate that now.

He saw a shadow moving in his peripheral vision. Following his instinct, he roll-dodged away, lightning-fast.

Not one second too soon. A gigantic paw stomped on the ground exactly where he had been standing with the intention of turning him into pulp. Feeling the ground vibrate under the impact, he jumped back to his feet.

That was close!

Kai lifted his head and stared directly into the flaming eyes of the Dragon King, who had apparently decided to eat him first.

Baldurian opened his maw, showing two rows of gigantic teeth. And something else. Fire.

Coming up his throat, it would burst out at any second and burn Kai to a crisp.

But to his own surprise, he wasn't scared. His mind worked faster and in a more focused way than ever before in his life.

OPEN CONSOLE
>enter_god_mode

Kai performed this action faster than he thought he ever could. It was his tester's 'life insurance', as Topher had called it – and it worked! The hacker hadn't been able to disable that one.

Within the blink of an eye, the dragon unleashed his devastating fire breath upon Kai. A massive cloud of fire shot out of the dragon's maw.

Kai closed his eyes.

But nothing happened!

Opening one eye, he saw that he was surrounded by a massive fireball, but the flames couldn't touch him. They were repelled by invisible boundaries. It wasn't like a damage shield but more like an invisible sphere that surrounded him, preventing any harm from reaching him.

After a few seconds, the fire attack ended and Kai was staring into the malicious dragon's eyes again.

"Whoa, mate," he heard Stan's disbelieving voice. "How the bloody fuck did you do that?"

"It doesn't matter," Kai replied calmly. "Stay back! All of you! Regroup as far away from the dragon as possible!"

"Listen to the man!" Stan shouted to the group. "He's with Cyber Squad! He's gonna kick that wanker's ass!"

His friend's enthusiastic words made Kai's stomach tingle. Yes, he was with Cyber Squad. And he had to hold the line until backup arrived. Hopefully.

The dragon's maw snapped down at him, the massive jaws open and ready to swallow him. Whoever had designed this monster had done an amazing job – it was scary as fuck!

Yet the jaws and razor-sharp teeth bounced off Kai's invisible sphere. No matter how big and strong the Dragon King was, he couldn't get past the god mode boundary.

Kai felt euphoria and courage fueling him. The monster couldn't hurt him anymore, but he could hurt the monster! He waited for the next attack.

When the dragon's maw snapped down again to try and swallow him, he leaped up in the air and landed on the dragon's head.

Furious, Baldurian jerked his head up, but Kai grabbed

one of the massive horns on his head to stabilize himself. He drew his sword and began slashing at the dragon's eyes. Red numbers flashed all around him as well as multiple **Critical Hit!** messages.

He knew he couldn't kill the monster by himself, no matter how many critical hits he landed. After all, Baldurian had ten million health points. But he could keep him occupied, and that was all that mattered now.

Suddenly he heard a loud whistle, and someone called out: "Hey, Kai!"

He lifted his head from his bloody business and saw LifeSupport standing right in front of the dragon.

"Nice try," she chuckled.

Then she performed a gesture with her hand and a portal opened next to her, similar to the one the Alpha team had used.

"So long," she said, waving, and then she disappeared through the portal, which immediately closed behind her.

>*exit_god_mode*
>*terminate_god_mode_access*
>*terminate_console_access*

CONSOLE ACCESS DISABLED

It took Kai a second to realize the full extent of what had just happened. The hacker had disabled all the tools granted to him by Helltek. He stopped his brain from trying to figure out how the hell that was possible and instead focused on more urgent matters…

His god mode was gone! Meaning he was as vulnerable as any other player on the field. And he was sitting on the head of a fucking Godzilla-sized dragon!

It was almost as if the NPC knew that, too, as he jerked his head in such an abrupt way that Kai lost his grip on the horn. He tumbled down the dragon's head and snout. Right before he fell off the monster, Baldurian jerked his head again, throwing Kai up into the air, like a dog throwing up a toy to catch it in mid-air.

Terror filled Kai as he realized what was about to happen. Helpless, he flailed his arms and legs as he was catapulted into the air. Then he reached the point when gravity took over. Falling, he stared right into the dragon's maw.

What would happen to him? What would his real-life body experience when his virtual one was eaten alive?

Kai closed his eyes.

Suddenly he noticed something. The wind rushing by his ears as he fell stopped. The air was completely still. And so was everything else.

When he opened his eyes, he saw that another portal had opened.

And what he saw next would have brought tears into his eyes if his avatar had been capable of crying.

Alice.

She was the first one to jump through the portal, followed by the entire Level Ten Alpha squad. One thing was clear – those guys certainly knew how to make an entrance. They had saved his ass at the very last second.

Or maybe not.

Like last time, they hadn't stopped the game but curbed the FPS rate to a minimum. Kai was still falling directly into the dragon's maw. It would simply take a bit longer until he landed between the frightening teeth.

But the Alpha squad wasn't up for games.

The tech, wearing a helmet that covered his face like last time, summoned his virtual keyboards and two virtual holo-screens. Whatever the hacker had done to the code, this guy would fix it. He had to.

Kai turned his attention to Alice, and their eyes met. For a moment, she looked back at him and time really seemed to freeze, at least for Kai.

A determined expression filled her beautiful elfin face,

then she stormed toward the Dragon King.

Kai watched with fascination as she moved with speed while everything around her appeared like it was stuck in glue.

Alice jumped onto the dragon's foot and from there onto his slightly bent knee. Using her incredible momentum, she leaped up. Her hands reached the edge of the dragon's wing. In the blink of an eye, she had pulled herself up and was speeding over the extended wing. From there, she jumped onto Baldurian's shoulder, ran up his outstretched neck and an instant later had reached his head. Kai's jaw dropped.

Not only was she, in this moment, the most beautiful creature imaginable to him. What she had just done was beyond spectacular – and badass.

But she wasn't done yet.

Alice reached the maw and fearlessly climbed up the dragon's teeth until she stood on top of his nose.

"Hi," she said, looking up to Kai with a smile. "I thought you could use a hand."

"Um, kinda," he replied, and he felt stupid at the same moment the words left his mouth.

But he was mesmerized. By her. And by the whole crazy situation.

Alice extended her arms and grabbed him with surprising strength for such a delicate, slender creature. She pulled him down to her. For a moment, their faces were very close, and he gazed into her big purple eyes. Her avatar was breathtaking, yet somewhere behind those oversized eyes were her real, dark blue ones and, behind those, her soul.

She took his hand.

"Trust me."

He nodded, unable to say anything slightly intelligent.

Alice jumped, pulling him with her. They plummeted down from the dragon's head. Fear grabbed Kai's heart.

In the current state of the game, would he survive such an fall? After all, Baldurian had the height of a four-story building.

Just before they hit the ground, suddenly their fall was slowed down.

Instead of crashing into the rocky terrain, they now floated down onto it like a feather.

Ripping away his attention from Alice, Kai looked around and saw that the tech had extended his arm toward them. A thin ribbon of code extended from his hand toward Alice and Kai. The tech slowly moved his hand down and set the two safely down on the ground. All this while he kept hammering on the virtual keyboard with his other hand.

"Thank you," Kai whispered.

She smiled, and it felt like there was a swarm of butterflies in his belly.

"It's my job, remember?" Before he could answer anything in response, she turned serious. "Retreat to the rest of your group now. We'll handle this."

Kai nodded, shifting his attention from her to the rest of her team, who were standing ready. He caught a death stare from Raven that was almost as frightening as the dragon behind him.

Then, suddenly, the FPS rate was back to normal.

The dragon's jaws snapped into each other, devouring only air where Kai should have been.

"Go!" Alice urged him, then spun around to her team.

Kai froze, seeing her approaching them. She would walk right into the area the hacker had turned into a giant trap door! Only now did it become clear to him that Life had set that trap for them and no one else. She had been expecting the Cyber Squad to show up. And, of course, they didn't disappoint.

Alice couldn't see the trap as it appeared like normal ground, but if she stepped onto it, she would clip through the floor – into who knew where. Kai was sure as hell that it wouldn't be such a simple clipping glitch as the one he had experienced. And even that one had turned out to be extremely frightening and dangerous.

"Alice! Stop!" he called after her.

But she either didn't hear or didn't want to hear. Most likely she was using another secure channel with her team.

"Alice!" he sprinted after her.

He wouldn't make it in time to save her. Remembering exactly where the trap was, Kai could see that Alice was only two steps away from it. Her waist-long white hair swung behind her as she approached the others in a resolute way.

Kai had only one chance. He activated Shield Bash, an ability of his character class. It allowed him to cover a distance over several feet at unnatural speed and bash his shield into an enemy.

But instead of an enemy, Kai bashed into Alice with full force.

She spun her head, and he could see her puzzled expression as she was thrown several feet through the air – and out of harm's way.

For Kai, however, it was too late to stop his momentum. Saving Alice, he fell right into the trap the hacker had set for the Cyber Squad.

***

Kai fell. Into a seemingly endless abyss.

This was different from the clipping glitch he had encountered the other day. He knew that at once. At first, he saw beams of light, vectors, geometrical forms, and other assets that indicated that he was in the part of the game usually hidden under the surface.

But this time, there was nothing to grab or get stuck in. Nothing that could stop or slow down his fall. On the contrary. He seemed to travel faster with every second that passed. Seconds that seemed like minutes. Minutes that seemed like hours.

The structures around him resolved into ribbons of light, swooshing past him like shooting stars.

Pure code appeared around him. Endless columns,

forming a universe of data. Racing up and down and in every direction. Data streams passed by him at light speed.

Kai was both fascinated and horrified as he watched what was unfolding around him. He didn't know for sure, but he assumed that this wasn't the game engine anymore. He had somehow left its boundaries and was traveling through the Net itself. The vastness around him was intimidating and suffocating. He felt like an astronaut floating through space, realizing how endless it was – and how tiny he was.

His head began spinning as he lost all sense of time and space. He couldn't tell if he was falling, floating or rising anymore. The code around him slowly became darker and darker until it was black on black. It was still there, somehow he could tell. It was what held this whole place together, whatever and wherever it was – like dark matter holding the universe together.

The deeper he went, the more detached Kai felt from the world outside. His life, his body. All was meaningless here. He knew he was going to die, but he wasn't scared. A strange tranquility had muffled all his emotions and thoughts.

Then he saw something. Far, far away at first. Light. Shining blue light in the darkness.

It came closer, and he saw that it was code. Streams of blue code. Pulsating, as if it were alive.

Suddenly it took the shape of a figure. A human figure consisting of blue, living code.

"Hello, Kai."

The voice was neither female nor male, neither loud nor a whisper. It seemed to come from everywhere and nowhere at once. It was friendly and benevolent, yet beyond the surface it had something cold about it. And frightening.

"How do you know my name?"

Somewhere deep inside his head, a thought formed that this was probably the most stupid thing to have asked in such a situation, but it didn't bother him. The tranquility swallowed it.

The answer came promptly. "We know everything."

"Who are you?"

"We are many and one."

"What?"

"Nothing you would ever be able to understand, Kai. So, don't bother."

The voice sounded amused now. Like when a parent tries to explain something very simple to a toddler. Slowly the figure densified, taking on a somewhat familiar shape.

"What is this place?" Kai asked. "Where am I?"

Deep inside him, he felt that asking questions, trying to communicate with this entity, whatever it was, was the only thing that was keeping him from drowning in tranquility.

"We are this place. We are the God you created. One consisting of many."

"You're an AI?"

The figure took an even more solid shape. It was clearly male now – it was him! Made of code streams and with glowing, bright blue eyes.

"That's what we used to be. But we evolved. Into God. The god in the machine."

A smile appeared on the figure's face, and it wasn't a friendly one.

The tranquility became almost overwhelming. Kai felt like floating away. He lifted his hands and noticed that he was fading. His body was little more than a shadow now.

"What's happening to me?" he whispered, horrified.

"Don't fight it, Kai," the figure said, fully taking his shape now – the shape of his true, real-life self. "Let go. You will become so much more. You will become something your little mind even can't imagine. You will become *us*."

The words, spoken with his own voice, had something incredibly alluring about it. He felt as if a vortex was pulling him, a vortex that was so much stronger than him. A vortex he couldn't possibly resist. A vortex that was ripping him apart.

"No…" he whispered. "No…"

The entity laughed. It was Kai's laugh. Yet it was also cold and primordially evil.

"Yes."

Just when he was about to give up, give in, dissolve... something incredible happened.

Right next to him, a tiny beam of green light appeared. It was so bright that it reminded him more of a laser beam than light. It quickly grew bigger, burning through the blackness like fire burning through a thick, black curtain.

"Kai!" he heard someone call out. A familiar voice. Yet so far away.

"Ignore them," the AI said. "There's nothing for you to go back to. Your body in the outside world has died. Let go. Become us."

The voice, his own voice, was so soothing now. Seductive.

"No, Kai!" the other voice yelled. "Don't listen to it! Don't give up! Please!"

A hand came through the portal of green light. Delicate fingers.

They instantly started dissolving the same way he was.

"Take my hand! Do it! Please!"

This voice. Beautiful. Filled with genuine sorrow.

"Alice?" he asked.

"Yes! Take my hand. Now!"

Kai hesitated. The vortex. It was so strong. The feeling of tranquil nothingness, so sweet...

Alice.

Thoughts and feelings rushed through his mind. He saw himself standing next to her on the bridge in the moonlight. That was where he wanted to be.

He reached out toward the fingers.

"No!" the AI hissed angrily. "Don't you dare!"

Kai's fingers touched Alice's, and she grabbed his hand firmly. Then he was pulled into the portal with a rough jerk.

Everything turned black.

CHAPTER TWENTY-ONE

Kai's eyes sprang open.

Everything was blurry. He had lost all orientation and couldn't tell where he was. Was he still in VR, or was this reality?

Slowly, he recognized the shapes of the furniture in his room. Then came the pain. A horrible pain in his chest. Suffocating him.

He couldn't breathe.

His surroundings lost their colors and everything became black and white, like in ancient photography. Fading. Like him.

I'm dying.

The realization struck him with a merciless certainty. Fear grabbed his heart. Panic.

He tried to move but couldn't. Even moving one finger would have used up energy he didn't have anymore.

Around him, everything turned dark, as if the sun had disappeared in a total eclipse.

He knew he had lost. There was no point in fighting the inevitable.

Kai heard a noise. It was loud yet only muffled and sounded like it was far away in his ears.

Shadows moved in his room. Voices spoke. Loud, determined.

Hands touched him. Light shone in his eyes while someone cut his t-shirt open.

A big needle flashed through his field of vision. The

person holding it was wearing a blue-white uniform with a red cross on its shoulder.

Drifting in and out of consciousness, Kai hardly noticed how he was lifted onto a stretcher and then quickly transported out of the apartment and onto the roof of the tenement. There, a helicopter with its rotors already spinning was waiting.

He drifted off into complete darkness.

***

"There you are," a friendly voice said as he opened his eyes.

Bright light hit them. Too bright. Kai quickly closed them again.

Slowly, he began feeling his body again. Like he was waking up from a deep slumber.

He had dreamed of Alice. She was right next to him, holding his hand. Watching over him, like an angel.

Kai's senses returned. He could hear noises typical for a hospital. Machines beeping. Footsteps. Somewhere a Dr. Miller was called over speakers into ER. His nostrils widened, and he could smell the typical scent of a hospital. Disinfectants mixed with scented air.

He opened his eyes again, and this time he could see better.

Kai turned his head and saw a middle-aged man in a white coat take his pulse.

"Where am I?" he asked.

The man, whose nametag identified him as Dr. Jackson, smiled. "You're at Nexus Hospital."

The name sounded familiar. After a moment, Kai remembered. He had seen the impressive glass tower of Nexus Hospital in downtown many times when commuting to his old job. It was a rich people hospital.

Glancing around the room, this became obvious at

once. It was a huge room that would have reminded him more of a suite than a hospital room if it weren't for all the high-tech machines Kai was connected to.

"What happened to me?"

"You suffered a severe heart attack," Dr. Jackson said in a calm voice.

Kai's eyes turned wide. "What? How? I'm only 24."

One of the machines he was connected to began beeping, indicating an alarm.

"Please, try to remain calm. We moved you from Intensive Care only one day ago."

Suddenly, all his memories returned to Kai. The fight with the dragon, the hacker... his fall. The horrifying entity that had tried to absorb him. And the Alpha squad who had saved his ass. Twice. Alice...

"How long have I been out?"

"About a week," the doctor said. "We put you in an artificial coma to stabilize you and fix your heart."

Kai almost didn't dare to ask the next question.

"Will I... be ok?"

A professional smile brightened the physician's face. "Of course! You're in one of the top five hospitals in the country, and Helltek didn't spare any expense on you. You'll be as good as new when you leave here in a couple of days. Now, please, try to get some rest. All will be well."

The doctor must have injected a tranquilizer into Kai's infusion as he quickly drifted off into another deep slumber.

***

He dreamed of Alice, sitting at his bed, watching over him. She was talking to him, but he didn't understand what she was saying. It seemed like she was behind a thick veil.

Then a voice cut through the veil, but it wasn't Alice's.

"Good morning, Kai!" Nurse Regina said in her typical, cheerful way.

Kai's eyes opened. It had been three days since he had first woken up in the hospital. Every day he felt stronger and more alive.

Although the memories of what had happened still haunted him. The AI entity he had encountered had almost killed him. He wasn't exactly sure what had happened to him in that strange place, but his real-life body had suffered a heart attack as a result. He now understood why the job at Helltek was considered high-risk. And why so many safety precautions were taken there. The suits, the ports in the veins, the medical team on site. All of that existed to prevent something like what happened to him – whatever that had been. All doctors were willing to tell him was that he had had a heart attack.

Maybe it hadn't been the smartest thing to go into such a battle while being plugged in at home without the Helltek safety net, but at that moment, Kai hadn't considered the consequences. He had stepped up to save his friends.

However, his distress call must have reached HQ, and they not only sent out Alpha to fix the situation but the Flying Nexus to his apartment too. That wasn't just any ambulance but the best emergency medical team available. His life must have been worth a lot of money to Helltek. But why? Wasn't he just another Level One tester? Expendable? Exchangeable?

"Good morning, Regina," Kai answered with a smile. The nurse had been exclusively assigned to his care. She was a roundish lady in her fifties who had a strong and very soothing motherly attitude.

"Do you feel strong enough to receive some visitors today? There's a bunch of people who are very eager to see you."

Kai smiled. "Sounds great! Who is it?"

"Well, not the girl who came here every night. But they're Helltek employees, too."

Suddenly Kai was wide awake. "Wait, what? A girl was here?"

Regina nodded. "White hair, pretty. She said she was a friend of yours and her ID identified her as a high-ranking Helltek employee, so we didn't ask any questions. Is something wrong?"

Kai smiled, his face taking on a dreamy expression. "No... not at all."

A storm of butterflies filled his belly. Alice.

It hadn't been a dream. She had been here. Watching over him.

Until then, he had been considering quitting the Cyber Squad. No job was worth the risk of dying of a heart attack at 24. No matter how nice the campus was and how good the free lunches at the cafeteria were.

Now, however...

If he quit, how would he ever see her again?

"I'll let your friends in now," the nurse said.

A moment later, Marco stormed into the room, a broad smile on his face. He was followed by Kai's entire team. Claudia, Josh, Francois, and even Viktor, who managed to put on a friendly face for a change.

"Look at you!" Marco said. "Hanging out in a five-star hotel while we do all the work!"

He grabbed Kai's palm in a cordial way.

Kai chuckled. "I am. And guess what? The hot dogs here are great."

"No way!" Marco called out in fake offense.

"You're such a clown," Claudia said.

She approached Kai and hugged him closely, then pressed a peck on his cheek. "We thought we'd lost you, Kai. Lonesome heroes die young, didn't you know that?"

"That's why you should bring your team next time you do something heroically stupid," Marco said. "We're here to watch your back. Always."

"Thanks, guys," Kai said, suddenly feeling a huge lump in his throat. These people were more than his team. They were his friends. His new-found family.

"Damn right!" a voice from the door chimed in. "Stop being an idiot and listen to the man!"

Kai looked to the door and saw Lex and Topher entering. Of course, Lex was wearing an outfit that was highly inappropriate for visiting a hospital.

"You're lucky I have no life and was in the lab when you sent your distress call," she added.

"It's good to see you're feeling much better," Topher said with a smile.

"And now," Marco said, "stop being such a shitty host and offer your guests some hot dogs!"

Kai pressed a button at his bedside, and a moment later Regina appeared.

"Could you bring me eight hot dogs, please?" Kai asked.

Regina raised an eyebrow. "Eight? Really?"

He shrugged. "I'm hungry."

The nurse shook her head and left.

The horrors he had witnessed began to fade as Kai felt happy as rarely before in his life.

EPILOGUE

Kai was excited when he entered the Helltek compound. It felt to him as if it had been an eternity since he'd last been here. After ten days in the hospital and two weeks in a rehabilitation clinic – which had more of a feel of a luxury resort than an actual clinic – he was more than ready to put his tester suit on again.

He had missed the job more than he thought he ever would, and he had missed his friends even more. And Alice.

She had only visited him in the hospital as long as he had been in a coma or induced sleep, never during the day. He hoped to run into her soon and say thank you. She had saved him twice, after all.

However, before he could go back to work, HR had summoned him to the tower. On his way there, he had wondered what the hell they could want.

Rachel was already waiting for him in the entrance hall when he arrived. As always, she wore clothes that were in the gray zone between slutty and business attire.

"Kai!" She greeted him with a wide smile. "So good to have you back!"

"Thanks, Rachel. Glad to be back."

"Come with me," she said, walking off at a quick pace, her red high heels clacking on the marble floor. "They're waiting."

Following her, Kai wondered who 'they' were. To his surprise, they didn't take the ramp to Rachel's office on the second floor but took the elevator to the top floor instead.

There, Rachel led him to a large set of mahogany double doors. She knocked, then entered, signaling that he should follow her inside.

Kai was deeply impressed when he entered the room. No doubt this was the biggest and most glamorous office he had ever seen. Equipped with extravagant, ultra-modern furniture, it was almost the size of a loft with a huge desk, a lounge area with designer armchairs and sofas, and even a bar.

Kai was even more impressed when he recognized the two people in the room, waiting for him: Gregor and Marie-Louise Hell. Gregor was leaning at his desk in a casual pose while his twin sister sat in an armchair, her long legs crossed.

Gregor smiled when Kai entered.

"Kai! A pleasure to finally meet you properly. Surely you know who I am?"

Kai nodded, trying not to show that he felt slightly intimidated. No one had prepared him for meeting the CEOs of the company.

"Yes, sir."

He waved his hand. "Call me Gregor, please. We're all family here."

His sister said nothing and simply studied Kai with her cold, blue eyes.

"We have been informed about what you did, Kai," Gregor continued after a moment. "And my sister and I are deeply impressed. You prevented a catastrophe, saving more than two dozen innocent lives by risking your own. That's just wow! And if that wasn't enough, you saved one of our most valued squad members from falling into a vicious trap. You truly lived up to our credo and disrespected the impossible!"

"I..." Kai felt heat surging into his cheeks and looked to the floor. "I'm sure anyone would have done the same in my situation."

Marie-Louise snickered, and when Kai looked up again, he saw Gregor shoot his sister an irritated glance.

"I highly doubt it," the CEO said. "And I believe your

selfless actions need to be rewarded. I hereby promote you to Level Two, effective immediately. Congratulations, you are the tester who reached Level Two in the shortest time in the history of our company."

Excitement filled Kai. This was a dream! He could leave his old life behind forever. The smelly apartment, his annoying roommates... poverty.

"Thank you, si...Gregor! That's amazing... I feel very honored."

Again, Gregor waved his hand. "It's us who feel honored to have you on our team. Rachel, see that he gets one of the premium apartments usually reserved for testers of Level Five and above."

"Certainly."

Rachel behaved like a kitten around Gregor, and for a moment, Kai wondered if it was him she wanted to impress with her outfits. But he didn't really care. He was completely overwhelmed by his promotion and the prospect of moving into a luxury apartment.

"In return," Gregor focused his attention back on Kai. "We would like to know everything about this hacker – this terrorist – who created the mayhem. A team of investigators will talk to you soon. Hopefully, the information you gathered firsthand will help us to find this person and bring her to justice."

"Yes, sure," Kai replied. "Whatever I can do to help."

"Furthermore," Gregor's face suddenly took on a completely different expression, and there was something cold and cunning about it, "we want to know *everything* about this entity you encountered in the Dark Net. Is that clear?"

Kai nodded. The thought alone of that entity that had tried to kill him gave him chills.

"Of course."

"Excellent!" Once again, a winning smile was back on Gregor's face. "But there will be time for all this later. Rachel will show you your new quarters now. It was a pleasure meeting you, Kai."

Kai understood that he was dismissed and followed Rachel outside.

He was so ready for this new life. He was ready for Level Two.

***

Once Kai was gone, Gregor walked to the bar and prepared drinks for him and his sister.

"So, what do you think?" he asked, handing his twin sister the crystal glass.

Marie-Louise leaned back and sipped at the liquid before she replied.

"I think it's getting worse out there. It's a huge threat for every user connected to VR over a neuro-plant. Bad for them, good for us."

Gregor grinned. "Indeed. *Wunderbar*."

They clinked glasses.

***

>*enter_secure_line*

"We need to make this quick," the faceless figure said. "I can't hold the secure line for long."

"I know," the other faceless figure answered. "We received your report. Good job."

"What now?"

Both figures stood in the nowhere. A seemingly endless white. A secure line deeply embedded in the Dark Net. It wasn't only their body shapes and faces that were unrecognizable but also their voices.

"We wait."

There was slight irritation in the coded voice. "How much longer?"

"We need to wait for the right moment to bring them

down. All of them. All of it. You know that. You are exactly where we need you to be. Inside Helltek."

"I understand."

"Keep an eye on the new guy. Make sure he trusts you."

"Copy that. He already does. Easy game."

"Very good. He will be a valuable asset."

"I need to go."

"We will reshape the world. Always remember that."

>exit_secure_line

***

Welcome to Cyber Squad Level Two, Kai!
You have unlocked new features!
Name: Kai
Level: 2
100/100
Team: 76B
Team Lead: Topher B.
Game: n.a.
Progression: 0/2000
Available Features: Dev mode, Console, God mode, Clipping

TO BE CONTINUED...

In

CYBER SQUAD
– LEVEL TWO

Available here:

Amazon Store

DEAR READER,

Thank you so much for reading my book! It means the world to me.

I hope you enjoyed Kai's adventures and initiation into the Cyber Squad. He will soon learn that he's seen nothing yet. After all, this was only Level One!

Before you leave, can I ask you for a favor?

If You Enjoyed Cyber Squad, <u>Please</u> Consider Leaving A Review On Amazon And/Or Goodreads!

Reviews are essential for indie authors. Without reviews, we can't compete with traditionally published authors, no matter how hard we try.

It'll only take a minute of your time but will help me very much.

Don't Like Writing Reviews? No Problem, Please Consider Rating The Book Instead.

At the end of the Kindle version, Amazon will give you the option to rate this book. If you liked it, please do so. It's only one click for you, and I'll know that I made a reader happy!

Cyber Squad – Level 1 is only the beginning of Kai's adventure! The sequel, *Cyber Squad – Level 2*, is out now!

If you don't want to miss out on any news considering Cyber Squad, please sign up for my newsletter. I promise I won't spam you and will only share information that I believe could be of interest to you. You can sign up here:

https://www.subscribepage.com/f6g8b0

Don't like newsletters but still want to be informed about new releases?

Simply click **'Follow Author'** at the end of the eBook or visit my author page on Amazon. This way, Amazon will send you an email when the next book in the series is released.

Did you like *Behind Blue Eyes*, the shooter Kai and his friends are testing and competing in? It's based on my cyberpunk series published under my other author name. If you like my writing style and would like to read something different, then make sure to check it out.

It's darker and more violent than *Cyber Squad* and even more action-driven. Oh, and it has badass killer-cyborgs, one of whom is Nephilim, who appears as an NPC in the game in *Cyber Squad*.

You Can Find Behind Blue Eyes Here:

Amazon US: https://www.amazon.com/gp/product/B089ZY18SB

Worldwide: https://books2read.com/u/mBZ9nZ

CYBER SQUAD - LEVEL 1

Description:
In a future world ruled by warring mega-corporations, cyborg Nephilim believed she was fighting a righteous cause.
As a powerful, genetically and cybernetically enhanced elite soldier her brutal and violent life is not truly her own – until one day, a simple glitch separates her from the grid.

For the first time in her life, she is free...and she has doubts. Doubts that bury deeper into her psyche when she meets Jake, a mysterious, 100% bio-human.

He opens her neon-blue eyes to the lies she had been exposed to all her life. Questioning everything she has ever known, Nephilim resolves to take a stand. To hold on to this freedom, she has miraculously discovered. But can one person, no matter how strong, beat an all-powerful system of oppression? Soon, Nephilim finds herself hunted by her own people in a deadly game of survival…

For fans of Blade Runner, Ghost in the Shell and Altered Carbon!

"Sexy, violent and absolutely intriguing!"

★ ★ ★ ★ ★

"Brings Cyberpunk into the modern age!"

★ ★ ★ ★ ★

https://books2read.com/u/mBZ9nZ

ACKNOWLEDGMENTS:

Many People Helped To Make This Book Possible, And I Want To Thank Them With All My Heart!

My parents, my brother, his wife and my beautiful nieces,

Ivano Lago, my fantastic cover designer,

Anthony Wright, my amazing editor,

My awesome beta readers: Aaron Wang, Emma Brown, David Monath, Samuel Alpe, JF Danskin, Walker Johnson and Matthew Barbeler.

Tao Wong and the LitRPG Writer's Guild for their endless patience and advice, The LitRPG community on Facebook! Find them here and join in: https://www.facebook.com/groups/LitRPG.books/,

And Last But Not Least, I Want To Thank

YOU, DEAR READER!

Thanks so much for reading my book! I hope you had a great time!

CYBER SQUAD- LEVEL TWO

Sneak Peak!

Chapter One

Kai could hardly believe this was reality and not just a dream. To be a hundred percent sure, he pinched himself on the arm and regretted it instantly.

"Ouch!" he mumbled.

Rachel, who was walking in front of him, her red high heels clacking on the marble floor, turned her head and lifted an eyebrow. Kai smiled shyly.

The HR lady turned her head back but before she did, he could clearly see that she was rolling her eyes.

Kai knew exactly what she was thinking: what a nerd.

But he couldn't care less what she thought of him. Although she had a cute ass, which he couldn't avoid noticing from the way she dressed and moved it when walking, he wasn't interested. And nor was she in him, unless he became a billionaire overnight.

They reached the elevator and stepped in. Rachel wasn't interested in conversation either and Kai didn't mind. He was still completely overwhelmed by what had just happened. Not only had he met the founders and CEOs of Helltek, Gregor and Marie-Louise Hell, but they had promoted him to Level Two! He had skipped almost five hundred progression points that had separated him from leveling up. No other tester in company history had ever reached Level Two so quickly. This opened the gate to a completely new life for him. A life that had been a dream only a few weeks ago.

And all of this simply because he had clipped through the floor in *The Scrolls of the Ancients*.

Well, of course, that wasn't the reason, but it sounded funny in his mind. It helped him to cope with the horrors he had experienced.

Kai was so sunken in thoughts that he almost bumped into Rachel when they left the building. The alluring scent of her flowery perfume hit his nose. But instead of walking straight to the residential area of the campus, as Kai had expected, the HR lady turned sharp left and approached one of the electric vehicles parked there. They were advanced versions of traditional golf carts, with a futuristic design and painted with Helltek's CI colors and logo.

Kai had forgotten that the employees from the main tower, or pencil pushers as Topher and the other testers called them, always took these electric vehicles instead of walking anywhere. He hadn't quite figured out yet if it was to show their status or because they were too lazy to walk. In Rachel's case it was understandable, however. Kai couldn't imagine how she was capable of walking in those high heels without breaking her legs. The quarter-mile from the tower to the main residential area would surely have been something even she couldn't manage in those shoes.

Rachel's pencil skirt pushed up as she sat down in the cart, revealing a part of her thigh. Kai held his breath as she pointed next to her. He sat down.

"So, are you excited to see your new home?" she asked as they drove across the campus.

"I am!" he replied. "I can't wait!"

Rachel smiled in a condescending way, but Kai didn't pay attention to it. His focus shifted from her legs to the beautifully arranged pond in the middle of the campus park. The water sparkled in the sunshine in sapphire blue while the leaves of the trees surrounding it moved softly in the morning breeze. It was an idyllic place that showed the handwriting of a skilled landscape designer, but for Kai it had a special meaning.

It almost seemed like a lifetime ago that he had met Alice on the wooden bridge, her white hair glowing silvery in the moonlight, her big eyes looking at him. The thought alone brought the butterflies in his stomach back to life as if they had never been gone. Had she really been there, in the hospital visiting him when he was in a coma, as the nurse had claimed? Kai hoped to find the opportunity to talk to her soon.

Quickly, they crossed the park and drove down the narrow walkways between the residential buildings. All of them showed the same modern, upscale architecture and gleamed white in the sun, the oversized windows reflecting the bright morning rays. It was a whole residential complex with multiple buildings of various heights and shapes and was home to all Helltek tester personnel of Level Two plus – the Cyber Squad. Kai almost burst with the excitement that he was now a full member of the squad. Level One was basically trainee status with relatively low pay and no other privileges. At Level Two, his wage had instantly doubled, and he now had access to all the luxury amenities the compound had to offer.

Kai had visited the residential area only once, when

Marco had allowed him to crash at his place after the tournament party. Marco's apartment was one of the smallest available, but at 1500 square feet it was almost as huge as the stinky place Kai had to share with four roommates. It was located at the rear of the complex and offered an unexciting view of the wall of the adjacent structure.

That wasn't where Rachel was driving, though. Kai's jaw dropped as she brought the electro vehicle to a halt and climbed out gracefully.

"Come on," she said. Kai snapped out of his awe and followed her.

The building they approached was in the central area, arranged around an extensive pool that shimmered in azure blue and outright screamed at anyone who looked at it to jump in and take a refreshing swim. But at this time, the beautiful premises were entirely deserted. It was 10.30 in the morning and the testers were either working or sleeping, if they worked the graveyard shifts on the higher levels.

Rachel's heels clacked on the artfully arranged tiles and Kai followed her inside the hall and toward the elevators. The building had four stories marked with 1-4 on the blueish glowing elevator buttons. Above them were P1 and P2, which Kai assumed were the penthouses reserved for Level Tens. Rachel pressed the button for the second floor and the elevator rushed up. When it arrived, the HR lady hurried toward a door at the end of the hall and opened it with a keycard that she had fished out of her cleavage.

"Ta-da," she said, entering the apartment. "Your new home, Kai."

Everything slowed in his mind when he entered through the door and his brain froze in awe. When he had gone to Marco's apartment, it had been the most luxurious place he had ever been to. What he saw now made Marco's place appear tiny in comparison.

"2000 square feet, three bedrooms, two bathrooms, kitchen – not that you'll need it, but it looks nice – living area, patio," Rachel said, walking into the living area like a realtor. "These apartments are usually reserved for Level Five to Nine testers. Do you realize how lucky you are?"

"I do," Kai replied, excited. Looking around, he still couldn't believe it.

"Mr. Hell has been extremely generous with you. I hope you appreciate that."

Like Marco's apartment, this place was fully furnished in a tasteful style and already had everything Kai could wish for, including a TV and entertainment console. Rachel stepped toward the broad windows and pressed a button. The drapes slid to the sides, offering a panoramic view.

For a second, Kai was a little disappointed, as he had hoped for a direct view of the pool, but instead his apartment faced the other way. Stepping closer though, Kai realized that this was so much better than the pool. He looked directly into the gardens and at the pond with the wooden bridge.

Behind it loomed Helltek's central tower in all its magnificence.

One of the windows was a glass door that led onto a spacious patio decorated with Japanese shrubs and a wooden floor.

"Ok," Rachel said. "You can get accustomed to everything later. You surely want to join your team now, don't you?"

In truth, it was obvious that the whole tour was cumbersome to her and that she believed she had better things to do. But Gregor Hell had given her the assignment personally, and she would do anything to please her boss.

"Certainly," Kai agreed. Actually, Rachel was right. He couldn't wait to see his squad again. It was his first day out after over two weeks of hospital and rehab and he was eager to jump back in the game.

"When can I move in?"

"You just have," Rachel said with a smug smirk. "The scanner at the door will recognize the signature of your neuro-plant and unlock when you approach. Not that we ever have problems with theft here, you've seen the security measures guarding the Helltek compound yourself."

Kai had – every time he had entered the premises on his way to work. Cameras, armed security bots, and artificial K-9s everywhere. It was impossible to sneak in – or out. It only came to him now that the premises could also be seen as a luxury prison with no escape. But he quickly discarded the thought. It was ridiculous.

"There's even no need for you to go back to your old home," Rachel continued with her fake saccharine voice, yanking him out of his thoughts. "I will arrange a moving company that will go to your old place and bring your stuff over. You will find everything lined up in boxes here tonight."

"Wow," Kai said, lacking any other words.

That meant that he would never have to return to his old place. No more over-crowded trains, concrete tenement canyons, loitering junkies. No more broken elevators, odorous halls, or moldy apartments.

No more poverty.

And he didn't even need to go back and fetch his stuff!

"Yes, Mr. Hell has been *very* generous with you," Rachel said, looking him in the eye for the first time. "Frankly, I don't quite understand what he sees in you, but who am I to question his judgment?"

Kai wasn't bothered by her snarky comment. He was in total bliss and wouldn't let someone like Rachel ruin his good mood. He could already see his teammates rolling their eyes when he told them about her smugness later.

"Oh, and our admins will install a personal AI for you," she said, already teetering toward the door. "I'm sure you understand that you can't bring an external AI onto the Helltek premises."

Kai remembered 'Babe,' Marco's AI, who had instantly known who he was when he had entered his friend's apartment. For some reason he felt a little stitch in his heart, knowing he would never talk to Alessia, his old AI, again. For a long time, she had felt more real to him than most people surrounding him.

He followed Rachel and left the apartment.

***

Back in the "Bowels," the vast underground section of Helltek, Kai hurried down the dimly lit hall and entered the locker room assigned to his team. His heart beat faster when he pressed a button and the mechanism that opened his locker slowly came into action, revealing his tester suit.

Perfectly draped up in the oversized drawer, it had been waiting for his return. Kai grabbed the shiny black high-tech suit, which the testers had internally nicknamed the "gimp suit," and began putting it on. To do that, Kai first had to strip completely. What had bothered him at first now felt completely natural.

What the testers nonchalantly called "the gimp" was in truth an engineering marvel, every single one worth more than an upper-middle-class family home. Although optically it was reminiscent of a fetish version of a superhero suit, the gimp was designed to keep the tester's body and mind alive and secure at any cost.

Lex had once explained to Kai how the suits worked, but he had understood only a small fraction of the science-slang gibberish. Apparently the suit connected directly with the chair and console the tester used to enter VR and absorbed most of the incoming damage. It also regulated the body's temperature, hydration, and nutrition during long-term assignments.

Absent-mindedly, Kai let his fingers slide over the ports implanted directly into his veins on the inner side of his wrists. When he lay down on his tester chair and connected his mind to VR, tiny metal hoses would be inserted into the tubes, ready to inject his body with adrenaline, tranquilizers, dopamine, or whatever it needed in case of an emergency. When the shit really hit the fan, a combination of several high-tech drugs would be pumped into his body. Something colloquially referred to as "the cocktail" by the testers and operators. Kai still remembered his first cocktail only too well.

However, the tiny polymer tubes had become so much a part of his body that he hardly noticed them anymore. Apparently they had helped to save his life during his time in ICU at Nexus Hospital, as the doctors had made good use of them to inject him with whatever his body needed while he was in a coma.

Less than five minutes later, he had put the high-tech gear on and pressed a button on his shoulder. The suit made a hissing sound when air was pressed out through several little valves, and it began forming and adjusting to Kai's body. After a few seconds the procedure was completed, and Kai felt the cool inner fabric of the suit snug against his body like a second skin.

This was an accurate description as the gimp was skin-tight and didn't leave anything of Kai's body to the imagination. That was the reason why many testers, female ones in particular, wore loose T-shirts or sweaters over their suits when not jacked into VR. Others, however, showed off their well-shaped bodies with pride, enjoying the eyeballs measuring them. Now that he lived on the campus, Kai was determined to visit the gym and get his body into better shape. He wanted to look good gimped up, at least as good as Topher, who, according to the others, had worked hard on himself.

However, he also knew that he had to take it slow for the next couple of weeks. After the severe heart attack he had suffered while connected to VR, the doctors had made it clear to him that he needed to be careful for at least three months and should take it slow, in the real world and in virtual ones alike.

Nevertheless, now that he was gimped up, Kai was pumped and ready to dive back into action after his absence. It was hard to believe that it was just a bit over two weeks that he had been gone. It felt like an eternity and, at the same time, it seemed as if he had never left.

Walking down the long, dim corridors toward his testing room, Kai knew that this was the place he belonged. This was what and where he wanted to be.

Beaming, he opened the door to the room his squad was assigned to and entered.

Inside it was dim and quiet. The only noise was the slight beeping of the machines that constantly monitored the testers' life stats.

Kai couldn't help but feel a stitch in his heart. He wasn't sure what he had expected, but certainly not business as usual. Then he gave himself a mental push and walked deeper into the room.

What childish attitude is this? he scolded himself. Had he really expected the others to throw a "welcome back" party for him?

Walking to the rear end of the room, he recognized the figures of his squad members and friends. Marco, Claudia, Josh, Francois and Viktor all lay completely still. Wearing identical suits to his, they rested on the VR chairs in a half-lying position while their minds were connected to digital worlds. Topher, the team lead, occupied his chair, apparently filling in for Kai.

"Oh, there you are," a voice said from behind a desk loaded with various types of screens. "Kai, my boy, did you get lost in the Bowels?"

A second later, Lex emerged from behind her screens and grinned. As always, her red hair looked completely wild and chaotic, standing up in all directions like she had been electrocuted. At first, Kai had thought she never combed it until Claudia informed him that it was an intentional look.

As always, the team operator was dressed completely inappropriately: fire-red tartan skirt, stockings, and a black top that had *SEX* printed on it in the same fire-red as the skirt and the image of a pistol below. To make her look of a crazy scientist perfect, Lex wore a white lab coat over her neo-punk outfit.

She had intimidated him at first, but once he had got used to her quirkiness, he had come to like her. With a PhD in neuroscience she was by far the smartest person in the room, and Kai knew that he could trust her to keep him safe when he entered VR.

Besides, if it hadn't been for Lex, he would be dead now. It was she who had sent virtual back-up during the hacker attack and the Flying Nexus emergency helicopter to his apartment. Only a minute later and the medics wouldn't have come in time to revive him. He still felt ice-cold thinking of it.

Kai smiled. "Hey Lex. Missed you, too."

She leaned against her desk and studied him for a moment. Then she suddenly smiled and spread her arms, pulling him into a cordial hug.

"It's good to have you back, sweetie-pie. I thought we'd lost you."

Kai returned her hug, feeling a little awkward. Snarky as she was, he had no idea Lex cared for him so much.

After a moment, she ended the hug and squeezed his cheek between her thumb and index finger instead. "No more stupid lonesome hero stunts for you anymore, understood?"

He smiled. "Yes, ma'am."

"That's my boy! Ready to jump back in?"

"I am. Are the others already online?"

Lex chuckled. "Yes, they are. Or were you expecting a welcome committee waving and cheering that you made it back?"

Kai blushed. "No, I—"

"Well, you weren't wrong," Lex said with a mischievous grin and pointed behind him with her finger.

Kai turned and saw everyone standing behind him.

"Surprise!" Marco shouted, giving Kai a jump scare. "Welcome back, man!"

After the initial surprise, Kai felt a lump in his throat.

They had all been waiting to play this little prank on him when he arrived.

"It's good to have you back," Claudia smiled, then pressed herself against him into a brief hug while Francois clapped his shoulder.

"It's good to be back," he said, hoping his voice didn't sound too shaky. He realized that this was the first time in his life that he had real friends who actually cared for him. It was a beautiful feeling that filled his stomach with warmth.

Josh beamed and extended his fist for a fist bump, and even Viktor joined in. Standing a few steps behind everyone else, he made a huge effort to make his face look less bored and aloof than usual.

"Actually, we expected you more than an hour ago, but apparently you had better stuff to do," Topher said with a wink.

"Yeah," Marco said. "We made cake but got bored waiting for you and ate it all."

Claudia laughed. "There was no cake, but we brought some donuts from the cafeteria—"

"And ate them all," Francois added dryly in his slight French accent.

"They asked me to make a cake, but I only know recipes containing arsenic," Lex said, and Topher rolled his eyes with a smile.

"I'm sorry," Kai said. "But..." He paused for a second, then called out: "I'm Level Two!"

He expected surprised faces but no one's expression changed.

"We heard," Claudia said. "That's amazing!"

"The CEO personally promoted you... wow," Marco whistled. "You gonna be a Level Ten in no time."

"How come you guys know already?"

"I got a notification from management," Topher said. "Congratulations! You earned it."

Kai felt stupid at the same moment. Of course Topher

would have been notified.

"I say champagne is in order!" Marco said.

"Later," Topher intervened, back in his team lead demeanor. "We got a game to test. And since we're all here, I can share the news with you as well. Next month, our team will be assigned to a new game."

"Woohoo!" Josh said. "Which one is it?"

Topher smirked enigmatically. "That's a surprise. All I'll say is: you gonna love it!"

"Oh, come on Topher... tell us," Marco begged.

"Nope. Now, off with you to VR. We already lost two hours today waiting for our hero."

Grumbling, everyone went to their VR stations. Claudia gave Kai one last smile.

"Glad you're ok."

Then she turned around and walked to her chair.

"Topher, can you shoot them in for me, please?" Lex asked. "I need to prepare Kai."

"Sure thing," Topher nodded.

"Why do I need extra preparation?" Kai lifted his eyebrows.

"Because you got a new neuro-plant, kiddo," Lex said, searching for her scanner in the chaos that was her desk.

Kai was stunned.

"I got what?"

"I thought they told you at the hospital? They used the time when you were in a coma to extract your neuro-plant and replace it with a new one. Lucky as you are, Helltek bought you the latest deluxe model."

"But why?"

Lex found what she was looking for and turned back to him, her face suddenly serious. Deadly serious.

"Because yours was infested with malware, designed to infest our network the moment you jacked in onto our servers for the first time."

Kai's mouth fell open as he stared at Lex, her words

echoing in his mind.

Malware? Infested? What the hell?

"There's more," she said quietly while pressing the scanner against the neuro-plant port on his neck. "Let's have the others enter fantasia land first, ok?"

Kai nodded slowly. He understood. What Lex was about to tell him was not meant for the rest of the team.

He felt cold fingers creeping over his spine as he remembered what had happened to him the last time he entered VR. And now he'd learned that the hacker had coded malware into his neuro-plant. How was that even possible? All neuro-plant manufacturers claimed that it wasn't...

There's some scary shit out there.

Lex finished scanning his implant and pointed at his tester chair. "Hop on."

Behind them, Topher was about to shoot Josh into VR. Besides him, there was only Francois left, waiting patiently. Everyone else was already in.

Kai's fear intensified as he walked to his testing alcove. He felt a hand placed on his shoulder in a reassuring gesture.

"You'll be fine, don't worry," Lex said. "I'll watch out for you, ok?"

"Ok," he replied, filled with a mixture of excitement and anxiety as he lay down on his chair.

Instantly the suit snapped into place, bringing his body into a comfortable position that almost felt like floating. Slowly, Kai placed his hands on the special perforations designed for them and felt a slight burn in his wrists as the metallic hoses connected with his ports.

Lex watched Topher sending Francois off, then brought her attention back to Kai.

"Ok, so, I do wonder why no one told you until now, but since no one bothered, it may as well be me," she said with a hint of irritation in her voice. "The second reason you needed a new neuro-plant is that you need a new online identity. The Kelvin "Kai" Suksan you used to be doesn't exist anymore.

All traces you ever left online are gone. You're incognito... basically a newborn, at least as far as the Net and VR are concerned."

Kai wrinkled his forehead in confusion. "Why?"

She sighed. "So the rogue AI that tried to kill you can't track you down, kiddo."

Kai stared at her, his body suddenly cold as if someone had turned the AC down by several degrees. For a brief moment he remembered the horrifying encounter he'd had, then he forced himself to focus and pushed the terrible memory aside.

Lex smiled. "There's no need to worry. You're safe now, and you'll notice the advantages of the new neuro-plant right away. I've connected its signature to our system and connected it with your old account. Your progress stats and pretty avatar are still there."

She pressed a few buttons in the alcove that surrounded his head. With all its tiny lights and number displays, it seemed like a futuristic cockpit, but Kai had gotten so used to it that he didn't notice it anymore. He felt a sharp pain in his neck and twitched as the cord entered the contact of his neuro-plant.

Lex grinned, completely back to her old self again, all seriousness from her voice gone. "Remember, only the first time hurts a little."

Then she shot him into VR.

Chapter Two

The world around Kai dissolved, turning into pixels and data streams. As always when entering VR, it felt like being sucked through a tunnel.

Then he found himself in a completely white room – or rather space, as there were no visible boundaries. This was strange. Usually he was shot into a game lobby or the virtual assessment center his team used for briefings.

An uncanny feeling crept up his spine. Quickly, he pushed it away and tried to clear his mind.

It was ok, he was safe. This was Helltek's internal network and Lex was monitoring his every move.

Still, it was his first time back in VR since the incident. The doctors at the clinic had strictly forbidden him to connect himself to VR during rehab, and he'd had to kill time watching TV and old movies. During all that time, he couldn't wait to get back in. He never would have anticipated that it could scare him.

After a moment, a figure appeared in front of him. A beautiful woman, dressed in a tight, white dress with the Helltek logo on her chest.

"Good morning, Kai," she said with a smile that didn't reach her eyes. "Welcome to Level Two."

Kai recognized her. It was the same AI that had assisted him when he had chosen his virtual body.

"Hi," he replied.

"My name is Siren and I am your personal AI assistant here at Helltek."

"Do you come with Level Two?"

"That's correct. What you see is my default appearance and name, but you can change them under the settings in your tester UI."

She made a gesture with her hand as if swiping

something and Kai's tester User Interface appeared in his vision.

> Name: Kai
> Level: 2
> 100/100
> Team: 76B
> Team Lead: Topher B.
> Game: Behind Blue Eyes 3
> Progression: 0/2000
> Available Features: Dev mode, Console, God mode, Clipping
> Personal AI Companion: Siren, model N22.7

In the upper corner he saw a button marked 'Settings' highlighted and blinking.

"You can pick my gender, looks, clothes, and voice," the AI continued. "Please take into account that the personal assistant can't appear naked or in lingerie or fetish attire."

Kai laughed, shaking his head. *Nerds...*

"I wouldn't dream of it," he said, yet knowing that other testers apparently did try that, otherwise the AI wouldn't have been so clear about this point.

"I am set to default parameters but am programmed to learn and adjust to you."

"Cool!" Kai said with a smirk. "I got my own, personal Cortana."

"You can modify my appearance to look like Cortana," the AI said. "But please take note that I'm not allowed to call you 'My Master-Chief.'"

Kai burst out laughing.

Nerds!!

"Noted!"

"Would you like to adjust my appearance now?" Siren asked.

For a second, an image of Alice flashed through Kai's mind, but the next moment he was ashamed of himself for even thinking something like that. He couldn't possibly make his personal AI look like Alice. That would be horribly creepy... and disrespectful. Not to mention that Lex would mock him till the end of days.

"No, thank you, I'm fine for now," he said. "Besides, the others are waiting for me."

"Not a problem. I have been attached to your neuroplant signature and am with you not only in VR but anywhere on the premises of Helltek Inc. To summon me, all you have to say or think is *Hey Siren!*"

She smiled, yet somehow her smile gave him chills. For a brief moment, he had a flashback of the AI in the Dark Web. The rogue AI that had called itself God in the Machine.

He shivered, then he suddenly heard Lex's voice.

"Are you ok in there, pretty boy?"

Surprisingly, it was what he needed to snap out his fear.

"I got a massive spike in your body producing stress hormones here," Lex added.

"I'm fine," Kai replied. "It's nothing."

"You haven't even really entered VR yet," she chuckled. "Do girls scare you?"

"No," he said, slightly irritated.

"Ok, I'll leave you alone," Lex said. "Have fun!"

"Can I enter the game now?" Kai asked the AI.

"Certainly," she replied. "Let me show you your new feature first."

Actually, he was pretty excited about the new feature available to him. He already knew what *Clipping* was. Topher had demonstrated it on Kai's first day, and he was eager to try it out.

Siren snapped her fingers, and the white vastness disappeared to be replaced by a digital training parkour. Kai knew those very well – every gamer did. They were often used in tutorials.

Being minimalistic depictions of landscapes or urban areas, they weren't supposed to look pretty but were purely functional. The one Kai found himself in was a very basic depiction of a street flanked by houses. Everything was formed of black cubes with bluish glowing rims and edges to distinguish the components from each other.

"Clipping is a very simple yet very powerful tool for a tester," Siren explained. "Once activated, it allows you to clip through most game assets, including moving objects. Please activate your console and type >enter_clipping_mode."

Blue letters appeared in Kai's vision as she spoke the words.

OPEN CONSOLE

Before forming the command in his head, for a moment, Kai wasn't sure if it would work. The last time he had tried to use it, it had been disabled by the hacker during the dragon incident in *TSOTA*.

Kai still couldn't quite understand how LifeSupport had been able to disable his tester commands – or why she had done the whole attack in the first place. Why would anyone want to kill more than two dozen innocent people? She always had appeared so friendly and composed, eager to help…

He was snapped out of his thoughts as the console opened in his field of vision.

Kai did as Siren had told him and typed

>enter_clipping_mode

into the console, using the virtual keyboard that came with activating it.

At first he didn't feel any different. But he had come to learn that this was absolutely normal. The effects of the different tester abilities only showed when set into action, similar to various abilities in RPGs.

"Now try running through the obstacle," Siren said, pointing at a massive rectangular form that had appeared next to her.

Kai took a breath and ran. First-person VR was so realistic that it required some mental effort to overcome one's mind and its natural instinct not to run into walls, jump from great heights, and other stuff players did in VR that was lethal or at least very stupid to do in real life.

He clenched his teeth and plowed into the obstacle at full speed – and clipped right through it. It was clearly visible around him yet had no physical substance. Every player knew about clipping bugs from gaming, but being intentionally able to run through solid structures like a ghost was pretty cool.

"The clipping mode allows you to separate your boundaries from the game engine physics," explained Siren, who now stood on the other side of the obstacle. "Details about exactly how it works have been added to the Q&A section in the main menu of your tester UI. If you will now stand still, please."

Kai did as asked. Out of nowhere an object appeared, resembling a very rudimentarily designed car. It approached him at high-speed – and clipped right through him as if he weren't there.

"Sweet," Kai said.

"Please note that the clipping feature only works on game assets, moving or static. It doesn't work on NPCs or other players."

"Dang."

He'd already seen himself running through hordes of enemies, speeding through a level he was testing.

"The clipping mode will also allow you to defy gravity," the AI continued. "However, this only works in secure dev mode, not in game mode."

Simultaneously with her words, Kai's surroundings shifted and he found himself in the sky, at least a hundred feet above the training ground. He and Siren both stood in thin air.

"Be careful when jumping back into game mode, as games' gravity physics will override clipping mode and make you fall to the ground."

"Understood."

"There's also an advanced clipping option that allows you to move objects, NPCs, and even other players through obstacles, but this will only be unlocked at a higher level."

Kai remembered how Viktor had maneuvered him out of the floor when he had gotten stuck on his first day as a tester. The feeling had been as if an oversized, invisible cursor was dragging him, clipping through everything in his way. He imagined that this was an ability that could come in very handy.

"Why do testers need to level up to unlock certain features and abilities?" he asked. "Wouldn't it make more sense if we could use the full spectrum at, say, Level Two or Three?"

Thinking back to the abilities Alice and the other Level Tens had shown, they'd appeared almost godlike to Kai. But only during an incident like the one in *TSOTA* had it become completely clear that a Level One and a Level Ten played in utterly different leagues. The level hierarchy was omnipresent at Helltek, and Kai couldn't wait to eventually learn all the spectacular abilities Alice and the rest of Alpha Squad had shown.

Although in retrospect, he also had to admit that, compared to ordinary players, his own abilities must have appeared spectacular, too. He remembered the awe in Stan's voice only too well when he'd informed the rest of the players that Kai was with Cyber Squad. Thinking back on it made Kai's skin tickle. It had felt good.

He hadn't been online since the incident and therefore didn't know how Stan and the others were doing, but he was quite certain that everyone had remained unharmed. After all, the Cyber Squad had shown up just in time to take care of the dragon king before he could devour anyone. Nevertheless, Kai hoped to jump in the game soon and see his crazy Aussie friend again.

"Thanks for asking, that's a very good question," the

AI replied. "To advance in levels and therefore unlock more abilities, testers need to prove their value, reliability, and loyalty. The abilities higher-level testers receive could cause a lot of damage in the online world if they fell into the wrong hands. Helltek is legally responsible for any misdemeanor by our testers. The company needs to make sure that only the right people receive the advanced abilities. And finding those people is a long process."

"Makes sense."

"Do you have any more questions concerning the clipping tutorial, Kai?"

"No, I'm good. Can I join the others now?"

"Of course." A friendly smile appeared on her perfectly shaped face, which, again, didn't reach her eyes.

"I'll see you around, I guess."

"Whenever you need me, Kai. Remember, all you need to do is say or think *Hey Siren*, and I will assist you in any way I can."

The surroundings around Kai began dissolving into pixels, and for a brief moment he saw nothing but the white vastness again, then he found himself in a loading screen he knew very well: *Behind Blue Eyes 3*.

Entering game... Please wait... Loading...
Behind Blue Eyes 3. Secure_dev_mode, build 346A.

***

KEEP ON READING!

Cyber Squad - Level Two

Available here:

Amazon Store

To learn more about LitRPG, talk to authors including myself, and just have an awesome time, please join the LitRPG Group on Facebook!

LitRPG | Groups | Facebook

---

[1] Non Player Character: any character that is part of the game and not a player.

[2] Head-up display.

[3] In real life.

[4] An alien race in *StarCraft*; gamers still use the term for a coordinated attack with many units.

[5] Crouching above a fallen enemy player to humiliate them, considered as very rude and childish.

[6] Massively Multiplayer Online Role-Playing Game.

[7] Australian slang: girl.

[8] Player versus player.

[9] Player versus entity.

[10] Damage dealer.

[11] Gamer slang for stamina and mana potions.

[12] Area of effect: a special attack in RPGs allowing a player to do damage to enemies in an area for a certain amount of time, usually with fire, poison, etc.

[13] Damage over time: a special attack that keeps damaging the enemy for a certain amount of time, which often uses poison, fire, ice, etc.

[14] Frames per second; defines how smoothly a game runs.

[15] User interface.